CW00499945

CHRISTMAS WISHES

A CHRISTMAS ANTHOLOGY

HANNAH MORSE JESSICA LONG C. E. LASHUA
ROSIE EAST KACI ROSE KRIS BUTLER
AVERY LAWRENCE STEPHANIE SCISSOM
ALEXIS TAYLOR BETH HENDRIX KATHERINE MOORE

BBB PUBLISHINGS

This book is a work of fiction. Names, characters, places, and incidents are the product of the author's imagination or are used fictitiously. Any resemblance to actual events, or persons, living or dead, is coincidental

Manufactured in the United States of America
First Edition November 2021

Cover done by Victoria Schaefer at Eve Graphic Design, LLC
Formatting done by Mystic Fortune Formatting

Created with Vellum

To you,

Thank you for being the wonderful person you are and loving me for all my faults. You are the peanut butter to my jelly.

Love you!

THE GINGERBREAD PRINCE

HANNAH MORSE

CHAPTER ONE

MOLLY

The dream job had not lived up to its name.

It hadn't even been close to fulfilling, or life-changing or any of the other lies management had promised. Walking out the doors of the multinational company, however, had upended Molly North's years of carefully laid out plans, changing her life forever.

A cold November breeze tugged at her hair, lifting the dark brown strands while sending a chill under her coat. Above her rose the three stories of the building she now called home. The first floor housed a coffee shop and bakery. Its sweet scents had been a big part of why she'd signed the lease since the minuscule third-floor walk-up studio had little in the way of comfort or charm.

Nothing bad could happen over a place called 'The Good Bean'.

Molly shut the door to her wagon with a thump. The tiny resident's parking lot was sandwiched between her building and the indifferent concrete wall of a schoolbook depository. How Seattle's school had so many textbooks that they needed their own building she had no idea, but they'd make for quiet neighbors.

From the trunk she hefted a cardboard box, staggering under the weight. The movers that morning had been nice enough, but she hadn't trusted them with her most precious things, such as the textbooks on the thermal properties of materials that filled the box in her arms.

With a little effort, she got the car's hatch closed. Mostly by imagining it was her previous boss' head she was elbowing into place. The jerk.

Molly keyed in the door code with her pinkie. Inside, the scent of rich coffee and baking gingerbread nearly overwhelmed her. Molly's mouth watered, accompanied by a gurgle from her stomach. As soon as these books were safely on the shelf, she'd get herself something to make up for skipping breakfast.

The narrow stairs leading from the ground floor creaked as she climbed them, accompanied by the sound of a radiator hissing in on the first landing. Not a good place for one, but for the price she was paying Molly was mostly happy to have heat. Seattle might not get down to below freezing often, but she appreciated being warm.

Pausing beside the pinging radiator, she blew her hair out of her eyes. The box seemed to get heavier with every step. Groaning, she hefted the books and turned to go up the next flight.

Her toe caught on the lip of a step.

Molly's stomach lurched as she started to pitch backward. It was really going to hurt when she landed on her back, crushed by the weight of the moving box.

A clatter of feet rushed down the stairs. Strong hands gripped her forearm and the edge of the box. Something metal pinged on the ground.

Molly yipped at being pulled upright.

"I got you," the man said, his voice rough with a Scottish accent.

"Ah," she said weakly, her heart still pounding from her near disaster.

Her superman was scruffy, with tidy light brown curls and bright blue eyes. He grinned at her and Molly upgraded him from cute to gorgeous. The dimples really sold his prince charming look, along with the streak of flour smeared across one cheek.

"Molly!" she blurted, and the man raised a brow. His hand was still on her, the warmth seeping through her sweater. "My name's Molly North. I'm moving into 3b."

"We'll be neighbors then, I'm 3a."

"Do you have a name, Mr. 3a?"

The tip of his ears flushed pink. "Please call me Fergus."

"Nice to meet you, Fergus. I suppose I should get out of your way." She tried to sidestep to allow him by, but he tugged at the box, keeping her where she stood.

"Let me help. I'd just popped up to my place to get a biscuit cutter."

Molly let him take the box, which he tucked under his arm like it weighed nothing. Her eyes dropped to the rest of him. Fergus wore a green apron with 'The Good Bean' embroidered across it. It was covered in flour and bits of dough. Several red sprinkles were stuck near the G of 'Good'.

"You're a baker?" she asked, feeling silly as soon as she asked. "I mean for downstairs."

Fergus bent and retrieved something from beside her sensible tennis shoes. They were comfortable, like the rest of what she had on. Why hadn't she opted for a less casual outfit? Something like a tiny black dress or a string bikini that'd make this gorgeous man with his kind eyes and kitchen knowledge notice her. She might have frozen before she got inside the apartment building, but then he could have warmed her up with skin-to-skin contact.

Molly put her mental brakes on that sort of thinking about someone she'd met two seconds ago. Instead, she focused on what Fergus proudly held up for inspection. It was a copper cookie cutter in the shape of a gingerbread man. Dropping it on top of her books, he turned and headed back up the stairs.

"Yes, to baking at home and at the cafe," he said over his shoulder. "It used to be more of a hobby for me, but I've been expanding my skill set. You'll not find a more delicious gingerbread man from here to…" He trailed off.

"Scotland?" she supplied.

"Aye, there."

She watched his jeans pull tight over his backside as she followed him up the steps. It was a very nice backside.

"I'm from Seattle." As always, mentioning her past lead to a minefield of things better left alone. Her parents' deaths, the years spent in foster care, how she'd clawed her way to a degree. She needed to get away from that fast. "Do you live with someone?" she blurted, wincing at his back. She couldn't be any more transparent if she was see-through.

"It's just me," Fergus said, shooting her a puzzled look. "I'm a bit of a homebody." His words were a balm and she relaxed. At least she wasn't drooling over someone's husband.

On the third floor, he stopped beside her door so she could let them in. The haphazard piles of boxes the movers have left would require hours of work to sort and put away. Molly didn't want to deal with any of it.

Fergus set the books down. He patted the one on top. "Just a little light reading?"

"I'm a materials engineer," she said. "Specializing primarily in home kitchen applications." The weight of her dying dreams landed square on her. "I left a position last month when it didn't turn out how I expected. My plan now is to take the ideas my boss tried to steal and create my own line of specialized bakeware." Finding out she was paid less than half what her male colleagues made had been the final straw.

Fergus's eyes lit up as he skimmed his fingers over the cover of a journal that peeked out from one side of the box, but then his brow furrowed. His gaze slipped from her to his shoes. Or at least she hoped it was his footwear and not the layer of dust coating the wood floor. Prior to move-in cleaning had not been a service the rental company offered.

Fergus looked like he was trying to decide something that required a great deal of internal debate.

Her phone rang, her best friend Chelsey's name popping up. "Hey," Molly answered. She crossed to look out one of the two large windows. It was an excellent view of the highway. The apartment seemed very small for her new ideas to take wing in.

"How's moving day going? Sorry I had to work." Chelsey's voice sounded chipper. They'd met when Molly had started the dream-job-that-wasn't. Chelsey was a security guard contracted by the building's owners. She'd liked the same salad bar as Molly and one day they'd gotten to talking and it'd turned out they got along like houses on fire.

"It's been fine, everything's here. Are we still on for lunch Saturday? I can't wait for you to see how small this place is." And maybe give an opinion on Molly's new neighbor. She glanced at him and he quickly dropped his eyes, but she was almost certain he'd been staring at her butt. Returning to the window she cocked a hip, just in case he was looking again.

"Postage stamp?"

"You're giving it too much credit, but the coffee shop is a bonus."

There was a muffled noise like Chelsey had put a hand over the phone's mic. "That's not an entrance," she snapped, voice distant. "Molly," she said clearly after a moment. "I'll call you later."

"Go kick-ass." Molly hung up and stuck her phone in her pocket. She turned to Fergus, who was right where she'd left him. "Thank you for the help," she said after a moment of silence.

"No problem." Fergus gave her a nod and shuffled towards the door.

Well, she supposed that was that. Maybe he'd sell her discount coffee downstairs.

When he was almost in the hallway, he paused and pushed a hand through his hair. Turning to face her, he leaned his shoulder against the jamb. That was really unfair, it made him look even tastier.

Wait, when had she decided she wanted to lick him?

"Do you have time for a chat over coffee?" He flashed her that disarming smile again, the indecisiveness of a minute ago having disappeared.

Molly's heart fluttered. She'd take coffee with him, or they could hide a body together. It's not like she was picky. "Sure," she said, instead of doing a fist pump.

Fergus' dimple showed up as his grin widened, sending Molly's thoughts right back to licking. "It'll be busy down there, we're a little short-staffed." His eyes lingered on her face. "I suggest a ginger biscuit along with whatever you get to drink. I'm working on the recipe before the holiday rush, and I think I might have perfected it this morning."

"You drive such a hard bargain. Coffee and a treat? You're speaking my language."

He tipped his head towards the hall. Everything else about her move could wait, she had something better to do than sigh over her lack of curtains. He led her back downstairs and through a door into the coffee shop.

"It smells so good," she said as they bypassed the line at the counter. A wiry man with thick gray hair was working the register. He glared at Fergus.

Fergus rolled his eyes at the man while pouring two coffees. "You'd hardly believe it was only November first in here, what with all the carols playing." He handed her a cup. Molly tried to ignore the little zings that flashed up her arm as their fingers briefly brushed together, but it was impossible. He made all of her zing in a way she'd believed didn't happen once you were out of your teens.

She concentrated on the carol playing, instead of how her body hummed. "It's too early." The lyrics were familiar. "And isn't that an Isle of Alba song?"

Fergus' gaze drifted away, and he shrugged a shoulder. "Maybe." His eyes narrowed, seemingly focused on something outside the window of the shop. Even standing on tiptoes, she couldn't see what had his attention. It was just the city's normal foot and vehicle traffic. With a shake of his head, he focused back on her and tapped the top of the bakery case. "Pick a biscuit."

Inside the glass-fronted case sat rows of cookies, each kind neatly labeled. Snickerdoodles, chocolate chip, oatmeal raisin, sugar, maple crème, mint chocolate, and a huge tray of iced gingerbread. Molly's stomach grumbled again. "Did you make all of these?" she asked. Every single cookie looked spectacular like it should be in a glossy food magazine. The icing on the gingerbread made her think of snowflakes.

"I did, keeps me busy." He set an elbow on top of the case and propped his head in his hand. "Which one do you want?"

"Gingerbread, of course. I've been promised the best."

He beamed while plucking a cookie from the tray and handing it to her. It was still slightly warm. Fergus claimed a snickerdoodle before finding them a table to sit at, their knees crammed together under the metal top. Molly didn't think she'd ever been so aware of someone else's legs before. A tiny shift and she'd be touching his thigh.

"We're really busy today," Fergus said, frowning at the register's five-person deep line. "I'll have to get back and help at the counter at some point, though trust me, I'd much rather be sitting here with you."

"I am glad I'm more entertaining than work." She took a bite of the cookie, the sweetness of the icing giving way to the warm spiciness of the gingerbread. Molly tried to hold it in, she really did, but a moan still escaped. "This is amazing."

Fergus leaned forward, the little table swaying as he put his folded arms on the top. "I'm glad you like them."

"I love them. You're going to be famous."

He ducked his head. "Nah, just want to help this place."

"If you want to help," called the man behind the register. "You can come make drinks instead of flirting."

Molly's cheeks burned. "I'm good if you need to go." Wasn't she the one flirting with him?

"He'll be fine for a few more moments. The ninny just needs to break down and hire help." Fergus took a big bite of his cookie.

Molly nipped at her treat as well, chewing thoughtfully. "I don't suppose you could use someone temporarily? I'm kind of between jobs right now and could use the money." Her savings would only last so long. Molly knew most people couldn't just walk away from a job, she'd been lucky to be able to afford to tell her boss just what he could do with himself. If she ever had power over the lives of other people, she would never treat them as disposable.

"Hey," Fergus called. "Molly here is going to start tomorrow. I'll teach her to open." Just like that, she had a job.

She finished her cookie with relish. Taking a risk, she bumped her knee against a very solid feeling thigh. A whole torrent of delightful zings raced up her leg. "I think I'm going to be very glad I met you, Fergus."

CHAPTER TWO

FERGUS

The plain grey sedan sat parked across the street, just beyond the circle of yellow light from a streetlamp. Fergus lifted a hand and waved at his security detail. With the dark tint of the windows, he could never tell if they waved back, but it was how he started every morning. Lowering the blinds, he plucked a clean apron off a hook. He tied it around his waist with a jaunty knot on one hip.

With a last run of a comb through his hair, he was ready for his early morning shift at the coffee shop. He loved getting the store ready to open, though probably his grandmother was turning over in her grave at him working behind a counter. She would have tutted about 'what has the Royal House of Kerr come to'?

He smiled ruefully. Grannie Kerr had been a force of nature. Anyone who'd tried to kidnap her would have been sorry very quickly, and she would never have fled to hide on the opposite side of the world for a year or two. Of course, she'd been Queen already at his age, which was slightly different than prince and heir apparent.

Fergus liked to think that spending a couple of years not being in the swirl of royal duties on The Isle of Alba would be good for him. So far, it'd been relaxing.

He eyed his door.

Molly North wasn't the tiniest bit relaxing. He had the notion she never did anything by halves. That included flirting. As a Prince, he was used to people making a fuss over him, though it'd been impossible to tell if the person was more into his string of titles, the power he'd one day wield, his bank accounts, or any one of the other things that'd defined him since his birth.

Molly had only seen the slightly awkward fellow from 3a, with hair that needed a trim and clothes that probably wouldn't stand up to being tailored, which meant she was interested in him.

What a terrifying thought. Fergus had only just started to discover who he was underneath the layers of duty that'd been his birthright. That man liked baking, terrible reality TV, and reading true crime stories. He also tended to not shave and let his hair have its natural curl. That alone made him look almost nothing like he had a year ago.

Well, he might as well get this over with. Fergus had faced much worse things than a smart, gorgeous woman at five in the morning.

He checked the peephole like he always did—there'd been a lot of intense training after the Marseilles incident—making sure it was clear. The hallway was empty. He exited, locked his door, and strode over to 3b, knocking forcefully.

Nothing happened.

He knocked again. After a second there was muffled cursing and the door opened. Sleepy eyes blinked at him.

"Huh?" Molly mumbled, though she must have been already up since she had a t-shirt, jeans, and one sock on. Its match dangled from her fingers. Her dark brown hair sat piled on her head, more a rat's nest than a bun. She looked adorable.

"Good morning," he said, striving for extra cheeriness. He couldn't help it. Molly obvious was not a morning person, which meant she'd hate that he was bright-eyed and bushy-tailed. There were endless opportunities for teasing ahead. He cracked his knuckles.

Molly blinked, yawned, and wandered back into her apartment. He crossed his arms, biting back a grin as she stared at the floor.

"Can I help you?" he asked after a moment. This was too much fun.

"I'm looking for my other sock."

"Have you tried your left hand?"

She blearily held it up. "Ah, there you are." A few hopping steps later and she had it on. It took her two tries to get her feet jammed into her trainers, but then she was pushing past him into the hallway, muttering something about 'too early'. Fergus followed her towards the stairs, his hand hovering over the small of her back. If she tripped on the way down, he'd be able to catch her. The gentle heat radiating from her to warm his palm was an added bonus.

A dangerous one. Fergus could just hear the lecture Pike would give him. His head of security, who'd followed him to Seattle out of some misguided sense of loyalty, had threatened to personally gut Fergus if he dared to get too close to someone. Pike trusted nobody, for good reason, even someone as obviously non-threatening as Molly.

Fergus simply couldn't fathom her being a honeypot sent to tempt secrets out of him. Mostly because she was too perfect. The sots behind the kidnapping attempts would send someone much more obvious, never knowing that his tastes ran to the brainy. Though Molly's tits did make him suspicious, they looked like they'd fit in his hand with a little leftover. Just the way he liked.

Not that he was looking at Molly's breasts, only her arse because she was walking slightly in front of him down the stairs. Generous hips, lush backside—maybe the bastards were hoping he'd perish of thwarted lust.

He needed to get control of himself. There were biscuits to make, dough to shape into croissants, and coffee makers that needed to be running.

Fergus let them into The Good Bean. When he flipped on the overhead lights, Molly groaned and closed her eyes. "Who invented switches," she sighed. "Because screw them."

He chuckled and directed her to behind the counter. "Alright, first things first. Let's make coffee." That perked her up. He showed her how the machines worked, gave her the training manual with recipes, and left her to sort things out while he got the ovens going.

Fergus loved this part of the morning, when things were quiet and the success of the day depended on him having his wits about him as he baked. It'd been a hobby he'd occasionally indulged in when he'd had the palace kitchens to flit to on a whim. Those cavernous, immaculate spaces had never felt as warm and homey as the cluttered, cramped quarters in The Good Bean.

What had started out as him running for his life had turned into him building a completely different one. Only Pike and his crew, flittering around the edges, reminded Fergus that there was no way for him to sink down roots here in Seattle. At least not how things stood currently. He wondered what his cousin would think if he suddenly found himself the heir apparent? Probably a lot of cursing once he'd sobered up enough to realize what was happening.

Fergus hefted the baking sheets he used from their shelf and banged them down on the counter.

"Everything alright?" Molly asked, appearing with two steaming mugs in her hands. The bitter smell perked up his nose and he gratefully accepted the cup, wrapping his hands around it to warm them.

"Aye, I'm fine. Lots on my mind this morning."

"I'm sorry." She yawned, following it up with a huge mouthful of coffee. "Is training me too much this morning?" Molly shrank in on herself as she spoke. He could imagine how many times a smart and enthusiastic woman like Molly had been told she was 'too much' over the course of her life. He wanted to kiss the frown forming at the corner of her lips, banish it so it could never appear again. Be the prince on a white charger coming to rescue her, only he was rubbish at being anything of the sort.

He settled for pushing the stack of baking sheets towards her. "Not too much," he rasped. Fergus cleared his throat. "Can you get these lined with parchment paper so the biscuits don't stick? It's there—" He pointed to the shelf the liner resided on. "After the first batches are baking, we'll open the doors for business." Thankful to have Molly doing one part of the morning routine, he started in on getting the dough mixing in the two industrial mixers The Good Bean boasted. They were old and refurbished, but he did have a lot of experience coaxing motors to keep running. True, those had been high-end sports cars, but the principles were the same.

Today, both mixers whirred contentedly, no need for him to fiddle with their innards.

One bowl of chocolate chip and another of snickerdoodle in hand, he returned to the work area to find all the pans neatly set out and lined. Well, all except one. Molly held that sheet up to the light, inspecting the dented and stained surface with some kind of tiny magnifying loop. "Why do you use these pans?" she asked, not looking at him.

"They're the ones the store owns?" He shoved a hand through his hair when she finally glanced up at him, her expression incredulous.

"Really?"

"Uh, yeah. I thought they were pretty standard."

A line appeared between her brows as she scrunched up her face at him. "I suppose, if you mean standardly terrible at baking cookies."

"Mine turn out fine."

She set the pan down with a clang. "I know. They're delicious." She ripped off a piece of the parchment paper, the sound of it against the metal teeth of the box more aggressive than he thought the flimsy thing would be capable of. "This isn't about your cookies, it's about a design that hasn't changed in a million years. Wouldn't you like to not have this extra step?" Molly waved the parchment paper at him before lining the pan with it. "And to not worry about burning the bottoms of the cookies, because the pan heats just right? If I could just tweak..." She trailed off and dropped her head into her hands.

Ah, bingo. It really wasn't about him, but about the ideas she had for the kitchen.

Fergus risked edging closer to her. When he was just within reach, he pressed a palm to her back. "I don't think I quite have the full picture of what landed you here, but I'm still sorry."

She turned to face him, lifting her buckwheat honey-colored eyes to his. They were shiny with unshed tears. "I apologize," she said stiffly. "I really am a professional. It just sort of hit me again how badly I was being treated at a place that was supposed to be my dream.

I hate that it turned into a nightmare." Her lids descended. His hand ghosted up from her shoulder to cup her cheek, and she turned into his palm as if seeking comfort from him, of all people.

Though he did suppose he knew better than most the difference between what people thought was a fairytale and actual harsh reality. If only he could explain that to her, but he couldn't. Keeping his lips sealed had kept him alive so far, now wasn't the time to start blabbing. Fergus had no idea how to help her without his money and royal clout, he just knew he wanted to make the world a little bit of a brighter place for Molly.

"What can I do to help?" he asked.

One of her eyes popped open. "Um, well, instead of listening to me complain, why don't you tell me what you do and do not like about these sheets? That'd be a good start for me, seeing what someone who bakes far more than I do considers important."

"I can do that." He rubbed his thumb over her cheekbone. "What about over dinner tonight? Nothing fancy, but there's a place that serves a mean salmon and chips half a block down." Fergus mentally kicked himself. He usually met up with Pike there every couple of weeks to be updated on things at home. Now he'd have to call his security to tell them about the fact he was taking a date there.

Pike would have his head on stake.

But Molly was worth a round of lecturing from the fellow. The no entanglements bit was a load of rubbish anyway. It'd always been an impossible goal.

"I'd like that," she said. "Thank you. And we better get these cookies in the oven. I don't want to get fired on my first day for distracting the baker."

"Right." He dropped his hand, even as nerves bubbled up in his stomach. Molly said she'd have a spot of dinner and a chat with him. A bloody proper date. "Um, let's…here, I have scoops. For the dough." He fumbled them out of the pan they were stored in and shoved one at her.

Smooth, Fergus, he mentally chided himself. For crying out loud, he'd partied with A list celebrities and been on dates with supermodels and---cripes, his hands were shaking. He tightened his grip on the scoop. This was different, it wasn't a PR stunt or part of an image-building strategy. He was taking a woman he fancied to a restaurant he liked because he wanted to know her better.

It was almost normal.

Fergus thought he could get used to normal.

CHAPTER THREE

MOLLY

"And then I told him to take the job and shove it." Molly tilted her pint glass and drained the last of her beer.

Fergus leaned forward on the pub's polished wood table. "You didn't."

"I did, in those exact words. I was promised so much and none of it was true." She dropped her empty glass on the table, trying to figure out if she wanted another. One was her usual limit, but Fergus was so easy to talk to that she wanted an excuse to keep going.

"Molly!" a voice hollered from beside her. She frowned and looked up into Chelsey's face, framed by her bright blonde bob.

Fergus looked equally confused. "Pike?" he asked, staring at the man standing next to Chelsey. Molly giggled at him. His biceps strained the arms of the plain t-shirt he was wearing and his hair was buzzed short. A tattoo peeking out from under one sleeve to complete the ex-military image.

"You didn't answer my text and you've been in here for hours," Chelsey said. "So I stopped on my way home to make sure you were fine. And I ran into this guy." She jerked her thumb at Pike. "Who is doing the same for your date."

"Ah, whoops, I didn't know it'd been that long." Molly pulled out her phone and winced at the collection of notifications. "Sorry."

"I am too." Fergus looked both upset and resigned. "We were having a good time."

Pike shrugged a shoulder, his gaze on Chelsey. Molly stifled a giggle at how pink Chelsey's face had become. "This lady had the right idea, coming in to check." Chelsey's blush deepened at the clipped Scottish accent. Molly was enthralled, Chelsey hadn't been interested in anyone since she'd been dumped a year ago.

"Why don't you two take our table?" Molly said, standing and collecting her coat. Both Pike and Chelsey stammered something to the effect that they couldn't, but they did it while sharing a look.

"I insist," Fergus said. "My treat." He patted Pike's shoulder as the man slowly sat. Chelsey sank down into the chair Molly had vacated. "We'll be fine." He shared a look with Pike, who nodded after a tense moment. Fergus flagged down a waitress and spoke to her in hushed tones, then directed Molly towards the exit. "Sorry about him, we shared a flat in college and he got used to keeping me out of trouble."

Molly wanted to ask how Pike had also ended up in Seattle, but Fergus slung his arm over her shoulders as they spilled out of the pub. She snuggled against his side, glad for his warmth in the chill damp air coming off the water. Her basic black dress was little protection against the cold. She tilted her head back briefly, looking up at the dark winter sky while around her the after-dinner crowd ebbed and flowed.

"You were right," she said, as they wove around pedestrians. "That salmon was amazing."

"Best I've had outside of Scotland. Have you ever been?"

She had a hazy memory of craggy mountains, green fields, a lot of trains, and omnipresent bagpipe music. "Once, when I was young. We hit all the major tourist places and finished with a jaunt out to The Isle of Alba to hear all about how it's a totally separate country that's never been conquered." It was her last good memory of her parents before they'd been swept from her life, and it'd ended up making the Isle feel like some magical place where families lived charmed lives.

"They're quite proud of that." Fergus shook his head, then turned unreadable eyes on her. "Did you enjoy the Christmas flavor of the Isle?"

"I was a kid. Of course, I loved a city named Yuletown that's known for being 'the home of Christmas'. It was magical, even in the middle of July."

He snorted. "Aye, I'm sure."

"Not as magical as tonight has been."

"That's the beer talking." He said it with a smile, and she elbowed him as he opened the door to their building for her.

She started up the stairs. "I only had one." Enough for a slight buzz. If she drooled, it was because of the handsome man following behind her, not because of the beer she'd downed with her dinner. Wait, he was a couple of steps below her. "Are you looking at my ass?" she asked over her shoulder.

Fergus nodded solemnly. "Yes."

Molly laughed, then nearly missed a step. "Whoops." She grabbed the rail.

A large hand cupped her rear. "No falling. I thought we already established that." The hand squeezed, then patted. "Not that I mind keeping this lovely backside in one piece."

Desire rushed through her, leaving her breathless. Fergus was smart, funny, good at what he did, and had she mentioned handsome? His curls practically begged to be held onto.

He gave her rear a little push, and somehow they made it up to the third floor with no more mishaps. Probably because his palm stayed glued to the back of her dress. They stumbled to a stop between their two doors. Molly knew they had a choice. They could wave good night and each head into their own places. They see each other in the morning, and maybe there'd be other dates, or maybe they'd just be good friends.

The other choice was that everything changed. Which was crazy. She barely knew him. Fergus hadn't been in her life for a week yet.

She swayed forward to lean her forehead against his shoulder. The rough knit of his sweater scratched at her. "I don't want tonight to end." Where had practical Molly gone? The Molly with a five-year plan and a bullet journal full of lists of goals for her career, life, and even what kinds of plants she wanted in her foyer.

Her new place didn't even have a foyer, but it did have a Fergus. Who'd laughed at her stories of awkward foster family meals and asked her endless questions about what she liked, from her favorite flavor of seltzer to if she liked dogs or cats more. He'd answered her questions readily too. She knew his favorite TV show and color.

Molly inhaled, savoring the hint of gingerbread that clung to him, sweet and inviting.

"Mols," he rumbled, nuzzling her cheek. "It doesn't have to. Come home with me, yeah?"

She shifted, raising her head. Their lips were less than an inch apart. Possibilities filled the air between them. Entire galaxies of what might be. A whole life, starting from this moment.

Pushing up on her toes, Molly kissed him.

Fergus' lips were soft as they glided against hers. The simmering heat in her belly ratcheted up a boil. He tasted of the beer they'd sipped, complex and hoppy. She needed more and fisted his sweater, pulling him against her. He groaned, his arms wrapping around her.

Always one to dive headfirst into a new project, Molly wanted to know everything about him. She wanted to research Fergus and find out what turned him on, what made him moan, and most especially, she wanted to discover every last detail about his body. Which meant he had far too many clothes on.

Fergus must agree because he palmed her ass again and ground against her. That was absolutely an erection pressing through his jeans to tease her hip. Her fingers dropped to the button of his pants, wanting him naked right that second.

"Hang on," he gasped, pulling back from her.

She snagged his belt loop to keep him from going any further. "What?"

"Hallway, we're in the bloody hallway. Bed?" He pointed at his door and she nodded an agreement. With a grunt, Fergus fished his keys out, let them in, and then crossed to the windows. He opened and closed a blind, which Molly couldn't puzzle out, but he was back in a flash and yanking his sweater over his head. The undershirt went with it, leaving him bare from the waist up.

Molly bit her lip. She must have won some kind of lottery, because jackpot. She laid both hands on his chest, the brown hair on his defined pecs crinkling under her palms. There was a lot more muscle than she'd been expecting as if he'd been training for something besides baking.

"I used to wax it," he said, eyes on her hands as she stroked him.

Molly shook her head. "I like it this way, very manly."

"Aye?" He sounded surprised and pleased, which meant he needed more kissing. She found his lips with hers, this time nipping at the pouty lower one. His tongue surged into her mouth. Molly sucked on it in welcome, delighting in the unrestrained noise of desire Fergus made.

She found herself being deeply kissed while also being directed to a small bedroom. A full bed took up most of the space. It was pushed against the wall and only had one nightstand, on which sat an empty water bottle and an ancient Isle of Alba cookbook featuring 101 different Christmas-related recipes. She'd bet at least ten were for gingerbread.

Fergus stopped her before she could sit. "Let me," he said, turning her to lower the zipper of her dress. It fell to the floor, leaving her in her lacy black bra and panties. "Fancy knickers," he whispered against the nape of her neck while unsnapping her bra. Down her arms it went, guided by his long fingers, before joining her dress.

The radiator in the living room hissed and pinged to life, but Molly hadn't even noticed a chill with Fergus wrapped around her. He was a furnace himself.

She pushed her rear shamelessly back against him while he cupped her breasts. This had been inevitable since the second he'd caught her on the stairs. Meeting him had been as fateful as getting into a highly ranked university. It'd changed everything for her.

He'd changed everything.

Fergus's fingers plucked at her nipples and she mewled. Now that she knew how talented his hands were, she was going to be jealous of the dough he worked every morning.

"I've been wanting to do this since I laid eyes on you." He groaned and nipped her ear. "Such lovely tits."

Continuing to play with one, he skimmed his other hand down her belly to her panties. One finger barely worked its way under the elastic.

"Can I touch you, Molly? Under your knickers?" He sucked at the sensitive spot just below her ear.

"Please, anything."

Fergus pushed his entire hand into her panties. "Wet for me already?" he groaned as he sent a finger questing between the lips of her pussy. She had to be, judging from the building ache deep inside and how good his touch felt.

The first stokes against her clit were soft, and she put her hand over his, the black lace of her panties trapped between them, to show him how she liked to be touched. He growled something about how hot that was, but it was the jerk of his cock against her ass that convinced her he hadn't minded Molly being a little bossy.

She knew she could be, both in bed and out, and it was a relief to know she wasn't about to disappoint him by trying to ensure they both enjoyed themselves.

"Thank you," she said.

Fergus pressed a finger into her channel. "For what?" She'd swear his brogue deepened by the moment. He added a second finger. Molly moaned her pleasure at the stretch.

"For being you," she managed. His cock throbbed again, and she couldn't wait any longer, she wanted to see it free of his pants. "Can you get naked?"

"But then I have to let go."

Molly looked at him over her shoulder. "I promise you can go right back to work."

He muttered something she thought was a curse word, but then removed his hands. She dropped her panties and scrambled on the bed, turning just as Fergus straightened up from pushing off his jeans. Her knees fell open. Because…wow.

Fergus curled his fist around his cock, stroking it slowly as he raised his head, meeting her gaze while wearing nothing but a shy smile. "Do I pass muster?" he asked.

"Yeah," she managed with a very dry mouth. He was gorgeous naked, and either baking was very good for muscle sculpting or he'd had a personal trainer at some point. There was enough definition in his arms, chest, and thighs—lord, his thighs—to scramble her mind without it being intimidating. His cock stood stiff and proud from a wiry patch of dark brown curls. The dark red head begged her to have a taste.

She patted the bed.

He tossed himself onto the bed, bouncing once before getting an arm around her. Molly ended up flat on her back, Fergus over her with his hands braced on either side of her shoulders.

"Ye want me, lassie?" he asked in her ear before teasing the outer shell with his tongue.

She turned her head and kissed him, scared to even try and answer the question, because she wanted him more than she could ever have dreamed of wanting anything, and she hardly knew him. He could wear socks with sandals or like pet spiders.

None of it mattered at the moment, not with his tongue in her mouth and his body pinning her to the bed. Bone-deep need flooded her, driving out every other thought except the desire to be closer to him. Molly gripped his firm ass, digging her fingertips in to spur him on.

Fergus shuddered and groaned. His cock ground against her belly.

"Mols," he gasped. "I need—"

"Please." She bit at his lip and arched her back, scrapping her sensitized nipples against his chest. With a moan he grabbed his thick cock and pressed the head between her legs, dragging it up and down her pussy. Molly's bit at his shoulder as pleasure coiled tight inside her. "There," she cried as he stroked the hot head across her clit.

"You like that?" Fergus asked in a near growl.

Molly didn't have words to respond with, just a wail as she crested into bliss. Her fingers clung to him, anchoring her body while everything inside her soared.

"Sweetness," he whispered. "My darling." He pressed soft kisses to her cheeks as she caught her breath. At last, she returned to earth. "I've got you."

"Fergus."

"I'm here. And I deserve a cookie for not forgetting myself."

"Forgetting?"

He mouthed her neck. "Rubber."

"Ah." Molly blinked up at him. "Condom, yes, thank you." She'd been so gone that hadn't registered, which wasn't much like her at all. A few kisses from this man and she lost her head entirely.

She didn't regret it one bit.

Fergus beamed, obviously proud of himself. He shifted to the side, bringing her with him, and fumbled around in a bedside drawer. He held up a condom after a moment, brandishing it like a prize. Laughing, she snatched it from him. With a shove, Molly sent him onto his back. His leg hair tickled when she straddled his thighs, and she clamped his thighs tighter with her own, turning the tease into a rough rasp. It sent a fresh wave of lust swirling through her.

The condom wrapper crinkled in her fingers. They shook with the force of her need. Molly bit her lip and concentrated like she was taking a final exam. She concentrated on the head of his cock, where precum beaded in a pearly drop. The condom rolled on easily enough, Fergus making soft noises of desire. His eyes darted between her breasts and where she was petting his cock. Her pussy throbbed with need, a beat that echoed warmly in the region of her heart.

Molly hitched forward. She spread the lips of her sex with one hand, folds slick with her honey. The cock in her hand, warm and hard, made her wish she'd had a taste of him before she'd slid the condom on. Next time, she promised herself. This was all too good to only be a one-time thing.

Positioning his cock at her entrance, she dropped down. The stretch had her groaning. He fit her like a key in a lock, letting free a torrent of pleasure. Molly mewled, her head falling back as she rode Fergus. His hands wrapped around her churning hips, encouraging her to move faster and rougher.

She pressed a finger to her clit, barely needing more than a light brush against it to crest again. She cried out, pitching forward against Fergus' chest.

He rolled them over, still thrusting, and pushed her thighs apart.

Molly pulled him into a messy kiss. He grunted and groaned against her lips. Fergus lost his rhythm. His hips stuttered, he plunged deep a final time and came with a harsh grunt. His cock bucked with release, and she gathered him against his chest, holding him as he spent.

They lay sprawled on the bed, panting, their limbs tangled.

"How long before we can do that again?" Molly asked when she had the breath to do so.

Fergus barked with laughter. "A few minutes, I'm not eighteen."

"I mean the date, well, and the sex. How are you not surrounded by adoring women?"

A shadow flickered over his face, but in the next second it was gone, and Molly wondered if she'd imagined it. "I don't think I want anyone besides you." He sat up and stripped off the condom, returning to cuddle against her side. "You like my gingerbread."

"Is that all it required? And you didn't answer my question."

"Honestly? I'm not sure I ever want you to go back to your apartment. I want to wake up with you, or do whatever it is you call opening your eyes in the morning."

She half-heartedly swatted his shoulder. "I'm just not a morning person."

"I noticed."

"And we could have breakfast tomorrow, then lunch, dinner again—"

"I like the way you think."

Molly laid her head on his chest, snuggling into him. A few days ago she hadn't known Fergus existed, and now she couldn't imagine a day without him in it. Her life's contours had changed in the blink of an eye, and she couldn't be happier.

CHAPTER FOUR

FERGUS

Six Weeks Later

Cracking the door open of his flat's oven, Fergus inhaled the spicy scent of the biscuits baking. The tops were still pale, so he closed the door to give them a few more minutes. He checked the slow cooker next, making sure the potato soup bubbling away wasn't too hot. Molly would be starving when she got home, and he couldn't wait to see her face when she smelled what he'd made her.

He wrinkled his nose. Maybe the soup and the gingerbread biscuits didn't complement each other well, but he needed to perfect his chewy gingerbread recipe. They weren't coming out as well as the regular rolled biscuits and he didn't know why.

Molly thought it was the pan, and she was probably right, as usual. Luckily for him, she'd used her contacts to get a few afternoons in a lab creating a prototype. He could hardly wait to get his hands on it and bake a fresh batch of biscuits straight away.

With a pause for a roll in the hay, either before or after the baking.

Before, he decided, he was missing her something fierce, and she'd only been gone a few hours. They were very rarely apart, and his world always seemed drearier without her to brighten it. Fergus knew he was absolutely gone for Molly, head over heels. Had been since the first moment he'd seen her if he was being truthful.

Brushing flour from his apron, Fergus paused to survey the decorations he'd spent the afternoon putting up. Faux greenery hung from the mantle, candles gleamed on the tables, and white fairy lights twinkled in the windows. He might not be able to return to the Isle, but he'd brought a little of his home to this place for Molly, even if she didn't know it.

With only two weeks to Christmas Eve, they had a tree, trimmed in red and green with twinkling lights, that sat in front of one corner. An assortment of gifts sat under it, including a small box with a diamond ring nestled in it. He'd never been so bloody nervous as he had been buying it with his meager salary from the coffee shop.

A salary he'd soon be living on.

Fergus was going to insist on speaking to his father in a few days to officially give up his claim to the throne. Along with it would go the lavish accounts, the yachts, the private jet. He didn't need any of it. His da might gift him enough for Fergus to buy a home for himself and Molly, but if not, they'd make do.

Without a crown looming over his head, he could just be plain Fergus Murphy, baker, instead of Thomas Hamish Fergus Murphy Kerr, heir to the throne of the Isle of Alba.

Fergus rubbed at his temple. He needed to tell Molly the truth, maybe after she'd agreed to marry the non-prince version of him.

His mobile rang, and his heart dropped thinking it was Molly saying she was going to be late, but it was only Pike.

"Hey," Fergus said, putting the call on speaker.

"How's it hanging?"

"Making dinner. Mols should be here soon."

There was a rustle on the line. "You, uh, have confirmed that Chelsey's going to be at your little get together next Saturday?"

Fergus rolled his eyes. "For the millionth time, yes. You really need to shag her and stop this song and dance." Seeing Pike, who Fergus had thought lived with a stick up his arse, get twitterpated over

Molly's friend Chelsey had been an unexpected bonus the last little while.

Pike laughed. "Right. I'll tell her you said that."

"Don't you dare." Chelsey could be scary.

Fergus looked at the phone. He took a deep breath. Pike needed to know he might soon be out of work as head of security for a prince. It'd turn out fine, he'd be reassigned with minimal fuss. Fergus loved his family, and his country, but they'd be alright without him. One figurehead was as good as the next.

"Hey, Pike, I'm going to ask Molly to marry me."

"Of course, you are." Was that laughter? "But don't forget there's the whole needing to do it publicly before the court clause."

Fergus pinched the bridge of his nose. "No, I haven't forgotten, but...I'm planning to renounce. Everything. My cousin can bloody have the throne. I want this life."

There was silence. "Fergus...I know how you feel about her. And I know you've not been thrilled with the responsibility that's been part of your life since before you could walk, but the Isle needs you. This world is only getting more difficult to live in. I'm not sure putting the fate of your citizens in your cousin's hands is a great idea."

"He'll be fine."

"I've watched him spend an hour talking to a plant at a palace party. The sod is not leadership material."

Fergus groaned. The fridge door squeaked as he pulled it open to grab a head of lettuce to tear up for a salad. "Probably not, but he'll do okay. Always the life of the party, that one."

"Your parents aren't going to be around forever, Fergus. I know it feels like they are, but you have to think past that."

He shredded the lettuce into near confetti. "Thank you for the guilt trip, but the Isle will go on just fine without me."

"Don't you want your children to know where they came from?"

"I'll buy them bloody Alba cheese at the grocers. And low blow, mate." Imagining Molly and babies at the same time also had the unfortunate effect of making his cock twitch. She'd make an amazing mother, and more than once she'd mentioned family. He wanted a big one, something he'd never had as an only child. Would his weans resent him later when they learned the life they could have led?

Maybe neither they, nor Mols, would ever have to know. A clean break might be for the best. His life as a prince was like a dream he'd had, with real life being Molly and their family. He needed more time to think.

Pike sighed again. "I had to try. But if Molly and hiding away in the States is what you want, then I won't stop you." There was a noise like Pike had leaned the seat in his car back. "I'm thinking I could move here permanently too."

"I'd like that." Fergus was glad Pike couldn't see him grinning. They were getting to be good friends, but Fergus would bet his left nut that the real reason Seattle seemed so appealing was one tall blonde bombshell, who oddly enough seemed to be interested in Pike as well. Love was a funny thing.

"Yeah," Pike said, voice a bit rough. "It'd be nice not to be looking after your royal arse for once."

Fergus chuckled. "It won't be royal soon. Then you'll just be staring at my arse. Might have to fight Molly for it."

"She'd win."

"Yes, she would. And she'll be here any minute."

The mobile beeped as the call ended. Fergus turned the radio back up, humming along to a Christmas song.

He arranged cherry tomatoes on the top of the salad, smiling when the flat door opened and closed.

"In the kitchen," he called, itching to have Molly in his arms.

Wiping his hands on a cheery red towel, he turned to greet her.

It wasn't Molly.

Fergus was looking at the business end of a pistol and the face of a man he'd hoped to never see again.

For a second he was back on the deck of a ship, the Mediterranean Sea hidden by dark and rain. The gun had been bigger then. The man holding it looked the same, black clothing, buzzed blond hair, and grey, dead eyes.

Fergus wiped at his eyes, even though this time they weren't fuzzy from booze and the downpour.

"Seems I found the little lost prince," the man drawled. Ice shot down Fergus's spine as he snapped back to his cozy flat. Any moment Molly could walk in, and end up with a bullet between her eyes.

This man had almost killed him once already. This time, his own continued existence didn't matter, Fergus wouldn't let Molly be hurt. The joy of a simple life, that a moment ago and seemed so full of promise, fell and shattered on the floor.

"Ivan," he rasped.

CHAPTER FIVE

MOLLY

The steady thump of the car's wipers kept time while Seattle drizzle blurred the holiday lights she drove past, making the whole world ethereal in the dark.

The unassuming nine by thirteen-inch pan resting on her passenger seat had a proprietary coating that'd taken far longer to be ready than she'd planned, but it was finally done. Fergus could make sure it worked how Molly thought it would, she could make any adjustments needed, and launch her bakeware line in the new year.

It wouldn't be the only new thing in her life in the next few months. Molly had stopped at a drug store on the way to her borrowed lab. The lines had formed a pink plus on all three pregnancy tests she'd bought, confirming what she'd suspected. Despite being careful, she and Fergus had created a new life.

Molly smiled and pressed a hand to her belly. She couldn't tell any difference, yet, but she had no doubt that next Christmas she'd have a baby in her arms. Fergus would make such a good father, the kind who would be endlessly patient and loving. Her heart tripped over itself. Somehow her year had gone from being a well of disappointment as her career had crashed down to an explosion of joy as she'd found a new purpose, love, and now a family.

Molly's stomach growled as she pulled her car into the lot behind her apartment. She looped a scarf around her neck and put her hat on before getting out. The winter weather was chilly, and the breeze off the water only made it worse. Hopefully, Fergus had something ready for dinner, she felt like she could eat a horse.

"I'm hurrying," she grumbled at her belly as it growled again. The baking pan went under her arm as she locked the car door. The coating on it was thick and smooth.

Maybe too thick. It needed real-world testing.

Molly let herself into the building, paused to inhale the sweet scent of The Good Bean, then rushed upstairs. She hated being away from Fergus and couldn't wait to snuggle against his chest.

Molly opened the door to his apartment, hung up her coat and scarf, and held the pan behind her back. She had so many surprises for him. Christmas music and the smell of gingerbread filled the high-ceilinged space. The curtains were still open, but the blinds were down, blocking out the night and rain. Their little home was peaceful and cozy, just how she liked it.

"Fergus?" she called. Molly was so in love she overflowed with it. "Honey, I'm home." Her stomach rumbled loudly. "It smells great in here. What are we having?"

She turned the corner into the kitchen and froze.

Fergus was on his knees, his hands up and behind his head. A tall man had a gun to his temple. Fergus's eyes were panicked. His lips moved. 'I love you', he mouthed, then yelled, "Get out, Mols, go."

She screamed and staggered back, still clutching the pan. This sort of thing didn't happen. People didn't just come into your home and hold your boyfriend at gunpoint. That was the movies, bad ones with ridiculous plots.

The hard-eyed man with the gun grabbed Fergus by the collar of his cardigan. She inanely recognized the sweater as the one she'd bought him because she'd liked the reindeer on it. It'd cost more than it should have, but it was warm and the dark green and crimson looked good on Fergus, so she'd splurged on it.

The gun that'd been aimed at Fergus rose to point at her. Molly's heart nearly stopped.

"She's no one, Ivan," Fergus said. "It's me you're after."

"Don't know," the man—Ivan—said. "Your parents pay for you, and you pay for her. Because I'm guessing the princeling has gone and fallen in love." He sneered the words in a Russian accent that sounded like it was out of a straight-to-DVD action movie.

"What's going on?" Molly asked. Her stomach was in knots. Who would want to hurt her or Fergus? They were nobody, just two people with little lives who lived over a coffee shop

Ivan barked with laughter. "She doesn't even know, does she? Some sweet little idiot with doe eyes you think you're in love with. What's she going to do when she finds out that you could buy most of this town and still have money left over to wipe your ass with?"

Molly locked eyes with Fergus. She didn't understand what Ivan was saying. "I think you've mistaken us for someone else." She tried to sound calm. Thankfully, Ivan seemed too busy gloating to notice she was holding something. Molly raised the pan with its thick coating to cover her abdomen. It made her feel a little better.

"Nah, I'm not wrong. I've been tracking this royal waste of space for months. You're a hard man to find." Ivan smirked as he shook Fergus by his collar. "But you did pick a pretty girl." The words made Molly's skin crawl.

Fergus grimaced. "You'll not touch her, you bloody bastard." He started to stand. Ivan swung the gun back to Fergus.

"Not so fast," Ivan said. "You got away once, but I'm not missing my payday again."

He'd taken his eyes off Molly. She had to do something. If she stood there like an idiot and let Fergus get hurt, she'd never forgive herself.

Her fingers tightened painfully on the pan she clutched.

"Maybe I'll just kill you, and make your father pay for your dead body," Ivan said, pressing the barrel of the gun to Fergus' skull. His jaw tensed, but his eyes never left Molly. As if she was the last thing he wanted to see in his life.

Ivan's finger moved.

"No!" She'd bash his brains out. Molly jerked the pan up.

Ivan turned and fired at her. The loud crack drowned out her scream. Searing pain raced up her arms.

Surprise etched on his face, Ivan dropped to the floor, blood welling out of a hole in his left shoulder. The gun clattered to the ground beside him. She lifted the pan, looking at the back. There was barely a scratch from where the bullet had hit and ricocheted off.

"The coating is too thick," she said, voice flat. It was supposed to help with sticking and getting an even heat distribution, not repel bullets. Numbness deadened her fingers and the pan slipped to the floor.

Fergus was across the room with his arms around her in the next second. He was warm and solid, and she held onto him tight, like a life preserver in high seas. Her stomach churned, threatening to rebel.

"I've got you," he said, pressing her close.

She was sobbing. When had that started? "I was going to surprise you," she said into his chest as she clung to him.

He didn't get a chance to respond before the door burst open, and Pike entered with a rifle in his hands. He wore black tactical gear and a grim expression. There were other men with him. Their heavy boots were loud on the floor. She'd be forever getting the dirt out of the rug.

"Car just took off from the corner," one of the men said in a crisp Scottish accent. "We're in pursuit. We don't know if there's anyone else."

"Get the prince out of here, take him to the backup location now," Pike barked. Molly blinked, too numb to even know what to make of her boyfriend's best friend being dressed like some super-soldier. It did look very natural on him. Chelsey would probably drool.

Her world spun again as two of the other men grabbed Fergus.

"No!" she yelled as Fergus was pulled from her arms.

"I'll bring her." Pike put a hand on Fergus' shoulder. "Sorry, you know the protocols."

Fergus was struggling in the grip of other men. "Molly!"

Pike pushed him towards the door. "I'll take care of her, but you have to let us do our jobs. Now go."

Fergus's shoulder's slumped. "I'll see you soon, Molly. Don't worry. It'll make sense. I promise. I love you." The last was shouted as he was hurried out of the door. Molly felt like she couldn't breathe.

"Good job, luv" Pike said, offering a hand. She ignored him and shakily pulled out her phone. "We already called the police." Pike glanced at where several men were surrounding Ivan. One had picked up his gun. Nobody seemed to be interested in stopping the blood leaking from his shoulder.

Good.

"Not calling the police," she replied, her voice tiny. Molly typed in a number and turned toward the Christmas tree. Its lights were off now, the cord laying on the floor like it'd been tripped over. Molly wiped at the tears on her cheeks. She didn't know what to think. Everything had changed and none of it made sense. The world that'd existed moments before had disappeared and she was drifting.

"Hello? Molly?" Chelsey answered on the third ring.

"Hi," Molly said, sniffing.

"What's wrong? What happened?" Chelsey snapping into professional mode felt like a lifeline amid the chaos.

"I don't even know. There was a man, and a gun, and now Fergus is gone."

Chelsey inhaled sharply. "What?"

"I think he's safe. I need...can you come?"

"I'm on my way."

CHAPTER SIX

FERGUS

Fergus paced back and forth in front of the enormous window of the penthouse suite's living room. The flat sat perched at the top of a high rise, leaving the city lights to shine like scattered stars at his feet.

He didn't bloody well care.

What he needed was Molly. Why wasn't she here? Where was Pike? The members of his team that stood mutely in the living room, their eyes fixed on the entrances, had all said they didn't know anything besides that both Pike and Molly were safe.

Which was good, but the need to touch her, to feel her solid under his hands, had become unbearable.

None of this, not the hotel, not the security, certainly not the media trucks parked on the street below, was what Fergus wanted. But his wishes for a quiet life shared with someone he loved had been tossed into the rubbish bin.

He raked his fingers through his hair, sending the curls into tighter knots.

Blast Ivan and whoever had sent him. He deserved far worse than a bullet in his shoulder and a life behind bars. He'd threatened Molly. The gun had been pointed at her. Fergus had thought he'd known fear, but he'd been wrong. True fear was believing that the one you loved would die. It hadn't let him go until Ivan had been bleeding on the floor and Mols had been in his arms.

And then they'd been dragged apart because protocols said to get him, and only him, away immediately to a safe location. Pike's security forces did their job by the book. Fergus ranting and raving wouldn't help anyone. Once upon a time he would have acted the spoiled royal brat, but he wasn't that man anymore.

He was a baker and a boyfriend. Someone who wanted nose kisses in the morning and tolerated Molly's freezing feet on him at night. He'd give anything to turn back the clock to when he'd complained about her chilly toes on his shins.

Would she even want anything to do with him now? Or would she just see a liar?

His mobile buzzed, clattering against the ornate end table he'd left it on. Fergus pounced on it, smashing the green accept button without looking at the number.

"Hello?" he said breathlessly.

"Please hold for King George Kerr of the Isle of Alba," said a perfunctory voice.

Christ on a cracker, he'd been expecting Molly, not his father. He nearly hung up, but then sighed and rubbed his temple. Might as well get this over with, there was no hiding any longer.

The line clicked over. "Hello, son," said his father. The rich sound of his deep voice brought up a thousand memories of stiff court functions and endless sessions of the man lecturing him on the long, long history of their family. It sounded like home.

"It's good to hear your voice." It really was.

"Yours too. We've all missed you. We'll get you on the first plane home that we can."

"No. I…my life is here now."

The king sighed. "What's her name?"

"What?" It couldn't be that obvious. "None of your business. Just tell me you have Ivan's crew in the crosshairs." Fergus' free hand clenched into a fist. They'd torn his life apart twice now. Enough was enough.

"They're cornered. There's a covert team intercepting them as we speak. Now tell me about this girl." His father's tone was warm, congenial like they were settling in for peppermint mochas and a long fireside chat.

Not bloody likely. "I'm going to marry her."

"That doesn't tell me much."

"She perfect. I've never met anyone I can talk to like her. She's warm, funny, brilliant, and beautiful. Works hard, even when she's not supposed to. Wants to make the world a better place."

"Excellent. Sounds like she'll be a fine queen."

"What, no, we're..." He trailed off and stopped pacing to lean his forehead against the cold glass of the window. "I'm going to renounce."

"Nonsense. Bring her here. We can do an official engagement ceremony at the Christmas Eve ball if you're dead set that this girl is the one. That part is non-negotiable, but you know we don't have the same nose in the air reaction to commoners marrying into the family that some royals do. Why your three times great-grandfather was a—"

"Terrific, but I have no idea if she's going to want that kind of life." Fergus pulled at a piece of fuzz on the thirteen-hundred-dollar cashmere sweater he was wearing. The woman who'd handed it to him had apologized that it wasn't better quality. He wanted the cardigan Molly had given him back, but right now it was being examined by security for whatever idiotic reason.

"Why don't you try asking her?" his father said kindly. "At least bring her for Christmas. There's nothing much that an Isle of Alba Christmas can't fix."

There was a noise at the main door of the penthouse and Pike came in, followed by Chelsey, who was wide-eyed as she stared at the posh penthouse. A very pale Molly trailed in behind them.

Fergus dropped his mobile onto the carpet and rushed across the room.

"Fergus," she whispered. He pulled her into a hug, a knot in his chest losing now that she was finally safe with him. Her embrace back was just as fierce.

"Let's go check out the kitchen," Pike said to Chelsey, then spoke up. "Alright, everyone out. Let's give these two some room." There were muffled footfalls as everyone left until it was only Fergus and Molly.

He unwrapped himself enough from Molly that he could cup her face in his palms. She appeared almost dazed, and her eyes kept darting around the living room. He couldn't imagine what she saw. To him, the gilt and gold were so much background noise. Even the view didn't impress him. He'd stayed in fancier places.

He leaned forward to kiss her, wanting to forget the penthouse and the entire night.

Molly stepped back. "What's going on, Fergus?" she said, voice shaking but with a note of determination. His arms fell uselessly to his sides.

He didn't know what to say. "Did you have something to eat?" he asked instead. "We can get anything imaginable here."

"I wanted soup."

He hung his head. This was a conversation he'd hoped to never have. "What did Pike tell you?"

"Not a lot, mostly that 'the prince will explain'. By which I assume he means you. And downstairs is a zoo. There are more television stations than I knew existed all fighting for space on the sidewalk. Who are you?"

"Fergus Murphy." He didn't look up, unable to meet her eyes.

"Who else?"

"That's the only person I want to be."

"I don't think you have a choice now. So I'll ask again, and I think I deserve an answer. Who are you?"

Fergus knew she was right. She deserved so many things. Starting with the truth. He said goodbye to the last of his dreams of things not changing. "I'm…I'm Thomas Hamish Fergus Murphy Kerr, Duke of Moray, and Prince of the Isle of Alba." He finally raised his gaze to her face.

Molly's forehead creased, but then she started laughing. She clapped a hand over her mouth like she could contain the giggles. "You are not."

"I'm afraid so."

She took a deep breath and let it out slowly, her humor fading. "What happens now?"

"Well—" Fergus rubbed the back of his neck. "I still want..." He broke off and sighed. The small ring under their tree should be on her finger, not in a box. He reached out and took her hand, lifting it to his lips. He kissed her palm, his mouth gentle.

Molly inhaled sharply as a tremor went through her. Her face looked pinched, her eyes tired, but she was here with him. She hadn't run. He pressed her hand to his cheek. There was still hope that she would want to be with him. "I was planning on renouncing everything. I'm still the same man. Bloody expensive sweaters that aren't warm enough and posh rooms don't mean anything. I love you."

Her fingertips scratched at his beard. "I know you're still you, but I can't believe I've been yelling at a prince to carry out the trash."

"I didn't mind."

She gave him a little half-smile before tugging her hand free. She pulled out her mobile and unlocked it, her fingers moving quickly over the screen. After a second, she held it up beside him. Her eyes narrowed.

"What are you doing?" he asked. The look of concentration on her face was adorable. Her nose wrinkled up and he wanted to kiss it. That morning he could have without worrying. That morning, with its coffee and toast, felt like ten million years ago.

"I still can't quite believe it. How could I not know?"

He craned his neck. She'd pulled up a picture of him from a few years ago. His hair was dyed lighter, he was clean-shaven, and the kind of skinny that a lot of partying without eating had got him. His eyes were red in the picture. Altogether, he looked like what he'd been, an irresponsible kid with more money than brains.

"I started going to the gym after that picture," he grumbled.

Molly brushed his hair back from his forehead, still comparing him to the picture. "You look so different." She lowered the phone, her eyes following the screen.

"That was the idea. Ivan and his crew tried to kidnap me in the Mediterranean. I hid. I went from baking as an occasional hobby to it being one of the most important parts of my life. The beard, the longer hair…it all seemed right. I'm not that guy anymore. I don't want to be him."

"What do you want?" Her voice was soft, the question tentative. Molly put her mobile away.

"You."

Her eyes closed, the lashes fanning out against her cheeks. "This is a lot," she said.

"I love you, Mols. I always will."

She bit her lip, and time slid to a stop. The dust motes dancing in the air stilled. The ticking of the white-lacquered grandfather clock paused. His heart ceased to beat.

Molly pushed up on her toes. Their lips met, and Fergus was reborn. His pulse thundered, air rushed in and out of his lungs, and desire surged through his veins.

His hand curled around her ass, urging her against him. With a moan, Molly jumped, wrapping her legs around his hips.

Fergus hoped she knew he never wanted to let her go.

CHAPTER SEVEN

MOLLY

Molly's head spun, from the hungry wildness of Fergus' mouth, from how ostentatiously wealthy the penthouse was, and from the fact that she hadn't known Fergus as well as she thought she had. That the child she carried, still more an idea than concrete reality, would itself be in line for a crown someday.

It all felt like too much, making it easier to focus on the man who'd been part of her every waking moment since he'd caught her on the stairs. Molly knew his tongue and lips, the grip of his hands and how his cock pressed eagerly against her thigh. She knew this Fergus, the one that couldn't get enough of her, the one that made amazing cookies and that liked to watch old movies. She loved this Fergus, it seemed impossible that her Fergus could also be royalty, the heir to the throne of the Isle of Alba.

His strong arms banded around her, carrying her into a bedroom she hardly looked at, it was just a blur of white walls with a huge bed. Fergus tossed her on it, then stripped off the sweater he had on. His pants followed, leaving him in just his boxer briefs.

Familiar tingling lust swept through her. She wanted him, like she had from the first moment she'd seen him. Molly scooted back against the mound of pillows at the head of the bed, her skin heating under his steady gaze.

She cupped a breast through her shirt, drawing Fergus' gaze to her chest and making him growl. Molly pulled her blouse off, tossed it away, and followed it with her bra. Sparks of pleasure lit her up as she returned to fondling herself, pinching and rolling her nipple.

Fergus' cock jerked in his underwear. He palmed himself, his eyes locked on her.

"What are you thinking?" she asked.

Fergus' lips quirked up. "That I can hardly believe you're here. That I could have died today. That you could have. But we didn't, we're safe, and I'm going to fuck you until you can't walk right."

Her stomach did a flip. She'd barely allowed herself to think about all that, she'd floated through most of the moments since. Time had become irrelevant, until she'd been brought here, to the man she loved. The man who would probably now fly back to Alba and realize that the girl he'd spent a few weeks with wasn't the kind that princes built a life with.

He didn't even know that, not yet. She had this last night when he would still be hers.

"I'm thinking about you," she said, truthfully enough.

"Good." He climbed on the bed, prowling up her body to her breasts. He nuzzled under her hand and claimed the nipple she'd been playing with. His mouth was warm, and his tongue flicked over her just the way she liked. "Nothing else matters right now, we're just us. And us is a good thing."

Molly didn't have an answer for that, because they had been good together, happy and making do in little apartments above a coffee shop. She'd bought him underwear for Christmas, and a new spatula.

He probably had twenty-five diamond-encrusted spatulas in his palace. She couldn't even imagine living in a castle.

Fergus let go of her breast and kissed her again, deep and demanding.

Molly kissed him back, her tongue in his mouth, wild to have a last taste of him. Maybe there could be some money for the baby, eventually, but certainly, no country would want her, a commoner, as the mother to the heir.

"Molly," Fergus whispered against her lips. "Are you here with me?"

"My head's still spinning." She opened her eyes.

Fergus kissed the end of her nose. "I know, god, I know. But we're safe. Alive. It's going to be okay."

What a dear, sweet man. "I know." She wanted him to remember this last time with her fondly.

Dropping to his side next to her, he fumbled with the button of her jeans. She sat up, finishing up with the zipper herself and shoving her jeans and underwear down her legs. They landed with a thump beside the bed.

"I love every part of you," Fergus rasped. He ran a warm palm up her thigh before dipping two fingers between her legs. "How bloody clever you are, how you throw yourself into new things, and how much you love the little things in life, like a good coffee in the morning." She moaned as he flicked a finger over her clit. "As long as it's not too early in the morning."

"Evil time of day."

He chuckled but continued rubbing her in sweet circles. "Entirely. I'm going to treat you to the very best from around the world, you're going to be amazed."

Molly needed him to not talk about an after that might not exist. His mouth needed to be filled with something. That gave her an idea, for something that would be a perfect and memorable last time together.

She gently pushed him back on the bed, kissing a path down his belly to his underwear. She hooked her fingers in the waistband and pulled them down his legs.

Fergus grinned crookedly at her as he stroked his cock.

Her heart cracked, close to breaking. She'd thought they'd really be together forever, the ones who beat the odds, but part-time baristas and princes weren't the stuff of fairytales, they were the stuff of terrible ideas and mismatched expectations.

Hope still fluttered determinedly inside her, which meant this would hurt all the more when it eventually ended. There had to be a lot of paperwork that would be required to make sure her child wasn't in line for the succession.

"That sounds nice," she said. "Though I really do like the stuff at The Good Bean, with a gingerbread cookie on the side."

Fergus beamed. "You have no idea how much it pleases me that you adore my biscuits."

"I adore a lot of your things." Like how his eyes lit up when she said that. Molly shuffled around on the bed until she could swing a leg across his belly, her foot grazing the planes and hair of his chest.

Fergus grabbed both her ankles. "Is this what I think it is?" he asked, sounding like a kid in a candy store.

"An early Christmas present." And possibly goodbye, not because she wanted to say it, but because reality would smack them in the face soon. One last stolen moment would have to last them, possibly forever

He hauled her legs toward him, pitching her forward so she ended up on her hands and knees, his cock right in front of her face. It was hard and ready, as tasty as any cookie. Mouth watering, she dipped down to lick the salty head.

Fergus moaned, his hands snaking around her thighs to grab her ass. A brief flash of embarrassment froze her, but she melted as Fergus slicked his tongue over her folds while making happy, appreciative noises. He pushed at her rear, and she spread her thighs wider to bring her pussy closer to his face.

"Can you breathe?" she asked.

"Don't care," he mumbled, voice muffled. "But yes."

His tongue found her clit and tapped it, making her moan as pleasure raced along her nerve endings.

Fergus' cock strained towards her, looking angry at being ignored. Wrapping her lips around him, Molly sucked, drawing his shaft into her mouth. He tasted familiar, male and salty, and she lost herself in it, hollowing out her cheeks and stroking him with her tongue. His thighs tensed, and she soothed one with a hand, not wanting this to be over too fast.

The pleasure between her legs built, distracting her. Fergus knew her so well, every flick of his tongue or press of his lips was perfect. A hand dragged down her ass, tracing it before he found her opening with his fingers and buried two of them deeply. Molly moaned, shamelessly gyrating her hips.

"That's it," he said. A third finger pressed inside her and she tensed, a muscle ticking behind her knee as she hurtled towards competition. She sucked harder, taking him deeper down her throat. Fergus groaned, the muscles of his legs standing out in stark relief.

She came, falling into bliss with a harsh whimper. Without thinking she sucked, messily and noisily, as her orgasm washed any other thoughts away. Fergus gripped her ass tightly, drawing out her pleasure by sinking his tongue deep into her channel.

It was only a minute later that he followed her, his cock bucking in her mouth as he released. He pressed his face into her pussy, moaning something that sounded like her name.

Briefly, they lay panting on the quilt. As soon as Fergus stirred, she scooted down and off him, turning around to lie in his welcoming arms. He looked blissful, his beard wet from her cream. Her cheeks heated as she snuggled against him, but she was glad for this moment. It would be a good way to remember him, satisfied and languid after lovemaking, the real kind, with actual love. It would carry her through whatever lay ahead, some future time when she'd just be somebody he used to know.

Molly hated that it fell on her to break the peace of the moment, but if she wanted to survive having fallen in love with a prince, she needed to get started.

"I'm going to go," she said.

Fergus turned his head, frowning. "What?"

"Look, I'm guessing you'll be going home soon and—"

"If you mean flying to Alba, yes, my parents are going to insist." He sighed and rolled his eyes. His parents, also known as the King and Queen. Molly couldn't quite wrap her head around that. She'd been living with a guy whose father's face was on coins. "You can come, I was whisked away earlier based on security protocols. That'll change. We won't be separated again."

Molly closed her eyes and lay her head on his chest, listening to the steady thump of his heart. "I need to get my head clear before I go anywhere. I'm not sure I can just stop my life and move to a whole different country."

Fergus stiffened. "What?"

"This is a big thing, I have to have the space to think about it." Her life had changed in an instant before, a stranger had shown up, told her that her parents weren't coming back, and had her put a few things into a bag before leaving the only home she'd known. This felt like that night all over again, the ground the thought was solid had turned to quicksand. She needed to pull herself free before making a decision.

"Oh." His hand stroked her back. He sounded desolate and she hated that she'd done that to him. "At least say you'll come for Christmas. Please, Molly." He rolled onto his side, pressing his forehead to hers. "Please."

Part of her wanted to say she couldn't, it was too soon, but her heart spoke first. "I'll try."

He sagged against the bed. "Thank you. I promise we'll work this out."

Molly was relieved he wasn't arguing with her or making endless empty promises. Her chest felt hollow, probably because he'd always carry her heart with him, but she had to do what was best for her. Maybe she was wrong, maybe there would be a place for her by his side, but they both needed to figure that out before things went any further, or became complicated by a baby.

She'd tell him soon, when their relationship became clear.

Molly pressed a soft kiss to his lips, worried it might be their last, before she stood and dressed.

Pike drove her back to her building, which was teeming with security personnel and Seattle police.

On the third floor, she glanced towards the open door of what had been Fergus' apartment. It sat completely empty, every last trace of their little shared life stripped away. Even the Christmas tree and gifts were gone.

Molly was too tired to ask why.

In her apartment, she flicked the lights on and off like Pike has asked to let him know she was safe. All the blind opening and closing Fergus had done anytime they returned from an outing suddenly made a lot more sense.

Molly poured herself a bowl of cereal and sat at her seldom-used kitchen table.

She'd never felt more alone in her life.

CHAPTER EIGHT

FERGUS

The chair Fergus sat on gouged into his back, the bloody kilt his mum had insisted on itched, and his freshly cut hair and newly trimmed beard left him feeling not like himself.

He sat waiting for a press conference—his father had instead on one—to start. He'd make his excuses for being gone, mumble something about the causes he was going to be championing, and then sneak in his mention of a big announcement on Christmas Eve. Fergus hadn't dared let it slip to anyone that he would be making that statement. The media would pounce on it and analyze the statement to death, most likely coming up with the correct solution, that he would be asking someone to marry him.

The requirement was to ask his intended bride for her hand in front of the entire court of Alba, and the next time they'd be assembled was the annual Christmas Eve party.

There'd be no mentioning Molly by name, she didn't need that spotlight right now.

He missed her so damn much. His days were endless oceans of missing her, wanting her. Everything that happened he always wanted to tell her first, but most of it he couldn't, due to state security issues.

Though he had taken a selfie in a mirror of him dressed up for the presser.

He pulled out his mobile, but there were no new messages. Ever since he'd been forced back into his role of prince, Molly had seemed distant. Though there was the time difference, and he had been hellaciously busy since returning to the Isle. He had to be reading things into her delayed responses that simply weren't true, but he never could quite work up the courage to ask if she was avoiding him because the answer might be too much for him to bear.

Fergus badly wished he'd been able to propose to her in the Seattle flat. Or the last time he'd seen her, before she'd left the penthouse. Maybe the distance between them wouldn't seem so vast if she wore his ring.

His knee jiggled.

Ignoring the niggling thought that she might not come for the holidays, or that he might not ever see her again. Fergus opened his text message app and sent her the picture. How do I look? he typed.

The bubble that indicated she was replying popped up almost immediately.

A kilt? She included a raised eyebrow emoji.

He grinned at the screen. It's traditional.

There was a pause, the bubbles appeared then disappearing twice before Molly's response arrived. And what do you have on under it? Two emojis popped up under the words, one sticking its tongue out and the other winking.

His blood warmed. It was the first flirty thing she'd said since he'd arrived in Alba.

Fergus typed quickly. Unfortunately, I can't be quite that traditional. I have to report that I have the approved royal boxer shorts on.

She responded with the laugh out loud emoji.

Knee jiggling faster, he asked what he had to know, the thing keeping him up at night. You are going to make it for Christmas? He sent it, paused, knowing wearing his heart on his sleeve might come back to haunt him, but then forged ahead. Molly deserved to know. I miss you, and it won't be Christmas without you here.

The dots appeared and disappeared. Time was running out, he was going to have to go on stage in front of the cameras in minutes.

I'm not sure I'm ready, Molly typed.

He leaned forward in the chair, heart hammering. Nobody was ever ready for the spotlight being part of a royal household brought. He'd been born to it and he still wouldn't call himself ready. But he suspected Mols might not hate it all as much as she thought she would. There were good parts, like being able to draw attention to things you were passionate about. There was also helping people financially or by raising their spirits by visiting them in the hospital or the like.

All of those were things he hadn't paid much attention to before he'd gone into hiding, more focused on the perks of being a prince, like partying on yachts, traveling to places like Brazil and Ibiza, and buying whatever ridiculous things struck his fancy.

He'd toss every car he owned in the ocean for another minute with Molly.

I bloody know it's a lot. Let me show you. If you hate it, then I'll step down. I was going to do that anyway. Not having you close is driving me around the bend. I haven't even told you how your pan is doing. It made all the difference when I had a chance to try the chewy gingerbread again. I also dialed back the molasses. I think the taste is more focused on the spices now.

Sleeping was nearly impossible when he didn't have Molly to spoon, so there'd been quite a few late-night sessions in the kitchen. Pike would sit in a chair nearby and snore, and usually, the head chef would appear to fuss. She'd eventually nod off as well. It all led to Fergus needing his own kitchen, and a little exploring had turned up just the right place. At the moment it was being gutted and needed appliances ordered.

"Your highness," Sebastian, his personal secretary, said. It forced Fergus to look up from the text messages, which made him scowl. Slight and on the shorter side, Sebastian always looked like a nervous whippet. "It's time, please hand me your mobile." Fergus glowered but handed it over after typing a quick goodbye to Molly.

Sebastian fluttered about him, straightening Fergus' lapels and making sure his pocket square was perfect. Sometimes Sebastian could be more of a nanny than an aide.

Finally, he stepped back and ran a hand over his slicked-down dark hair. "You'll do."

"Thank you." Fergus strode to the side of the small press conference stage and waited until he was called to the podium. A round of unexpected cheers from the press took him aback. "It's good to see you too," he said with a polished smile. Before the attempted kidnapping, he'd fended off biting questions from reporters about whoever his rumored love interest was, or whatever scandal he'd caused at some party.

Feeling welcome was brand new.

His smile became more genuine. "I'm sorry I was gone so long without a word. I know that the basic story has already been released. Today I'm here to assure the Isle that we are safe and secure. The trail of the mercenaries has been traced back to one of the large oil companies upset that we're ending offshore drilling in our waters. They played hardball and lost. To show my dedication to the future of our country, after the Christmas season, I will be part of the effort to change all Royal properties to use only renewable energy."

Or he might be, the actual events after Christmas Eve entirely depended on Molly. He hated that he might be lying to the country, but if he returned to the States it'd no longer be his problem.

"What did you do while in hiding?" asked a balding reporter from the Isle's major newspaper.

He leaned casually against the podium. "Do you really want to know?"

Several of the reporters shifted forward in their seats and nodded.

"I wish I could tell you I was busy being James Bond, but mostly what I did was bake." A murmur went through the room. "I perfected several personal recipes, including one for gingerbread. It's based on traditional Isle of Alba methods, but I like to think I made it my own. Currently, I'm working on a chewy version."

"Will you be releasing a cookbook?" asked an older woman.

"That's an excellent idea, I also make a very tasty snickerdoodle." He beamed at her and she flushed. This was much more fun when it wasn't an interrogation on the media's part.

In the rear of the room, Pike pressed a finger to his earpiece, then signaled for Fergus to wind things up.

He straightened. "I'd like to stay and chat, but I'm being told my time is nearly up. One last thing before I go. On Christmas Eve at the Royal Ball, in front of the entire court, I will be making a very important declaration."

The room erupted with shouted questions. Fergus stepped away from the podium, gave the older woman a wink, and walked away. Behind him, the buzz increased exponentially.

"That was fun," he said when Sebastian met him backstage.

"You were very charming, Sir. Though now the entire Isle will be erupting in speculation about who the lucky lady is."

Fergus grimaced. "I'm not sure she'll agree with the lucky part." He accepted his mobile back from Sebastian. "And I'm not telling you a thing," he added to the man's questioning look. "I won't give it away, not even to you. So don't expect any clues."

Sebastian sighed. "You have a meeting with your mother about upcoming appearances in fifteen minutes."

"I'm going."

Walking towards the private family wing of the palace, he unlocked his mobile's screen.

At the top of his notifications was a text from Molly. He punched the air, nearly giddy as joy bubbled up.

He read the words over and over.

I'll be there.

CHAPTER NINE

MOLLY

Molly sat squished in a window seat of the small plane winging its way across the North Sea to the Isle of Alba. The flight was packed, like the ones from Seattle to Dulles and on across the Atlantic to Glasgow had been. Below, clouds raced over the blue-grey water of the ocean. She hadn't slept a wink, too nervous about what waited for her at the end of the journey.

Chelsey had been much more relaxed and had nodded off about thirty minutes out of Dulles and not awoken until they were descending into Scotland. She was awake now, drumming her fingers on her thigh and eyeing the other passengers. Everyone on this flight seemed much cheerier than the others, they chatted excitedly while wrapped presents crowded the overhead bins and poked out of carry-on bags.

It seemed the spirit of Christmas even inundated flights to the Isle. Too bad it couldn't seem to touch her.

"You're frowning," Chelsey said. "It's okay to be mad at him. He did a really idiotic thing."

"It's complicated." Very complicated, in ways she had never expected her life to be. Chelsey didn't even know the half of it. The baby was still Molly's secret. She'd been terrified to tell anyone, in case word got back to Fergus before she'd had a chance to speak with him about the child. Telling him via text message or over the phone didn't feel right either. She'd do it in person. Soon. When she'd worked up the nerve.

The two middle-aged women sitting in front of her, who'd had their heads together since takeoff bickering over the correct ratio of salt to baking soda in sugar cookie recipes without coming to a consensus, finally turned their attention to the newspaper one of them had brought.

"Doesn't he look all grown up?" one said, holding up a section of the paper. A picture of Fergus from the press conference a few days ago graced most of the page. The headline above blared: Who could she be?

Molly wished she could hide under her seat. The American media hadn't carried much about Fergus saying he'd make an announcement on Christmas Eve, but the closer Molly had gotten to the Isle, the more speculation she'd heard. It threatened to overwhelm her.

The other woman tutted. "Wouldn't kick him out of bed for eating crackers."

Okay, that was just weird. He was her boyfriend.

"I wonder who he's marrying?" the woman continued. "I bet she's one of those Hollywood starlets. They're all blonde and busty."

The first woman snorted. "He wouldn't marry an American. My money is on some Swedish princess."

Molly slumped back, trying to tune out the words. Those were the kinds of women the entire country expected him to marry. Movie stars and princesses. Not out of work materials engineers. Especially not ones who got pregnant before the wedding.

Chelsey leaned close to Molly and spoke in a low voice. "I'm serious. You can be mad and him and his handsome face. And just ignore the gossip."

As if it was that easy. "I am mad," Molly whispered back. "But, as I said, it's complicated."

"Do you want to tell me why? Because of the money? It is weird that not only could he buy you a mink coat, but a whole farm of minks if that's what you wanted."

"No, that's not…" She trailed off while chewing on her bottom lip.

Chelsey took her hand and squeezed. "Whatever's bothering you, tell me. I can't help unless you do."

The temptation to have one person on her side while walking into the frenzy they were flying towards was tempting. Molly had brought Chelsey along as moral support, but Chelsey couldn't do that if she didn't know everything.

Molly lowered her voice further, though no one was paying any attention to them. "No repeating this." Chelsey nodded. "Not even to Pike. You can't tell a soul."

Chelsey let go of Molly's hand. She mimed locking her lips and throwing away the key.

"I'm…I'm pregnant."

"Oh shit."

"Yeah."

"You haven't been drinking enough water."

"What?" That wasn't the response Molly had expected.

The flight attendant light dinged as Chelsey jabbed it.

The attendant bustled down the aisle. "Can I help you?" she asked with a practiced smile.

"Bottle of water for my friend, she needs to stay hydrated." Chelsey glared at Molly.

"I'm fine, really." Though Chelsey immediately worrying over her lifted some of the burden she'd been carrying.

"And here I thought all the crying was because you were upset," Chelsey muttered.

"I haven't cried that much." Well, except at the commercial with the puppies, and every time Jingle Bells played because it was her favorite carol. Molly grimaced and bumped Chelsey's elbow with her own. "You're a good friend."

"I might cut off his balls for not taking better care of you when..." She gestured towards Molly's middle.

"He doesn't know."

Chelsey's mouth fell open. "Oh my god. You're just as bad as he is, Molly!"

"It's a surprise, for Christmas."

Chelsey dropped her face into her hands. "Just drink your water."

The flight attendant reappeared with a bottle, and Molly took it gratefully. She was thirsty. The water, some Isle of Alba brand with a label showing a crystal-clear lake, tasted like heaven. She chugged the entire bottle in one long drink.

"Is everything there going to taste this good?" she asked, coming up for air.

"You'll have to tell me." Chelsey tried to waggle her brows, but it mostly looked like she was very confused.

"Stop, I don't even know if we're going to be doing any of that. I don't have any idea what's going to happen. I mean, we're not even in first class."

"Phew, I'm glad I'm not the only one who expected that. I'm going to kick him in the shins for putting us in coach."

The urge to defend her boyfriend welled up. "Maybe he's just used to how things have been this last year, or put cost first, or it didn't cross his mind because he's overwhelmed with prince duties or whatever." The email with a link to the tickets had come from a generic Royal House of Kerr email address, so Molly had assumed a secretary had sent them. Fergus had been very busy the last few days with only sporadic texts, mostly asking if she'd be there soon.

Chelsey rolled her eyes. "Fine, I'll just think about kicking him in the shins."

"I'm good with that."

The overhead speakers crackled to life, the pilot letting the crew and passengers know to prepare for landing. Molly gripped the arms of her seat. She looked out the window of the plane just in time to see the ocean change to a rocky coastline. Her stomach roiled as the plane dropped, from pregnancy and nerves as well as the rapid descent.

Snow-covered fields gave way to the outskirts of a city. It hit her that this could be her new home, that she could someday be responsible for many of the people on this plane, that she'd get to know the names of the streets whizzing by under the belly of the plane.

Molly closed her eyes and gripped the arms of the seat tighter.

She didn't move until the plane had touched down and taxied to the gate.

Chelsey touched her shoulder as if Molly was merely asleep and not close to panic. She blinked at her friend and Chelsey helped her up and shooed her down the aisle. Cold air nipped at her in the jetway. She barely had time to wrap her coat tighter before she stepped out of the gate and into the airport.

Christmas assaulted her from every direction. Cinnamon and cloves swept up her nose, and an actual choir sang carols in a corner of the lounge. Every surface was covered with garlands and twinkling lights.

She swayed on her feet, from exhaustion, hunger, and way too much holiday festivity.

"You okay?" Chelsey asked, grabbing her arm.

"This is a bit much."

"Yeah," Chelsey agreed. She led Molly to the baggage claim where an older man in a cap and coat was holding a sign that read 'North'. Molly and Chelsey's luggage sat beside him.

Disappointment dribbled through her, but it wasn't as if the crown prince of Alba could mosey down to the airport on a whim.

"That's us!" Chelsey chirped.

The man tugged at his cap. "Name's Liam, I've got the car all nice and warm waiting on you."

"Thank you." Molly picked up her bag and followed Liam out into the weak afternoon sunlight, where they stowed the luggage in the trunk of a gray sedan. Molly got in the back seat and scooted over to give Chelsey room. A tiny Christmas tree sat on the dash.

"Did you ladies have a nice trip?" Liam asked as he pulled into the flow of traffic.

"It wasn't bad," Chelsey said. "Do you drive lots of people to the palace?"

"This time of year, aye, there's rather a lot of royal guests."

Molly winced. Was that all she was? A "guest"? If she'd flown all the way here to be royally dumped, she was going to be so mad. After she got done crying. She dropped her head into her hands. It shouldn't surprise her, but some part of her still believed in fairy tales. The part that'd hoped each new foster home would be the last one, that she'd finally found a place to belong.

As Liam navigated the narrow city streets, she stared out the window at the beautifully decorated streets and quaint houses and shops covered with a dusting of snow. It was lovely and festive, and Molly hated that Fergus wasn't the one showing them to her.The car turned a corner, and Chelsey gasped. Molly whipped her head around to peer through the windshield. Her jaw dropped. She'd seen pictures, but no number of images could have prepared her for the reality of the Royal Palace.

At the end of the wide, tree-lined avenue sat a huge building, the edifice a stately white marble. Window after window glinted in the afternoon light, the sashes decorated with cheery red bows. A black wrought iron fence surrounded the building, its harshness muted by evergreen garlands.

"Damn," Chelsey breathed.

Molly couldn't even speak as Liam drove them slowly past the imposing structure. They turned a corner, then into a gate with a manned checkpoint. A guard checked the driver's badge and Molly and Chelsey's passports before waving them through. Gravel crunched under the car's tires as Liam pulled up and parked in front of a set of glass doors.

A porter in a green uniform appeared and whisked away their luggage. Chelsey thanked Liam, while Molly stood and gaped at the vastness of the palace. Through the doors was an ostentatious lobby. A woman with grey hair pulled into a tight bun glared at them.

"Molly North and guest?" the woman asked. Molly nodded. "I've assigned you a double room," she sniffed. "Space is at a premium during the holidays, so you'll have to share."

Molly pasted on a smile. Another bit of hope slipped away. She'd imagined spending her nights with Fergus, safe in his arms. She shouldn't have come. This dismissal would have been so much easier to take thousands of miles away and over the phone.

"This way." The woman marched down the hallway. Molly shuffled after, a worried-looking Chelsey beside her. They rode an elevator up, then walked down another long hallway. The decorations were pastel landscapes and dark, heavy wood furniture, the tops festooned with Christmas greenery. The woman stopped in front of a door. "Room 515, remember it in case you get lost and need to ask for help. You are in the south wing. You are allowed anywhere in it. If you need transportation or other services, ring the front desk." She shoved a key at Molly. It sat cold in her palm.

"Thank you," Chelsey murmured. The woman nodded once before turning on her heel and stalking off. The inside of the room was generic, two beds with headboards, a television on a dresser, and a small table. It could be a hotel room anywhere in the world. Chelsey made a face. "Where's your prince?"

"No idea," Molly said. "I thought...I don't know. That I'd be different from other guests." She really had, but the whole trip had been mundane. She plunked herself down on the foot of one of the beds. The beige walls mocked her, reminding her just how lacking in status she was. She picked at a loose thread on the quilt.

Chelsey paced. "I expected you two to run to each other through a field of poinsettias, or whatever the Christmas version of lovers reuniting is."

"Yeah, well, me too."

"I'm going to pee." Chelsey marched into the bathroom but immediately bounded back out. "Molly! You have to come see this!"

Molly rose slowly, not very enthusiastic about whatever could be in a hotel bathroom. She peeked in. Chelsey stood cackling while trying to take a photo of the toilet.

"Wait," Molly said. "Is that what I think it is?"

It didn't make up for her missing boyfriend, but the bright gold glint of the toilet seat did spur her into action. She pulled out her cell phone, which had a lack of messages, and snapped a photo. The traditional gold toilet seats of the Royal Palace were mentioned in every guidebook Molly had borrowed from the library. Apparently, they were not to be missed if you were a tourist.

Chelsey bent over the commode. “This thing is well attached, there’s no walking away with it.”

“Huh.” Molly hadn’t expected a toilet seat to drive home just how much she didn’t belong.

Chelsey’s fingers sped over the screen of her phone. “I’m texting Pike, but he’s probably at work and won’t be able to respond for hours. Why don’t you try Fergus?”

“He most likely doesn’t have his phone either.” She hated that she didn’t have a way to contact him. Another pulse of loneliness spiked through her.

“Just try.”

Molly stared at the screen. She brought up the picture of the toilet up and sent it to Fergus with the caption: Even for guests?

He didn’t reply.

Resigned, Molly retreated to the simplicity of unpacking her bag. Chelsey joined her after a minute, and they worked in silence.

It stretched until it became uncomfortable, while Molly’s thoughts whirled with what difficulties the future could bring.

“Do you think I should ask for child support?” she said as Chelsey put neatly folded underwear into a drawer.

“I think you should shove a—”

She was cut off by Molly’s phone ringing shrilly. Molly pounced on it. “It’s Fergus,” she hissed at Chelsey, who froze. Molly answered the call. “Hello?”

“You’re here?” Fergus barked.

She frowned at the angry tone. “Isn’t that what you wanted?”

“When? How? I thought…it doesn’t matter. Where are you?” He sounded extremely angry, in a way Molly had never heard before.

“Room 512, south wing.”

“What the bleeding fuck are you doing there?”

The snarl in his voice put her back on her heels. "Look, I just got here. I'm exhausted. At least now I know where I belong. In the guest wing." She could be angry too, damn it. Her muscles tightened. "You could have broken up with me over the phone, I don't know why you dragged me here to do it."

The line went dead.

CHAPTER TEN

FERGUS

It'd been pure luck that he'd seen her message. Fergus had been in the middle of getting his formalwear fitted for the Christmas Eve ball, trying to hold himself together because the event was only a few days away and he'd yet to hear any travel plans from Molly. The fear that she'd decided he wasn't worth the trip had started to creep in. He'd been afraid to call and ask again, not wanting what could potentially be his last conversation with her to be a row.

Desperation had been plaguing him, and he'd gone as far as asking Pike to dredge up the paperwork required for Fergus to initiate the renouncement of his titles and his claim to the throne. One late night he'd baked an entire flurry of gingerbread snowflakes, filling out the forms with everything needed, excepting his signature.

Molly might not want the prince, but she'd damn well craved him when he'd been simply Fergus, the bloke who lived next door. He could be that again. He could be anything for her.

The tailor had been writing something down when Fergus had peeked at his mobile while attempting not much up the half hemmed formal kilt the tailor was working on.

The only notification was from Molly. He'd opened it, and his heart had nearly stopped. She was here, in the palace, and he'd had no idea she was even on her way. When she'd answered on the first ring, her voice strained, he'd nearly gone round the bend.

His mobile had made a satisfying crunch as he put a dent in the wall with it, and then he was out the door, the tailor left behind as Fergus strode towards the South Wing. Guest room, the love of his life was in a bloody guest room.

Fergus rounded a corner, nearly running into his secretary.

"Are you quite done with the fitting?" Sebastian asked, eyeing the open white dress shirt with its unfinished sleeves and the asymmetrical kilt Fergus had on.

Fergus grabbed him by the lapels of his green jacket. "Why did you not inform me that Molly North was arriving today?"

Sebastian's eyes went very wide. "Who?"

"Molly North, from the states." Fergus shook Sebastian, who fumbled his mobile, nearly dropping it before raising it with a shaking hand.

"Oh, um, yes. your highness. As asked, I added her name to the official list of guests you invite to the ball and had a travel agency arrange the transportation. I had no idea you wanted to be informed of arrivals. Also taking up residence today are the Duke and Duchess of---"

Shite, Fergus hadn't told his assistant to keep him informed about Molly. He let go of Sebastian, who immediately smoothed his hair down. "Anything about Molly comes to your attention, you tell me immediately. I don't care what time of the day or night it is. And get me a new phone, one with all the bells and whistles."

Sebastian drew himself straight. "Of course, sir."

"And message Pike, tell him to meet me outside of South Wing room 515."

"Doing so now, sir."

Fergus grimaced. "And I'm sorry, still angry, but I apologize for being out of line."

"Very good, sir." Sebastian's fingers flew over the keyboard on his mobile, but his expression was mollified. "Though I am glad your family no longer fancies beheadings for those they're displeased with."

"You better hope not," Fergus muttered. Sebastian scurried behind him, darting onto the elevator as Fergus punched the button for the floor Molly was on. The damn Palace was suddenly far too big, and it took nearly ten minutes of almost running for him to reach the entrance to the South Wing, which had controlled access.

The woman seated at the desk glanced up as he rapped his knuckles on the counter, then did a doubletake and shot to her feet. "Your highness," she sputtered. "How may I assist you?"

"Let us through, Betty," Sebastian said in a soothing voice before Fergus could snap at her.

The door unlocked and he pushed it open hard enough to slam it into the wall. He walked faster, his undone shirt flapping behind him. The doors, pristine white with the room numbers indicated in neat brass plaques, flashed by until he reached 515, which looked the same as every other.

"Is there a problem, your highness?" a woman in black slacks and a tight grey bun asked.

Sebastian trotted down the hallway, face red, not having been able to keep up with Fergus' mad rush. He was too far away to blunt the edges of Fergus' anger this time.

"There is a blasted big problem. Let me in this room, now," he bellowed at her.

"I sorry, sir, private guest quarters--"

"I said now," he yelled, and she took a step back. "If I have to tell you again, you'll be out on your arse in the snow."

The woman swallowed but raised her chain. She opened her mouth. Fergus growled, satisfied when she snapped her jaw shut again.

"Have you tried knocking, sir?" Sebastian panted as he arrived.

Fergus bit back another retort and brought his fist up, but the door swung open before he got a chance to bang on it. Chelsey, blonde hair mussed, made a face at him. "Fergus? What are you wearing?"

He grabbed her sleeve and tugged her into the hallway. "Pike will be here any minute. Have him take you for coffee." He shoved past her and slammed the door behind him.

Molly stood near one of the blandly decorated beds, looking worn out with bags under her eyes, her mascara smudged like she'd been crying.

In the next instant, he was across the room and sweeping her into his arms, raining kisses on her brow. Molly slung her arms around his neck, looked up with her big brown eyes, and promptly broke into sobs.

"What's wrong?" he asked. "Molly, I'm sorry, what can I do?" Fergus had no clue what had earned him her tears.

"I missed you," she sniffled, pressing her face into his chest. She sniffed again. "You smell good." The sobs got louder.

It was very tempting to tell her she should have simply come with him, but he knew better than to say that out loud. She might not have figured out how she felt until right this minute.

"I'm sorry there was mix up," he murmured. "Won't happen again. I'll have your things moved to my room."

She hugged him tighter, molding her body to his. "We should talk, I have something to tell you."

Alarm bells went off in his skull. "Is it that you're going to run off and live with wolves?"

"Not that." She gave a shaky laugh. "I'm not dressed for it."

"Then whatever you want to say can wait until after I make love to you." That hadn't been his plan, but his rage was fast pivoting into raw desire.

Molly nodded. "It can." She took a step back, her gaze roving up and down him. "What the hell are you wearing? I'm not complaining, exactly, but you look like you should be wandering a windswept moor somewhere."

He put his hands on his hips. "If you must know, I was in the middle of a fitting for the Christmas Eve ball."

"Do you plan to wear more than just an open shirt, or should I accessorize with a stick to keep people from trying to hump your leg?"

The desire exploded into pure lust. He launched himself at her, gathering into his arms. Twisting, he landed with his back on the bed and her on top. He sank a hand into her travel-tangled brown hair and directed her mouth to his. The kiss was hungry and desperate, he couldn't get enough of her taste or her moans.

Molly seemed just as eager as him. Her lips glided against his, their tongues entwined, but then she nipped his bottom lip, only to immediately soothe it by licking and sucking at the spot. That tiny bite of pain drove him crazy. He pawed at her shirt, finding the hem to slide a hand under, the feel of her bare skin against his palm burning like a brand.

Her hands were everywhere, combing through his hair, her nails raking through his beard, fingers splaying over his chest. "I missed you," she murmured, tears still in her voice. He kissed her again, wanting to show her that she had been just as missed. His cock strained, as desperate as the rest of him to touch her.

The ball, the media, speeches, none of it mattered, not when he had his Molly in his arms.

She abruptly pushed back and stood. A whimper escaped him at the loss, but in the next instant his mouth twitched up in a smile as Molly wrestled with her t-shirt.

"Shit," she grumbled, her arms tangled in her shirt as she tried to pull it over her head.

Fergus pushed himself to his feet. He swept his hands up her sides, over her breasts encased in a lacy black bra—they were even more generous than he remembered—and up her arms until he could help pull the shirt up. It inched up her face, revealing her kiss-swollen mouth. Unable to resist, he leaned in and caught her lips with his again, teasing her with his tongue as he pulled the shirt the rest of the way off.

Arms free, Molly attacked her trousers. "Hurry," she gasped. "I need you."

"Aye, I can tell." He shed his shirt, pausing after dropping it to the floor. "Mols," he said. "I don't suppose you brought rubbers? They're not usually something I bring along to a fitting."

She undid her bra. "Don't worry about it, I promise I can't get pregnant right now."

"Right, sounds good." Fergus trusted her, plus he wasn't inclined to argue at the moment. And he couldn't help but be a wee bit excited about going without. He felt around the waistband of the kilt. It fastened somehow, in some way he couldn't figure out as Molly's bra slid down and off her arms.

"What's taking so long?" She narrowed her eyes at him, and he gave up on getting the damn kilt off. "Do you need some help?"

"I have no clue how it's fastened, but I'd love a little help with my shorts."

Her lips quirked. "Oh, of course, your highness." He couldn't figure out a comeback, most of his blood having surged to his cock, before Molly dropped to her knees in front of him. She slid her hands up his legs, sending goosebumps skittering over his thighs, she tugged his boxers down, and he belatedly managed to kick off his loafers so she could get the underwear off.

Wearing a wicked grin, she shoved the front of the red and green kilt up, leaned in, and sucked his cock deep into her mouth. "Fuck, Mols, you feel so good." She hummed a reply, the vibrations making his toes curl. She bobbed her head, eyes closed, expression blissful. He tenderly cupped her cheek even as she did her best to make his eyes cross.

Her hand dropped between her legs, and she rocked against her fingers, moaning around his prick. He'd come too bloody fast if she kept that up.

"On the bed," he murmured. "Missed you too much for this to take long." Fergus helped her to her feet and onto the mattress. Following her, he knelt between her thighs to admire her sweet pussy. It glistened with her cream, inviting and sweet. "Later I'll lick you senseless, take you nice and slow, but right now all I can think about is being inside you."

She nodded, spreading her legs further apart. "I thought," she whispered. "I thought you wouldn't still want me. Not once you were here, once you remembered all you could have."

"I'd give every bit of it up in a heartbeat for you," He wrapped his hands around her calves and hitched her legs over his shoulders. "I'm going to take you deep."

"Quit talking about it and do it," she snapped, bracing her hands on the bed.

With a huffed laugh he pulled up the kilt, took his cock in hand, and thrust the head into her. Pleasure raced through him. At last, he was where he belonged.

He pressed forward, Molly's body tilting up to take all of him. She moaned as he sheathed himself entirely inside her, the root of his cock grinding against her clit.

Face flushed, mouth open in bliss, she gazed up at him.

Fergus pulled back, then plowed forward again. Her inner walls pulsed around him. "I'm going to marry you, Molly," he said. "You are my life. If you don't want all this, then I'll simply be a baker."

"Weird proposal," she gasped.

He paused, muscles straining. "I'll have to ask again, in front of the court, it's—"

"Tradition."

"That, but if, after you see everything here you don't want any part of it, then the night of the ball I'll abdicate. Surprise all those old bastards."

"You still haven't asked."

Fergus locked gazes with her, giving another deep thrust to make her shudder. "Molly North, will you marry me?" His heart stopped.

"Yes."

He lived again, heart hammering with relief and joy. He plunged into her, pistoning his hips, declaring his love for the one person in the world that'd seen all of him and still wanted what she saw. She made him feel like a true prince.

Molly moaned, the fingers of one hand plucking at her nipples before descending to her clit.

She barely had to press her index finger against it before she came, her channel pulsing around him as she cried out.

The feel of her pleasure drove him right to the edge.

"Molly, Fuck, Mols, I'm going to come."

She pressed a hand to his cheek. "I want to feel it."

The rhythm of his hips became ragged. He thrust hard and rough a dozen more times before he fell headlong into an explosion of pleasure that rushed through him like a supernova. He thought he might have roared something, but mostly he was consumed with the rush of his release.

When his cock stopped pulsing, he rearranged Molly's legs so he could crash to the bed beside her.

She stroked his hair and murmured softly to him.

"I have to get back to the tailor," Fergus muttered far sooner than he would have liked. "He needs to get me out of this thing."

"I like it." Her hand moved lower to slide over the pleats. She squeezed his bum while making a happy little noise.

"Then I'll live in it, forever. Never take it off."

Molly laughed and pushed at his shoulder. "I'll go with you, if you promise we can have something to eat after." Her nose wrinkled up. "Do you have any cookies? I mean yours, gingerbread with icing? I suddenly want one in the worst way."

"I have tons, it's been hard to sleep and you know I stress bake. Sebastian can bring you up one while the tailor fusses over whatever I've done to his work."

She patted his chest. "Better make it three."

CHAPTER ELEVEN

MOLLY

The woman in the mirror couldn't be her. But when Molly made a face, and so did her reflection.

"Stop it, or it'll freeze that way," Chelsey said. She looked like she'd been born to wear the frothy white gown she'd was in. Sparkling clips held her blonde hair back from her face.

Molly scrunched up her nose. "Will not." The off the shoulder red ball gown she wore, designed by someone whose name she should probably recognize, clung to her breasts and sides before cascading in a shimmering waterfall of crimson to the floor. Her hair had been styled to hang in curls over one shoulder, making her look like anything but the materials engineer she was. Ponytails had been her signature most of her life.

Chelsey spun around in her dress, the hem flaring out. "This is amazing. I've never had my makeup done for me before. I feel like a star."

"I don't even recognize myself."

"You look great, and like yourself, just a more made-up version." Chelsey inspected the toe of her pump. "I think these shoes cost more than I make in a month."

Molly leaned towards the mirror, batting her brand-new fake

eyelashes. She couldn't decide if they looked good or like moths had decided to cling to her face. "I don't know if that says more about the shoes or the fact you are not paid enough."

"I would say both," said a new, feminine voice from behind Molly. She spun, nearly tumbling over as she teetered in her own pair of outrageous heels.

A woman with auburn hair pulled into a sleek bun and wearing a cream-colored sheath gown stood in the doorway. The floor heaved beneath Molly like the sea. The queen of Alba, and quite possibly her future mother-in-law, was staring at her.

"Your Majesty," Molly gasped, bobbing a curtsey as Chelsey did the same.

The queen laughed softly. "We will have to work on that."

Molly's face burned. "Am I late? Fergus said—"

The queen waved a regal hand and floated more than walked into the room. "Call me Anne, and no, I know we're supposed to formally meet before the ball, but it's impossible to talk frankly when everyone is hanging on every word you say." Anne crossed to a round ottoman and sank onto with a sigh. She kicked one of her pumps off. "Evil contraptions."

Molly shared a look with Chelsey and they both broke into giggles. "Terrible," Molly agreed. "It's nice to meet you."

"I'm sure we'll get along quite well, and I feel like I already know you, my son has become incapable of saying anything that doesn't somehow involve you."

Molly winced, but Anne only beamed at her.

"There is a lot of tradition here, isn't there?" Molly asked, her gaze sliding to the evergreen garlands tacked up along the wainscoting of even this out of the way room. "I've been reading the books Fergus gave me, on the history of this palace and his, er, and your, family."

Anne raised a brow. "I can promise you that we do not, as a rule, behead nearly so many people anymore."

Molly tried not to, but she couldn't hold back a snort of laughter. "Good to know."

"I'm willing to guess what you really want to say is something more than comments about Isle of Alba tradition." Anne's relaxed manner fled, replaced with a piercing stare. "I won't ask my son to stay, though his cousin is going to make a mockery of this family, and yes, I know about Pike doing the research and Fergus getting his paperwork ready, but what I don't know is how you feel about it all."

Molly hoped that a rogue pack of Albian wild sheep might burst through the wall and trample her. When the wall remained stubbornly intact, she cleared her throat. "Ah." She swallowed. Chelsey edged over and took her hand, squeezing her fingers. Molly met the queen's gaze. "I have no frame of reference for any of this. I'm terrified." Self-consciously, Molly dropped her hand away from her stomach, where her palm had somehow come to rest.

Anne's gaze was far too knowing. "It's not always easy, there's a public face you have to have, that Fergus has had since he was very young. That public face protects you, keeps you safe. Those you love know you, your family knows you. All my best memories are from when Fergus was small, when my father was still alive and ruling. I grew up in this palace too, there is no better place to be a small child." Anne grinned with a mischievous glint in her eyes. "There are secret passages, and entire rooms forgotten by time. I loved it. I still do, but you should ask Fergus. That boy used to drive me daft with how many hours he'd spend gallivanting about the place."

"I will." Molly still had a decision to make. She didn't think that Fergus could simply walk away from his heritage like he thought he could. It'd take more than a signature, and what would she tell their children when they learned they could have had all this, but instead their mother had been worried she wouldn't fit in? That, more than any other concern, had stopped her from suggesting she and Fergus elope.

"It's okay to be scared," Anne said, proving again how observant she was. "But know we're all ready to welcome you with open arms. The press might be grumbling a little about an American stealing the prince's heart, but most of those articles boil down to: at least you're not English." Anne glanced at a clock on the wall, one probably older than her and Chelsey put together. "We should go, Fergus will be down in a moment and my husband is dying to meet you."

"Me?" What could a king possibly want with her?

Anne laughed a little, tinkling laugh as she slipped her heels back on. "Be prepared, he has a degree in chemistry and has been delighted with the experimental coating you developed. I know it's for baking, Fergus has been using the pan and raving about it—really, as a princess establishing a bakeware line and then donating the profits to help programs to provide food to the elderly would be an excellent thing—and it didn't even dent from a bullet shot at close range. My husband is fascinated, he thinks it could be used on helmets or vehicles as a lightweight bulletproof material, and he is going to talk your ear off about it."

Molly perked up. "I did go a little overboard with its durability."

"Thank god," Chelsey murmured. "I'm going to go find my date, I'll see you soon." She bobbed another curtsey. "It was nice to meet you, your majesty."

Anne nodded at her. "Remind Pike he actually has the night off, that man works too hard."

Chelsey grinned and nearly ran from the room, leaving Molly alone with the queen.

"I love him," Molly said, still looking at the closed door Chelsey had escaped through. "Whatever happens, just know that I love him, and I want what's best for him."

Anne moved to stand beside her. "I know, and he's head over heels in love with you. Whatever happens, I'm happy for both of you. Now let's go get this photo-op done so we can dance. I've heard the decorations are very well done this year." She stood taller, shoulders back, chin high.

Molly copied the posture, trying out her own public face. Could she actually do this? Be an inspiration as well as a wife and mother? She followed Anne from the room, past knots of people, some of which she recognized as upper crust Isle of Alba citizens. Anne put a hand out to stop her at the foot of the broad staircase that dominated the formal entryway.

"There he is," she said, gesturing with a slight nod to the stairs. "I'm going to find my husband. He's probably ranting to some poor sod about the evils of offshore refineries. You two catch up with us as soon as you're able."

Molly nodded, then raised her gaze to the stairs. Fergus stood on the landing, speaking to Sebastian. He patted Sebastian's shoulder before turning to descend. Her breath caught. The preview she'd had of his outfit hadn't done it justice. The dress kilt hung to his knees under a black jacket and vest. Green kilt hose, black brogues, and a bright red bowtie completed the outfit. His hair was tamed, and his beard freshly trimmed.

He looked very princely.

Her heart nearly hammered out of her chest as he stepped off the last riser and took her hands. "Hello, gorgeous."

She swayed. "You look very...regal," she managed. If she hadn't already been pregnant, she might have ended up that way just from looking at him.

Fergus smiled, his eyes crinkling at the corners. "You alright?" His grin was wicked, he must have guessed the reason she couldn't find her tongue. Damn him.

"I'm peachy." She leaned in closer, inhaling whatever woodsy cologne he was wearing.

Fergus pressed a kiss to the corner of her mouth. "What am I doing tonight?" he asked.

"Me?"

He barked with laughter. "Besides that, though these bastards are lucky I'm not stripping you naked in the middle of the room. Waiting to get my hands on you is going to be difficult." He curled a strand of her hair around his finger. "But tell me, Mols, what am I going to do in that ballroom?"

CHAPTER TWELVE

FERGUS

Fergus swayed to a slow song with his entire world in his arms. Molly, a goddess in her ball gown, curled against his chest, where she belonged. The ball was in full swing, guests dancing, hobnobbing, and eating. The room throbbed with Christmas cheer.

Molly had made a good show as his parents had dragged her around the room, introducing her to every world leader, ambassador, and royal they spotted. All grace and smiles, Molly had managed to sound both enthusiastic and pleased to hear about everything from the year's harvest of sugar beets in Poland to the Irish ambassador's long-winded stories about her wolfhounds.

He was extraordinarily lucky to have her by his side.

When her smile had started to flag, he'd whisked her onto the dance floor, where all she had to do was lean against him. Fergus could almost pretend it was only for her benefit.

Molly mumbled something against his chest.

"What was that?" he asked, stroking a hand down her back.

She tilted her head up. "I miss our Christmas tree. The one here is nice and tastefully decorated, but I think it's larger than my entire apartment."

"Norway donated it."

"Should I watch for trolls?"

"Probably, but I was just explaining how we managed to have such a grand fir."

She sighed and put her head against his shoulder. "It's gorgeous, but I was so looking forward to tomorrow morning, with our little tree and the few gifts under it. Whatever happened to those packages? Everything just disappeared."

"Pike kept track of them, they're safe and sound here. We can open them tonight if you'd like." One of the gifts was nearly burning a hole in his pocket. His mum had offered any one of the many heritage diamond rings his family had accumulated over the years, but Fergus had declined, he wanted to give Molly the ring he'd chosen for her. "There's just that one thing I have to do first."

"Oh yes, that. Better get on with it, before I change my mind and run off with one of the trolls from the tree." The playfulness in her voice unwound a knot in his chest. Fergus searched the crowded room, finding Pike dancing with Chelsey, both of them lost in their own little world. At last, he caught sight of Sebastian, who appeared entirely in his element with a blue tooth speaker in his ear and his fingers dancing over his tablet's screen as he directed security, media coverage, and the placement of plates containing the gingerbread biscuits Fergus had baked.

The reviews of them had so far been spectacular, and it was nice to hear more about that than the usual questions about whatever scandal he'd been adjacent to that year.

Though the press dubbing him 'The Gingerbread Prince' was a bit much. However, they'd be talking about something else very shortly. Fergus caught Sebastian's eye and nodded. The man whirled into action, barking orders into his earpiece.

A murmur swept through the crowd as space was cleared in front of the enormous Christmas tree, green velvet ropes marking off a semi-circle. The press started circling like vultures, setting up cameras and jockeying for the best position.

"You ready?" he asked, bringing them both to a halt.

Molly took a step back, tilting her face up to his. "Yes. I feel like I'm jumping off a cliff."

"Mols, we don't have—" He paused as she held up a hand.

"But it's okay, no matter how long the fall, I know you'll be there to catch me."

He swept her into a hug.

"And," she added, voice muffled against his chest. "I am thrilled to be first in line for all your baking."

"I love you," he murmured into her ear, his heart near full to bursting with it.

"I love you too, Prince Fergus, now you better ask me to marry you, the important people are all in place."

"None of them matter, you're the important person to me."

She rolled her eyes and pushed him in the direction of the tree.

Keeping her hand in his, he led her to stand in the open space before the tree. It soared to the high ceiling of the ballroom, festooned with twinkling white lights and an entire army of green and red ornaments. They were all traditional and felt like old friends.

"Do you see the sheep about halfway up the tree? The one that's your favorite shade of green?" He said to Molly as he directed her with a hand on her lower back.

Her brows drew together for a moment before relaxing. "He's got curly wool hair."

"That's my favorite. I nearly broke him when I was five, because I needed to give him a hug and stole him off the tree."

"Did you get in trouble?"

Fergus shook his head. "No, and he was returned safe and sound. I like seeing him every year. So while this tree might be brand new to you, to me it's as familiar as the back of my hand." He pointed at an intricately carved wooden star. "That one was made to commemorate my birth."

Molly lit up. "Is that a tradition?"

"There's an official Royal ornament maker, they'd be offended if they weren't allowed to."

"I love it."

Seeing her excited over something so closely tied to his country and his family warmed him all the way through. Everything might be new and different for her, but she was finding her way. The thought of someday standing right here and ceremonially hanging an ornament marking the birth of their child...that did something to him.

He needed to get her out of here and to somewhere he could properly show her how much he appreciated her.

Fergus turned to face her, ignoring the cameras. A few clicked, but Molly didn't glance towards them. Heart nearly hammering its way out of his chest, despite knowing her answer, he sank to one knee. The sound of the shutters sped up. He slipped the black velvet box from his coat pocket.

He squeezed her trembling fingers, hoping his own nerves wouldn't make him stumble over the official proposal. He opened the case, with its small princess cut diamond.

"Molly North, before the monarchs and peers of the Isle of Alba, I, Thomas Hamish Fergus Murphy Kerr, a Prince of the Isle, do ask you to be my wife, for the good of the land and of its people, and for the good of mine own heart."

Phew, he'd made it.

Molly's eyes were suspiciously shiny, but her mouth twitched into a soft smile. "I, Molly Louise North, a materials engineer, accept."

He pulled the ring from the case and slipped it on her finger before rocketing to his feet and sweeping her into a hug, spinning her around in an excited circle. When he stopped to set her back onto her feet, there were absolutely tears in his fiancée's eyes, but she was grinning. The kind of wide grin that it was impossible to fake. Happiness radiated from her.

The ring on her finger glinted as he picked up her hand and kissed the back of it before turning towards the cameras and crowd. "May I present my bride to be and your future queen, Miss Molly North."

"Small ring," someone hollered.

"I bought it for her when I wasn't a prince. It's a reminder that we fell in love when there wasn't the promise of money or power, just good company—"

"And excellent baking!" Molly said, drawing a round of laughter and a chorus of 'awww' from the crowd.

"This way!" Pike hollered, Chelsey hanging off his arm and mouthing 'congrats'. Pike pointed to the side of the room, where Sebastian guarded a side door that stood open.

Fergus tugged Molly's hand, feeling like he was five again and absconding with the sheep, only this time nobody would be able to pry his prize away from him, they dashed through the door, which shut and locked behind them.

Molly's laugh got louder as she took stock of where they ended up.

"The portrait gallery is not my favorite part of the palace," Fergus grumbled. He let go of Molly to open up a carved chest that graced one wall.

"I can't believe how much you look like so many of these people, even though I know your family has been ruling this island for close to nine hundred years." She squinted at a painting of one of his very great grandfathers. "That could be you dressed up for Halloween."

"That's King Hamish the Third. Despite the resemblance, I hope I'm nothing like him." Fergus pulled out the cheap reindeer cardigan he'd stashed in the chest the day before, swapping his formal jacket for it. He tossed a pair of trainers to Molly, who squealed like he'd just given her the crown jewels.

She hopped around, tugging off a pump. "If I remember from my reading, he was very stabby."

"Very is quite the understatement."

Molly freed herself of her shoes and stepped into the trainers with a relieved sigh. Fergus mentally patted himself on the back.

"That's quite the nose," Molly said, frowning up at a painting of a dour woman with grey hair wearing what had been the height of Victorian fashion.

"I've heard stories about how much she enjoyed looking down it at everyone. Queen Anne Kerr the first."

"Ah-ha, she was the one who issued the decree about gold toilet seats in the palace."

Molly really had done her homework. "It was her." He counted light sconces until he reached the right one. A quick pull and a hidden door swung open.

"That is amazing." She followed him into the passageway, which quickly became a staircase that wound downward. A few bare bulbs lighted their way. "Back to the toilet seats. That has to cost a lot."

"More than it should, though the ones in the guest quarters are some other metal dipped into just enough gold to cover them. Only royal rear ends get solid gold. The story is that my great grandmother was so shocked that wash closets were being installed indoors—plumbing wasn't her strong suit—that she issued the decree for the seats to at least make the loos in the palace seem fancy."

"Huh, well, couldn't you just un-decree it when you have the chance?"

He paused, stopping to look up at Molly. She halted and raised a brow. "It's not that easy. For more than a hundred and fifty years, there's been a family who makes their entire living supplying those toilet seats. There's more than one documentary about their business, which only uses traditional methods. Remind me to show you their maker's mark, it's a work of art all on its own. If the palace ceased buying from them, the business would shutter fast, and I hate to think of the backlash. Every kid on the Isle gets dragged on a field trip to see the workshop at least once during primary school."

Molly winced. "I have a lot to learn."

"And you'll be brilliant at all of it. I know it, you're an amazing person. Who else would have countered 'prince' with 'engineer'?" He loved her so blasted much. "C'mon, I can't wait to show you what I've got going on down here in what is absolutely not a repurposed dungeon."

Molly shook her head. "Stabby."

"I have never personally stabbed anyone. That's what Sebastian and Pike are for. These days all beheadings and stabbing are delegated."

"I'll make a note, now show me the dungeon."

"Worst pick-up line ever," he said, laughing as he reached the bottom of the stone steps. The heavy door squealed as he pushed it open.

The other side was less conspicuously old Alba. It gleamed with white tiles and white walls. Stainless steel appliances shone, ready to be used.

"A kitchen!" Molly gasped. "It's gorgeous."

"This is my kitchen, so I stay out of the way of the palace chefs. Through the door there is your space."

Molly trotted over to peek. "It's empty."

"Aye, because I have no idea what a genius engineer and future princess needs in a personal lab."

"I…thank you." She wiped at her eyes.

"Talk to Sebastian, he's got a budget and the connections to get you whatever you need."

"I never imagined—" She broke off with a gasp. "Our presents!" On a wooden table sat the rest of the packages from Seattle. Molly shoved one at him and ripped at the paper on one bearing her name. She held up the socks with Christmas Llamas on them. "Just what I wanted!"

She'd exclaimed over them during a trip to a big box store before reluctantly putting them back and he'd fought tooth and nail through the holiday shopping crowds to get them for her. He'd been bursting with pride when he'd checked out with the last pair in the store, and seeing her cooing over them now made the fight worth it.

She'd always be worth it.

Fergus opened the package in his hands to find a box with a new spatula and a blank cookbook. He thumbed through it, imagining filling it up. "Thank you," he said, holding the book up. "For believing in me."

Molly jumped up, sitting on one of the unused counters. "Always." She put her socks on, holding up her foot to admire them. "You don't have to open the other packages right now. It's just new underwear and a scarf. I didn't know you'd have all the fancy high thread count stuff."

"But it'll be better because it's from you."

"I still think the fancy stuff will feel better. I do have one more present to share."

He put his hands on her legs and spread her knees, filling up the space between them with his body. "Yeah?"

She made a pleased sound but shook her head even as she ran her hands over the fine linen of his shirt. "Fergus, I'm pregnant."

He reeled, the ground shifting under his feet. "What? That was just a couple of days—"

"I was already pregnant then." Her cheeks flushed. "I think it was the very first time together, when we almost got carried away." She bit her lip. "The little plus sign showed up on three tests I took the day I came home to find…" Molly's eyes dropped to where her fingers clutched at him. "To find everything had gone sideways."

Joy left him breathless. "I'm sorry that happened, but we're safe, we're here. Oh, bloody hell, I'm going to be a father." He put a finger under her chin, tilting her face up to his. "I've never been happier."

"I can't wait to see what ornament is made for this baby." She put a hand on her belly, smiling cheekily at him. "Maybe a little carved gingerbread man."

"Maybe." The possibilities danced through his imagination, spinning out into a whole life blessed with Molly and their children. He kissed her, heat flaring between them. "I think this wins as the best gift ever."

She chuckled. "You sure?"

"The spatula is a close second."

Molly pressed her forehead to his. "Merry Christmas, Fergus."

He cupped her cheek and brushed a thumb over her lower lip, making her shudder. "Merry Christmas, Mols." Her arms went around him, and he knew he was right where he was always meant to be.

The End

ABOUT THE AUTHOR

Hannah Morse is the author of contemporary and historical romance novels. She lives in New Mexico with her high school sweetheart and too many Chihuahuas. She can be found binging Netflix shows or reading steamy novels when she isn't hard at work writing a happily ever after. Receive a free high-heat romance for signing up for her newsletter.

www.writesmorse.com

OTHER BOOKS BY HANNAH MORSE

The Sea Treats Series

Cake

Chocolate

Churros (2022)

The Ramsbury Estate Series

High Strung

Hothouse Bloom (Coming Soon)

Dancing Lessons (2022)

Anthologies

Reluctant Groom

Anonymous Part 3

Christmas Wishes

Backbone: A Single Parent Finding Love Anthology (February 2022)

The CARE Inc Series

Royal Boy (Coming Soon)

Standalones

Snowed In with the Scot (January 2022)

THE CHRISTMAS ORNAMENT

JESSICA LONG

TRIGGER WARNING

This book contains scenes that may be a possible trigger for some people. Read at your own risk.

CHAPTER ONE

"Shawna?" Tara asks quietly after I hang up the phone, her eyes wide and her face full of concern. "What is it? Are you okay?"

Questions swarm inside my head, demanding answers that no one can give me. I don't know how to articulate my feelings. How can I sum up a million different emotions running through my mind?

The words feel foreign on my tongue, but I push them out. "My dad is dying." My voice cracks.

Those four little words contain all of my emotions and fears.

Why?

Why is he dying?

Why can't I do anything to stop it?

Why now?

Why him?

"Oh, sweetie." Tara puts down the mixing bowl that contains our special maple gingerbread cookie dough before rushing over to me.

Unable to move, I embrace my best friend. Tears stream down my face as the future becomes blurry.

Maybe it is just my vision that's blurry. I swipe furiously at the tears.

A few days ago, I made plans to spend this weekend shopping with my dad. He was going to come here and we were finally going to get him a tree and some new decorations.

I teased him because Christmas is one week away and he hasn't put up one decoration.

Now, it seems like this is going to be his last Christmas.

"I need to go home. I need to finish Cartwright's wedding cake. I need to get the order together." My to-do list is already a mile long and growing by the second.

"You head home and stay as long as you need, I'll take care of everything here." Tara gives me a squeeze before heading back to her maple gingerbread cookie dough.

"Are you sure? That is a lot for one person to handle. Hell, that is a lot for the both of us to handle." Sure, we usually have help in the afternoons but she can't be here at four in the morning and close in the evenings.

"I'll get my nieces to help out, my brother will love the downtime, the girls will love being here, and all it will cost is a handful of cookies each day." Tara laughs and continues to stir the batter.

"Thank you. For everything." I say, hoping to convey my gratitude.

"That's what friends are for. Now go before I realize how much work I need to do today and hold you hostage." Her teasing helps keep the tears at bay.

I hang my apron on the hook, grab my keys, and say one last goodbye. "Call me if you need anything."

"You too, and I mean anything. I can be back here in a couple of hours."

I've never had to leave the bakery for an unknown amount of time. Ever since I first opened the doors, I've been here, nonstop.

This has been my dream for as long as I could remember. Ever since I was a little girl, I dreamed of making all the cookies for Santa in my town. Of course, the older I got the dream morphed into cakes and other pastries. It became my true passion.

Until I met Jasper, but that is a story for another day.

My bakery is in a different location, but it is successful and for that I am thankful.

Without wasting any more time, I rush upstairs to my apartment and pack a bag. I grab everything I can think of and head to my car.

Throwing my bag in the trunk I hit the road, intent on making it to my dad's before nightfall.

As luck would have it, traffic is already insane. The roads are full of holiday shoppers and the weather has taken a turn for the worse. Snow falls in piles, ice coats the asphalt. So what is normally a two-hour trip, has turned into a five-hour shit show.

Impatiently and emotionally, I finally pull into my childhood home's driveway. It is well after dark but every light is on in the house.

Grabbing my bag from the trunk, I inhale deeply, letting the icy air calm my nerves. It has been far too long since I've been home.

For years I've stayed away, afraid of facing the life I left behind. Afraid of old feelings coming back if I ever saw him again.

"I'm in here." My dad calls from the living room.

His normally strong voice is gone, replaced by a different, unfamiliar voice that is frail and full of vulnerability.

Walking into the living room, my heart breaks into a million pieces. My dad looks completely different. He is fully sprawled out in his recliner, covered with his favorite blanket. His skin is pale and lifeless. His breathing is labored.

How could things get this bad in such a little time? A few days ago, Dad was full of life. We joked. We laughed. We talked for hours.

Tears stream down my face. I'm not ready for this. I tried to prepare myself for the worse, but this is beyond my imagination.

"Dad..." I whisper, my voice cracking.

"It's good to see you, Shawna-bear" My dad whispers back, tears welling up in his eyes.

I chuckle at his use of my childhood nickname. It brings back sweet memories that have me sobbing like a little girl.

"Don't cry. Everything will be alright." Dad lightly pats the arm of his chair.

Sitting down like I used to, I lean my head on his shoulder and close my eyes. I want to pretend things are how they used to be, just for now.

After several long quiet minutes, Dad breaks the silence.

"Who told you?" Dad mumbles into my hair.

"I got a call from Mrs. Edith this afternoon. She just wanted to let me know what was going on since you were adamant that no one call me until the weekend." I give him a stern look.

"Of course she called. I should have known. That woman loves to gossip. I didn't want to bother you with this nonsense." Dad holds his hand up when I start to protest before continuing, "We were going to see each other this weekend anyway. I didn't want to pull you away from work, knowing this is your busiest time of year."

I sigh. "There is always work to be done. You will always be more important, especially since..." I trail off, not able to finish that thought or sentence. The emotions continue to hit me like the surf pounding the shoreline.

"Let's just enjoy the time we have together." Dad chimes in.

As much as I'd love to forget the reason I have come home, I need answers to help calm my nerves and soothe my mind.

"How bad is it?" I know what Mrs. Edith said but she is just the hospital administrator and didn't have all the facts.

Dad's smile is small but hopeful. "The doctors think my chances don't look so good. They are saying less than a year, but miracles do happen."

I feel like I'm in a deep dark pool, struggling to stay afloat. "Well, lucky for you, I plan on being here for as long as you need. Before you protest and tell me you don't need the help, I want to be here and I already have the bakery situated to allow me the extra time to be here."

"Tell Tara I said thanks," Dad says before closing his eyes.

Giving him a hug, I whisper, "I'm going to unpack my bag, let me know if you need anything."

I head up the stairs, running my hand along the large oak railing, remembering when Dad and I tried to slide down it when I was twelve years old. He fell and broke his toe, I fell on him and bruised my left eye. Mom was pissed because we had family pictures the next day and had to reschedule.

I let out a chuckle as a tear runs down my cheek. Mom passed away unexpectedly almost a year ago. I thought it was going to break Dad, but he stood tall and strong and continued to live life as Mom would have demanded.

Now, Dad is fighting for his life and I can't help but to wonder what Mom would do in this situation. Would she still celebrate Christmas to its fullest, like usual? That would mean trying to dress Dad up to attend the town's Christmas Eve party. Or would she keep what could be the last Christmas Dad has intimate and small- just the two of us?

Turning on my bedroom light, I look around at all the trophies still lining the upper part of my walls. They aren't from sports competitions, instead they are from baking contests and championships. Ever since I was little, I knew I loved to bake and wanted to open my own bakery in the city. I dreamed of living far far away and making it big.

Looking around, I see that Dad hasn't changed anything here. My white painted desk sits in the corner of my bedroom, papers and magazines stacked on top. Old photos of us with Mom are still taped to my closet door. My old television still sits atop my four drawer dresser, just like it did all four years of high school.

Sitting down on my bed, I place my bag next to me and cry. I let the tears pour out, no longer able to contain them past my facade. I cry until I no longer have tears.

Realizing how long I've been up here, I dry my eyes and quickly unpack my bag, placing my clothes in my empty dresser and my toiletries in the spare bathroom.

Once I am back downstairs, I notice Dad is no longer in his chair. Worry crosses my face, dread fills my veins.

"Dad?" I yell.

"In here." He calls out from the kitchen.

"What are you doing? I told you to let me know if you needed anything." I scold.

"Well, technically, I didn't need anything. I just wanted a small glass of eggnog." Dad's smirk brings a smile to my face.

I let out a little laugh. "Technicalities are always right in the name of the game," I remember Dad always saying it to Mom.

"That's right, so that means I'm right." Dad gloats before laughing.

His laugh turns into a coughing fit. Worry replaces my smile as I help him sit down in one of the chairs.

Just for a moment, it is almost like old times. We are laughing, joking, and having fun and his illness isn't present.

"Well, at least let me pour the eggnog." I grab two of Dad's favorite crystal glasses and fill them up with the homemade eggnog.

I hand a glass to Dad before taking a sip. The creamy cold liquid coats my tongue. The vanilla spice sends my taste buds soaring.

"Mmm. This is really good. Just like Mom used to make." The thought makes me sad.

This is our first Christmas without Mom, and quite possibly could be Dad's last Christmas. I could use a drink or two.

Luckily, my stomach interrupts the sadness and growls loudly, echoing off the kitchen walls. Dad and I laugh, all problems and concerns seem to drift away for the moment.

"Have you eaten yet? I can whip us up something." I need the distraction right about now and I can fill my noisy stomach.

"Actually, I ordered dinner some time ago. It's been a habit of mine for the better part of half the year. My guest brings me food and keeps me company. Occasionally, he eats with me too. It should be here any minute now. If I had known you were coming, I would have ordered more food." Dad drinks the rest of his eggnog and puts the glass in the sink.

Who can this mystery guest be? And why hasn't he ever said anything to me about this?

"I brought enough food to feed everyone." The deep, very familiar voice says from the doorway.

I can't believe my eyes. "Jasper? What are you doing here?"

CHAPTER TWO

"I'm bringing your dad food." He says as if we have never met each other before.

"Jasper has been my dinner guest for a while now. He came over one night about eight or nine months ago and brought dinner and we just talked." Dad chimes in.

"Talked about what? How he broke my heart? How he slept with my best friend? Or maybe it was how he landed in jail the night we were supposed to celebrate our graduation." I am bewildered at how this friendship came to be.

All this time my dad has been talking to and hanging out with my ex-boyfriend. I would have rather him be secretly dating someone rather than inviting Jasper into our house, especially after everything Jasper has put me through.

"It's not like that, Shawna." Jasper tries to de-escalate the situation but it only makes me madder.

"Then what is it like? Because from where I am standing it looks like you and my dad have been lying to me this whole time, and I am the fool in the end." Not that I've talked to Jasper in a long while, but I am hurting and letting the words pour out of my mouth without a care in the world of who might get hurt.

"Shawna-bear," Dad starts but I can't deal with the nickname right now.

"I need to go. I'll be back later; don't wait up." I grab my necessities and head to my car.

The old creaky screen door doesn't slam behind me and I know I am not alone.

"What do you want?" I say, turning around to face Jasper.

He doesn't speak. Instead, we both size each other up. The years have been good to Jasper. His normally lanky body has filled out, replaced with piles of muscles. What was once shaggy, shoulder length hair is now cut short. His eyes are still dark and expressive but his jawline is more angular and covered in a five o'clock shadow.

This new Jasper leaves me craving for more. He makes me want to make bad decisions and pull him up to my room.

A part of me never got over him. My heart still longs for him; my pussy still remembers every night we've spent together.

My mind reminds me of the heartache and the distrust. He slept with my best friend!

Well, that is a sobering thought as a cold wave washes over me and distinguishes the lust flame.

"Are you done checking me out?" My tone is bitchy but doesn't catch him off guard.

"Nope." He says like an asshole. "You look good. The city has been good to you."

His voice is smooth like twenty-five-year-old whiskey.

Changing the subject, I ask, "Why are you here? Why can't you leave me and my family alone? Haven't you done enough?" Tears threaten to fall, but I blink them away.

Fuck him. Getting in my car, I don't wait for his response. I head to the only open place in this small town- the bar.

We might not have stoplights in this town, but we do have one of the best bars I've ever been to.

I park my car in the gravel extended parking lot and lock my doors, ready to forget about today.

Walking into the bar is like dejavu. This is the locals favorite hangout spot from teenagers to old retired folks and everyone in between. I'd even been known to pound back several shots in my teenage years.

For a second everyone looks my way, conversations pause as I am greeted by the bartender.

"Fucking hell, I must be going blind!"

"Well if it isn't Uncle Sam, I must be going blind as well." I tease as conversations resume.

Sam is now in his seventies but is young at heart. He's the best bartender in town, who pours the biggest shots, but we accredit it to him being a retired Marine.

His beard can rival Santa's, but everyone will know he is a fake based on his vocabulary. Besides, even though he is now older and retired, he has been able to keep most of his Marines day physique.

"I'm sorry to hear about your dad." He pours me a double shot of whiskey. "On the house."

"Thank you." I gulp down the offered shot. It slides down my throat and immediately warms me inside.

"I'm assuming that is why we have the pleasure of seeing you here again?" Sam's voice is low and full of concern.

"Yes. I am planning on being here until he doesn't need me anymore." Hopefully it is because he survives the illness.

I don't even want to think about the alternative.

"Well, I'm glad you are staying a while. How's the bakery? Your dad shares his packages with me all the time. I secretly think it's because he is jealous I am still in shape after all these decades. He's been trying to fatten me up." Sam chuckles as he pours me another double shot.

"The bakery is doing great. We have more orders than ever before so I'm staying busy." I make sure to include that because Sam has been known to try and play matchmaker, especially this time of year.

"That's great! I'm happy for you, but also a shame. A young woman like yourself deserves to have someone to celebrate life with. Isn't there anyone in the city that is into you?" Sam asks bluntly.

"No, there isn't anyone and that's the way I like it." I'm not going to admit that I still have a thing for Jasper and seeing him, in my house, has stirred those feelings back into rotation.

I worked hard to suppress those thoughts and feelings and now they are coming back full force.

"You know, Jasper still loves you. Even after all these years, I'd bet he would try again with you. He has turned his life around and even opened a garage. He's a damn good mechanic. Honest too. You should make time to swing by and see him." Sam being blunt is something you can always count on. He doesn't sugar-coat shit or coddle you.

I down the other shot and place the glass back on the bar. "Oh, I don't think that's a good idea. Plus, I already saw him. He was bringing Dad some food. Hence why I am now here drinking."

"I'm not going to tell you what to do, but every story has three sides: your side, his side, and the truth. Give him a chance to tell you his side of the story. I remember what it was like being young and in love. I made several stupid mistakes. Thank God my wife was patient and understanding and gave me chance after chance." He smiles a small smile before his look changes to sadness.

"How is Meredith?" It is unusual that she isn't here. Normally she is running around chatting with patrons and downing shots with the best of us.

"She is at the hospital with Abigail and Alexa who are both currently in labor with their first child." His grin widens as he thinks about his first, and second, great grandchild.

I can see the love in his eyes. He is absolutely over the moon.

"That is incredible! How are you feeling, Great Grandpa? Do they know what they are having or is it a surprise?" I am grateful for some happy news to get the focus of the conversation off of me.

"It is going to be a surprise. Although, I am hoping for one of each. I have heard you don't know love until you have a grandchild, but nothing beats having great grandchildren. I am fortunate enough to have not one but two coming." His grin lights up the room.

He opens two beers, claiming one for himself.

"This is just the news I needed to keep my mind at ease and off current situations." We clink our beers together and take a sip.

"Let me know if you need anything else," Sam says before walking to the end of the bar where a couple just sat down.

I get lost in my thoughts. Was Sam onto something? Is there more to the story that I have neglected to see or listen to for the past six years?

Do I want to risk more heartache by hearing his excuses?

Waving my now empty beer bottle at Sam to order another one, I see movement out the corner of my eye before smelling the musky sandalwood cologne. I immediately know who is now occupying the seat beside me.

"I figured I would find you here." Jasper whispers in my ear.

The warmth of his breath in combination to the alcohol I have just consumed makes me moan out loud.

I see a shit-eating grin grow on his face.

"That's the alcohol speaking." I turn to see Sam holding two beers and fighting to hide his smile.

"Thanks Sam." Jasper takes the offered beer.

I watch in slow motion as he raises the ice cold bottle towards his mouth, his lips parting just the right amount to allow the liquid to slip past. He swallows several gulps before licking the beer taste off his lower lip.

Face flaming, pussy dripping, I turn back to my own beer. I don't speak for fear of saying something stupid like inviting him into my bed and eventually my heart.

We sit in silence, each consumed with our own thoughts. After we finish our beers, Jasper spins to face me. I refuse to look at him and decide to play with the tiny white napkin laying on the bar.

Drinking on an empty stomach might not have been the smartest idea. The alcohol starts to affect my stubbornness and before I can reason with myself, I am turning to look at Jasper.

"I'm sorry." Jasper blurts out.

I see the truth in his eyes. He really is sorry. This is the most sincere I think I've ever seen him. The sight almost breaks my heart.

"I can't do this right now. Today has already been too much for me to handle alone without piling on repressed feelings and past relationships." I grab my wallet and lay down several bills before waving goodbye to Sam.

Jasper follows me out to the parking lot. "You don't have to go through this alone. I am here for you. No matter what we have been through I know what you are going through right now and it isn't healthy to pretend things are alright. You need time to process all of this. You need time to cry and scream, to let the feelings out. Drinking like that isn't the answer."

Pissed and a little drunk, I interrupt him. "And what is the answer? You? Believe it or not, I've done just fine pretending things are okay. For the past six years, I have pretended to be alright, and guess what? I am finally okay. I've moved on from you and you should move on from me." I lie but I refuse to let him think he has won.

"I'm happy for you, honestly. You deserve to find happiness with someone that treats you like a queen." He stares into my eyes and I can feel the wall crumbling.

"Shit," I mumble, knowing I am already sinking in too deep.

Jasper, not being able to read my thoughts, assumes I am thinking about my drunkenness and my inability to drive myself home. I don't correct him.

"I'll take you home in my truck and can bring you back to your car in the morning." Jasper leads me over to his truck and helps me in.

"Thanks," I whisper as he leans over to help me get my seatbelt buckled.

His face is so close to mine, his cologne still a favorite of mine. When he turns to look at me, I lean forward and press my lips to his.

For a moment, he lets me kiss him. I'd even bet that he's enjoying this kiss.

"I want this more than I've ever admitted. I need you, Jasper." I mumble against his lips, my heart beating fast and hard.

"Me too, but not this way." He says before pulling away and closing my door.

Disappointed and feeling rejected, I close my eyes as he drives the short way to Dad's house.

"Thanks for the ride home." I slowly make my way inside, only stumbling a couple of times. I refuse to look backwards at him, ready to forget the kiss and the feelings that have resurfaced.

CHAPTER THREE

Waking up hungover was not part of the plan, and neither was kissing Jasper and practically throwing myself at him. What am I doing with my life?

Groaning, I roll over and cover my face with my pillow. It's too early to be up, even though I see the sun's first rays peeking through the blinds.

Rich aromas drift in through my open door. Sniffing, I smell what appears to be breakfast cooking and coffee brewing. My stomach growls letting me know that it is indeed time to wake up.

"I'm never going without dinner again. Or drinking that much on an empty stomach." I climb out of bed and grab a change of clothes before heading into the bathroom across the hall.

Clean, awake, and dressed for the day, I head downstairs to see why Dad is cooking when he should be resting.

"Dad, didn't I tell you to let me know if you needed anything? You shouldn't be on your feet cooking. You need rest." I finish saying just as my feet hit the tile flooring.

"I am resting," Dad says from his chair.

He is fully reclined with his favorite cover on. I can see his reindeer slippers poking out from the end of the cover. He has had them since I was a teenager. He claims those are his favorite slippers and that is why he won't replace them.

Confused, I walk into the kitchen to see Jasper standing in front of the stove, frying eggs and bacon. I shouldn't be surprised to see him here cooking for Dad, but after making a fool of myself last night, I'd rather not see him when he looks so damn good and I look like a train wreck going through a hangover.

What does surprise me is the fact that he is listening to Christmas music. He was never really big into the holiday, claiming it was all a scheme for consumers to spend more and be more gluttonous.

I, on the other hand, absolutely love Christmas. I love the decorations, lights, food, and of course the cold weather. Most of all, I love how everyone seems to relax this time of year and enjoy time with friends and family.

It could be the increase in baking, but I always feel at peace this close to Christmas. Well, I did until recently.

"Like what you see?" Jasper asks in his sexy voice bringing me back to reality.

"I wasn't staring at you." I say defensively. "Actually, I was just thinking about how peaceful this time of year usually is for me, despite being busier at work."

I trail off, not wanting to voice my problems and concerns this early in the morning.

"Until I came along and changed your plans." Jasper teases, bringing a smile to my face.

"I will admit, I was surprised to see you and I apologize for what I said."

He cuts me off. "You don't have to apologize. Actually, I wanted to see if you would like to accompany me today. I have some shopping to do and we need to get your dad a tree."

"That actually sounds great. I need to find something for Dad." I am completely lost as to what though. "And Tara." I add. I usually get her a spa day gift certificate and a bonus but I want something more since she is watching the store while I am gone.

"Who's Tara?" Jasper's voice is full of intrigue.

"My assistant and best friend. Before you ask, no she is not single and no you can't sleep with her." At his scowl, I add, "Okay, I shouldn't have said that and I'm sorry."

"Eh, I had it coming. Want to help me plate?" He motions to the pile of plates, silverware, and napkins sitting on a tray.

Glad for the conversation change, I hold the plates as he places eggs, bacon, and toast on them before placing them back on the tray. I fix Dad's and my coffee the way we like it with just a tiny bit of sugar before turning to Jasper.

"How do you want it?"

He raises an eyebrow and cocks his head to the side. The look would normally remind me of a dog, but he makes it look downright sexy.

I quickly add, "Your coffee. How do you like to drink your coffee?"

My face blushes bright red as he visibly checks me out. My attire isn't sexy, it's functional and fleece, but he looks at me like I am in nothing but thin strappy lingerie.

"Black. All black." His voice is strained and deeper than normal.

I quickly glance downwards and see a bulge forming in his jeans. Fuck. I should not have done that.

Needing to distance myself from him, I pour his cup and quickly carry the tray to the living room.

Carefully placing the tray down, I turn towards the recliner. Dad looks like he is sleeping, but I know he can't sleep when food is cooking. He used to wake up out of a deep sleep whenever Mom started cooking breakfast.

"Are you ready to eat, Dad?" I whisper so I don't startle him.

His eyes open and a weak smile crosses his face. "Yep, I feel starved. You know I can't sleep if food is being cooked."

At least he has an appetite and is making jokes. I wait for him to sit up before placing his coffee cup in his cup holder and his plate on his lap.

His voice is feeble. "Thank you Shawna-bear."

I wait until he takes his first bite. "I didn't cook, Jasper did."

Handing Jasper his coffee and plate, I carry mine to the couch and sit down. The coffee is hot and the food is flavorful.

"This is either incredibly amazing or I am just starving." I look over at Jasper to see him staring at me.

"Well, you didn't eat last night." He mentions before taking a bite of his toast.

"But she did drink." Dad chimes in.

"Well, I needed a drink after the revelations yesterday," I explain.

After eating the rest of the meal in silence, Jasper loads the dishwasher as I grab my wallet, phone, and keys.

"Anything you need while we are out today?" I lean down and hug Dad, realization setting in that he's not doing too well.

"Nothing comes to mind. Have fun. I'm just going to nap for a while." Dad leans the recliner back and closes his eyes.

I help him get his cover right. "Call if you need anything. Get some rest, we will be back as soon as we can."

Following Jasper out to his truck, I swipe the lone tear off my cheek.

"Hey, are you okay?" His voice is sincere.

"Yeah, this is just a lot to take in right now. I feel utterly useless, there isn't anything I can do to make things better." I let out a long sigh.

Jasper backs the truck out of the driveway and heads to the Christmas tree farm. "The next few days, weeks, months are going to be tough. You will question every little thing, whether it is relevant to the sickness or not. You will go through intense periods of sadness, anger, and hurt, but it will all be alright in the end. You have me. I'm not going anywhere."

Jasper's mom died our senior year. It tore him apart. Once the doctors found out what was causing her to lose weight at an impossible rate, they knew it was too late.

Two weeks later, she passed away. I stood by his side the entire time, afraid of what he would do if I was gone.

I almost withdrew from college before it even started, but that is when he cheated. Things went to hell and all I could think about was getting away and starting a life far from him.

He parks the truck and helps me out. We spend a few minutes looking around at all the trees they have to offer before selecting the perfect one. After it is loaded in the back of his truck, we hit the road. Jasper drives slow, letting me reminisce.

"I figure it is about time I stop blaming you for leaving and apologize for what happened all those years ago." He starts.

"Why now?" I ask with no hate in my voice, just genuine curiosity.

"Talking with your dad has opened my eyes to the things that matter most in my life, or at least what I hope will be in my life. Though some of the rumors are true, most have been taken out of context and I want you to know what really happened that night." He explains.

"Did you really sleep with her?" I can't bear to say her name.

"No."

That one word sends a wave of emotions over me. Relief that he didn't, anger for the lost relationship, and confusion as to why so many people said he did.

As if reading my mind, he says, "I'll explain everything that I know."

"Okay." I want to sound confident but it comes out as a frightened whisper.

"From a very young age, Mom was extremely protective over me and I didn't know why. In school, kids picked on me and I hated her for embarrassing me. It wasn't until I was older that I found out I was the result of my Father raping my mom. He was abusive towards her and eventually, he took his anger out on me. She did everything she could to protect me, but I refused to let that man touch her."

I grab his hand, linking my fingers with his.

"Why didn't you ever tell anyone?" My heart hurts for him, for the rough childhood he had to endure.

As he drives past the high school, he grips the steering wheel tighter, until his knuckles turn white.

"He always threatened me. I thought it was for the best especially after losing my mom. Anyway, the night of the party, the night that forever changed things, was the worst beating I had ever gotten. I left the house with the intent of getting drunk and couldn't find you so Mandy kept me company. After the tenth or so shot, the night got fuzzy. I remember her saying you were waiting at your house for us so I left with her. Obviously, that wasn't the case." He pauses to give me time to process everything so far.

After a moment, he continues," I might not remember all of the details but I know that I never slept with her. How could I have had sufficient time when we got into an accident a block from her parent's lake house. I went home, she went to the hospital. My father was pissed and kicked me out so I turned to drugs to afford bills. I was arrested a few months later and spent two years in jail."

"Wow, I didn't know." How do I convey sympathy for something that happened so long ago? Something that I've been pissed about for far too long.

"No one really knew. They knew the rumors and some knew bits and pieces but no one, until your dad, knew the whole truth. Now, you also know the whole truth." He looks at me, staring, and waiting for me to respond.

"I am so sorry you had to deal with all of that at such a young age. What I don't understand is why you didn't ask for help? You could have stayed at my house. My parents loved you, they treated you like you were family. Why resort to drugs? Any place in town would have helped you get a job and a place to stay." That is one of the good things about this small town.

He pulls into my driveway, but neither of us move.

"It's not a good reason, but I needed a lot of money as quickly as it could come in. I was ashamed of my father and what he had done. I needed to do it on my own." He looks embarrassed, ashamed.

We are interrupted by the front door opening. Dad stands in the doorway holding a royal blue ornament in one hand and a piece of paper in the other.

"What is that?" I ask, closing the truck door behind me.

Dad waits until I am standing in front of him to speak. "Your Christmas gift. From your mom."

ABOUT JESSICA LONG

Jessica Long is a stay at home mom during the day and an author at night. You can find her traveling often, gaining inspiration for scenes in upcoming stories. When she isn't traveling or writing, she is crafting.

She loves writing a variety of genres from contemporary to paranormal to reverse harem. Romance, Love, and Smut all with a happy ending.

Join the FB group:
https://www.facebook.com/groups/365103847822906/

FROSTED HEARTS

SNOWFALL DUET BOOK 1 (EXCERPT)

C.E. LASHUA

CHAPTER ONE

The snow swirling outside the window was beginning to get on my nerves. Footprints from a few hours earlier were nowhere to be seen, giving off the impression that the cabin I was currently living in was abandoned.

Oh, well. I doubt anyone would trudge through this blizzard to come and rescue me. Especially considering they all sent me up here to begin with. The thought of me waiting around for some guy gave my skin the crawls. I was really kicking myself in the ass for not taking all those wilderness and survival classes Mark used to push on me.

The image of him popping into my mind came with a flood of unresolved emotions I wasn't nearly ready to delve into. Heaving a sigh, I tampered the rising panic and pulled the overly fluffy blanket tighter around my shoulders.

The frost captured my gaze, inching its way higher and higher up the glass, tiny little snowflake crystals competing to see which would reach the top first. The highest flakes leaving behind the first ones that cleared the path for them. In my mind, I could vaguely see myself in them, a tiny little snowflake at the bottom being left behind. Trampled upon and pushed down, being forced to make way for those who thought they had bigger dreams than me. Bigger aspirations.

I'd show them, though. The tiny flake that everyone else used was slowly growing larger, becoming strong enough to forge its own path.

Learning by example, leaving the other snowflakes in its wake, it was making its way to the top of the window. So close. It was almost there. The end was only a couple of inches away now.

The tiny little flake that all the others cast aside was within reach of its goal.

A pounding on the door rattled me to my senses.

Looking back at the frost that obviously hadn't moved an inch, I shook my head, forcing myself back into reality.

I had clearly been in the cabin alone for far too long.

Another bang at the door echoed through the room, making me jump.

It was probably just another tree limb that broke off. When the wind first picked up three days ago, there was debris flying around, hitting the house at every angle. The first time it happened, I crawled under five layers of blankets and hid for the entire night. I swear, the isolation was getting to me. In my defense, it sounded like the abominable snow monster was getting ready to break down the door and eat me alive.

I wouldn't complain about reading something like that in one of my books, though. For some reason, I've been on a weird monster romance kick lately with bloody gore and massive… appendages. Anyone could tell just by looking at my e-reader. But real life? Nope. No way. Hard pass, thanks.

Before I could contemplate whether to investigate or ignore it, the rap came louder this time. Harder and faster, before the doorknob jingled.

"Hello?" The shout came muffled under a combination of the barrier of the door and the howling of the wind. Positive I was going delusional; I slowly rose from my position in the window, clutching the blanket a bit tighter as if the thickness of it would protect me from whatever was out there.

Reaching the door, I gingerly began unfastening the locks as if whatever was out there was about to attack me as soon as the door opened. It had to be some wild animal, right? I mean, it was obviously talking to me, but there was no way any sane person would be out in the middle of this storm.

Not alive, anyway.

"Hello?! Anyone in there?" The voice came again, surprising me with the gruff undertone laced throughout it. He sounded like a rugged lumberjack; someone I'd expect to find living in the middle of the woods by themselves.

And if he lives in the woods by himself, he knows the land, the territory. Maybe he ran out of food and was there to kill me for more. Maybe he was lonely being up here and needed comfort, willing or otherwise. The thought popped into my head, making my hand come to a standstill on the last lock.

"That's ridiculous," I whispered, more to reassure myself than anything. Still, my hand didn't move.

"What's ridiculous?!" The voice came again, surprising me back to my senses and away from thoughts of cabin retreat murders.

"If you're done talking to yourself," another unfamiliar voice added, "we'd like to come in. It's a bit cold out here." That was the understatement of the year. The fresh voice belonged to someone more refined. Or at least more reserved.

Huffing a little laugh, I undid the final lock to open the door, hoping against all hope it wasn't a couple of serial killers on the other side.

Stepping back, I held the door open just wide enough for them to get through, trying to keep most of the wind out. At least I thought I held it wide enough. Their voices may have been completely different, but their frames were both wider than the space I left them. Clearly, they were packing some hidden muscles under those coats. Not that I could really call them coats. They were more like designer coats meant for fashion and worn by people in the city.

Coats like Mark used to wear when he went to work–.

Shaking my head, I dispelled that thought before it took root.

Subtly glancing at the strangers, I quickly shut the door and began refastening what felt like a million locks. I tried not thinking about the fact that I was locking myself in the cabin with two would-be murderers. I chose to think of it more as me being the good Samaritan and earning some much-needed positive karma.

If they didn't try to torture me in my sleep, I didn't foresee any problems. It's not like they were hard on the eyes, either.

"Thanks for opening the door." This was the lumberjack voice, with snow coating his pitch-black hair, his build slightly bulkier than his companion's. Swinging a pair of green eyes in my direction, he threw out a warm smile that seemed to reflect in those pretty emeralds, effectively brightening the entire room.

Stunned by his beauty, my mouth hung open like a fish gasping for breath. A snort of laughter finally drew my attention away, settling on the less bulky but equally defined man next to him. He was wearing a cocky grin that instantly made me want to shove him back outside into the snow.

The smirk only grew the longer he looked at me, as if he could tell what I was thinking. Arching an eyebrow, I dared him to say anything.

"I'm Luke," the first man said, drawing my attention back to him as he began taking off his wet clothes. "And this is my brother, Jasper. We're sorry to drop in on you like this."

"No, we're not," the one called Jasper chimed in. He waited until we were both looking at him before he continued, his green eyes locking on mine. "It's a shitshow out there. We needed shelter. I'm not sorry about that."

So, he was the unapologetically practical one, huh? Good to know.

An uncomfortable laugh sounded from beside me as Luke attempted to cover for Jasper's rudeness.

"Either way, we appreciate you taking in a couple of strangers, Miss–?"

He looked at me expectantly, and it took my mind a moment to catch up with everything that was happening. I admit, it had been a few rough days being up here with no human interaction.

"Avery." The word came out as a tiny squeak before I thought better of it, kicking myself for not giving them a fake name. They might be gorgeous, but I didn't know who they were.

"That's a beautiful name, Miss Avery." Luke's expression as he looked at me was so friendly and open, a complete contrast to the shrew look I was receiving from the other man. Both had the same angular cheekbones and defined Roman nose. However, when Luke talked to me, he had this look about him that told me I could confide in him and he was willing to listen. When Jasper gave me that same look, it was glancing down the length of his nose at me like I was some type of bug and telling me he didn't trust a single word that came out of my mouth.

"Avery. Just Avery," I corrected. Though, I had to admit I really liked the sound of that rough voice calling me 'Miss.' Clearing my throat, I pointedly looked away from their faces and down to their clothes. Not without missing the fact that Jasper's smirk grew another inch.

"Just Avery?"

I nodded, refusing to look up.

"Well, Just Avery–." The smirk was starting to leak into his voice.

"You guys should probably get out of those wet clothes," I cut him off before he could say anything else. "I'll go check for some extra clothes for you."

"Thanks." The confused whisper followed me as I retreated to the bedroom, hurrying as fast as I could without running.

Leaning against the closed door, I let out a tiny sigh, trying to remember what the self-help books taught me.

Never use the word 'just.'
It's a protector word and diminishes the value of whatever words follow.

It might seem ridiculous to some people, but those books are what helped get me to where I was. I was a nobody, merely another employee that was working long hours with little pay. Now? A potential CEO to a multibillion-dollar corporation. Potential as in a year or two away, if Mark didn't continue to get in my way, and the current CEO's plans to retire didn't change.

The thought of him instantly put out any attraction I was feeling toward the two strangers in the next room.

Fucking Mark...

CHAPTER TWO

I could hear them.

On the other side of the door.

Whispering.

They were probably wondering what was taking me so long with the clothes. But there I was, leaning against the door, trying to gleam the slightest bit of information that I could get out of their hushed conversation.

Not getting anything useful, I leaned back, pulling the door open with me. As soon as I stepped out, bundle of clothes in hand, two pairs of sea-green eyes swung towards me, one with caution and the other with mirth. It was hard to miss the intense looks on their faces, though, before they hid the expressions. From the looks of it, they're not exactly a picture-perfect family.

But then, who is anymore?

Again, Mark's conceited face thrust itself in my mind.

Forcing a smile, I made my way out of the room, handing them each a set of clothes.

Regretfully, I had switched out my fluffy blanket with a thick sweater to move around better. Or really, so I could make a break for it better if either of them tried to come at me.

"They might not fit perfect. The owner's a friend of mine and her husband isn't quite built like the two of you." Realizing belatedly how honest that was, the red that had nothing to do with the cold colored my cheeks, I attempted to backtrack.

"I mean, he's not as large as–."

Eyebrows shot toward the ceiling.

"What I meant was, his muscles aren't as–."

Identical grins formed on their faces. It was then I realized they were actually twins. Somehow, their personalities changed their entire facial features and made each look completely different.

"Are you twins?" The question blurted out of me before I thought about how invasive I was being with their lives.

This time, the eyebrow arch was out of surprise instead of humor.

"Excuse me?" Jasper asked as his stare bore a hole into the side of my head.

"Well, it's just that–." There's that word again. So much for all those life coaching books.

"Just that what?" Luke hedged, as if attempting to smooth over Jasper's surly response.

"You guys seem so different for brothers. You didn't look at all alike when you stepped through the door. I mean, besides the eyes and hair," I added, waving a hand toward their heads.

Holy hell, it was going to be a long snowstorm.

A low chuckle reverberated through Jasper's chest as Luke's face darkened even more.

"As fun as this is, I'm getting out of these clothes." Luke started toward the door I had come out of before turning back to face me with a glint in his eye. "Unless, of course, you want to help."

My breath hitched at the image of this random man, built like a UFC fighter, stripping down bare in front of me...

"Stop teasing her, Jasper," Luke chided, throwing me a sympathetic glance. It was Jasper's turn to chuckle before disappearing.

Damn me if that sound didn't do something fierce to my insides.

"Don't mind him. He's just an ass." A brief laugh escaped as I smiled up at the remaining brother.

"Thanks, I'll try to remember that."

There was another rule broken. I've known these guys for all of two seconds and they seem to revert me back to old habits already.

Never say "I'll try."
It implies no confidence in your abilities to accomplish your tasks.

"You can use one of the upstairs bedrooms to change if you want." I turned away from him, pointing in the direction to change the subject. "There's five more bedrooms up there, so take your pick."

"Five?" His surprise caught me off-guard. From the looks of him and his clothing, he had to have come from some type of money. Especially if the Rolex on his wrist was anything to go off.

"Mhmm. It's mainly used as a vacation home for my friend and her family. I won't need to use all of them."

"All of them? You're here by yourself?"

"Yesssss," I cautioned slowly, dragging out the word. "But don't get any ideas of trying to axe-murder me in the middle of the night." Pointing a finger in his direction, one hand on my hip, I sent him my most intimidating glare. Granted, it wasn't very effective. Even less so when he doubled over laughing.

"I'll keep that in mind," he said between breaths.

"Good." I couldn't help the smirk that snuck its way across my face.

"Thanks for the clothes." He started toward the stairs, throwing over his shoulder, "I'll try not to let my large build ruin them."

I didn't need to see his face to hear the laughter or see my own to know how red it was.

Hopefully, the snow would let up in the next few minutes.

Making my way through the kitchen, unfastening the locks, I looked toward the woodpile in the corner. It was slowly dwindling down, but there was no way I was making my way out into the freak storm to replenish it. There was still a good amount of it left, covering the entire wall, but I did not know how much longer this storm was supposed to last. Heaving a couple logs into my arms, I twirled around, bumping face first into a lean chest. Inch by agonizing inch, I raised my head to be met with Jasper's questioning gaze.

"You don't have any electricity."

I arched an eyebrow at his obvious statement.

"Nope. I sure don't."

"I tried to take a shower to warm up."

"In case you haven't noticed, there's a big storm outside that probably affected the power lines."

Narrowing his eyes at the sarcastic tone, he looked down at what I was carrying. Or attempting to carry since he felt it was necessary to continue blocking my path.

"What are you doing?"

"Carrying wood." Lifting my arms higher as if it wasn't obvious.

"Why?"

"To heat the house?"

"How?"

"What?"

"How do you use the wood to heat the house?" I stared for a moment, unsure of how to answer. I wasn't sure if he was being serious or if he was messing with me.

"With the fireplace."

"Where is that?"

"In the living room?"

"Is that a question?"

"No?"

Smirking, he grabbed the wood out of my hands and started back into the house.

"Wh–hey!" Was this guy for real? "What are you doing?"

Looking over his shoulder, as if I was the dense one, he replied, "Warming the house. I'm cold."

"Okay…" What else was I supposed to say? It was one of the strangest conversations I've ever had.

Reaching the living room once again, we were met by Luke, sitting in the middle of the couch with his arms stretched across the back. He didn't seem to hear us come in as he stared into the fireplace, the flames dancing across the shadows in his eyes.

"Luke." Jasper's voice came out a demand. Whether that was to snap him out of it or to not let me see the anguish, I wasn't sure which.

"Luke." Still no response. Suddenly, a high-pitched whistle sounded right beside my ear, ringing throughout my head. Instinctively covering my now-sensitive ears, I looked to the culprit for an explanation, but he wasn't even looking at me. Surprisingly, he didn't do it to be a dick like I had expected.

It was more to get a reaction out of Luke, which was met with success, judging by the glare he was leveling in our direction. Luke, to his credit, didn't give a reaction; merely walked over to the fireplace and gently put the new logs on.

Against my better judgement, I wondered about how they got there and what kind of relationship they have. It's not like they actually get along or anything, so it makes a person wonder.

"Oooooookay then." Once again, stretching out the sounds to fill the awkward silence. "You guys hungry?" Before either could answer, I continued, "I bet you are. I'll go get you some food. I've got some leftover chili. You guys like chili?" They opened their mouths to respond, but I beat them to it, again. "Awesome! I'll get you some chili."

"Chili?" Luke's voice trailed me as I hightailed it through the doorway and into the kitchen.

Confrontation has always made me uncomfortable. That's why Sarah insisted I come up in the first place. She made a very convincing argument, telling me I'd need a lot of rest and relaxation if I was going to go head-to-head with Mark for the CEO position. Sarah wasn't wrong, of course. She rarely ever was; that's part of what made it so frustrating. If she could see me now, she would still say it was a good idea.

'Two dicks make a much better stress-reliever than one.' Then she'd hit me over the head with that damn notebook of hers, asking why I haven't made a move yet. There'd be no reason telling her that I just met them, and they clearly had a lot of baggage going on.

Would that matter to her? Hell nope.

Imagining how that conversation would go was enough to bring a smile to face, exhaling a bit of the tension that was in my shoulders.

Opening the fridge as fast as I could manage, I grabbed the container with the chili and slammed the door close again so the little cold that was in there wouldn't seep out. Not that it mattered. I could've just taken everything out and stuck it in a snowbank outside and it'd stay cold just fine. Probably a bit frozen, though.

Standing in the middle of the kitchen with the bowl clenched between my hands, I was unsure what to do next. No electricity meant no heating the chili. What good was cold chili?

I really hadn't thought that one through.

Debating for a moment, I set the bowl on the kitchen island and rummaged through the pots and pans. Finding what I was looking for, I grabbed everything and made my way back to the living room.

Something must have happened while I was gone. When I walked in, I was met with an uncomfortable stare-down between the brothers. Ignoring the obvious tension, I walked straight in between them and plopped down in front of the fire. There was no reason for me to feel on edge here, and I refused to.

Feeling their stares, I opened the container and dumped the contents into the cast-iron pot.

"What are you doing?" Jasper appeared over my shoulder, his breath tickling the side of my neck.

"What does it look like? I'm cooking food."

"How are you going to put the pot over the fire?" Luke positioned himself over my left shoulder, his whispers caressing the sensitive lobe.

"Well, you know." I held up the heat-proof gloves I found with the pot and slipped them on.

"You're joking, right?" Jasper deadpanned from one side.

"She has to be joking." Luke confirmed from the other.

Slowly shaking my head, I looked back and forth between the two.

"Do you guys have a better idea?" Silence. "I didn't think so." I held the pot by the handle, getting ready to thrust it above the flames, when a pair of brawny hands reached out, grasping them.

"Hey!"

Jasper took the pot from my grasp, looking me straight in the eyes. "Luke can hold it. Give him the gloves."

"But–."

"Please, you think you're going to sit there for however long holding a heavy-ass pan over a fire, but far enough away not to burn yourself?" He scoffed. Unable to think of a good comeback, I sat there pouting, pursing my lips, making him give a snort in return.

"Please, Avery." I turned to find Luke mere inches from my face, pleading with me. "You were nice enough to take us in out of the cold. The least we can do is heat up some food."

"Okay," I relented, quietly. I watched in silence for a moment as Luke put on the gloves and took over. "I've never cooked anything over a fire before."

"No?" The question came from my left.

"Nope. Don't get me wrong, I've had to work my butt off and accomplish everything in my life on my own. I've always fended for myself. But somehow, I always managed to escape the glory of camping." I felt a small chuckle as it reverberated through my left shoulder. When had Luke started leaning against me?

"I can't say that I blame you. We've never been camping, either." He nodded to his brother, who was now sprawled on his side, head in hand, looking up at me.

"Nope," Jasper confirmed. "I probably would've used a regular kitchen pot, too."

A comfortable silence followed. I watched as the flames licked the bottom of the pot, lending their heat to our survival.

"So." I decided to be the one to touch on the inevitable subject. "How did you guys end up way out here in the first place?"

More silence.

"That big of a secret, huh?" I laughed, attempting to play it off, flipping my blonde locks over my shoulder and twirling the end. It was a habit I couldn't seem to break. "That's okay. I'll go first."

CHAPTER THREE

They waited as I searched for the right words to start. Taking a deep breath to calm my nerves, I began picking my words carefully. It wasn't like I was going to spill all my life's secrets to these guys, but it would be nice to have some people to talk to while we were all forced in such proximity.

"My friend made me come." I gave a little laugh when their eyebrows shot to the ceiling, looking at me as if I had lost my marbles. "She thought I could do with a break. A stress-reliever. I'm getting ready for a huge promotion at work, but I'm up against a couple other people for it." If I didn't single him out, maybe I wouldn't think about him. "Anyway, she can be very convincing. She forced me up here with my books and told me to delve into the darkest, smuttiest romance books I could find."

I started talking without a filter, forgetting who I was talking to as I remembered Sarah, and, before I realized it, I was telling them about my lady porn.

Suddenly, the fire became very interesting as I intently started, refusing to move a muscle. I couldn't believe I told them that. I never told anyone that before, Sarah excluded.

"What–ahem–what do you mean by darkest?"

"What do you mean by smuttiest?"

Each question was catapulted at me, breaking the stillness of the room.

A nervous laugh escaped as I continued to twirl my hair around my poor finger.

"That's–uh–not the point." I tried to deflect, but they weren't having any of it.

"Please?"

"Pretty please?"

"What kind of smut is it?"

"How smutty is it?"

"Scale of one to ten?"

"What kind of things do they do?"

"Guys, please stop," I begged. "I really shouldn't have said that. I don't know why I did. Sometimes my mouth runs away from me without me realizing it. You'd think I'd learn by now, but noooooooooo. How many times, Avery? How many times will it take for you to completely embarrass yourself before you'll stop over sharing things that you really shouldn't? How many–?"

"Hey, hey, hey." I felt soothing circles on my back as I pulled my knees up to my chest, burying my face out of sight, my hair cascading over them. Effectively hiding me from sight.

"It's not that big of a deal. Everyone watches porn. What's the difference between that and reading it?" That was definitely Jasper trying to comfort me.

Apparently, a few hours was far too long to spend with a stranger without giving them very personal information about you.

"Excuse me while I go crawl in a hole."

I stood up to escape their stares of amusement. I had no clue where I was going. The cabin was pretty big, but it felt far too small at that moment.

I needed to get out into the fresh air. Maybe if I hurried, I could make my way to the mini cabin, which wasn't really mini at all. The one they used as a guest cabin out back. Reaching out for the coat by the front door, I shrugged it on. Grabbing my hat and gloves, I was about to do the same when I heard a movement behind me.

Turning, I came face-to-face with a broad set of shoulders, just like I had earlier. Strange to think I've only known them for a few hours.

"What do you think you're doing?" Surprise shook his voice as Luke held onto my wrist.

"I need some fresh air."

"Have you looked outside?" The incredulity in his voice was setting my nerves on end. I looked over his shoulder to see the pot laying haphazardly on the floor with chili flowing out of it.

"There's another cabin," I tried to explain.

"Absolutely not." His voice thundered around the room, more deafening than the howl outside, making me flinch back in response.

Before I could even begin to think about how to handle the situation, the door behind me flew open and an entire snowbank came cascading inside. Twirling, squealing in surprise, I leaped back straight into Luke's iron-grasp. We stood there, staring in disbelief, Luke's hand on my shoulders no doubt in an attempt to keep me in place, as Jasper stood in front of us with one hand held out toward the incoming snow.

"See?" Did that damn grin ever leave his face? "We're snowed in now. There's no escaping."

"Well, when you say it like that," I gave a little laugh. "It sure makes me want to stay in here even more and get strangled in my sleep."

Smiling broadly, he reached down to pack a handful of snow into his hands, carefully shaping it as he continued to look at where his brother's hands were on my body. Instinctively, I felt them tighten against my skin. Even through the gloves he was still wearing, I felt the fingers dig into my skin as if they didn't want to let go.

Jasper saw the same.

"I mean, if you're into that kind of thing," Jasper replied with a flirtatious wink, making my insides turn to knots.

One second, we were in a standoff. The next, there was a massive snowball slamming straight into Luke's face, knocking him off balance. It wasn't enough force to knock him down, but he took a step backward to steady himself, giving me the chance to escape in a fit of laughter.

Ending up next to Jasper, he reached out a hand, offering me the next snowball. Only hesitating for a moment, I accepted the challenge. Waiting until Luke raised his head to fire it straight into the middle of his forehead. This one caught him more by surprise. His foot slipped in the snow that was melting from the heat of the cabin, taking him down to the ground.

"Oh, you guys are in for it now." A fierce look dominated his features as he lunged toward us, grabbing fistfuls of his own snow. Running back to the living room, Jasper and I took cover behind the couch, waiting for our moment to strike.

"You don't need to be so embarrassed; you know. About the books."

The seriousness of his voice caught me completely off-guard as I turned to look at him. This time, though, he wasn't just close. He was right there. Our lips grazed accidentally, as I opened my mouth to reply. We both went stock-still as the situation sank in.

"I'm sorry," I muttered, leaning back. "I didn't mean to–."

"That's a shame," he muttered. "Because I did."

Luke chose the perfect time to interrupt, popping his head up behind the couch, launching a counterattack straight into the side of both of our faces, and popping back down.

Jasper and I looked at one another for another moment before nodding in agreement, launching ourselves over the couch. Battle cries ripping out of both of us, we threw the rest of our ammunition into Luke's hard frame.

I should've been paying a bit more attention to where I was stepping because the next thing I knew, I was slipping in the snow. Grabbing a hold of Jasper's arm to steady myself, I ended up taking him down with me, crashing straight into Luke. The three of us fell headfirst into the snowbank peeking through the door.

By the time we caught our breaths, we were all doubled over in laughter. Attempting to get out of the tangle of limbs, I set my hand down to push my body up, only to fall further into the bank. There were hands groping my butt, knuckles brushing my nipples, legs entwined everywhere. I didn't even want to think about the places that my hands were touching, otherwise my face would be as red as the fire that continued to crackle.

After a couple of minutes of struggling, we all seemed to give up for the moment to take a breather.

"He's right, you know," Luke said, eyes resting closed.

"Huh?"

"Jasper. He's right." I looked over at the man in question to see him looking back. "You don't need to worry about being embarrassed with us."

"Oh." What else was I supposed to say? How could I not be? I wasn't used to anyone, let alone strangers, knowing intimate details of my life.

"We're serious, Avery," Jasper chimed in.

"Yup." Being the one who started the conversation, Luke sure seemed like he was going to fall asleep at any moment in the freezing snow. "No worries here. We should relax and enjoy the peace. I'm sure it's a rare thing for all of us."

"You're one to talk," Jasper whispered, the edge to his voice returning from earlier. He had the same set to his jaw from when I walked in on them.

"No worries," Luke repeated. Whether he didn't hear his brother or was blatantly ignoring him, I wasn't sure. A yawn escaped him as he cushioned himself further into the bank. "No family. No pestering friends. No inheritance. No jobs. No Sarah. No Mark."

I went still. The blood in my veins turned to ice, and not from the snow. Jasper was gaping at his brother as if he was surprised he said anything.

Suddenly, Luke's eyes popped open to stare straight into mine.

"How the fuck do you know about Mark?!"

To be continued...

THANKS FOR READING!

Are you as obsessed with Avery and her men, Luke and Jasper, as much as I am?

Frosted Hearts is now up for preorder and will be releasing early 2022.

Curious about my other works?
Those can be found on my website:
www.celashua.com

I'm always up for meeting new friends so make sure to stop by and join my Facebook Group:
Stalkers of Chaos

SNOWED IN WITH YOU

ROSIE EAST

CHAPTER ONE

HOLLY

It was finally time for my Christmas getaway. I'd been counting down the hours until it was my holiday. My case was packed and now I had to make the drive up to the hilltop lodge that I had booked for the week.

One week in a secluded mountain lodge two hours away from my hometown—just me on my own with no work or distractions. The lodge had an open fire, an alpine view, and plenty of comfortable chairs. I'd been so overrun at work I'd barely had an opportunity to sit down and have some time to myself. My family would hardly notice I wasn't home; they'd be too busy fawning over my older brother and his newborn baby.

Before I took my case down to the car, I checked my stock of books and DVDs to keep me entertained for the week. Boredom wasn't on the agenda. Running around my flat, I picked up another handful to be on the safer side and grabbed my handbag with my chargers in it to make sure I would still be contactable.

Walking outside one last time, I inhaled deeply. The smell of winter filled my nostrils, even though the cold air stung slightly. I only knew it was going to get colder the higher up the mountains I got, but it would be worth it once I curled up with a blanket and a hot chocolate in front of the roaring fire.

Sitting in my car, I clicked my seatbelt in before turning the radio on. Driving for two hours in winter, it was wise to be wary of quick changes to the weather. The local stations would keep me updated.

Beginning my journey, I could feel the tension easing in my body already. I needed this holiday more than I realised. I just had to cope with the drive first.

Pulling into the carpark, my drive had been relatively painless. I'd made it. Checking the instructions on my phone, I read that I had to head to the nearby cafe to collect the key. Trudging through the shallow snow, I smiled, taking in the mountainous scene around me. The trees seemed to go on right up to the horizon. Soon, the sun would set. I couldn't wait to watch it, I might even photograph it. Sunset was my favourite time of day.

Entering the Mountainside Cafe, I noticed the small candles scattered around the room. I wondered if they lit them at night. The scent of freshly baked pastries overwhelmed me. I wasn't planning to get anything from the cafe, but after smelling them, it would be difficult to resist.

Approaching the desk, I was convinced I could resist. That was until I saw the man behind the till. Baked goods were going to be the least of my worries. It had been years since I'd last been in a relationship, after that I'd thrown myself headfirst into my career. I had no time for men. Something about this man though was making my insides flutter. I licked my lips as I took in his dark hair and stubble, even his tartan shirt and fitted jeans that I could see over the counter.

He cleared his throat, and his gravelly voice cut through my thoughts. "I asked if you were okay. Can I help you?"

Shit, had he already spoken to me? "Oh… Yes, I'm good. Sorry, I was just admiring the cakes." What a load of lies! If he was observant, he would know perfectly that I was not looking at that cabinet at all.

"Our cakes look amazing, don't they? Would you like any?" His husky voice sent shivers down my spine.

In my mind, I wanted to ask if any part of him was on the menu, but that wasn't appropriate. He was a stranger. "I shouldn't..." I trailed off.

"Why shouldn't you?"

He had a point. I did have a car full of bags to carry to the lodge, so that seemed reasonable. "I'm only here to collect the key for the Pine Lodge. My booking said that I needed to come here. Is that right?"

His smile widened; it was a little concerning to me, but I knew that was probably just me overthinking things as usual. "Yes, you are in the right place. Can I ask for your name, please?"

"Of course, it's Holly Frost." That really was my name, my parents clearly had a cruel sense of humour. I was shocked they hadn't named my brother Jack.

I heard the person behind me snigger in line, before turning to their friend to make a snide comment about how that must be a fake name. I'd become accustomed to people making jokes out of my name at this time of year. I hated it, but after twenty-three years, I'd toughened up, so it didn't affect me anywhere near as much as it used to.

I caught the man behind the counter glaring at the next customers, however, he seemed to manage to hold his tongue. "I've got you here on our list. Here is the key. Do you need any help carrying your bags across? As a guest of the lodge, you are able to get breakfast here every day for free, and if you need any help, we are your closest neighbour."

In my mind, I knew I could carry my belongings to the lodge alone, but my heart and my gut were telling me to accept help from this man. "You know, help with my bags would be great. Seeing as I'll have help now, I should manage to carry a cake too." My words surprised me, but I went along with them.

"I will get my mum to come through to watch the shop, then I'll get your cake. Two minutes, Holly." The deep baritone of his voice, paired with his sharp eyes when he said my name, sent shockwaves of arousal through my body. Coming to the Mountainside Cafe every morning was sure to become the highlight of my holiday, especially if he was working here. While he was speaking to his mum, I couldn't help but think through potential ways to subtly ask him about his plans for the holiday and his name. I was a planner; I had to think through every possible outcome before taking any action. Maybe it was time I started taking risks.

CHAPTER TWO

JACK

Walking into the kitchen in the cafe, my mum scowled at me. "Jack, what are you doing back here? You're supposed to be manning the till today."

"I know. The booking for the Pine Lodge has arrived and asked for help with their bags. Will you be able to watch the front while I help them, please?" I gave her my best puppy dog eyes, hoping she wouldn't be able to resist. I was her baby boy after all.

"Jack, what is going on? You never offer to help people with their bags. What are you up to?" Her eyes narrowed in suspicion. She knew me too well.

"She asked for help, who was I to refuse?" I attempted to dodge her question.

She raised her eyebrow. "Oh, it's a she. Very well. Yes, I will come through. Did you tell her about her free breakfast from us? Did you tell her about..."

I rolled my eyes, before interrupting. "Yes, Mum, I told her about the lodge being closest to here and us being able to help. I know the script now." I'd been working there during holidays for the past six years in an official capacity and helping out as long as I could remember.

"Good. I'll come through now, then."

"Thank you, Mum," I beamed, turning to walk back to the counter to get Holly her cake.

The petite blonde girl standing at the counter with her sparkling blue eyes took my breath away for the second time. She seemed so different from all the locals. In a room full of people, all I could see was her. Confidence radiated around her, and everyone could sense it.

"Holly, my mum will come through in a minute, then I can help you with your bags. Now, which cake would you like?" I hoped she couldn't catch on to how attracted to her I was from the way I was behaving. She probably wouldn't be interested in the small town mountain boy anyway.

"Thank you. Would I be able to get the butterscotch tart and a slice of the brandy cake, please?" Her soft voice sounded angelic to my ears, but maybe my mind was just obscuring everything about her because she was a beautiful girl.

"Of course, let me get those for you and then we can head up to the lodge. I hope you have strong shoes on—it's a long way up." I heard the patronising words leave my lips. God, why was I so useless with women? I hoped she didn't now think I was an arse with my need to mansplain things for no reason.

I didn't dare say anything else, God forbid another stupid thing came out of my mouth. I headed to the cabinet and began serving her cakes into small paper bags we used for takeaways. My mum appeared beside me and placed a hand on my shoulder just as I deposited the first of the cakes onto the counter.

"Okay, I'm here, you can head up when you're done," she spoke confidently while eying up Holly. Likely curious why I was taking a sudden interest in helping the lodge guests. I noticed her subtle nod of approval in my peripheral vision. Clearly, my mum liked something about this woman too.

I finished serving the cakes with a small smile on my face while my mum took the payment. After handing Holly her cakes, I untied my apron, hanging it up and moving around the counter. "Right, let's take you up to the lodge and get you settled in."

She sniggered at me slightly. "That would be great. I can't wait to see it." She must have noticed I was coming across as a bumbling idiot. I needed to redeem myself quickly.

"It's gorgeous up there, you'll fit right in." I couldn't stop myself from saying it. I wanted this woman to know that she looked amazing. I'd only just met her, I would never normally say that to anyone, but here we go. She was bringing out a confident side to me that I didn't know existed. Until now, I always waited until I was certain there was a mutual interest, or even for the woman to make the first move, but not with Holly.

"Oh... thank you," she said as a blush crept up her neck from under her polo shirt to her face. I wanted to know what was under those layers she wore. I just hoped I would get to find out before she left.

Walking to her car in silence, I took her in as she looked down the main street curiously. Did she want to explore before going to the lodge? Should I ask? Why was I so uncertain about everything when it came to her? She makes me act like a blabbering, clueless teenager again. "Holly, do you want a tour of the town before we take your bags up to the lodge?"

"I would love one, but don't you need to head back to the cafe and let your mum get back to what she was doing?" She chewed her pink lip into her mouth.

"She will understand that I need to show our guest what a welcoming community we are." I winked at her.

A soft laugh erupted from her. The sound sent my blood rushing south to my cock. I wanted to get to know this woman better as soon as possible. I had to start thinking about anything other than her so I didn't walk around town sporting a serious hard-on. "Okay, a tour would be lovely. I suppose I'd better know the name of my guide then."

"My name is Jack."

She burst out laughing. "Please tell me your surname isn't Frost too?"

"No, it's not. It's Claus..." I joked, grinning as I said it.

"No way. Shouldn't your name be Nick then?" she questioned.

"That's my dad." I winked at her. "My surname is actually Walker."

"Oh no, that's not Christmassy at all. Suppose I'll just have to ignore you telling me that and continue believing you are the son of Santa himself." She seemed slightly disappointed.

"For you, I will be Santa's son. Maybe I will put some presents in your stockings too." I flirted with her, hoping she wouldn't be too weirded out by what I'd just said.

Thankfully she wasn't. Instead, she just burst out laughing. "Jack, I think we're going to get on great. I'm glad I met you."

"I hope we will. Let's get on with this tour then, shall we?" I offered her my arm, anticipating she would link arms with me. When she did, goosebumps covered my skin, her touch electrifying my very senses.

CHAPTER THREE

HOLLY

I'd been here for three days, but I felt like my week was just flying past me. Since the first day, I'd been spending more time with Jack each day. I had hardly read any of the books I'd brought with me because I'd been out doing things with him. So far, we'd taken a tour of the town, and visited the ice-skating rink — a sport at which I was terrible. Today, he was coming to meet me with breakfast for a surprise. He'd said he would arrive at ten, but it was now ten past. A seed of worry bloomed in my chest.

I looked out of the window and upon gazing at the snow falling around the lodge, I wondered if he was going to be able to get up to me. I really hoped he would. It was quarter past ten when a knock sounded on the door. I practically ran to open it to be greeted with the sight of Jack wearing a large jacket and holding a few bags of what looked like shopping.

"Hey. What's in the bags?" I asked curiously.

"We're set for a few days of heavy snow so I brought you supplies. I can't stay with you because I have to help at the cafe, so I thought I'd make sure you were stocked up, in case you get stuck."

I swooned slightly. This man cared so much, even though I'd only known him for a short time. "Thank you. What have you brought me then?"

"Take a look, I'm going to light the fire. I thought, today, instead of going out somewhere, we could just sit in front of the fire together, maybe watch a film. Does that sound okay?"

"That sounds perfect. That's what I had planned for my whole trip, so why not? I have a stack of DVDs in my case," I replied, hoping it wouldn't come across as strange that I'd intended to spend my whole trip alone in the lodge. That was also before him. Sometimes, the world just shoved signs in your face that you should be doing more than sitting alone. Jack was that sign for me.

"Great. Do you want to choose one while I start unpacking the supplies?" he inquired, seeming desperate to shoo me away. What was he hiding?

Entering the bedroom, I smiled at the tartan throw on the bed where I'd neatened it this morning knowing he was coming up to visit. Dragging my case out from under the bed, I was careful not to scratch the hardwood floor. Even when I wasn't at my own flat, I was still scared about the cost of potential repairs. I looked at the stack, unsure what sort of film he would be into.

Quickly, I discarded the ones I didn't feel like watching just now. Looking at my remaining options, I realised that one was a classic and I hadn't watched it during this festive season yet. Pulling my slippers on, I headed back to the living space. Comfort first, after all. Normally I would put my pyjamas on, but I didn't think I was quite at the point with Jack that I could do that.

Opening the door from the bedroom, I was hit with a decadent waft of bacon. Had he sent me to choose so he could cook me breakfast?

"Hey, what are you cooking?" I decided to test my luck.

He jumped at the sound of my voice breaking through the silence. Turning to face me, he scowled slightly. "Isn't it obvious? I'm cooking breakfast for a beautiful woman."

Heat travelled up my face. I loved all the sweet comments he'd showered me with, even though they may have started a little prematurely after meeting. They made me feel special but embarrassed that he thought that. I'd never been with a man who said such wonderful things. "I mean, what's for breakfast?"

He playfully rolled his eyes before answering properly. "I'm making you bacon and cheese croissants."

Tears pricked my eyes, I'd mentioned that my family always had bacon and cheese croissants at Christmas and I would miss it this year. He actually took it to heart and had taken it upon himself to make sure I still got that. Something about this man seemed too good to be true, but I wasn't going to start complaining now. I was leaving in four days and would probably not see him again afterwards. "Thank you," I whispered, attempting to hide the emotions bombarding me.

"You're welcome. Go and get the film set up. I'll bring it over when it's ready. What are we watching?" he called out as I walked away to the sofa.

"*Home Alone*," I shouted back. In the sitting area, I was met by an already roaring fire and two mugs of hot chocolate with cream on the table. *How long had I been in the bedroom?* He seemed to have done so much in such a short time.

I wasn't sure if he replied since I was too busy picking my jaw up off the floor about how perfect he seemed to be. Attempting to distract myself from thinking about the man in the kitchen cooking my breakfast, I concentrated on preparing the film before getting myself comfortable on the sofa, all curled up with a blanket. Today was going to be perfect.

I hadn't been sitting for long, skipping through to the menu on the DVD, when Jack walked in with our breakfast. "Here you go, breakfast is served complete with hot chocolate."

"Thank you. Jack, how are you still single if you do things like this?" I couldn't stop myself from asking him what'd been on my mind.

"I haven't met the right woman before now," he answered while gazing into my eyes. My heart began thumping erratically in my chest.

I didn't know how to answer what he had just said. I was rendered speechless, and that never happened.

Beginning to overthink his words and my lack of actions, I hit play. Relationships had never been my strong point, no matter how short. The much-needed distraction of *Home Alone* filled the lodge.

CHAPTER FOUR

JACK

I couldn't believe she had chosen one of my all-time favourite Christmas films to put on. I wished I could just spend all the time she was here with her, but I had to help my mum in the cafe because my brother was away. My dad did what he could, but he wasn't always able to do much. My mum had given me the morning off, but I needed to be back before one to do the afternoon shift, which meant we could only watch one film.

The more time I spent with Holly, the less I wanted her to leave. The conversation between us seemed so natural. It was like I'd known her my entire life, and not just a few days. I was close to finishing university and all my friends were beginning to get married and move on to bigger and better things. Meanwhile, I hadn't had a long-term relationship since my high school girlfriend, and even then, I wouldn't really count that as a proper relationship. I was convinced she only dated me to get a discount at the cafe.

Shaking my head slightly, I needed to stop thinking about my past and my friends, and focus on here and now. The beautiful girl beside me was all that mattered. I didn't know how much time we would have together, so I had to make the most of it.

Our breakfast quickly disappeared. She smiled once she finished it, facing me. "Don't ever tell my family about this if you meet them, but that was the best bacon and cheese croissant I'd ever had. How did you make it so amazing?"

I smirked; it was an old family recipe that was passed down the generations. It also could only be given out to family. "Sorry, Holly, I could tell you, but I would then have to kill you. It's a family secret."

She fluttered her eyelashes at me and softened her gaze into a pleading look. "Are you sure you can't tell me?"

"I'm sure," I replied sadly. I wished I could tell her, but I just couldn't, owing to our family tradition.

"It's okay. I was just messing with you anyways. Although, if you ever change your mind, give me a call." She smiled and softly kissed my cheek.

Fuck, that was the first time she'd kissed me. I focused on the film even though I'd seen it about five times per year since I was six, I couldn't think about her touch. It seemed that was all she wanted me to think about though, as she shuffled along the sofa and wrapped her arm around me while resting her head on my shoulder.

I slipped my arm around her and rested my head against hers. The berry scent of her shampoo filled my nostrils and I knew I would never be able to smell that again without getting turned on. Our heads resting together in the warmth, we quickly fell asleep.

Waking up, I saw the screen had returned to the menu screen of the DVD. How long had we been asleep? Gently, I rocked her shoulders. "Holly, wake up," I murmured into her hair.

She drowsily moved, beginning to stretch her body out. Every move she made, I was aware of where she was — she'd moved closer to my lap. Her hands were now dangerously close to my cock. I couldn't act on it though, I needed to get to work soon. "Sorry, I didn't mean to fall asleep. What time is it?" she spoke groggily, rubbing her eyes as she sat up.

I reached over for my phone to check the time and it was now half past twelve. I let out a sigh of relief, I had time. "It's half twelve. I need to leave." I told her as I scrolled through my notifications. Dread settled in my stomach as I saw the number of missed calls and texts from my parents.

When I read one message, I figured out why I had a sense of dread. *Snow is really heavy. Hurry down before you get stuck.* Checking the timestamp on it, I knew it was too late. How could I tell Holly we were potentially stuck here?

"Holly, I need to check what it's like outside. If my messages are correct, I think we're stuck here," I told her while I strode towards the door. *Please don't be as bad as I think it is,* I thought while I walked. I opened the door and my fears were confirmed. The snow was easily two feet deep. How did that happen so quickly? Shit.

The door still open, I paced around the cloakroom. Holly placed her hand on my arm — when did she walk up to me? "What is it? You seem stressed, and you left the door open. It's freezing in here."

"Did you look outside?" I snapped at her slightly. Did she not understand what two feet of snow meant?

"Yeah, the snow is pretty deep." She nodded while chewing her lip. "Oh shit, that means you can't get back to work, right? We're stuck here?"

I watched as an array of emotions crossed her face as she realised the situation we were now stuck in together.

Her face looked content. Was she waiting for my confirmation of what she had just said? I was sure my face reflected the reality of the situation we had now found ourselves in. "Yeah, we're stuck. I'm going to try and call the cafe to let my mum know. Go and wait on the sofa. You may as well choose another film. We'll probably not be leaving any time soon," I called after her as she walked away.

I'd put on a brave face even though I knew in reality, depending on how bad the storm was, that we may not be able to get out of here for at least a few days. I felt a special connection to this woman, but I didn't know how she would feel about potentially being trapped in a small lodge with me for a prolonged period. Maybe by the end of it, she wouldn't seem like such an anomaly.

Dialling the number for the cafe on my phone, I was surprised when I couldn't get through. Ending the call, I checked my screen. My worst fears were confirmed seeing the No Service icon. The storm might've knocked out the towers; it usually happened every few years. I decided to try the landline even though I knew that if the mobile tower was down, the phone lines would be too. I had to try; I couldn't just leave my mum in the lurch for the afternoon shift. Although, if the storm was as bad as it seemed, she would have to close up to make sure she made it home safely.

Holding the phone up to my ear, all I heard was the dialling tone. My suspicions confirmed — we were not reachable. I felt relieved seeing the message from my parents that they had made it through before the service dropped if nothing else. There was nothing more I could do except enjoy my time here in the lodge with Holly. The views and company would make up for being trapped.

CHAPTER FIVE

HOLLY

I picked out a selection of DVDs before returning to the sofa. My gut was telling me that we weren't going to be getting out of the lodge today. Sitting down, panic and relief washed over me. I was stuck here, but I was glad to not be alone, despite the intention of my trip being isolated.

Jack entered the room and sat beside me with a loud sigh. "How did the call go?" I asked him, despite his hunched shoulders and crossed arms telling me it wasn't positive.

"It didn't," he grunted.

"Oh, I'm sorry. Is there anything I can do?" I rested my hand on his knee, hoping my move would show some support, even though I was certain I wouldn't be able to help much.

"Not really. Let's just put the next film on and enjoy our time together." He shrugged.

I began to worry that being snowed in with him was not going to be as fun as I'd first thought when we'd made the discovery. Picking up the stack of films, I narrowed the choice down to two, offering him the choice. "*Rise of the Guardians* or *The Grinch*?" I asked him as I held the two boxes out towards him.

He raised an eyebrow surveying my selections. "Is this some sort of irony? Jack Frost and The Grinch? Maybe it's a metaphor... English never was my strong suit. Is it supposed to be a reflection of us?"

"I didn't mean it to be. Sorry, I just find when I'm feeling sad or stressed that a children's film always makes me feel better," I apologised quickly while chewing my lip and avoiding eye contact with him, afraid I'd only upset him more.

"Hey, Holly, look at me." He lifted my chin, forcing my gaze to meet his. His soft touch sent a shiver down my spine and goosebumps prickled on the back of my neck. My body's reaction definitely wasn't because of the cold as we sat in front of a still roaring fire. "That's better. What was the whimper for, though? Are you scared?" he rambled on, but I sat dumbstruck.

"What whimper?" I furrowed my brow, unsure of the meaning of his question.

"I touched you and then you whimpered. I didn't hurt you or scare you, did I?" His eyes softened and his features relaxed.

Guilt washed over me as I realised my unconscious reaction to his touch had caused him to worry. Maybe this man really could be part of my future. "No, you didn't. My body is just traitorous."

His knee jerked slightly at my words before I heard his deep intake of breath. "Traitorous, how?" The response was just as I hoped it would be.

"I didn't want you to know what your touch does to me... it drives me wild. My body decided to let you know anyway," I told him honestly, while actively trying to hide my nervousness about what I'd just admitted. Who said that to people they hardly knew?

"The feeling is mutual. So, what do you want to do about it? We have to amuse ourselves somehow... it's not like we're going to be interrupted." His low voice became huskier as he spoke, his arousal clear.

I paused before answering. I was always so well behaved; this was out of character. I'd heard of people having holiday romances, but not ever having one myself. It was time for me to live in the moment rather than vicariously through my friends. "I think we should act on whatever this thing going on between us is. Chemistry, sexual frustration, whatever it is, the answer is the same. Are you up for that?"

He smirked. "Of course, I'm up for you... I mean that. I do have a little fantasy about this lodge though..."

He piqued my interest with his comment. "I could help you with that, but only if you tell me what it is." I teased, partially because I knew what I wanted, but first, I had to find out what his fantasy was. If it wasn't something out of my comfort zone, I was all for it.

Leaning in close to my neck, he pressed a kiss on my neck. The unexpected contact made my back arch with delight, and a gasp escaped my lips. "I've wondered what it would be like to fuck on the rug in front of the fire. Would you be willing to find out together?"

The corner of my mouth turned up as I let out a small laugh. "It's not like you could find out alone? I am happy to help you," I reassured him.

"Good," he growled, pushing my legs apart and positioning himself between them. Wrapping his strong arms around my body, he lowered me onto the floor. "I hope you're ready for this, Holly." His low voice and his words sent a wave of arousal through my body. Wanting to get closer to him, I wrapped my legs around his body, which now smothered mine as he hovered over me.

"I am," I confirmed.

"In that case, let me start taking some of these layers off you."

I nodded, at a loss for words anymore. His weight shifted from over my body, resulting in him straddling across my thighs. Watching his hands make light work of my dressing gown tie and blouse buttons, I couldn't help but think about what those hands may be doing very soon. They seemed so deliberate with their movements.

His strong hands parted my blouse, leaving my bra visible to him. I feared a wave of cold was about to hit my newly exposed skin, but being so close to the fire meant that it never came. "Beautiful," he mumbled, desire heating his already dark gaze.

My mouth dried as I anticipated his next move. I couldn't bring myself to interrupt him — the intensity of his gaze made me relinquish my control. I smirked at the irony... All it took for the control freak to lose control was a look. Everyone I knew would be so shocked to hear that, if I could ever tell them about what was about to happen.

CHAPTER SIX

JACK

Holly's green eyes darkened as her pupils expanded. Her silence was turning me on more than anything she could ever say. The expression blanketing her face told me that my moves were reciprocated and I was pressing all of the right buttons for her.

Her full breasts spilt out from her floral bra. Seeing them for the first time, without all the layers she usually wore, just emphasised how perfectly she fitted her figure. Shifting from her body, I slid her loose lounge trousers down her smooth legs so she was just resting on the soft rug in only her underwear.

I rose to stand, making sure she could see me. Unbuttoning my jeans, I examined her body, taking every feature of her in. Her long blonde hair splayed out around her head. Against the black rug, her body stood out. I smiled seeing a small birthmark on her hip. Her eyes roamed over my body as I pulled my jeans down onto the floor before unbuttoning my tartan shirt. Dropping my shirt to the ground, I watched her pull her plump bottom lip between her teeth.

Bending down over her, I dropped down to my knees while I pressed my lips against her soft lips. Connecting our mouths for the first time, she wrapped her arms around my body, pulling me firmly against her. I smiled against her kiss, satisfied with the way she was reacting to me.

Moving to deepen the connection between us, I slipped my tongue against hers and massaged her mouth with it. Hearing her moans beneath me and feeling her hips rising up to get her core closer to me, only made me harder. I wasn't going to be able to last long if she kept this up.

She slid her hands down my body to the waistband of my boxers, scraping her nails down my sides as she went. The soft contact of her nails would normally have tickled, but rather I found it erotic. Her fingers continued down inside my boxers and slipped them down to my knees. My cock jumped hearing her gasp as she laid eyes on my naked body for the first time. I didn't want to move my body from hers to remove them completely, but I couldn't keep them on and allow them to restrict my movement either.

Needing to strip her completely, I hooked my fingers into her pants and slowly began to pull them down her thighs, then did the same with my boxers. Both of us now free from our underwear, I took it on myself to remove the final obstacle to her nakedness.

Pushing my lips against hers again, I guided her up until she was seated to allow me to pop the clasp on her bra open. The fabric fell away from her body while I guided the straps down her arms. She wrapped her hands into my hair and forced me back in close to her, kissing me passionately, and taking control of the situation.

She pulled me down to the ground so she was lying flat again, with my body hard against hers. Releasing me slightly so she could speak, I took a breath. "Jack, please hurry up. I need you."

I couldn't resist her request. My weight moved away from her and I used my knee to spread her legs apart so I could position myself between them. Supporting my weight with my arms, I grabbed a condom from my discarded jeans. Rolling it on, I watched her face as she looked at me in fascination. Satisfied she was ready for me, I lined the tip of my cock up with her entrance. "Are you ready for me?" I asked her, unable to resist teasing her a little more.

"Yes, Jack," she replied breathily.

I smiled cheekily. "Wrap your legs around me then." My bossy side came out when I was turned on, but women loved it, so I didn't control it.

She obeyed me, the move allowing her to make the first move by pulling my hardness inside her. I remained still as she coated my cock in her wetness. The tightness of her pussy stretched to accommodate me. Enjoying playing with me, she moaned as she pulled back until my cock was almost out of her.

Holding just the tip of my cock in place inside her, she paused. She watched my face with her head tilted to the side curiously. Without saying a word, she used her feet to force my hips against her. Our groans matched each other as my cock buried to the hilt.

"Fuck, Holly. You feel amazing," I gasped. My words had the desired effect as she began to move her body, using her strong legs to control the speed and depth I was able to reach. She was using me for her own pleasure, and I was happy for her to do it. We were going to be stuck here so I'm sure this wouldn't be the last time, especially if she enjoyed herself.

Her walls began to clench around me while I attempted to hold on until she came around me. I wanted her to fall first. I could feel my balls beginning to tighten with my cum. Needing her to come, I dipped my head down to her chest and sucked one of her pert nipples into my mouth.

Making contact with her rounded breast with my tongue, her pussy tightened around me as her spasms began. She was close. Using my tongue and teeth, I teased her stiff nipple, pulling it up gently as our rhythms matched each other. Feeling my body begin to betray me in her tightness, my movements became erratic.

Her eyes closed and her head dropped back as her orgasm overcame her. "Fuck… Jack… yes!" she cried out as her pussy clamped tightly around my cock, drawing my own orgasm from my body. I felt my body tighten as my muscles clenched, and I collapsed down against her, supporting some of my weight off her, allowing her to ride out her orgasm without hurting her.

Lying against her, our bodies covered with a sheen of sweat, I listened to the crackling of the fire and Holly's breathing. Alone with her, I was thankful I'd come up here this morning. Snowed in or not, I was certain this woman was my perfect match.

I wasn't sure how long we had been lying in silence when her small hands pressed against my chest. "Sorry, I'll get off you," I spoke softly, not wanting to disrupt the quiet.

I pulled myself out from her before slumping down onto the rug beside her. Moving beside her, she snuggled into my side, kissing my chest as she did.

CHAPTER SEVEN

HOLLY

On the rug, naked and satisfied, I felt the weight lift from my shoulders. I didn't realise how much I had needed that. I still wasn't sure if there was something more going on or if it was just sexual tension manifesting as something more. Feeling my eyelids getting heavy, I continued thinking through what was happening between us until eventually, my brain stopped.

I stirred, and the smell of food filled my nostrils. I couldn't figure out what it was, though. Waking up, I realised I was in bed again. Had today all been a dream? Climbing out from the bed, I noticed it was dark outside. How long had I slept for?

I pulled my pyjamas on before heading into the living area. Seeing Jack walking around the kitchen wearing only grey sweatpants, I groaned slightly. Did he really want to go for round two already? I wouldn't complain, but I was hungry.

Jack's voice broke through the silence. "Hey, did you sleep well?"

I looked around confused by how he knew I was standing here. "I did, thank you. How long was I asleep for?" I asked, curiously.

"It's now half past six, so about five hours. Are you hungry?" he replied quickly.

"I'm ravenous. What are you making?" I was keen to find out what the wonderful smell filling the room was.

"Come and take a look. It's a Christmas curry my mum started making a few years ago. It sounds weird, but tastes amazing." He beamed as he showed me the pan on the hob which he was mixing.

Sitting at the table, we chatted easily while he cooked. I enjoyed watching the muscles in his upper body move as he moved.

Finally, the Christmas curry was ready and he served up my plate with a berry cider to drink. "This looks amazing, thank you," I said as I tucked into the meal.

The remainder of the evening passed in a blur of food, films, and chatting. Before I knew it, I was tired again. We hadn't discussed sleeping arrangements, but I knew we needed to. "Jack, I'm tired. Do you want to share the master bed with me?" I asked while wringing my hands together nervously.

"If that's okay with you, sure." He nodded, not wanting to assume.

"Of course, I wouldn't have suggested it otherwise," I said, shaking my head slightly at his answer.

The smile on his face widened and his eyes lit up. "Great, let's go to bed then."

I began to lose track of the days passing while spending time with Jack. I had forgotten we were stuck here together until the morning of the third day. We woke up beside each other, naked from the previous night's entertainment.

Groggily, Jack spoke, "Good morning. How are you today?"

"I'm good, I just woke up beside you again," I said, honestly. My feelings towards this man had been growing in our time together while eating, drinking, watching films, and fucking.

He rolled towards me and pressed his lips against mine. I immediately reacted, moving to deepen our kiss when I heard a knock on the door. He pulled back away from me. "Was that the door?" he asked while running his hand through his hair.

"I think so? We should check," I replied, nervously. I didn't want our time together to end.

Nodding, he climbed from the bed and pulled on some jogging bottoms and a t-shirt from beside the bed. He left the room, and I followed him to the door where I would be able to hear.

The door creaked as he opened it. "Hello, Dad."

"Hello, Jack," came a masculine voice from outside the door.

I waited for him to realise we weren't snowed in anymore. "Dad, how did you get up here?"

"I walked. The snow has melted a lot. It's just dusting now. It actually has been since yesterday, but your mum told me to leave you a few more days. I was going to, but then your girlfriend's family showed up to see her."

I watched Jack's jaw drop and the colour drain from his face. Unable to stand and watch any longer, I approached the door, thankful I'd thought to pull my dressing gown on. "Hello, Mr Walker, I'm Holly," I introduced myself to the man standing at the door, who was almost the spitting image of his son.

Reaching his hand out, I took it in an act of politeness. "Nice to meet you. Please call me Nick. I've heard so much about you."

I sniggered; no way was he actually called Nick. I'd thought Jack was joking when he said that. Needing to say something quickly, I diverted back to what he had mentioned about my family. "Did you say my parents were here?" I asked, scowling and doubting it was true.

"Your whole family is here. They said you stopped communicating with them and they got worried, so they came up to check you were okay. I've not told them about Jack being here with you. I did explain about the snowstorm, but everything else is on you." He winked at me, and I could see immediately where Jack got his cheekiness from.

"Thank you, Nick. I suppose I'd better go and change if I'm coming down the mountain." I felt the weightlessness and easy-going nature of the last few days dissipate. My shoulders began to feel heavy again. I had to face reality.

CHAPTER EIGHT

JACK

I was annoyed that our time together had come to an end even though it was inevitable. Her family was here though, so it was time to go back to the real world. She would probably leave with them and I'd never see her again. At least I'd always have the memories of the petite blonde I spent my holiday with.

Trying to hide how I was feeling, I dressed back into my jeans and jacket, ready to go down the mountain. Although I had been trying to hide my emotion, Holly picked up on it. She walked up behind me and wrapped her arms around me. "Just because my family has appeared, that doesn't mean this is the end." Her reassurance made sense, but it wasn't enough to convince me of it.

"I hope not," I mumbled.

"It's not. I like you too much to never contact you again. You go back to university soon anyways, so we'll be closer to each other than ever. Maybe, just maybe, we could continue this whole relationship thing we have going?" She pulled on a loose bit of skin on her lip with her teeth.

"Really? That sounds amazing!" I hooted tearfully.

"Great. Let's go down to civilisation again and introduce you to my family as my boyfriend." She smiled softly and planted a kiss on my cheek.

My heart felt full of warmth, relieved that this wasn't the end for us. I just hoped her parents liked me. Entangling my fingers with hers, we walked down the mountain together. Being snowed in together really had given us the push we needed to act on our feelings.

The End

ABOUT ROSIE EAST

Rosie is Scottish born and bred, still living in Scotland with her husband and dog. Reading and books had always been a part of Rosie's life. As a child she would often say she wanted to be an author (or a dog) when she grew up.

As an adult, writing didn't feature highly due to university commitments. Upon graduating university, ideas bombarded her mind and one day decided to sit down and write something.

Her other hobbies include baking, reading and watching films. Marvel is her favourite thing to watch while writing.

Also by Rosie East:

Wrapped Up In You: A Second Chance Romance Anthology

FOLLOW ROSIE

Facebook - https://www.facebook.com/rosieeastauthor
Facebook Group - https://www.facebook.com/groups/rosiesromancers
Instagram - https://www.instagram.com/rosieeast_author/
Bookbub - https://www.bookbub.com/profile/rosie-east
Goodreads - https://www.goodreads.com/author/show/21412080.Rosie_East
Newsletter & Website - https://rosie-east-author-y4d2f0.mailerpage.com

SAVING LUKE

KACI ROSE

CHAPTER ONE

BROOKE

"Is there such a thing as too many Christmas lights?" Lexi asks, as I string up some lights over the large, two-story, stone fireplace mantle.

"No, there isn't. Not when this is Oakside's first Christmas! Come on, help me and hand over some tinsel," I say.

Even though this is the first Christmas at Oakside, we are filled with injured military men, who have no desire to celebrate it. They want to focus on healing, well, most of them anyway, and then get the hell out of here.

I can't blame them, but if they will beare going to be stuck here over the holiday, then they should at least be able to celebrate it in style, right?

Well, how do you make a group of people celebrate the holidays, when they have no intention of doing so? This is what Lexi and Noah have tasked me with this year.

"Whoa, it looks like a fairy threw up in here." Lexi's husband, Noah, says.

"You," I point at him., "Aare not helping."

"See, I told you. Too many twinkle lights," Lexi says.

"No such thing," I tell her.

I step back and take in the large fireplace in the lobby. This is one of my favorite rooms, with big windows overlooking the courtyard. I imagine the fireplace going on a cold, winter day, and I can't help wishing for snow, because it would be the perfect decoration with the fireplace lit. Though sadly in southern Georgia, we hardly ever get snow.

"I still think the Christmas tree is too small," Noah says, as he comes up and wraps his arms around Lexi.

"That tree is twelve feet tall, and it took eight people to get it in here. It's plenty big, trust me." I reassure him.

"Well, in this room it looks small," he retorts.

"Because this room is massive," I tell him.

"But it's cozy, and i. It's still one of my favorites in the whole building." Lexi says.

Lexi owned this large, southern plantation home and was waiting for the home to show her its purpose.

Lexi is Noah's wife, and they started Oakside together earlier this year. They met, while Lexi was visiting her brother in the hospital, when he was injured on deployment. Noah was in the bed next to him. Long story short, it ended with Lexi never leaving his side.

Noah was badly burned in a fire, so he has a lot of scars on one side of his body and face. It took a lot of time to heal. Once he recovered and was cleared for PT, there was no place for him to transition to out of the hospital.

That's how Oakside was born. When the hospital completes what they can do, then Oakside gets involved. Once the men and women who are fully healed of anything that could cause an infection, then they're referred to us. We provide physical therapy and doctors, as well as having them work with therapists. If needed, we'll bring in specialists like plastic surgeons, or someone to fit prosthetics. Currently, we are putting the finishing touches on the barn and will be adding equine therapy, too. Also, we're starting on an aquatics center with an Olympic sized pool.

There are all sorts of programs at Oakside that helps the soldiers transfer to civilian life, before they leave. That means making sure they have a job, or if they're going back to school, and then they have a place to live, and a means to support themselves.

Since I was Noah's nurse, I got to know them both really well. When they asked me to come to Oakside, it was a no brainier. Though, I might have thought twice, if I had known I'd be in charge of Christmas festivities this year.

Noah leans over and kisses Lexi on the top of the head, and I can't help, but to want that kind of relationship. Lexi pulled Noah through the worst time in his life, and now, there' is no one more devoted than Noah is to Lexi.

"I like your hair like that," I tell Lexi.

She has her light blonde hair done up in a braid across the front of her head and down over the shoulder.

"Thanks., I've been trying some new styles. Well, mMore like Paisley has been trying them, and I just wear them," she smiles.

Paisley is Easton's wife. Easton was a patient here earlier this year and is now part of the security team. He was a prisoner of war, and Paisley was bringing her therapy dog in to help the soldiers. Her dog, Molly, took off right to Easton. Turns out, Easton was her brother's best friend growing up. They both had crushes on each other, and Paisley was determined to help Easton, and that pushed them together.

When everyone around you is falling in love, you can't help but wonder, when it will be your turn.

I move to get some more decorations for the fireplace mantle and see a man in a wheelchair with a woman, neither of whom I've seen here before.

Like Lexi can read my mind, she's answering my question, before I even ask it. "That's Luke. He's the new patient I told you about."

Ahhh, yes. I get briefed on all the patients, since I run the nursing staff here. Luke was in an accident and thrown from a Humvee. He has swelling around his spine that' is preventing him from walking. His doctors think he'll make a full recovery, but it's a waiting game for the inflammation to go down. Because he needs PT, the hospital sent him here.

We encourage family and friends to spend as much time with their soldier, because it really helps with their rehab. Lexi even went as far as to turn some old buildings on the property into cabins for families to use, when visiting from out of the area.

This woman looks like Luke's girlfriend, and I'm glad she's sticking by him through all this. Most don't, and it actually slows their progress down.

It's as if Luke can feel my eyes on him, because he turns my way, and his piercing, green eyes focus on me. He has several days of stubble on his face, and his dark brown hair has grown out of its military cut. And I have to say, he's one of the most handsome men I've ever seen.

Crap, he's with his girlfriend, and here I am, crushing on him. I offer him a smile and nod my head, before turning back to my task of decorating.

Thank goodness I'm not his nurse.

LUKE

As I look around the lobby of Oakside, I have to admit it looks much better than the hospital. Though, I didn't want to leave the hospital, my sister insisted on me transferring to Oakside, because she's heard really great things about their success with recoveries. She's determined to get me better, even if it's against my will.

Since it's just the two of us, I would do anything for her. Our parents died months after I joined the military, and she was still a few months away from graduating high school. Thankfully, her best friend's parents took her in, and let her stay with them, and finish school. She already had a full- ride to Tennessee University lined up. So, I sent her money to give them for rent, or buy what she needed each month. I have always made sure she was taken care of, and I will find a way to do so now.

Right now, I hate that it's just a waiting game for the swelling to go down, but that's where I' am at. At least, it gives me time to figure out my next steps, because moving home and having her wait on me hand and foot, isn't an option.

"Okay, I got you all checked in. Your nurse is on her way down, and she'll take us to your room, and we will get you all set up. You get your own room, so you will have some privacy. I was reading online the rooms are more like staying at a bed-and-breakfast than at a hospital, so I really think you'll like it better here."

That isn't what captures my attention, though. The woman decorating the lobby area, which looks more like a large living room, holds my attention. She's beautiful with her dark brown hair that falls down in waves.

Her smile is huge, and you can tell she's enjoying decorating the room for Christmas. Like she can feel my eyes on her, she turns to me, and our eyes lock. I always thought, when people say the world stopped spinning, they were full of crap, but I need to make some phone calls and apologize, because holy hell, it's true.

Everything stops, and I don't hear or see anything, but this beautiful woman. When she smiles at me, I'm a goner. I need to find out who she is, but preferably, without my sister in tow. The beautiful woman gives me a nod, and then turns back to her decorating.

Just then, a nurse walks in wearing scrubs, and she starts talking to my sister, but I don't hear anything, until the nurse places her hand on my arm.

"Okay, let's get you to your room and settled in. Today, is a free day for you, but your appointments start tomorrow." She starts wheeling me down the hall and stops at the elevator. *Crap.*

"Is my room on the second floor?" I ask.

"Sure,Yes, and in my opinion, is it has the best view right out the front and down that long tree lined driveway. It's my favorite part of the property." The nurse keeps talking, but I ignore her and close my eyes.

Gabbie grabs my hand. She had to deal with me in the elevator leaving the hospital earlier and knows this is a problem for me. I squeeze her hand, and she just runs her thumb over the back of my hand.

Ever since the accident, I can't be in small, confined spaces that move, like, elevators or, the transport plane back stateside. Cars aren't so bad, as long as all the windows are down. Gabbie knows this, even if she doesn't know exactly why. I also don't plan on telling her.

Even thinking of the appointments Gabbie set up for me tomorrow, doesn't help, because as soon as I feel the elevator start moving, my heart races, and I gasp for air.

"Stay with me, Luke., I'm right here. You are at Oakside, and you're safe. You' are with me, and. I'm not going anywhere." Gabbie says, and I focus on her voice.

Before I know it, the doors are dinging, and we are off the elevators, but my heart is still racing, and I feel like I just ran two miles with my rucksack on.

When we enter my room, I have to admit it's really nice. It's almost like a small apartment. On one side is a bed against a reclaimed wood wall. The queen-sized bed is set with extra pillows and blankets, and then a nightstand on each side. In front of the bed, is a seating area with a couch, coffee table, and two chairs. They're all done up in brown leather with throw pillows, with a TV on the wall across the couch, and windows behind the couch.

Opposite the bed, is an exposed brick wall and a desk with drawers, perfect for working on or setting up a laptop.

I have my own bathroom. It's done in black -and -white tiles with a large walk-in shower, and a mock claw-foot bathtub that has a door for those who need easier access. The mirror looks like it was made from an old wood dresser and done in dark wood to match the rest of the room.

Thise place is twice as big as my hospital room, and I shared that with another guy.

"This is all mine?" I ask, almost in shock.

"Yep, you will be here in recovery, so it might as well feel like home. Lexi refused to let you guys feel like you were stuck in the hospital again. That was Noah's big complaint, and I c. Can't say I blame him. Now, there's a packet on your desk with a map of the place. Also, there's a calendar with all of your appointments, a schedule of events, a list of TV channels, menus, and more. You are free to move about the grounds, but please just write on the whiteboard by your door where you'll be. You can't leave the grounds without a doctor's approval and checking out at the front desk. I will be in with your medications. Morning rounds are at eight a.m., and nighttime rounds are at eight p.m."

She goes on to show me the buzzers in the room, by the bed, and in the bathroom, if I need her, and then explains mealtimes, and a few other things.

Gabbie stays with me a while, getting me all set up and organized, unpacking my clothes, and having dinner with me in my room.

We talk, and before she leaves, she turns to me.

"You focus on getting better. Nothing else matters, okay?"

I agree, as s. She doesn't need to know that all I can focus on is finding the girl from the lobby.

CHAPTER TWO

BROOKE

A few hours after decorating the lobby for Christmas, I'm heading into work, when Lexi stops me.

"Okay, it's been a stressful morning already, and I know you'll get briefed, but I wanted to let you know from me we had to move Luke to one of your rooms," Lexi tells me.

Instantly, I'm alarmed.

"Why? What's wrong?"

"Well, we didn't know he had an issue with confined spaces, and he can't use the stairs and refused to use the elevator, so he wasn't leaving his room. So, we did some shifting, and moved him downstairs, and assigned him to you."

"Why me?" I ask.

I've been doing so well at avoiding him. The feelings I felt by just looking at him still run through me, when I think of him. I don't want to be tempted, especially since he has a girlfriend.

"Other than you are the head nurse, and the best one we got?" She gives me a look, like I've completely lost my marbles.

Hell, who knows? Maybe, I have. I've never had feelings for a patient before, and it's a line I'm not willing to cross.

"Yes, other than that," I say with a straight face.

"Honestly, he reminds me of Noah. He's lost in his head, and I think you can help him better than anyone here," she admits.

Well, I sure as hell can't say no to that. So, I just nod.

"Okay, I'm going to go get my briefing, and then, I'll talk to his old nurse and see what I need to know."

I head to the conference room where I get briefed from the nurses on anything major going on, and also anything I need to know for my patients. When Lexi asked me to come to Oakside and run the nursing staff, I agreed, and only if I got to still see patients, too. That's my favorite part of my job, helping someone, e. Even more so, when I'm helping a soldier.

After hearing the report and discussing the needs of the other guys I' am taking care of, Luke's old nurse comes in and sits down.

"It took me a bit to figure out why he was refusing to go to his appointments. I wish the hospital had told us, so we could have put him on the ground floor from the beginning," Maria says.

I agree with her there.

"They may not have known. In the hospital, the doctors and all staff come to you, so it might have only been an issue, when he was discharged." I try to comfort her.

"No, he was agitated in the elevator on the way to his room the first day, but I was talking on and on about the place and didn't think much of it. Many of the guys are anxious, when they first get here. New surroundings and all."

"His doctor was going up to see him, so he didn't really miss any appointments. The physical therapist gave us a list of exercises to work with him, but he's still wheelchair bound. They expect him to be walking some in a few weeks or so as the swelling goes down more."

She goes over all the technical stuff from the hospital, his background, and family information. I see that he only has his sister listed as next of kin.

"Have we asked about his parents?" I ask her, wanting to make sure his forms are filled out properly.

"Yes, they died a few years ago, so it's just him and his sister. She's the one who insisted he come and has been to visit him a few times that I have seen."

"Good. Guess it's time for me to go introduce myself." I say, as I stand up.

I look over his files one more time on my way to his room, and stop outside of the door, and take a deep breath. In school, we learn how to hide our emotions. Emotions aren't good in high-intensity situations, and I try to use that skill now.

Even though the door is open, I knock on the door frame, as I peek my head in. The room he's in is set up and decorated the exact same way as his room upstairs, with but the only difference being is the Christmas tree I added in the corner on a small table.

I find Luke sitting up on his bed, reading a book. He' is dressed in sweats and a tT-shirt, which seems to be the uniform the guys choose to wear around here, because it's easy. He sets his book down and looks at me.

"Hello, Luke. I'm Brooke. I'll be your new nurse and wanted to come in and introduce myself. Have you done your exercises from your physical therapist yet today?" I ask.

He shakes his head no.

"Okay, I' am going to take your vitals, and then we will work through those exercises. I see here you like to eat in your room. Now that you are on the ground level, do you still want to eat in here?" I ask.

He nods.

"Okay." I make a note on my tablet I carry, so the kitchen staff will bring his food to his room.

During the entire time I check his vitals and work with him on the exercises, he doesn't speak a single word.

Over the next week, each day is the same. I come in and do all the talking, and he says nothing, but complies with his appointments, and exercises.

Needing to find a way to get through to him, I sit down with Lexi and tell her how he's been.

"I told you he needs someone to get through to him," Lexi says.,

“Aand I really think that could be you. Talk to him, and f. Find a way to get him to open up. You know as well as I do, the longer he stays shut down, the longer his recovery will be."

"I know. I will think about it and try to get him to open up. Mind if I tell him Noah's story? I feel like that's a story he might relate, too."

"As you know, my husband always likes to share his story. He’s so dedicated to helping these guys, that he’ll tell it over and over again, if it helps them." Lexi smiles with pride.

I head home to make my plan of action that mixes in some holiday cheer. Poor Luke has no idea what's coming at him tomorrow.

LUKE

It's been a few days, since I switched rooms, and a few days, since Brooke has become my nurse. Of course, the girl I had my eye on was to become my nurse. Why wouldn't she be? It adds a whole new level of confusion to everything.

We have a routine down. She comes in each morning and checks my vitals, gives me my medication, and helps me do my physical therapy exercises. Then, she takes me down to the dining room for breakfast.

She makes sure I attend all of my appointments. Which is normally physical therapy in the morning, followed by a doctor's appointment, if I have one. Then in the afternoon, I have my required therapy session, and then a meeting with a counselor, who is meant to help me figure out my next steps in life.

Brooke makes sure I eat lunch and dinner, before coming in again to check on me before bed and do more exercises.

I have yet to speak a single word to her, but I have been watching her. She smiles, and talks, and is really good at her job. Everyone here seems to like her. She’s friends with Lexi, who is one of the owners of the place.

So today, when she walks in with a determined look on her face, I know something is different. She's in scrubs, though her top is Christmassy with Santa, reindeer, and stockings on it, and her pants are a dark green to match. Her thick chestnut hair is pulled up in a messy bun, and her lips are light pink, which I have come to learn is because she likes to use cherry Chapstick. I don't want to think about how many times I've thought of kissing those lips just to taste them.

"So, tomorrow is the Secret Santa drawing for patients here. Lord, who thought putting on something so simple was so much work!" She goes to tell me about the event set up, as she takes my vitals and gives me my medication.

"Still not talking to me, huh?" She makes herself comfortable, sitting down on the edge of the bed. She's fFairly close to me though, as I'm sitting up against the headboard. It's my favorite spot in the whole room, because my back is to the wall, and I can see anyone who comes in, and normally, it's before they can see me.

I still don't answer her. What do I say? No, I don't trust myself to talk to you? Then, I would have to explain why, which will just make this weird, since I'm sure she has a boyfriend or husband waiting on her and wants nothing to do with a cripple like me.

"You remind me of Noah, you know," she says.

That's when I cave. "What?" I ask.

Her face breaks out in a huge smile, and my heart skips a beat.

"Ahhh, there he is," she says. "I was Noah's nurse, before Oakside. It's how we met. He was one of my patients in the hospital, and Lexi never left his side. Because he was there the longest of almost any patient I had, the three of us bonded pretty well. When they started Oakside, I came over with them."

She smiles with a faraway look, lost in a memory, before continuing. "Noah was stubborn at first. Lexi had to drag him kicking and screaming through the healing process, b. But he was a fighter like you. He taught me the most important thing about recovery."

She pauses, so I sigh. "What's that?" I ask her.

"You need something to fight for. Guys with the most basic injuries take forever to heal, if they have no motivation. I've seen men like Noah heal much faster than anyone ever thought possible, because they have the right motivation. So, what's driving you?" Sshe asks.

"My sister," I say without thinking.

"Well, no offense, but she isn't enough." Brooke says without missing a beat.

"What? She's all I have. I have to get better for her."

"But she isn't motivating you to get better. You're still stuck in this holding pattern. Eventually, you need to find your ultimate impetus to push yourself. Now, let's do these exercises and get you down for breakfast. Also, you are going to do this Secret Santa no matter what. I put in too much work for you to tell me no," she says adamantly.

"Yes, mMa'am," I smirk. Everyone has been so careful thinking I might break, and here she is giving me sass. I love it.

She stands up and runs a finger up the bottom of my foot.

"You feel that?" Sshe asks.

"Barely," I say.

"Better than not at all." She says, doing the same thing to the other foot, which feels the same.

Then, she starts helping me with basic leg movements, and like every day, her hands on me feel like heaven, and I have to think of not so pleasant things, so I don't pop wood just from her hands on me. It's a daily struggle, but I wouldn't have anyone else help me.

My sister tried once, and it wasn't the same. I told Brooke that night I hadn't done them just so she'd do them with me again.

As she wheels me to the dining room, I wish time would slow down and give me a little more time with her.

"After breakfast, it will be time for the Secret Santa. So, don't go anywhere, as I'll be back for you. You also have a PT appointment right after," she says.

Already waiting for her to come back to me? I realize, who am I kidding. I'm already in too deep.

CHAPTER THREE

BROOKE

"Okay, you ready for Secret Santa?" I ask Luke, as I walk up to take him to the event room.

"You don't have to do this. I' am just happy to be spending Christmas back stateside this year. I don't need anything over the top," he says.

"This isn't over the top. It's a simple gift exchange, and I'm not letting you out of it. Everyone needs a little holiday cheer, and who knows, the guy you get might need your Christmas cheer more than you need his."

"If you say so." He crosses his arms, as I push him down the hallway in his wheelchair.

"Okay, look at it this way. This is your chance to help another guy out. Everyone is here for some reason, and you know that. Some guys just have it worse than you. At least, you will be able to walk, when you leave. Not everyone can say that." I try to appeal to his practical side.

It works, because he takes a deep breath and uncrosses his arms. "Okay."

I pat his shoulder, "Thank you."

Though, it's hard to ignore the heat racing up my arm from that simple touch. It's been happening every day, when we do his exercises, and it's more difficult to ignore than you might think.

Lexi is running the Secret Santa, so when we get to the event room, I park Luke at a table, and then pull up a chair to sit with him. But I'm also ready to help Lexi, if she needs it.

After going over the rules and all the fun stuff, Noah and Lexi each walk around with a basket for the guys to pull names from. When it's Luke's turn, he hesitates and looks at me, so. I give him a nod of encouragement, and he picks his name.

"Who did you get?" I ask.

"Alex," he says.

"Oh, he's a nice kid, and I stress, kid. He was hurt on his first deployment out of boot camp. His family doesn't live nearby, but will be here for Christmas. So, do you need me to take you Christmas shopping?" I ask him.

I know I shouldn't. Not because I can't take him shopping, because I can. He's one of the few permitted to leave the grounds with supervision. I shouldn't take him, because it might feel too much like a date, or at least to me. With all the confusing feelings, I should put some space between us.

But when his eyes go big and full of hope and excitement, I know I can't back out.

"I can go out in town?" He asks, like a kid asking if he can open his Christmas gifts early.

"Yes, with supervision, and as your nurse, I'm on the approved list," I tell him. "On my next day off, I'll come to get you, and you can help me do some of my shopping, too."

"What about your other patients?" His excitement seems to dampen a bit.

"Well, they will be ordering online, because they either don't want to go, or aren't approved to leave the grounds," I tell him.

He nods, and the excitement is back.

"Okay, but be warned., Iit will be all things Christmas. We will even get our picture taken with Santa," I tell him.

"Fine," he grumbles.

"And we'll get Christmas cookies and hot chocolate at the food court."

"I like cookies," he shrugs.

"I'll play Christmas music there and back."

"I doubt you can be more annoying with them than my sister," he says.

I smile, "Challenge accepted. Now, let's get you to your physical therapy appointment."

The rest of the day goes by in a blur, as I think about all the Christmas things I want to do on our day out.

The nurse in me is also making checklists on what we'll need and making sure he doesn't overdo it.

Before I leave, I go and find Lexi in her office. I knock on the door, before stepping in.

"Hey, I just wanted to give you a heads up. I'm off the day after tomorrow, and I'm going to take Luke into town to go shopping for his Secret Santa. Since I planned to do my Christmas shopping then too, it works out." I tell her.

She sits back in her chair and looks at me.

"I think it will do him some good to get out of here for a bit. But remember, he seems to have panic attacks with elevators," she says.

"Yes, his file says the car will be fine with the windows down, and I was thinking of going to that outlet mall that has the food court and the carnival in the summer," I tell her.

"I think that's perfect. Make sure to fill out the forms and sign him out. You know the drill. Call me if you need me, but I trust you know what you're doing."

Lexi has a lot of trust in me, I think as I head home. I hope I don't do something stupid to break that trust.

LUKE

Today, is the day Brooke is taking me shopping. I shouldn't be so excited about this, but I am. Not just because I get to get out of this place, but because I get to get out of this place with Brooke. I didn't even tell my sister, because I know she'd want to take me herself, or she would want to come along. But I need to do some Christmas shopping for her, too.

My other nurse that works, when Brooke doesn't, is here today, and she helped me get ready. I hated every minute of her touching me. Maybe, because it wasn't Brooke, or maybe, because it was just another woman, but I can't be sure. It gave me the motivation I need to figure out how to get myself ready on the days Brooke isn't here for me.

I had breakfast and am sitting in my wheelchair in the lobby, waiting for her. Looking around, I take in all the Christmas decorations she put up. The tree is one of the largest I've ever seen and decorated in blues and silvers. There are decorations from all the military branches, and lots of southern themed decorations, too.

I guess Oakside has a southern themed Christmas. I'm not sure what it means, but that's what I've heard. On the wall heading upstairs, is the a photo of a man in uniform and under it is a shadow box with a folded flag and a few medals, one being a purple heart. I instantly know this man was killed in action.

When I wheel over to get a closer look, I see his name, Tyler Bates.

"That was my husband, before I met Noah," Lexi says, as s. She offers me a sad smile. "He died on deployment, but he always made sure I was taken care of. Enough so, that I was able to buy this house. For a few years, before I met Noah, it was just me, living alone here. When we started Oakside, Noah insisted his memory be out in the open. He's the true reason we're all here today."

All gave some, and some gave all.

You hear that quote in the military, but it never has meant more than it does right now.

"Here you are!" Brooke walks up. I turn to find her in jeans and a sweater just like the first day. I've gotten used to her in scrubs, but I like her like this, too.

I look back at Lexi, who smiles at me. "Go enjoy your day of freedom."

Smiling, I head over to Brooke, who is bubbling with energy.

"Okay, I have a whole day planned, but if it becomes too much, you are to tell me. Do you understand and swear on whatever the holiest thing to you is?" Sshe asks.

"I promise. Though, I'm not sure how it will be too much, if I'm sitting down all day. At most, my arms will get tired, and then you'll just push me,"," I shrug.

"Point taken. Okay, let's go."

I like that she doesn't try to push her way into helping me into the car. She lets me figure it out myself. It makes it easier that her car is a sensible four- door sedan, unlike the jeep my sister drives.

When I stop her from closing my door, she doesn't question it. I take a few deep breaths to steady myself. She gets in, starts the car, and rolls down all the windows. I must give her a confused look, because she shrugs.

"It was in your file." Is all she says.

I close the door and buckle up. She doesn't ask why, but I feel like the question is hanging there.

"I was tossed from a Humvee. I aAlmost didn't get out, so now confined spaces bring me back to that day. I'm working on it," I say.

"Listen, I get it. We all have stuff in our past that makes us who we are, good or bad. This is a safe space with me always. If you don't want to talk about something, we don't talk about it. But I'm always here, if you need someone to, even if it's just hear you ranting about something that doesn't make sense to no oneanyone but you, okay?" Sshe says.

Not sure what to say, so I change the topic.

"I would like to shop for my sister, while we're out, if that's okay," I tell her.

"Of course, and your girlfriend too, right?" Sshe asks.

"What?" I ask, completely thrown off. *She thinks I have a girlfriend.*

"The girl I saw you with, when you checked in., I haven't seen her since, though." She says hesitantly.

I can't help but burst out laughing.

"That's my sister, Gabbie, and a world class pain in my ass. She's in school and studying for finals. Once she's on winter break, she'll be around more."

"Oh, sorry., I just assumed," she says.

"It's okay. I don't have a girlfriend or a wife for the record. Do you?" I ask bluntly.

"I don't have a wife," she smiles.

"Boyfriend?"

"Don't have one of those, either. I pPut all of my energy into Oakside, once it opened, and that hasn't left much time for dating, which makes my brother happy," she smiles.

"Tell me about you," I say.

"Ask me anything, but be prepared to answer the same about yourself."

"Well, you know my parents are gone, and the only family I have is my younger sister, Gabbie. So, what about you?"

"My parents are gone, too. I have my grandma, and my brother, who is married and has two kids."

"They live here?" I ask.

"Yep, we see each other at least once a week for dinner, if not more. You and your sister close?"

"Yeah, my parents died right after I joined the military, and Gabbie was in her senior year of high school. Her best friend's parents let her stay to finish out school, since she had a full- ride scholarship. I sent them money to help out, and Gabbie money, so she didn't have to work and could focus on school. She's in her last year now and will be graduating early, because she took summer classes."

I smile at the thought of how hard Gabbie has worked, but the smile fades, when we pull into a shopping center.

"What is this? It looks like the North Pole exploded here." I say.

"They go all out for Christmas, and it's why I love shopping here this time of year. Come on."

Just like with getting into the car, she stands by in case I need help, but lets me do all the work, getting out of the car and back into my wheelchair.

"Don't think just because you can't walk that you won't be carrying my bags," she says.

I smile and know then this girl is something special, e. Even if she' is trying to kill me with all things Christmas.

CHAPTER FOUR

LUKE

"Okay, any idea on what you want to get your sister?" Brooke asks me.

"Yes, a Coach bag. She has had her eye on one for years, but even though I know she has money saved, won't buy one for herself."

There' is a Coach outlet store here, and we make it ourt first stop. The salesgirl is very helpful, when I describe the one my sister liked. While they don't have it, they have one that's close, and even gift wrap it for me.

"We can store that in Lexi's office, so your sister doesn't snoop and find it," she tells me.

"Good idea."

"Okay, this store has stuff from locals and lots of *'one of the a kinds'* type of stuff. My sister-in-law loves this place, and so does my grandma, so I'm going to do some shopping here. Look around, and y. You might find something for your Secret Santa."

We go our separate ways, and at one point, I notice Brooke tries on a dream catcher necklace, but puts it back. I've noticed she seems to like dream catchers, and she even had on a dream catcher scrub top with a set of dream catcher earrings. So, when she's on the other side of the store, I pick up the necklace, and take it to the counter, and tell the clerk I'm buying it for her, and then ask her to box it up, while I keep shopping. She winks at me and does as I ask.

Still unsure of what to get my Secret Santa, I look at some quotes on wood plaques, and when I see one that makes me laugh, I decide to get it for him.

'Punch today in the face.'

It's perfect for what we all face each day at Oakside. If nothing else, maybe it will make him laugh.

I make my purchases, and then wait by the door for her to finish up.

"We done shopping?" I ask, taking her bag from her.

"Nope, I've got gifts for my grandma and sister-in-law. Now for the hard ones, the kids, and my brother. Plus, we still have to get our picture taken with Santa," she smiles.

I totally thought she was joking about that.

"Well, if we are going to be out much longer, can I interest you in having lunch with me?"

I know this isn't a date, but I really wish it was, and asking her like this, feels a bit like it is, b. But I know it's not.

"Well, I'm going to have to insist on it." She smiles, and we make another stop where she's able to cross her brother off her list before lunch.

"Man, I know I'm a girl, but shopping really tiresries me out. I don't know how some people do this all the time!" Brooke remarks,ed as we went head towards the food court.

The moment we step inside, my skin starts to crawl. The space is too big, too many unknowns, and the noise seems to amplify.

Almost like she can pick up on how uncomfortable it is, she grabs my wheelchair, and we go right back outside.

"What's wrong?" I ask her.

"It's too noisy. If you don't mind, there's a sit down place over there," she says, pointing over her shoulder.

I smile, "Sounds perfect."

Over lunch, we talk about all the things normal people talk about. No doctor appointments, or physical therapy talk. She tells me about her family, and I talk about my sister. We share stories of growing up and bad first dates, not that I have many to share.

For the first time since the accident, I actually feel normal, and I didn't realize how much I really needed that.

"So," Brook says., "I think I'm going to shop for my niece and nephew online. My sister-in-law did some online wish list, and I'm just going to buy off there for them and include some candy. Then, that's all I'll need for the kids." She says, as we leave the food court.

"So, anyone else to shop for?" I ask her.

"Nope, not today. Ready to head back after our Santa photo?" Sshe asks.

"Yes, I think so. You sure Lexi won't mind holding the gift in her room?" I ask again.

"I know she won't mind, but I can take it home with me, if you want. I have two spare rooms, so putting it in a closet is no big deal."

Though, I know Lexi's office would be fine, something about having it at Brooke's place feels right. Plus, then I know I have an excuse to talk to her, and maybe, see her like this again.

"You don't mind?" I ask.

"Nope, let's put it in the trunk with my stuff, and I will take it home with me."

The line for Santa photos isn't very long, so we pose for a photo, and even get a candy cane, before heading back to the car.

Something shifted today between us. I know it did. This was such a normal activity. Something friends could do, and it was so easy and fun, but it was us, and it was perfect.

So, when she gets in the car, I don't even think twice., I just lean in and kiss her. She hesitates only a moment, before she's kissing me back. Her hands in my hair pull me closer, and my lips tingle, as they touch hers. I don't remember a kiss ever feeling like this. It's overwhelming, yet I can't stop. I don't want to stop.

Thankfully, it's her who has the strength to pull away, because I don't think I would have been able, too. When I search her face, all I see is the huge smile on her face.

The oneOne I'm sure that matches mine.

This feels right. More right than anything in my life has felt before.

BROOKE

I just dropped Luke off at Oakside, and am I'm now driving home and can't keep the smile off my face. It's been a long time, since I've felt like this for a guy, t. The butterflies and giddy feeling. It's been even longer, since a kiss had made my heart race and turned me on, like no one's business.

I pull up and find Lexi waiting for me.

"I just got done shopping for Noah, but he's a snoop. Can I wrap these and leave them here?" Sshe asks.

"Of course. I got some gifts to wrap of my own," I say.

"Then, I'd like your help ordering some stuff for the guys. I want to make sure everyone has something to open other than their Secret Santa gifts." Lexi says, as we unload our bags.

"Just set up here in the middle of the living room. I can put on a Hallmark movie, and we can have a mini wrapping party," I say.

"Sounds good. Oh, who's getting a Coach bag?" She asks, eyeing the bag I'm taking to the guest bedroom.

"Luke's sister. Apparently, she likes to snoop, too. I suggested he leave it in your office, but he seemed and bit hesitant, so I offered to keep it here in my guest closet." I tell her.

"Nice. Not only is he close to his sister, but he also spoils her. Another check mark for him," she says.

I put the bag away and grab my wrapping supplies.

"How many points does he have? And why does he have points at all?" I ask.

"Oh, Brooke., I see how he looks at you, and how you look at him, when no one is looking."

I feel my cheeks heat, so I turn and head into the kitchen to get us something to drink.

Changing the topic, I ask, "So, what did you get Noah?"

Lexi gives me a look, like she knows exactly what I'm doing, but thankfully, she gives me a break.

"That man is so hard to shop for! I had him make a wish list, which included mostly tools by the way. Then, I took that list into the store and asked a sales guy for help and pointed out what I wanted to get him and here I am. I also went shopping for my brother, his wife, my nephew, and my parents. We still have Noah's family to shop for, but he's going to have to help me there," she says.

"You sound like you were as busy as I was. I bought for my brother, his wife, and my grandma. Though, I gave up and will be ordering for my niece and nephew online. Kids are too hard to shop for these days. They want this toy or game, but it has to be a certain color, or character, and or heaven forbid you get it wrong. Then, you get the stink eye on Christmas." I tell her.

"Well, what did you expect, when you bought her the wrong jeans?" She laughs, remembering last Christmas, when I tried to get my niece the jeans she wanted and got the name mixed up.

The ones I got were pretty horrible, once she tried them on. I felt so bad and tried to make it up to her, but the damage was done. I am not the aunt who gives bad gifts. A title I doubt I will ever live down.

We spend the next hour wrapping gifts, before hopping online and going over some possible ideas for Christmas gifts for the patients that fit in our budget.

"Why don't you talk to Mandy to see if she can do some quick fundraiser, asking for gift donations or money for gifts? Every little bit will help. I think we should get the guys something practical they can use." I tell her.

"Good idea. In a perfect world, we could gift them all laptops to help with school, or the job search, when they are discharged, but laptops for twenty-four patients right now just isn't in the budget."

We bookmark a few ideas and decide to ask the other staff for some suggestions, too.

When Lexi leaves, I head over to my grandma's for dinner.

"Well, it's about time you get here. I was beginning to think I'd have to send the cops to do a well visit to check on you!" Grandma says, as soon as I walk through the door.

That's my grandma, always over dramatic. That's how you know she cares about you, though.

"Sorry I'm late. I was doing some Christmas shopping today. Then, Lexi came over, and we wrapped gifts and did some shopping for the guys at Oakside." I tell her.

"Well, help me finish setting the table, and then you can tell me all about it." She says, as I follow her back into the kitchen.

She made her famous lasagna. Not because she knows I like it, but because it will give her leftovers for a week, and she'll just have to warm it up. She made garlic bread and a salad, too.

We sit down and Grandma makes me say grace, before we dig in. Then, she turns to me, "Tell me everything that' is going on at Oakside."

Grandma is one of the biggest reasons I took the job, when Lexi and Nash offered it. I was working at the hospital, and the job was comfortable. Because I had been there a few years, I had a good shift, great benefits, and a stable routine.

When Ggrandma heard of the job offer, she was my biggest advocate to take the leap and do it. She has always had a soft spot for our men in uniform, and she helps them out every chance she can. If it all went south, she promised I could move in with her. Though, I think both of us knew it wouldn't, as the community at large has been very supportive for a small- town in southern Georgia.

Then, I tell her about the Christmas decorations and festivities, my Christmas shopping, and taking Luke with me. I leave out the kiss, but Grandma still eyes me, like she knows I'm not telling her the whole truth. Let her wonder.

"So, with the holiday's coming up, you got yourself a boy to take to all these events?" Grandma asks, as I take my second helping of lasagna.

"Yes, with all this extra time I have." I roll my eyes.

"Well, the winter carnival will be soon. Take someone, and I expect to see photos," she says.

"Why don't you go with me?" I ask her.

"Girl, dispute despite my astonishing good looks, I am no spring chicken. You need a good strong boy to hold on tight to during those rides that whip and flip you," she says.

I almost shoot sweet tea out of my nose at that.

"Grandma, when you talk about rides that whip you, I don't think you are giving me the mental image you are thinking of," I laugh.

This earns me a glare, "You know exactly what I mean, young lady!"

"I promise I will find someone to take to the winter carnival," I tell her, because I know she won't let it go.

"I want photos, and it better be a man," she nods.

Great, let me just whip one out of nowhere.

CHAPTER FIVE

LUKE

Today, I'm having lunch with my sister, and I'm really looking forward to it. She's been busy this week with finals, so this is the first I've seen her in a week.

I' am waiting out in the lobby, when Brooke walks by on the phone. She smiles and waves at me, as she goes back to where I know a few offices are. I'm watching her, so I don't notice, when Gabbie walks in, but she beelines right for me.

"Luke! Oh, I' am glad to have a few hours of no books and being able to eat real food. Come on." She goes behind me and pushes my wheelchair, instead of letting me do it myself, which I'm perfectly capable of doing.

That's a big difference between her and Brooke. Actually, Brooke has stopped helping me and expects me to do more and more, and she likes to see where my limits are. Gabbie would baby me forever, if she could.

She picks a table towards the back of the large dining room, but next to a window that overlooks the garden.

"I will go get our food. Be right back." She says, setting her stuff down.

The food is served in a buffet style line, and it's good food, even if it's on the healthier side. It beats the hospital food by a mile.

"Meatloaf today! One of your favorites," Gabbie comes back and sets the tray in front of me.

"So, tell me about school," I say, as we start eating.

She tells me about her finals and her study group. One of the boys in her study group asked her out, and she agreed, if he was willing to wait, until after Christmas, which he was. I make a mental note to do some digging into this guy. It won't be hard as my sister is very active with her social media.

"So, what have you been doing this week?" Sshe asks.

"Well, my nurse, Brooke, made me join the Secret Santa thing going on here. Then, the other day, she took mey shopping out in town," I tell her.

My sister narrows her eyes at me and bites her lip. I wish I could tell what she was thinking.

"I was able to get your gift, and it's not in my room, so don't waste your time snooping." I try to joke.

"Why did she take you shopping?" Gabbie asks.

"What do you mean? I had to get gifts for the guy I picked and you," I tell her.

"Is she taking all her patients into town shopping?" Sshe asks.

"Not that I know of." I set my fork down.

"So, just you. What else did you do?"

"We had lunch, and then she brought me back here," I tell her.

"It sounds like a date." Gabbie says, not missing a beat.

Of course, this is the moment Brooke walks in to the dining room and catches my attention. My eyes follow her, and like she can feel them on her, she searches me out and offers a smile and a small wave.

My sister misses none of it and pinches my arm to get my attention.

"You are here to get better, not to get laid!" She hisses at me.

What the hell? She has never talked to me like this. Not to mention, I am the older one here.

"That's not what it is, and besides, my sex life is none of your business," I cringe at mentioning my sex life, or lack thereof, to my younger sister.

"It is my business. You are here to get better, so you can come home to me. No distractions." Gabbie saysid a bit louder.

"Will you knock it off? I won't have my younger sister telling me what to do, or what is right for me. I don't even know where I'm going after this, so don't start planning out my life for me." When the hurt washes over Gabbie's face, I instantly regret my harsh words.

Before I get the chance to say anything, she stands up and walks out, leaving me at the table alone with people around us, staring at me. I groan and bury my face in my hands. Someone sits down across from me, and hoping Gabbie is back, I look up, but it's not Gabbie, it's Easton.

I've often seen him around the property, and he's head of security here at Oakside. He appears to be studying me, but says nothing. When I see him around, he seems to be a man of few words, and it's one of the things I like about him.

"What's wrong?" Hhe asks.

Needing someone to talk to, I spill everything. From going shopping with Brooke and to the kiss to the fight with my sister. How I want more with Brooke, and I don't want my sister babying me.

Easton listens to it all and lets me get it all out.

"When we are at war, we often forget it's just as hard on those back home having us there, as it is for us to be there," he says. "You know I was a patient here, too?"

His words make me think, and then I shake my head. "No, I didn't know."

"I met Noah, when we were in the hospital. They had healed all my physical wounds, but mentally, I wasn't okay. The hospital wouldn't release me, so when Noah and Lexi started Oakside, I was the first person they brought in. See, I was a POW, prisoner of war, and was kept in a dark room with no windows. The only people who were there caused me pain and tortured me."

His Adam's apple bobs, and he takes a deep breath. That's when I notice a dog by his side. While he's speaking, she stands and rests her head on his chest. He pets her and continues talking.

"For months, all I did was stare out of the window of my room. I didn't care what the view was, just that there was one. I couldn't stand to be touched. Then, one day in walks Paisley," he says, grinning.

"More like Molly dragged me in." A woman walks up beside him and smiles. She also has a dog at her side. Easton's face lights up, as he pulls her down onto his lap.

"Hi, I'm Paisley." The woman says, holding out her hand. She's has dark brown, almost black hair, a nice tan, and high cheekbones. While she's pretty, in my eyes, she doesn't hold a candle to Brooke.

"Luke," I say and shake her hand.

Easton wraps his arms around her waist and continues his story.

"She gave me a reason to heal, to move on, and to be better. Sometimes, we need that push, a reason to be better than we are. Family and friends, they will accept us no matter what version of ourselves we are. But finding the love of your life? You have to prove yourself," Easton says.

"I tell you it's not going to be easy on whoever the lucky lady is either, so just be patient," Paisley adds.

"Maybe, I should go talk to my sister," I sigh.

"Nah, let her cool down. If she is anything like Paisley, when her and her brother fight, she needs some time to calm down," Easton says.

"Great," I grunt. I can only imagine what plans my sister is trying to put into place.

BROOKE

Luke was in a weird mood yesterday after lunch. I figure it was something to do with his sister, so I let him be. He's still in a strange mood, when I go in to check on him this morning.

"You going to tell me what's bothering you?" I ask, as we work on his exercises.

"My sister is just being crabby. She has this whole life planned out for us, but it's not exactly one that I want. We fought about it yesterday is all," he says.

"Family always has your best intentions at heart, but sometimes, you need to put your foot down on what is right for you. She'll come around," I tell him.

Once we finish his exercises, I drop down on the couch next to him.

"I was wondering, and you can totally say no… " I start, but lose my train of thought, when he grabs my hand to hold.

Starting over, I clear my throat. "Maybe, you'd like to get out of here for a bit. There' is a winter festival going on in town. I have off tomorrow, so we could go get some fresh air," I suggest.

He's quiet for a moment, before meeting my eyes. "Can we invite my sister? I want you two to get to know each other, and I think she'd like the carnival."

"Of course. I can't wait to meet your sister," I smile.

Why is it that I can hear my grandma's voice in my head whispering…?

Famous last words.

Luke's sister insisted on driving Luke to the carnival and meeting me there, so I'm sitting on a bench in front of the gates, waiting for them. When I spot them, they are about ten minutes late and both look a bit irritated. Luke is still in the wheelchair, and his sister is pushing him. Knowing Luke prefers most of the time to wheel himself around, I bet this is part of the irritation.

As sSoon as Luke's eyes meet mine, the annoyance falls away, and a grin splits his face, making his sister scowl a bit more. Oh, my., Ttoday is going to be fun.

"Hey, guys."

"This is my sister, Gabbie. Gabbie, this is Brooke." Luke makes the introductions.

"Nice to meet you." Gabbie says, even though she doesn't look like it is.

"So, where do you want to start? I'm thinking we scope out the food, get some now, walk it off, and then grab some more food, before we leave," I say.

Luke chuckles, and Gabbie fights a small smile.

"Sounds good," Luke says.

We follow our noses to the food section, and everything looks good.

"Is that fried Oreos?" His sister says, slightly giddy.

"On a stick, apparently," he says.

"I love fried Oreos," I say, trying to find something to bond with her over, but she just scowls at me.

We buy our fried Oreos and keep walking. We end up at the gGingerbread house competition and have some fun checking out the different categories and casting our votes.

"Okay, my favorite is by far the old time hotel with the horse-drawn carriage in front," I tell them.

"No way. The collapsed gingerbread house with the hand drawn tornado over it was the best," Luke laughs.

"Which one did you like the best?" I ask Gabbie.

"Yeah, which one?" Luke asks, when she doesn't answer me.

"I liked the beach hut that was sitting over the blue gel water. It even had sand and palm trees," she says.

"Yeah, that one was really creative. It had starfish in the sand, and Swedish Fish in the water." I say, but earn no response from Gabbie.

I sigh, asnd Luke and I share a look. I'm sorry he mouths, and I just shrug my shoulders.

"So, what are you in school for?" I ask Gabbie.

"I'm going to be a teacher." She gives Luke a glare.

"What grade?" I ask.

"Middle school. I want to teach history."

"If you love history, you should sit down with Lexi. The history on the Oakside property is amazing. Lexi looked up a lot of it, when she bought the place." I tell her.

She just nods, as we end up at the petting zoo next. Gabbie walks off to feed some of the animals, while Luke and I hang out by the fence.

"She's a bucket of sunshine," I say, when she's out of earshot.

"I'm so sorry. I thought she'd be over this fight we had by now."

"Oh, she isn't mad at you. It's a girl thing. I'm encroaching on her territory, so no matter what, I'm the enemy. It's okay, and it will just take time. She needs to see I have your best interests at heart." I tell him.

He reaches over and takes my hand. I sit down on the bench next to him, so we are at eye level.

"You are amazing, y. You know that? If she wasn't here, I'd kiss you right now," he says.

"I'd let you. But for now, I'll take a rain check," I smile into his crystal-like green eyes.

He brings my hand to his lips and kisses the back of my hand. Even this small gesture, sends tingles up my arm and turns my insides to mush. Of course, this is the moment Gabbie walks back up and clears her throat.

Luke sighs and shoots me an apologetic look, before turning back to her.

"Why don't we do the tunnel of lights next?" Luke suggests.

I nod and stand, and waiting for Luke, but his sister sighs and goes to push his wheelchair, which makes him look irritated again.

"Why don't you help him more?" Gabbie asks.

I give Luke an apologetic smile. "Well, I've learned Luke likes to do things for himself, and it's better the more they do, because the faster they heal. If you baby them constantly doing everything for them, they don't heal as fast." I tell her and shrug.

I don't want to make her mad, but it's just my experience. Though, the dirty looks she sends me, tells me she thinks it's a dig directly at her. After that, she ignores me, as we walk the lights that are synced to Christmas music that' is currently playing "Jungle Bell Rock."

I try to not to let Gabbie get to me, but something says that, if I can't make nice with the sister, I won't have a chance in hell with Luke.

LUKE

"I think I'm ready to go home," I say, finally sick of how Gabbie is treating Brooke. I regret asking her to come with us, because she has completely ruined the day.

"Okay, let's get you back," Gabbie says.

"Actually, I'd like Brooke to take me back," I say in my stern older brother voice that leaves no room for arguments.

Gabbie looks hurt, and then pissed, before hugging me, and then heading out without a word to Brooke.

True to form, Brooke walks beside me and lets me wheel myself, which I prefer to do.

"I'm sorry about this. I had no idea she'd be like this. We fought a bit, but I thought she'd be over it and be nice to you. I shouldn't have invited her., I ruined the whole night." Finally, I stop rambling, when Brooke places her hand on my shoulder.

"Luke, it's fine. I'm glad you invited her, and I got to officially meet her. We might not be BFFs anytime soon, but it's a step." She says with a small smile.

"You are just being nice, but d. Don't. Gabbie is a handful on her best day." I shake my head.

Once in the car, I turn to Brooke. "Take the long way back?" I ask.

"I can do that," she says.

We play music and talk about the carnival and Christmas traditions our families had growing up. She' is laughing and smiling, and this is how our day should have been.

When she pulls into Oakside, I stop her from getting out of the car.

"Even with everything and Gabbie's behavior, I'm really glad you asked me to go. I had a good time." I tell her.

"I did, too," she smiles.

Then, I lean in and kiss her, wrapping my hand around her neck and pulling her into me. She wraps her hands around my neck, as she responds to my kiss, but by deepening it. Her soft, warm lips on mine are like a drug I can't get enough of.

When one of her hands trails over my shoulder and down my chest to rest just above my heart, I feel like this kiss gets taken to a new level. I trail kisses down her jawline.

"Luke," she whispers.

I keep kissing down her neck to her collarbone, and then back up the other side of her neck to her ear. Exploring her, learning what she likes, and soaking in every little moan. I give her earlobe a light tug with my teeth, and she gasps. My lips meet hers again, and she trails her hand to my waist, and then slips under my shirt. When the heat of her hand rests on my stomach, it's my turn to gasp with pleasure.

Pulling slightly away, Brooke's luminous eyes move over my body, and then she looks into my eyes. Then, she leans in and gives me a quick kiss again, before moving away.

"Let's get you inside. You have a busy day of appointments tomorrow."

She wasn't lying. My day starts off with a visit to my physical therapist. He puts me through my paces, which kicks my butt.

"You're looking very good!" Vince says. "If you keep up this progress, I don't see any reason we shouldn't have you walking by Christmas."

"Really?" I ask a bit shocked.

"Yes. Now, you won't be running marathons or anything, but you should be walking around here pretty easily. Keep doing your exercises each morning and night, and I will see you tomorrow," he says.

My next meeting is with my counselor. Each person at Oakside is assigned one, and they are supposed to help with the transition from Oakside back into civilian life. According to the packet of papers I got from here, this included everything from further education, to job finding, to getting us set up with VA benefits, and even helping us line up a place to live, reaching out to family, and more. Basically, anything we need, we are supposed to go to the counselor.

"Hey, Becky." I greet her, when I get to her office.

Becky is always bubbly and upbeat;, the kind that makes you wonder where she gets all the that energy. Then, when you leave her, you can't help but feel better no matter how you felt, when you got there.

I've also learned that she' is Lexi's sister-in-law and best friend.

"Luke! So today, we are looking at your plans for after Oakside. Have you thought about it, since the last time we talked?"

"A little. I always help set up my unit's deployments, and was wanting to see how that could translate into a civilian job." I tell her.

"We can do that. Let's go over what you would do, and I will make some calls," she says.

She listens, as I tell her everything I would do to get ready for deployments, gear checks, itinerary setups, making sure everyone's papers were in order, etc. After I finish, she has a few ideas for me, and we set up a time to meet next week.

My last appointment of the day is after lunch, and it's a meeting with my therapist. This is by far my least favorite appointment, but I know he has to clear me to leave Oakside, so I try.

"Luke, come in," Dr. Tate says. "I thought we'd start working on your issue of confined spaces."

It's a small thing, but the guy earns points for not saying fear of small places. I hate it, when Gabbie says it like that. But for her, I grin and bear it.

We spend time talking about the accident, about how I couldn't get out of the Humvee, as it started rolling, and then being thrown from it a second before it exploded. The nightmare it's been causing, and how it's led to my issue of confined spaces. How I'm okay in a car, as long as the windows are open, but in an elevator, I almost hyperventilate.

He asks questions, and I answer them. As much as I don't want to talk about all this, I have two very good reasons to push forward. Two girls depending on me to work on myself, and who will drag me kicking and screaming from this dark place, whether I like it or not.

CHAPTER SIX

LUKE

I'm in my room later that day, when Lexi knocks on the door.

"Can I come in? There' is something I need to talk to you about," she says.

I'm sitting on the couch, so I gesture for her to join me in the chair across from me. Closing the door behind her, she takes a seat.

"So," Lexi says., "I just had a talk with your sister, and a. A not so nice one at that. She just left my office after trying to file a complaint about Brooke."

"What?" I say louder than I intend, and Lexi flinches slightly, but then takes it in stride.

"She came in saying Brooke was being inappropriate with you. Of course, I sat her down, because I was concerned and wanted to hear what she had to say. As she started talking about what she felt was an inappropriate relationship, I listened closely. But I've talked with Brooke, and she's told me about your outings. Just so you know, Brooke was Noah's nurse, and she' is now a friend. We talk." She looks at me, letting me know without words that she knows things.

"So, after I calmed Gabbie down, I told her you had been making moves on Brooke as well. Then I said, because of the situation, I would watch it, but unless you yourself filed a complaint, there wasn't anything I could do." Lexi continues, "But I felt like I should tell you and see if there' is any truth that it's gone too far?"

"No, and if anything, I pushed Brooke too far yesterday. I really like her. She makes me feel... normal again. Not broken, and something that has to be fixed, like Gabbie does. Though, I love my sister, but she's young and sometimes too damn much to deal with. I don't always know how to handle her." I lean forward, resting my elbows on my knees, looking at the ground.

"Sometimes, you have to be blunt. They will get upset, but she's family, so she'll forgive you for it. I see it time and time again around here. Family and friends want to help so much, that they forget that the men here must help themselves first. They need to back up, let go, and be on the sidelines. You are the only one that can heal you. We are here to help with that, but we can't force you to heal."

"Does Brooke know about Gabbie?" I ask.

"Not yet, but I have to call her and tell her," Lexi says.

"Will you tell her I'd like to talk with her too, please? I know she has the next few days off," I say.

The nurses here work three twelve-hour shifts, and then have four days off, but not Brooke. With her being head nurse, she works four ten-hour shifts with three days off. It means I see her more than I normally would.

"Of course," Lexi says, before getting up to leave.

I have the TV on, but I'm not really watching it, as I think about what Gabbie did.

There' is a soft knock on the door, and when I look up, I find Brooke there in jeans and a t-shirt.

"Hey, come in," I tell her.

Her face is closed and emotionless. I can guess what's coming next, and I know I'm not going to like it.

"I just talked to Lexi," she says.

"She told me what Gabbie said. I will talk to her," I say.

"Luke, I can't risk my career, and my reputation, and everything I've built on this. I worked too hard to get where I am, and I love my job. Had she gone to anyone else but Lexi, I'd be put on probation, pending an investigation. When it came out what was going on, they would be letting me go to prevent medical malpractice. It wouldn't matter whether or not you initiated it."

"Come on, Brooke., Iit's not that bad," I say, but, in my heart, I know she's right. I know we got lucky this time, but if Gabbie tries to push this, it could get ugly.

"No, Luke, we can't go on. I just wanted to come here and tell you face-to-face that we need to end this. I can't risk it, and she's your family. You need to focus on getting better for her, and she needs you. If nothing else, this shows she needs you more than you realize."

"Why do you think that? Because from where I'm sitting, I see an ungrateful brat who I spoiled too much and is now throwing a temper tantrum, because she isn't getting her way," I say, now irritated.

Brooke stands and takes a deep breath.

"When people act out, it's when they need love the most." She looks torn, as she turns to leave.

"Brooke, don't leave it like this," I beg her.

She just shakes her head and walks out of the door. We haven't been that serious, and it hasn't been that long, but it doesn't stop me from feeling like she' is taking my heart with her. And with every step she takes away from me, it doesn't ease the pain that fills me.

❄

BROOKE

I leave Luke's room and head right to my friend Hailey's house. After my talk with Lexi, I texted her to make sure she was home. Lexi assured me everything was fine, but to say I'm a bit freaked out would be an understatement.

Hailey is a nurse at the military hospital, and we worked together for many years. I've been trying to convince her to come work at Oakside with me, but she likes it at the hospital, so I don't push too hard.

She meets me on the front porch with a hug. "Come on, I have some drinks set up on the back porch."

In my mind, Hailey is a true southern bell. She has the blonde hair done up in what I think is a fancy messy bun. The kind that' is meant to look lazy, but it took her a while to perfect. Her perfectly applied makeup, and hot as hell clothes amplifies her image. Along with her charming southern accent, and, of course, her quintessential southern house, s. She reminds me of Reese Witherspoon.

Her back porch is my favorite. It''s done in white wood, has large two story ceilings, and it's been enclosed as a sunroom, with glass walls on three sides. She's using it as a sitting room, and has decorated it beautifully, but my favorite part is the swinging sofas, hanging from the rafters.

Though, the hanging sofas are relaxing to sit on after a stressful day, they're not a good place to sit after you have been drinking. Trust me on that one, as we both learned that the hard way.

We both curl up on the swing, facing each other with some sweet tea and cookies.

"Okay, you have the *'I have a problem, and I need to talk to you about it'* face, so spill it," she orders.

"I think I'm falling for a patient," I tell her outright.

This causes her to sit up straight. No more relaxed friends chatting, she' is getting down to business. I tell her about Luke from the first day, and how I felt just seeing him, and to him being reassigned to me. I don't leave out any details about his sister, taking him shopping, going to the cardinal with him, and how his sister acted.

"Then, I get a call from Lexi today, asking me to come in, because she needs to talk to me. When I get there, she locks us in her office, which she never does, and then proceeds to tell me Gabbie tried to file a complaint against me for taking advantage of Luke. Lexi thankfully stopped it, saying she has seen Luke putting the moves on me, Lexi's words not mine, and unless Luke comes forward, then she isn't able to do anything. Gabbie is pissed. Lexi told Luke, so Luke is pissed, and I'm just... scared," I finish.

"Have you talked to Luke?"

"Yeah, right after I got done with Lexi and before I came here. He kept saying he'll talk to Gabbie, but I ended things. I can't lose my job and everything I've worked for. If this had been the hospital, I'd be on leave right now," I say.

"Not necessarily. Remember Marla?" Sshe asks.

Marla was another nurse we worked with at the hospital.

"Yeah?" I ask curiously, wondering where she's going with this.

"She met her boyfriend, while she was his nurse. The mother tried to make a stink about it and went to the hospital board. Yes, she was put on leave, while they investigated, but her boyfriend stood up and said the mother was causing problems and trying to be controlling. He gave this huge speech, and Marla was cleared. They were told to keep it out of sight, until he was released, and they have been together ever since. She didn't have a history of dating patients, and neither do you," Hailey says.

"She got lucky. What would have happened, if he hadn't stuck up for her?" I say.

"I was curious about that too, so I asked around. Apparently, they would have reassigned her and put her on probation. Yeah, it would have been on her record, but if it's not habitual, it wouldn't have been an issue. Only when it becomes a pattern, do they really step in. They frown about dating current patients and discourage it, but there isn't anything in the handbook that says we can't., Aat least, not yet, anyway."

"This just sucks," I say.

"Listen, you can be friends, so be his friend," she goes on. "Once he's discharged, you can see if it goes anywhere, but with the bitchy sister, you might have dodged a bullet. No one needs the sister-in-law from hell to deal with."

"I don't think I can work with him every day and just be friends," I say.

"Then have him reassigned."

"It's a small place, and he's already been reassigned once, and I don't like the idea of anyone else working with him."

"Now you are just being difficult," she laughs.

"This isn't just a crush. I want to date him. What I feel for him is... stronger than I have ever felt before. There' is a pull to be around him. When I'm with Luke, I'm calm and relaxed, and. I can be myself. That kiss? I've never felt anything like it and want to experience it again and again."

She looks at me and bites the side of her lips, as she thinks.

"I guess this comes down to you. Is this so strong that you don't want to give it up, but you'd give up your job at Oakside, if it came down to it? If so, then by all means go ahead. But if Oakside is more important, then you need to stop, even if it's just until he's released. This is a decision only you can make."

"Why can't finding a guy be easy? Why is there always something complicated?" I lament. "Why can't we know if this is the guy? If I knew he was *the* guy, then I'd be fine risking it all. But the thought of stepping away from Oakside for him, and it not working out, would crush me."

"Give it time. Maybe, just be friends and see. You will know, when you know, and you can't rush these things," she says.

"I know you're right. So, you are seeing anyone?" I ask.

"For a split second, but after the third date, he got all handsy. I couldn't help thinking that for him date three meant sex, and that was the end of that."

Hailey is a sweetheart, beautiful, and kind. But she' is very picky, when it comes to men, though. Very few make it past date three. She knows what she wants and isn't willing to settle.

I wish I waswere as sure as she is.

CHAPTER SEVEN

LUKE

It's the day after my talk with Lexi and Brooke, and I'm still fuming at Gabbie. So, when she comes to visit, I know we have to talk this out.

"Did you really go to Lexi about Brooke?" I ask the second her butt touches the couch.

Her back goes ramrod straight, h. Her sign that she' is preparing for a confrontation.

"Yes. You came here to heal, not find a fuck buddy," she snaps.

"Damn mit, Gabbie. We aren't sleeping together," I growl.

"You expect me to believe that? I saw you two together!"

Well, this isn't a conversation I wanted to have with my little sister.

"Gabbie, s. Stop and think. My legs aren't working right now." I say, hoping she'll put two and two together.

"You don't need your legs, if she does all the work." Gabbie says, some of the fight leaving her, and her cheeks turning pink.

"Damn mit, I haven't even gotten hard, since my accident," I glare at her.

She looks down at her hands in her lap, refusing to make eye contact.

"I wasn't happy, when you joined the military, and now, here you are. I won't let anything derail your healing," she says.

"*You* are derailing my healing. You baby me. Did you notice that not once did Brooke step up to push me around at the carnival? She expects me to do it myself. She expects me to get in and out of the car myself, which I can. If I need help, she's there. Though, she pushes me to do as much on my own as I can. I'm not as helpless as you think I am." Gabbie looks at me, almost in shock. So, to prove my point, I stand from the chair I'm sitting in and move myself to the wheelchair next to it. Then, I wheel myself to the door.

"I love you, Gabbie, and will I'll always be here for you, but Brooke is important to me, too. and Yyou messing with her career like you did is unacceptable. I know you had it hard after Mom and Dad died, but I think I've been too easy on you, because now you are acting like a spoiled brat. So, I'm thinking it's time for you to go and don't come back, until I call you." I say without looking at her.

"You're kicking me out?" Sshe asks.

"For now. I'm so mad that I don't want to do something I can't take back."

She stands and walks to stand beside me.

"You are all I have left. I can't lose you, too."

"You are not losing me, but after your little stunt, it almost seems like you want to push me away. If you want to keep me in your life, you will not take this any further. Do you understand?" I say in my most authoritative voice that' is a lot like our fathers.

She hesitates for a moment, before she nods and walks out.

I sit there and think of my sister and Brooke. Gabbie is family, but if it came down to it, could I walk away from Brooke? The thought of it is too painful, b. But I know I can't walk away from Gabbie, either.

Needing to talk this out, I head out to the lobby and find Lexi at the front desk.

"Hey, Luke., Iis everything okay? Gabbie looked pretty upset," Lexi says.

"Yeah, we just had a talk, and she' is pissed she didn't get her way. I also told her not to come back for a while, so we could can both cool down."

"Ahhh, sometimes it's best to let things settle." Lexi nods.

"Yeah. Hey is Easton around by chance?"

"He is. Hang on." She picks up her phone, asnd her fingers go flying across the screen.

"I found him. He's in the library. Ddo you know where it is?" Sshe asks.

"Yeah, I remember passing it recently," I say.

She points to my left, "Take this hall, and i. It's right next to the PT room."

Going down the hall, I pass the dining room, before I get to the library. I haven't been in this room before, but it's amazing. On my right and left, the walls are nothing but floor to ceiling bookcases, as is the wall with the door I just came through.

In front of me, most of the wall is glass with French doors that open to a courtyard that' is shared with the lobby windows. In the center of the room, are desks with computers, and along the windows, are couches and chairs.

I spot Easton with his wife, Paisley, over there, and he waves, when he sees me.

"Hey, man., Eeverything okay?" Hhe asks.

"Can we go outside? I'd like to talk," I say, not wanting to disturb the people in here.

"Sure. You okay here?" He asks his wife.

"I'm good." She holds up her book.

We walk outside and sit on a bench where he can still see Paisley.

"Paisley was your best friend's sister, right?" I ask, trying to remember some of his story.

"Yeah."

"Was there ever a point where you had to choose between the two?" I ask.

"Ahhh. When her brother found out, it wasn't pretty. He saw it as a betrayal on my end. By that time, I was already in love with her, and couldn't walk away from her. So, I that's what I told him. Then I said, not to make me choose, because if he did, I'd choose her. He wasn't very pleased, but when he saw how happy she was, he came around. Having trouble with your sister?"

"Yeah," I say and go on to tell him about the winter carnival, and my sister going to Lexi, and the fight we had just now.

"I think you both need to cool off. Now, she's afraid of losing you in a whole new way. You are the only family she has left, and I'm willing to bet she had plans of you two living together and being a family. If things with Brooke get serious, those plans go away. At the same time, you are right that she can't keep babying you, if you are going to recover. Though, you need to heal in more ways than one, to be good for anyone."

He's right. I need to get my life on track to be worthy of anyone, especially Brooke, to prove to her I'm worth taking a chance on.

"Channel what you are feeling right now into your recovery. You will be shocked how fast your progress is," Easton says.

It's time to put that to the test.

LUKE

All my resolve leaves me, when Brooke walks back through the door for the first time in a few days. I had planned to respect her wishes and keep some space between us for now, but the moment her eyes lock with mine, I know that was a fool's dream.

I need her so much more than I wanted to admit to myself.

"So, I hear you are up and walking." She says with a forced smile.

"I can walk around the room. I'm still not very steady, but anything outside of that, I'm still in the wheelchair," I say.

"Can I see?" Sshe asks.

This right here. She wants to see what I can do, because she wants to cheer me on. I need this, and I need her. She' is always pushing me to be better, and I know I can do that for her, too. I just need to stop getting in my own way.

She' is standing across the room, leaning on the door frame, so I stand up and hold onto the furniture along the way, instead of using the walker they gave me. I slowly make my way over to her. Once I'm right in front of her, I place my hand on her waist. Her sharp intake of breath is the only sound, though she doesn't say anything.

"Let's go look at Christmas lights tonight after your shift," I say.

I want some time with her. Some time to just be us.

"Luke... " she says.

"My therapist says I need to be in smaller spaces and work on controlling my feelings in them," I say.

I know this is playing a little dirty, but I know she'll have a hard time saying no to something that will help with my recovery. When she sighs, I know I'm right.

"Okay. I will clear it with Lexi first." That's the best I can hope for. She then helps me work through my PT exercises, before heading out. I fill my day with appointments, and during lunch, Brooke comes and finds me. She sits down with me to eat her lunch.

"Lexi cleared it with your doctor, so we are down for Christmas lights tonight, but I am to encourage you to keep the car windows up," she says.

I nod, because I knew that would be the case. While I'm dreading that part, I am still looking forward to my time with her.

That evening, once night falls, Brooke helps me out to her car, and we go look at lights.

"My brother has already mapped out some routes, because he took the kids out to look at lights the other night. So, I have the scoop on some of the good stops." I can't take my eyes off her tonight. With the way the lights hit her face, she looks so carefree. Even though she' is still in the scrubs she wore to work, she' is the most beautiful woman I've ever seen. When we hit the next traffic light, I lean over and kiss her.

"Luke." She mumbles against my lips, but she kisses me back.

When the light turns green, I pull back, and she has a huge smile on her face. So, at the next traffic light, I do it again. Another traffic light, another kiss. It's the perfect distraction for me that I don't concentrate on the windows being up, and I'm in a confined space. Between lights, I have my hand on her leg, and I inch closer and closer to her core, until I finally brush over it.

"Luke... " she moans.

But this time, when we get to a traffic light, I don't kiss her, but I rub her over her leggings. She leans her head against the headrest and closes her eyes. Then, she lifts her hips, trying to increase the pressure. When the light turns green, I take my hand away, and she lets out a frustrated groan.

At the next light, I trail my hand up her leg and circle her clit. Again, she lifts her hips, trying to get some relief, until the light turns green.

This time we hit a residential street with a lot of lights, and the traffic is going slow, taking in one house after the other. Brooke keeps looking at me, and I'm looking at her, not paying any attention to the lights.

"Let's go back to your place," I say, and she nods.

In the fifteen minutes it takes us to get across town to her house, it seems like the longest drive in the world. I keep playing with her during each stop, but not letting her fall over the edge.

The moment she pulls into her driveway and puts the car in park, she moves in for a kiss and runs her hand over my cock that has been hard as steel the whole time I've been in the car with her.

"Inside, or we won't ever make it there," I whisper against her lips.

Then, we are unbuckling and making our way inside the house, as fast as we can. Even though I'm still unsteady on my feet, I want to get inside as fast as possible. Dragging her with me to the couch, I pin her down, wasting no time making her comeum this time. I've had her on edge all night, so it doesn't take but a few strokes of her clit, before she' is digging her nails in my shoulders and screaming my name.

As she catches her breath, I remove my shirt, and her eyes follow my every move. Then, she stands and removes her shirt and pants. I've never seen anyone more beautiful. In her panties and bra, her body is luscious with just the right amount of curves and breasts that I can't wait to see free. She turns, and I'm so entranced watching her walk down the hallway, that I don't even question why is sheshe's walking away.

Before I can question it too long, she has returned with a condom in her hand, and a smile on her face. Before she even makes it to the couch, I've removed my pants.

While I know I should do the gentlemanly thing and tell her we don't have to do this, and t., That this isn't what I came here for, but right now, all I can think about is, if I don't get inside her, I'm going to die.

She straddles me on the couch and scoots back just enough to pull my cock out and give it a few strokes, which makes me even harder.

"I love your hands on me, but if you keep doing that, this will be over, before it even starts," I groan.

She only smiles and opens the condom, sliding it on for me. I bite my lip, because even that movement feels too good. Then, she stands and removes her panties, before straddling me again.

"You sure?" She asks me.

"Shouldn't I be asking you that?"

"I'm more than sure."

"Me too," I say and grip her hips, as I slowly pull her down on my cock. She's so wet from all the teasing, that it doesn't take much, until she' is fully seated on me, and we both moan.

As she rocks her hips, I let my hands explore her body. Running by hands up her side, enjoying the feel of her smooth skin, I finally get to her bra and push it up, letting her tits spill free.

They are perfect and round. I lean forward catching one of her raspberry tipped nipples and sucking it into my mouth. Her breath catches, and she arches her back, giving me easy access. I'm so concentrated on playing with her nipples with my tongue that I'm not prepared for the swivel she does with her hips, and I almost lose it.

But the look on her face, tells me she knows exactly what she did. Bringing my hand between us, I start playing with her clit, because there' is no way I'm going without her having an orgasm.

I love how sensitive she is, but all the teasing tonight has put us both on edge. When I feel her pussy start fluttering and gripping my cock, I can't hold back, asnd I start to cumcome. I cCouldn't stop it, even if I tried.

Looking into her eyes and feeling her grip on my cock, is the single most earth shattering feeling in the world.

This woman is going to break me, if I let her.

CHAPTER EIGHT

BROOKE

It's been a few days, since I went to look at Christmas lights with Luke, and I'm walking into work, when I see Gabbie, getting ready to leave. She doesn't look happy, but I decide to chance it, anyway. Taking a deep breath, I give her a smile and walk over to her.

"Can we talk?" I ask.

She looks hesitant, and I can't say I blame her. Looking at the door, then back at me, and then back towards Luke's room, she gives a big sigh.

"Yeah," she says.

She follows me into the dining room, and we each get some coffee, and then sit in a back corner. At least, we are out of the way, if this doesn't go well.

Once we are sitting down, she looks at me and purses her lips. I guess she isn't going to make this easy on me, and so I'll try to make this as friendly as possible.

"I'm just wondering why you are so against him dating," I ask her point blank.

For a moment, I think I see a ghost of a smile on her face, but it's gone just as fast.

"He's all I have, and he left me alone to go to the military, and it's time for him to come back and for us to be a family," she says.

"You and I both know, when he enlisted, that he had no idea what was going to happen to your parents. I don't know all the details, but from what I do know, he's bent over backwards to make sure you are taken care of. That sounds a lot like family to me," I say.

She drinks her coffee, but she says nothing. She just stares me down, so I continue.

"Okay, let me ask you this, then. You put all of this energy in to preventing him from dating, then you find the a guy, get married, and start a family, and then he's left alone. How is that fair to him?" I know she isn't going to answer me, but I had to try.

"He just needs to focus on getting better, while he' is here." Is all she says.

"It's never a bad thing to have more motivation. I want him to get better, too. Every day I push him to make sure he' is doing his workouts, getting to his appointments, and doing what he should be. But right now? He's miserable with you two fighting. He tries to push it aside and work past it, but I see it. Even if he won't admit it, he's regressing."

For a brief moment, she looks guilty.

"I get the only family thing. I went through it with my brother. Then, he met his wife, and when they got married, I gained a sister, who has become one of my best friends. I now have a niece and nephew to spoil." I tell her, hoping maybe we can relate to something.

"I don't need any more friends," she says.

"Okay, I don't know if what we have is forever, but we won't get the chance to find out, if you don't let him, because I know he'll always choose you. As he should, and because that's Luke. One It's one of the many things I love about him."

I decide it's best to end things here and stand up.

"Thank you for hearing me out," I say and walk away without looking back.

I head right to Lexi's office and am thankful I find Noah there, too. I close the door and collapse on the couch.

"So, I'm in love with Luke, his sister hates me, and if I keep pursuing him, I risk ripping them apart, losing my job, and my heart. How's your day?" I say.

They look at each other, before looking back at me.

"Well, nothing worth it is easy," Noah says.

I don't even hide my eye roll, as I throw my head back on the couch and dig the heels of my palms into my eyes.

"What happened?" Lexi asks.

"I jJust talked to Gabbie," I say. "She doesn't care about anything, because all she wants is her brother, and her only family. I get that, but nothing I said seemed to reach her. The longer the fight, the more Luke is going backwards, instead of healing."

"Have you talked to Luke?" Lexi says softly, as she sits down next to me.

"No, he's stressed enough and doesn't need this, too. Maybe, you should look at moving Luke to another nurse. Aat least, to save your asses," I say.

"Nope, Luke is making amazing progress, and I stand by you. You pushing him is a huge reason for his improvement. We have watched you, when you don't realize it, and you are always professional on the grounds, and there's nothing to warrant it, especially when Luke contradicted what Gabbie said," Noah says.

"I'm not worth risking all this," I tell them.

"We think you are, and I bet Luke would think so, too," Lexi says and gives me a hug.

"You need to talk to him. At least, tell him how you feel and see where he is. If Noah and I learned anything, it's that communication is key. In the early days of our relationship, all we could do was talk." Lexi smiles at Noah.

Noah returns her smile with a look at Lexi filled with nothing but love, and it's how any girl wants their guy to look at them.

I remember when I was first assigned to Noah and seeing them, and the way he looked at Lexi, I had thought they had been together for years, not weeks.

"You two just got very lucky," I mumble.

Lexi smiles back at Noah. "Yeah, we did. But you have now, too."

LUKE

I' am looking over some of the paperwork my physical therapist gave me on some new exercises, when Gabbie walks in. She stands at the door, unsure if I even want her there, but I don't want to fight, and I don't want to push her away either.

"Well, you going to stand there all day, or are you going to sit it down and visit?" I ask her.

She looks relieved, as she takes off her coat and sits on the chair next to the couch.

"I was hoping to nail down our Christmas plans," she says.

"Well, I'm doing Christmas here. Part of my rehab is participating in the activities. I want you to join me, so we can support the other guys." I say, and her face falls.

"I was hoping we could do Christmas just the two of us, as a family," she frowns.

"I know Gabbie, and I get it. This is the first year I'm back. But this is where I am, so we can do Christmas here."

She looks at me, like she knows I'm not telling the full truth. It's because I'm not. I don't want to commit to plans, because I want to spend time with Brooke. I want to see what activities I can get her into. But I can't say that to Gabbie, because I know it will set her off again. At this point, the last thing I want is to fight any more.

"Okay, what are we doing here?" She seems to take the change in plans in stride.

"Well, there' is the gift exchange for members later today, and then some crafts tomorrow. They are preparing a big Christmas eve dinner, which I'd like you to come to next week."

She nods, "I will be here. Now, what do you want for Christmas this year? You know you are already hard enough to shop for."

"Just you here in a good mood is all I want," I tell her.

"You have to give me some ideas, so you have gifts to open."

I bite my tongue, because I want to go off and tell her the only gift I want is for her to let up on Brooke, and so we can be happy. But in the back of my mind, I can hear my mom scolding me and telling me to be patient.

"Well, I have been reading a bit more, so those thriller books you used to send in the care packages, more of those. My therapist has me doing some adult coloring books for stress and anxiety, so coloring books with intricate geometrical designs and some coloring pencils. Also, lounge clothes, t-shirts, and sweatpants."

Gabbie is making notes on her phone. "Good, this gives me some ideas." We spend the next hour talking, before Brooke peeks her head in, and Gabbie's posture goes stiff.

"Sorry to interrupt, but you have a PT appointment," Brooke says.

I look at the clock. "Time got away from me. I'm on my way." I say to Brooke with a smile.

"Gabbie, you are welcome to wait, until he's done in here, or there are some other family members in the lobby. I can show you to the library too, if you want," Brooke says.

I hold my breath, waiting for her reaction.

"I'm actually going to head out. Luke finally gave me some ideas for his Christmas gifts, so I need to go shopping. I will be back tomorrow." She gives me a hug and leaves.

Brooke watches her go, and then turns back to me. "What kind of gift ideas?" Sshe smirks.

I just smile and shake my head. The ideas I have for Brooke are much dirtier than anything I'd talk about with my sister.

"I have a PT appointment to go, too. I want to walk. Will you go with me?" I ask.

She looks uncertain, but I have been cleared to walk, as long as I take breaks, when it gets to be too much. It almost seems like Brooke is battling the nurse who wants to encourage her patient, and the girlfriend who doesn't want me to overdo it. I see the moment the nurse in her wins out, because she straightens her back, takes a deep breath, and nods.

"Let's go."

She wraps her arm around mine, and to anyone looking in, it appears like we are just out for a walk. What they don't realize is I'm leaning on her more than needed, as we walk through the lobby.

I make it to PT and sit down. "That wasn't as bad as I thought it would be."

"Well, I can always get the wheelchair, if you are too tired to walk. Remember, after this is the gift exchange in the lobby." She reminds me.

PT flies by, as I think of Brooke and our night together after the Christmas lights. Brooke is my secret weapon to pushing myself in PT and still being able to walk out to the lobby for the gift exchange. I may collapse onto the couch, but I still made it.

"How was PT?" Brooke asks, as she sits down next to me.

"Kicked my butt in a good way," I say, as I watch two guys in suits walk over by the Christmas tree.

"Who are they?" I ask.

"The couple with the two little girls? That's Owen and Ellie. Lexi met Ellie at a fundraiser, and they hit it off. She volunteers here sometimes. Owen owns a company in Knoxville. He's super rich and is always donating and helping out here. The other couple is Teddy and Mia. Teddy is a former patient, who inherited a company, and over the summer, Ellie's best friend, Mia, was volunteering, and that's how Mia met Teddy. They are always here doing stuff for the guys." Brooke says just as Teddy steps up.

"Hello everyone. I'm Teddy. I was patient here, just like you. My unit came under fire, and when I woke up in Germany, I was told I was the only survivor. To say I didn't deal with it is an understatement. This place and, the people here saved my life and helped me heal. Because of them, I met my amazing wife Mia and am able to honor the men who didn't make it home." He turns to smile at his wife.

Pointing to the other couple, he says, "This is a good friend of mine, Owen, and his wife, Ellie. Ellie is friends with Lexi and can't seem to stay away from Oakside. So, because of that and because we know what it's like to spend Christmas alone, we decided we weren't going to let all of you do that. Under the tree, are some gifts for each of you, and some for the staff, because I know how hard they work. Allie and Becca here will help pass them out. The gifts for the patients are ones we hope will help you with your next steps." Teddy nods towards the two girls, standing next to Owen.

There' is a round of applause, and then Christmas music starts, and the kitchen staff brings out cookies and eggnog.

Each patient gets a brand new laptop, and a. A high tech one, too.

"Are they serious?" I ask.

"Yeah," Brooke laughs. "When I say these guys are rich, I'm not joking. They are billionaires."

"Hence the suits," I say. "Open your gift, I'm interested to see what they got you," I tell her and nod towards the presents in her lap.

Inside are a coffee mug, some coffee, and a card. When Brooke opens the card, her jaw drops, and her eyes tear up.

"What is it?" I ask, and she turns the card towards me and inside is a grocery gift card with a note that they want to pay for her groceries and gas for a year. On the gift card is a crazy high amount.

"Wow. That's amazing." I say in shock.

Brooke stands and walks over to Teddy and pulls him in for a hug, and then does the same to Mia. When she turns to Ellie, Ellie is pulling her in first, and while Owen refrains from hugging her, he still places a hand on her shoulder.

I know it's all friendly, but having another man's hands on her, is irritating me. When Brooke walks back over to me, she' is just shaking her head.

"I wasn't Teddy's nurse, but I worked with him on days his nurse was off, and the progress he's made, well, it's just night and day." She says, watching him.

We hang out for an hour, talking and enjoying the Christmas mood, before she helps me back to my room.

"Listen, I'm having dinner tomorrow at my place with my brother, his wife, their two kids, and my grandma. I'd like you and Gabbie both to come."

I turn to face her and can't imagine why she should would want Gabbie at her house after the way she has acted towards her. Like she can read my mind, Brooke sighs.

"For better or worse, Gabbie is your sister. Since she's the only family you have, I won't stop trying to reach out to her. Maybe, seeing my family isn't much different than hers will help. Or maybe, my brother can get through to her, or maybe, it will all blow up in my face, and five years from now, I'll turn to my brother and say remember that dinner when? Who knows, but I have to try," she adds.

Putting a finger under her chin, I tilt her head towards me and place a kiss on her lips. With just this small kiss, a jolt of electricity runs between us.

"We will be there, and. Gabbie will drive me., Lord, help me." I smile at her shining eyes.

As Brooke heads back to check on her other patients, I sit on the couch and try to think of how I could bribe Gabbie to be on her best behavior. That's if I can even get her to agree to go at all.

CHAPTER NINE

BROOKE

I'm running around the house, making sure everything is in place, when my brother steps in my path and pulls me in for a hug.

"It's going to be okay. Everyone here is on your side, so she won't dare try anything tonight," he says.

I broke down and told my brother everything, including that Gabbie doesn't like me and our run-ins so far. He knows what this dinner means to me, and I know he'll do everything he can to make it a success.

"This has to work. If I can't win her over, I will lose Luke, and I'm too far down that road to be able to accept that," I say what I mean without saying the words, but thankfully, my brother gets it.

When the doorbell rings, I know there' is no turning back. So, I open the door to find Luke smiling at me, and Gabbie just staring. She isn't glaring or looking pissed off, so I take it as a win.

"Hey, guys., Ccome on in. Oh, and drink whatever my grandma hands you at your own risk. The stuff she makes could be used to remove tar." I warn them.

Luke chuckles and leans in to kiss me on the cheek.

Guiding them into the living room, I introduce them, "This is my brother, David, and his wife, Jill. Their kids are running around somewhere, and their names are Clark and Cassie. This is my grandma..." I say, but get interrupted.

"You can call me Betty. Want a drink?" Grandma says.

"Ahhh, no., Ccan't have any with the medicine I'm on," Luke says.

Grandma looks at him with a twinkle in her eyes and says, "Damn doctors always putting you on something."

"I'm driving, so I'll pass," Gabbie says.

"Plus, she isn't old enough," Luke adds.

"Oh, posh," Grandma says.

"Anyway, this is Luke and his sister, Gabbie," I say, as we sit on the couch.

Everyone starts talking and laughing, as t. The kids are playingplay card games on the floor, dragging in anyone who will play with them. I watch Gabbie, and she' is on her best behavior. While I have yet to see a smile grace her face, she' is polite and talks to anyone who speaks to her, and she watches everyone, especially the kids.

When we all sit down to eat, food gets passed, conversation flows, and Luke finds little reasons to touch me, and the smile seems to never leave his face. After dinner, while we are cleaning up, I see Gabbie slip out on to the back porch.

"Hey, I'm going to go talk to her." I say to Jill, who practically pushesd me out of the door.

"Hey, you, okay?" I ask Gabbie, as I slip on to the back porch.

She' is leaning up against the railing, looking up at the night sky filled with stars.

"You were right. I do want him to be happy," she says.

I say nothing, but go stand beside her.

"I haven't seen him this happy, since before Mmom and Ddad died. He's smiling and fits right in. I enjoyed myself, and if my brother is happy and starts a family, I can see myself slipping into the same role you did. I won't get in your guy's way again."

"Thank you, Gabbie. He' is pretty happy in there, huh? I'm surprised him and my brother get along so well," I say.

"Yeah?"

"Well, the last guy I dated, my brother showed up to my house with a shotgun over his shoulder, talking all about hunting, and what a great shot he is. How nothing can run from him, and the entire time I'm staring at the guy. I didn't hear from him after that."

Gabbie laughs. "Well, I can say I haven't gone that far."

"Just know, when Luke sees you starting to date, it will be the same thing. He'll be protective, and it will be as both the big brother and the father figure. He'll take on the role of giving the guys the dad speech. My brother is probably giving it to Luke right now," I say.

We are quiet for a moment longer.

"This doesn't mean we are best friends or anything," she says.

"Nope, b. But I do hope you know you can talk to me about anything. When Luke gets overbearing, or when you start dating, I'm the perfect one to put him in his place." I tell her, and that earns me a smirk.

"I should probably get going." She says, and we turn to face the house.

Through the glass French door, we can see Luke playing cards with my brother, niece, and nephew.

"Why don't you let me take him back to Oakside? Let him play a bit more."

"Okay," she agrees with a shrug.

Several hands of cards later, everyone is gone, and so are all the Christmas cookies my grandma brought over, and it's just Luke and me.

"I can't believe you won Gabbie over," he says.

"It was only a matter of time," I smirk.

"No one has tried before, not like that." He takes my hand. "Thank you."

Then, he pulls me in for a kiss. It's soft, gentle, and sweet, but it still sends a tingle down between my thighs. When I try to take things further, he pulls back from the kiss and looks me in the eyes.

He gazes at me, like he' is searching for something, as if he's looking straight into my soul.

"I love you, Brooke." His words take my breath away.

It hasn't been that long, but what we have between us, is so intense and strong. While I don't doubt what I feel, the only thing that has been holding me back is how we can make it work. With Gabbie now on board, I have no doubt that we can go forward and make plans.

"I love you too, Luke."

More sweet kisses turn into more hot kisses that I don't want to stop, but I have, too.

"We have to get you back to Oakside," I say.

On the way, Luke doesn't let go of my hand. When I park at Oakside, I turn to him.

"On Christmas Eve, Oakside is doing a big thing for the patients, but my family is doing Christmas dinner at my brothers. Why don't you and Gabbie join us? The kids will demand you put together their new toys, and I will wrap Gabbie's gifts and put them under the tree. There will be cookie decorating, and it will be fun."

"We will be there," he says.

LUKE

Before I even open my eyes, I can tell Brooke is in my room, as i. It smells just like her.

"Why are you up so early? It's a holiday," I groan.

She laughs, "I volunteered to work, so anyone who wanted the day off, could have it., Pplus, that means I get to spend the day with you. I promise once Gabbie gets here, I'll make myself scarce, so you can have family time. Just don't forget about tomorrow."

"Dinner at your brother's., I won't forget." I smile, as I sit up in bed.

"Now, let's get your exercises done. No rest just because it's a holiday," she says.

I don't need help anymore with getting ready, or my daily exercises PT gives me. We both know that, but I like her around, and I like her hand on me, so we are always finding little ways for her to help.

After my exercises, I shower and get ready, and she moves on to her other patients.

Sitting down in the dining room for brunch, I'm waiting on Gabbie. But instead, Noah joins me with a big smile on his face.

"You did it," hHe says.

"I did what?" I'm not awake enough to read between the lines.

"You got the job., As soon as PT clears you, it's yours." Noah slams my shoulder from across the table, and I sit there stunned.

"You're serious?" I have to be sure.

Noah laughs, "Yes! I told you that many places love hiring veterans, and having Oakside behind you, is a huge boost. I talked to your doctor, and he really thinks you will be released, before New Year's, if you don't mess up between now and then. You will need to still keep seeing your therapist for the enclosed spaces issue, but that isn't a reason to keep you here."

"Oh, and this came for you." He hands me a package, and I smile.

"I was worried it wouldn't be here in time. This is Brooke's Christmas gift." I tell him.

"Brooke is a special woman. She was there for me and supported Lexi through everything and has become a really good friend to Lexi and me. You treat her right, and after you get released, we will set up dinner at our place for the four of us."

"I'd like that," I tell him, just as I see Gabbie walk into the dining room.

She walks over hesitantly and smiles.

"Am I interrupting?" She asks, almost shyly.

"Nope," Noah says., "Jjust wishing Luke here a Merry Christmas and giving him some good news. He's all yours." Noah stands up and starts talking to other people scattered in the dining room.

"What good news did he have for you?" Gabbie asks, as she puts her small purse over the back of her chair and sits down.

"You will have to wait, until tomorrow to find out. Speaking of Brooke, she invited us over to dinner at her brother's. I plan to go, and I hope you will join me."

Gabbie eyes me, and I know she won't pass up a chance to spend time with me, especially outside of Oakside, but I know she isn't happy that I didn't give her much of a choice.

"That sounds good. I liked her grandma. She's snappy," she giggles.

"There' is one more thing I want to talk to you about, and I'm not sure you're going to like it," I tell her.

She settles her hands on the table and sits up straight. "Let me have it."

"I love Brooke. She' is it for me. I feel it in my bones. I'd like to ask her to marry me." I watch her reaction.

She does very well at keeping her emotions under control, but she runs her eyes over my face, like she' is waiting to see if I'm joking. She bites the side of her cheek, before she speaks.

"Brooke and I talked the other night at her house. Watching you interact with her family, I finally got it. You two together? I wasn't losing you, but I was gaining a family. I would be getting a brother, sister, grandma, niece, and nephew all to spoil." She smiles, "When do you plan on asking her?"

"I'm not sure honestly," I tell her.

We spend the next hour eating brunch and talking about different ideas. Together, we look online and find everything from extravagant to the simple. But I know the idea, when I see it, and Gabbie agrees.

We decide to exchange gifts tomorrow, since Brooke says the adults will do a gift exchange, once we get there. Then, we head back to my room with some hot chocolate and watch some Christmas movies, and it reminds me a lot of the days, before I left for boot camp, and how easy going things used to be.

"Savannah has some good schools," I tell Gabbie, as she' is getting ready to leave.

"I had a feeling you were going to stay in the area, so I already put in a transfer for next year. I have to finish this year out, though."

I hug her. "We will make it work. Come down for spring break, and I will go up for weekends here and there."

"Yes, we'll make it work," she repeats.

"Now, go get some sleep and be here tomorrow at seven a.m.," I tell her.

"It's a holiday! Don't people sleep in anymore?" She grumbles, as she heads out the door.

Tomorrow is going to be a day for the books. Brooke and Gabbie getting along, some big news, and I can’t wait to see the look on Gabbie's face, when she opens her gift.

CHAPTER TEN

BROOKE

I slept at my brother's house last night, because his kids get up at the first crack of dawn on Christmas day, and I didn't want to have to drive that early. I' am woken up by them jumping on the bed.

"Auntie Brooke, Santa has been here!" Clark says.

"We were really good this year! There are more presents than last year," Cassie squeals.

"Did you wake your parents already?" I ask without even opening my eyes.

"Yes, Mommy said to tell you she' is starting coffee," Clark says.

"Your mom is my favorite person. Go help her with coffee, and I will be there in a minute." I tell him.

They bolt from the room, and I want to go back to sleep, but sure enough, the smell of coffee starts to fill the house. So, I drag myself from bed, throw my hair up in a messy bun, and go out to get some coffee, while calculating my chances of getting a nap in today. They are looking pretty darn slim, since Luke and Gabbie will be here in a few hours to spend the day with us.

The next hour is spent watching the kids unwrap gifts that include everything from clothes and books to the latest video games they wanted, and even gift cards to the ice cream place they love.

I remember what it was like to be a kid like that, and when I catch my brother's eye, I know he's remembering it, too. Back when life was simple, nothing bad happened, and our biggest worry was making sure we didn't get grounded, so we could still go to our friend's house.

After all the kids' gifts are opened, they run to their room's to start playing, and the adults get ready and presentable for company.

As I am just getting out of the shower, I hear my grandma yelling, "Looks like a herd of hyenas got to your gifts!"

"Grandma!" Tthe kids yell running to her.

By the time I make it to the living room, she has the kids cleaning up the mess, and David and Jill are in the kitchen starting brunch.

We are just setting the table, when Luke and Gabbie show up, and the kids run to greet them, much the same way they did Grandma. Luke's eyes zero in on me and pull me like a tractor beam to him. The moment I'm in front of him, he pulls me in for a hug.

"You look beautiful." He whispers in my ear.

I'm not in anything fancy, just some jeans and a silk blouse.

We sit down, and over breakfast, the conversation flows, until Luke speaks up.

"So, I got a job. They are holding it for me, until after the first of the year, when my doctors think I will be released." He says, and my eyes shoot to him.

Almost like he can read my mind and can see the questions racing through it, he continues.

"It's on the base here, doing basically what I was doing in the military, but now as a civilian contractor. There will be no more deployments."

"Luke, that's wonderful!" I tell him, more relieved than I should be, because he's staying in the area, but it means he won't be near Gabbie.

Then, Gabbie says, "I put in for a transfer to change schools starting next year. So, I have one more semester, before I can move down here."

These two have to have a connection to my head today, and it's kind of creepy.

"Well, that means we will have another girl to hang with, right Brooke?" Jill says.

"Yep, and one more for wine nights," I say, smiling big.

"When she turns twenty-one." Luke narrows his eyes at me.

"Sure, sure," I joke with him, and he just smiles, and so does Gabbie.

"Okay, time to open gifts!" Jill says, and the adults move to the living room. My brother gets Jill the watch she had been hinting hard at for months. My grandma gets my brother and me our yearly gift card to go buy clothes.

My brother got me the most adorable scrubs with military logos on them. I might have a slight scrubs addiction, since I wear them all time.

Luke gives Gabbie the purse he bought her, and she squeals louder than the kids did.

"Luke! Are you serious? Oh, my Ggod., I can't believe you got me this bag. I've never had anything this nice! I swear I will take care of it." She' is already moving everything from her old purse to the new one.

I hand Luke his gift.

"Now, this is from all of us, and there' is no arguing, okay?" I tell him.

He gives me a skeptical look, before ripping open the wrapping paper and opening the box.

"I can't believe you guys." He pulls out the a brand new phone with a bunch of accessories my brother swore he needed.

"You need a reliable phone for work, and we might have gone overboard. But thanks to my brother, it's all stuff you will need," I tell him.

He sets the box down and pulls me in for a kiss that's a bit longer then what I'd have expected being in front of my family and all.

Then, he and my brother share a look that I can't read, before Luke stands and hands me my gift. It's a small box, and as I continue opening it, I see a velvet jewelry box just perfect for a ring.

My hands shake, as I open the box and find the most stunning princess cut diamond ring I've ever seen. When I look up at Luke, I find him down on one knee in front of me.

As I glance around the room, everyone is wearing smiles, and Jill is taking pictures.

"Eyes on me." Luke whispers, and my eyes snap back to him.

"I knew the moment I stepped into Oakside and saw you that you were someone special who I wanted to get to know. Those first few days after I was transferred to one of your rooms, I remember being so dumbfounded. I had no idea what to say to you, but I was just happy to have you in my space. But the more I got to know you, the harder I fell in love with you. It took me a bit to admit that to myself, but it's true. I' am head over heels in love with you. Now that everything is lining up for when I leave Oakside, there' is just one more piece of the puzzle to put together. I want to marry you and start our life together. I want to be your husband and for you to be my wife. Will you marry me?"

My eyes dart to my brother, who is wearing a huge smile, and he nods slightly. Looking at my grandma, she wears a matching grin and nods as well. My eyes land back on Luke, and his eyes never left mine.

"Yes," I say, and the whole room bursts into cheers.

"Does this mean you will be our uncle?" Clark asks.

"Sure, does, little man," David says.

"Yes, another man in the family! We were way too outnumbered." Clark says, as he runs off.

What a Christmas to remember.

EPILOGUE

LUKE

I can't believe today is my last day at Oakside. I'm walking out with a job, a fiancé, and an entirely new family, who has welcomed me with open arms.

Everything has fallen into place. As I sit in the dining room, waiting for the final paperwork, before I head out, Levi comes up to me.

Levi is a new transfer. He's lost part of his leg and is having to relearn some of the basic everyday things. One thing I said to Brooke, when I met him the first time is he's just too upbeat. Like he's trying to convince everyone else he's accepted everything and is okay.

She agreed with me, and said she's seen it as a coping mechanism, and he has to work through it.

"Hey, man., Yyou ready to bust out of here?" Hhe says.

"Yeah, my girl will be here to get me soon," I say.

Brooke has today off work. After I proposed on Christmas, I started looking for a place to live, but Brooke insisted I move in with her, since she already has a place. When Gabbie isn't in school, Brooke also insisted she stay with us. With most of her free time, she's been getting the place ready for us.

"Man, I hope to be in your shoes soon. I met the girl I'm going to marry." He says with a huge smile on his face, but a bit of worry in his eyes.

"Yeah, who is she?" I ask.

"A gGirl I went to school with. I ran into her again the other day. Damn, she got hotter. How is that possible?" He shakes his head. "Shoot, I got a PT appointment, and I'm gonna be late. If I don't see you, before you leave, you take care."

"You too," I tell him, as he heads off in his wheelchair.

This place has started to feel like home, and I'm thankful Gabbie insisted I transfer here, instead of staying in the hospital. I need to remember to thank her for that.

I don't want to think about how different my life could have been.

Read more about Brooke and Oakside in the **Oakside Military Heroes series by Kaci Rose.** Lexi and Noah's story starts off the series in *Saving Noah*.

ABOUT KACI ROSE

Kaci runs on coffee, chocolate, and Oreos. She loves her book boyfriends with tattoos, muscles, beards, and a little dirty.

Kaci loves romance books and has been jotting down ideas since she was in high school and is now putting the ideas down on paper.

She believes in satisfying, happily ever afters with a lot of steam on the way.

She is known for her Cowboy series, **Rock Springs Texas** and her Military Romance series **Oakside Military Heroes.**

BOSH BELLS & EPIC FAILS

KRIS BUTLER

TO ALL THE MAGICAL CHRISTMASES WE'VE HAD, AND ALL THE ONES TO COME. MAY YOU NEVER STOP WISHING FOR CHRISTMAS MIRACLES.

PROLOGUE

Snow began falling softly outside the window as I watched, and I couldn't help but become excited. The first snowfall of the season was always something to celebrate. I'd been excited all day, the smell in the air, and I knew it would be soon. Everyone thought I was crazy when I announced it, but I could; I could smell the snow. Maybe it was the one weird gift I had, but it was mine, no matter how much other people tried to convince me otherwise.

Arms wrapped around me from behind, snuggling into my neck, and I rested back in his arms. "You were right. It's snowing." He chuckled, giving in to my amazing gift.

"Mmhmm."

"You can be smug about it. I clearly haven't learned to respect this weird gift of yours over the years. Though, I think I just like to give you a hard time. It's my favorite pastime."

"That you do!" I acknowledged, laughing. "I like it, though. It keeps me humble."

"How hard was it for you to say that?"

"So, hard!" I admitted, laughing even more. "I like to flaunt my wins so much. At least you're a good sport about it. I can't say that for everyone else."

"Well, that's because I'm obviously the more mature of the bunch."

Turning in his arms, I smiled up at him. "Oh, is that what it is? And here, I just thought it was because you liked having sex with me." A burst of air left him in a guffaw at my words, causing me to smile even wider.

"Well, there is that, but I thought that went without saying." He bent down to kiss me, and like every time our lips touched, I fell even more in love with him.

"Hey guys, sorry to interrupt, but this one is starving, and the others are clambering to open gifts." The interrupter held up a baby, tears streaming down her sweet face as she reached out to me, her little lip quivering. "Mama."

Heart-melting, I left the embrace of my husband and took my child. "Thanks, go ahead and start, and I'll be out after I finish feeding her."

The guys both turned, but my husband stopped, giving me a knowing look. "Don't fall asleep or get caught up in that journal of yours."

"Me? Never! I'll be down in a bit."

They both nodded, knowing smiles on their faces as I sat back in the rocking chair, the blonde beauty already sucking away at my breast. Smoothing her hair away, I thought of all the dreams I had for her, all the hopes and wishes for her future. Despite what my husband had warned against, I grabbed the notebook off the side table, the pen already on the last page I'd gotten to, reading over what I'd written earlier.

Once she had her fill, her little baby coos the soundtrack to my thoughts, I laid her down in the temporary crib we had set up at my parents. Laying across the bed, I started to write, telling her the story of how I fell in love. When I'd written for a while, I knew I had one more thing to say before I closed it, bargaining with time to close my eyes for just a few quick minutes.

My Dearest,

By now, I hope you can see how much we all love you, and I hope that whatever happens in your life, you too have love. I think there is magic at Christmas that doesn't exist at any other time, so I hope you embrace and love it as much as I do. And if for whatever reason I don't get to spend a million Christmas' with you, may you always have these. For what is Christmas without magic bells and epic fails?

Boring.

Merry Christmas, dearest one.

Love,

Your mother

CHAPTER ONE

SAWYER

DECEMBER 2020

Christmas music rang out through the store as I ran around the corner, hiding behind a large blow-up penguin. It hadn't been my brightest idea to start a game of hide-and-seek tag in the largest Christmas store known to man, but after two hours here, I'd gotten bored. Ollie and Soren had easily fallen into my trap and were playing with me. We'd all come with Rhett to the megastore a few towns over, thinking it would be fun to pick out Christmas decorations for the house. It was BOSH's first Christmas, after all.

None of us had understood the implications of that request.

Out of all the people who'd be a Christmas snob, I never expected it to be Rhett, our resident grumpy bear. Elias had given me an eyebrow raise when I suggested we'd all go, but he'd kept his mouth shut. I'd be paying that favor forward later when I teased him and then left him with some Christmas blue balls to match the decor.

Challenge accepted, Elias.

Rhett had a mile-long list, and everything had to be a specific brand, color, and aesthetic. It was cute for the first hour, but by hour two, I wanted to poke my eyes out with the candy-cane-shaped lights. Peeking around the massive Chilly Willy, I didn't hear the person who snuck up behind me, the motor of the blower covering their footsteps.

"Gotcha!" Ollie chuckled, grabbing me on the sides and hauling me up into his arms. Squealing, I didn't fight it and went easily as he spun us around. Throwing my arms around his neck, I smiled up at my ginger-bearded boyfriend. Ollie had the rugged hockey player look down, and right now, with his hair longer and his beard growing out, he was a delectable sight to behold. I'd added flannel shirts to my Christmas shopping list and had some plans to live out some lumberjack fantasies.

"Hey, boyfriend."

"Hey, pretty girl."

His smile was brilliant as he leaned down and kissed me. We might've gotten lost in our kiss as the sound of a throat clearing brought us back to the land of snowflakes and mistletoe.

"You guys are so busted."

Leaning against the shelving of every shaped wreath imaginable, stood Tyler. His golden-brown hair flopped against his forehead, his green eyes pierced me as he stared. I motioned with my finger, and he walked over, a sly smile on his face.

"Well, what do we have to do in order to avoid being in trouble?" I asked, batting my eyelashes.

"Oh, wildcat. I can think of so many things… but Rhett is up at the checkout, and he's waiting for you to bring the items you three hooligans said you were getting half an hour ago." He gave me a pointed look, clearly knowing we'd been up to no good and not gathering any items like we'd said.

"Oops."

"Yeah, oops. Luckily, I'm a good boyfriend, and I got it for you. So, let's go before Papa Elf gives us all workshop duty or something," he muttered, turning in the opposite direction. Ollie set me down, and we followed Ty together. When he started to shake his rear extravagantly in front of us, we both chuckled, appreciating the view.

"Now, that's some hot crossed buns!" Ollie whistled.

"Not again with the Christmas puns," I groaned, rolling my eyes. Ollie had been non-stop with his Christmas jeers.

"It's not even a Christmas one, babe," Tyler yelled over his shoulder, winking.

Ollie peered down to me with a raised brow, and I shrugged. "I don't know what they are," I whispered, and Ollie chuckled, not admitting if he knew or not. Doubtful.

Thankfully, he didn't make any further punny statements. As soon as it hit midnight on November 30, my world had become a tidal wave of red and green. I hadn't celebrated a real Christmas in years, and *never* to this extreme. Victoria had been festive, but even this was a level all of its own.

Rhett had lists upon lists, and within twenty-four hours our house had started to become a Winter Wonderland. He'd even gone and helped his mom with the B&B. It was a whole new side to him I never would've expected. It was cute, if not slightly annoying, when I didn't put the correct amount of ornaments in one section of the tree.

With the new additions in our lives, the Brotherhood of Sawyer's heart, or BOSH as we'd shortened it, Rhett had decided some new decor and trees were due to represent all of us. There were already four trees in the house, and now we were adding two more. As much as I griped about it though, it was beautiful inside and out, and it did feel like a magical Christmas world inside.

I told Rhett he should hire himself out to decorate for people, but he hadn't been interested. I guess he only liked doing it for places he had a connection to, his annoyance for people outside of our circle shining through.

We came around the corner and found Mateo and Rhett waiting for us. My sweet nerd smiled before heading down the checkout lane to grab a cart. His glasses concealed his eyes, his dark floppy hair falling across his forehead, but I could tell he was amused with me, chuckling softly as he went. The two with me handed off the items we'd gathered and escaped down the aisle with Mateo as well.

"Traitors!" I hissed.

They only laughed, not caring as they escaped to the safe zone.

Rhett stood waiting, his famous eyebrow raised, as I crept closer. I couldn't read his emotions from here, so I kept scooting along, dragging my feet a minuscule amount closer.

"Baby, why am I not surprised you were the one creating a ruckus?"

"Who, *me*? I'd never! You've got me mistaken."

He shook his head, a grin spreading on his face as I neared. The damn boy knew it was my weakness, and I sighed, finishing my trek to him. Rhett took the ribbon I held and dropped it and the other items on the conveyor belt. He kept staring at me, his eyes boring into me, ignoring everyone else.

The cashier scanned the items, slowly bagging them as she looked me over. I couldn't tell if she was annoyed I'd held up her lane or if it was because I was with all the guys. Either way, I didn't care. I'd had enough of girls giving me the stink eye to last a lifetime. Wrapping my arms around Rhett's waist, I clung to him like a barnacle. My arms barely reached around him, my fingers locked for maximum effect.

Rhett looked down at me while he paid and just patted me on the head. He scowled at the cashier as she tried to get his attention, and it only made me love him even more. He was a grumpy old man at times, but he was mine. They all were.

Once she handed him back his card and receipt, he went to shove it in his pocket but was stopped by my presence on his body. "Baby, I need to put this in my pocket."

"Use mine. I'm not moving."

Chuckling, he reached down, but instead of putting the items in my pocket like I asked, he lifted me by the ass, pulling me up in one motion. This man and his arm muscles, Lord have mercy!

Yipping, I gripped around his neck, wrapping my legs around his waist. "You know, grump, I probably look like your disobedient child like this." I twisted myself, so I was on his back instead of like a toddler on his hip. He grunted as I koala'd my way around but didn't stop me.

As we exited the store, a cider stand was near the door, and I eagerly pointed at the hot beverages. Rhett didn't say anything but walked over and handed her some money. He went to grab a cup, but she slapped his hand, and he pulled back in alarm. I was about to go off on the lady when she picked up a decorated cup with a lid and presented it to me.

"For the lady, may it bring all of your Christmas wishes." She bowed her head as I took it, and I looked at Rhett as I hung over his shoulder. He smirked at me, finally letting me down.

"Thanks."

She didn't say anything else but turned to wait on the next customer. The weird thing was she let them pick their cup. Rhett and I exchanged a look, but the cold had me shaking off the weirdness and jumping in the truck that pulled up. We'd borrowed one to get the trees because Rhett insisted these two be real ones. Oliver was in the driver's seat, looking sexy as fuck behind the wheel. Henry sat in the passenger seat, but climbed out and got in the back with me when he noticed Rhett. There was no way Rhett would fit back here with his 6'7" frame.

The rest of BOSH waswere in an SUV up ahead, idling at the front of the entrance waiting for us. Ollie took off as soon as we were all situated, and I laid my head against Henry as I sipped my drink. It tasted different than any cider I'd had before, but it was tasty, and I found it gone within a few minutes. Since we had a bit of a drive, I snuggled closer to Henry and closed my eyes, the guys' conversation lulling me to sleep.

"How long has she been sleeping?" I heard a voice ask in the distance.

"For about six hours. She slept through lunch and dinner. When I checked on her again to see if I could get her to eat something, I noticed her fever. Is she going to be okay?"

A wet cloth was placed on my forehead, and the coolness felt nice against my skin. I blinked my eyes open to find the guys, along with Rhonda, Rhett's mom, crowded around the bed. I tried to focus on them all, but it was hard, everything was fuzzy around the edges. Suddenly, a sharp pain in my abdomen had me sitting up with a gasp. The person who'd been leaning over me barely had time to move out the way before I nailed them with my forehead.

"Ow," I cried out, clutching my stomach.

"Where does it hurt, Sawyer?"

"It's like a sharp pain," I gasped. "Fucking hell," I winced. "Sorry, Rhonda."

"It's fine, sweetie. Does anything else hurt?"

"No, but I really need to pee."

"Okay, I'll help you," she offered, reaching for my hand.

"Okay."

She had the guys clear out while she helped me to the bathroom, and the most excruciating pain imaginable pierced through me as I peed.

"Fuck, oh my God, that burns something fierce."

Breathing through the pain, I gingerly wiped and waddled to the sink. Bracing my hands on the counter, I took some deep breaths until I could fully stand and wash my hands. Wobbling to the door, I opened it and found Rhonda waiting for me.

"Any symptoms?"

"Um, yeah, it burns when I pee," I cringed.

She chuckled. "Rowan wanted to name our WiFi network that," she joked and then realized I wasn't in the mood to appreciate the hilariousness of that. "Well, sweetie, I think you have a UTI. Honestly, I try not to think about what you get up to with all of those boys, but yeah..."

It was at that moment I realized what she was implying, which meant, of course, I had to make it worse, code orange style and word vomit all over her, awkward Sawyer style. "I haven't even had a proper orgy! This is so unfair."

Realizing the words I'd just shouted at my boyfriend's mom, I groaned, covering my face. Thankfully, Rhonda was the coolest and only laughed. "Honey, more power to you if you can wrangle them all. Come on, we're gonna need to call in a prescription. Rest and relaxation are in order for the next few days until the worst of it passes."

Nodding, I shuffled to the bed. I was glad someone had called her. Isla and Sampson, my newfound biological parents, would've been way more embarrassing to have to discuss this with. Samson might've even tried to shoot one of the guys. It would be better to keep this on the down-low to save me ultimate humiliation from my parents.

Getting comfortable in the blanket and pillow masterpiece Soren had made while I'd been in the bathroom, I was surprised when there was a knock at the door. Looking up, I found the last person I expected to be there—Mr. Hawthorne. I glanced at him curiously, but he only nodded in greeting.

Mr. Hawthorne was in his forties, with blonde white hair, crystal blue eyes, and clean-shaven, he always took me by surprise. He was dressed in one of his typical expensive suits, looking out of place in my bedroom. As always though, his smile was kind and welcoming.

"Mr. Hawthorne, what can I do for you?"

"Please, Sawyer, call me Logan. I was wondering if I could have a moment of your time?"

"Um, now's not the best. I'm not feeling the greatest."

"Oh, of course. I'm sorry you're under the weather. Perhaps, I could just drop this off then, and we could talk more when you're feeling better?"

He raised a brown leather journal wrapped in twine and holly. "Um, sure." I didn't fear him anymore, but he was still a stranger to me for the most part. I knew he was important to my adoptive mom, so I wanted to give him the benefit of the doubt. He'd also inevitably saved us all, so there was that to consider. It was just awkward, when my vagina felt like it was on fire, trying to have a heart-to-heartheart to heart with the man.

"This was your mother's, or Victoria's. I thought you might like it. It's about some of her better moments here before everything became about taking down the Council. Isla and Samson are in it as well. I thought you'd be able to get to know a different side of her, and them. And well, perhaps, me too. I'd like to be in your life if you'd let me."

He seemed so sincere, I could hardly say no, even if the thought made me a little uncomfortable. "That's kind of you. Thank you. When I'm feeling better, maybe we could get some hot chocolate or something?"

"That'd be nice. You know, your mother always said cider and hot chocolate had magical qualities about them at Christmas. It would be nice to share some of that magic with you."

He handed me the journal before squeezing my shoulder, making his way out the door. I didn't have much time to open it before the guys returned, arms full of food and their own pillows and blankets. Rhonda returned and told me there would be some medication delivered soon and to rest up.

"You okay, bite-size?" Ollie asked as he snuggled up behind me. I grimaced slightly as I was moved, my abdomen still feeling painful.

"I'll survive. Though, I'm mad at all of you."

The seven of them turned, shocked expressions on their faces. "Why? What did we do, sweet pea?" Soren, my golden snowboarding Adonis asked, his handsome face creased in confusion.

"You all hypnotized me with your dicks, and now it burns when I pee," I cried.

Of course, they all found that hilarious, the fuckers. Huffing, I curled onto my side and ignored them as I opened the journal and began to read about the first woman I called mom, Victoria, while the sounds of "A Christmas Carol" played in the background on the TV. At some point, my head drooped, my eyes closed, and I fell asleep on top of the journal.

CHAPTER TWO

SAWYER

I was dreaming. I knew I was dreaming, but it didn't stop the dream from happening. No matter what I tried, I couldn't wake myself. Pinching my arm for the millionth time, I gave up when nothing happened. At least I wouldn't bruise in my dream, right?

Accepting I was in a dream state, I looked around the room I'd found myself in, wondering what in the hell was going on and how I found myself here. This seriously had to be a dream.

Why did I believe I was dreaming?

Well, I didn't usually wake up with a penis between my legs!

Okay, scratch that. I sometimes woke up with a penis between my legs, but it wasn't like *this*. Nope, not like this at all.

Looking down, I checked again, and sure enough, the foreign appendage was still there. Was this what happened when you had a UTI? I'd never read about this online before. Perhaps no one spoke about it because it was too weird to comprehend. There could be hundreds of girls out there walking around with a dick now, too afraid to say anything.

Or maybe it had been that cider? Now that I thought more about it, the whole exchange with the women had been weird. The way she'd slapped Rhett's hand and made sure I had a specific cup, it could only mean she'd doped me!

Unless this was all part of my high fever delusion? When I thought about it, I did feel flushed.

Feeling relieved at the notion it was all some weird delusional fever dream, I decided to accept the opportunity to be a guy for a time. Looking closer at the room I was in, I could guess it was a dorm, and my roommate was still fast asleep. I peeked over to see if I could recognize him, but it was too dark to tell.

The realization I was in a dorm room stood out to me. Why would I dream about being in a dorm room? I hadn't even been in the dorms on campus that I could recall. My feverish delusion had apparently been smoking crack. Perhaps I needed to venture out more than just around campus or read more books. Now, that was an idea! Mine and Soren's book club was my favorite type of book club, after all.

The alarm next to the bed of the boy I was peering at started to go off, and I jumped back just in time to avoid being smacked with his arm as he reached out and turned it off. I was impressed he only needed it to go off once, and then was *bam!* awake. He rolled over, catching me staring at him as I stood frozen to the spot. His white-blonde hair was tousled over his forehead, and his crystal-blue eyes regarded me with suspicion as he swung his legs over the edge of the bed.

"Chase, why are you standing over me?"

Stuttering, I managed to get some words out, "You can see me?"

The boy gave me a weird look, turning up his lips in a rye smile. "Of course I can see you. You're standing two feet in front of me. Did you hit your head or something? Coach will be pissed if you're off your game. Move. I'm grabbing the shower since you seem to be taking your time this morning."

"Coach?"

The boy stood, pushing around me, and walked to a dresser on the far side of the room to grab clothes. My question had him turning around, doubt in his gaze now as he assessed me. "Yeah, Coach. For the hockey team? Seriously, did you eat strawberries or something?"

I blinked. Man, I had weird dreams. I must be channeling Ollie and Ty with the hockey team. "Strawberries?" I mumbled, but the boy shook his head, his brow creased as he headed to the other door in the room.

Sitting down, I tried to pinch myself again, but still, nothing happened, and actually, it was beginning to hurt. Looking up, I jumped back in fright when a ghostly version of Aggie, my mothers' mentor and tea-loving friend, appeared.

"Aggie! What are you doing here? What's going on?"

"Oh, sorry, dear, running a bit late. I never do seem to make it on time to these things. Nevertheless, you're here, and I'm here, might as well get on with it."

"And where exactly is here?"

"The past, of course!" She exclaimed as if that cleared it up.

"The past… who's past exactly?"

"Ah, well, *that* I'm afraid I can't tell you. Rules and all." She shrugged her ghostly shoulders, and I wanted to shake them. "But," she hedged, and I gritted my teeth in annoyance. I didn't find this side of Aggie fun, at all. Bring me back the grandmotherly version any day. "I am allowed to tell you that you have a day to figure out what you're supposed to learn from this."

"Wonderful, and here I thought waking up with a penis was the weirdest thing that would happen to me today."

"I did think that was rather genius of me." She giggled, and I wondered if she'd been spending too much time with me. "Enjoy!" Aggie gave a finger wave and poofed out of the room.

Yep! I've clearly lost it. Sighing, I braced my head in my hands as I contemplated the craziness of my delusion. Penis growing, Aggie poofing—Holy facial hair, batman!

Feeling my face, I stood to take in the man beard I had in the small mirror on the wardrobe door. Considering I was a teenager, it was pretty impressive. The door opened causing steam to roll out and my mysterious roommate returned. Of course, he found me fondling myself in the mirror and rolled his eyes at me.

"You're so obsessed with that beard, man."

"What's not to like?" I chuffed, wanting to stand up for whoever I was.

"It's scratchy and makes you look old."

"Well, maybe I like it."

"Whatever, man. You better get a move on it."

He'd been dressing as we spoke, and I realized when he finished, he was fully dressed now. Jumping, I opened the wardrobe fully and pulled out a uniform. At least it made it easy. Except as I hopped down the hall chasing him, putting on my shoe to try and catch up, I found myself cursing the invention of ties. Who thought teenagers knew how to tie a tie! What was wrong with these people?

Righting myself once I had my shoe on, I dug around in the bag to see if I could find a phone, anything to give me a clue to who I was and what past I was stuck in. I should've looked in the room more, but my roommate extraordinaire hadn't waited, and I didn't want to be clueless about who I was and lost. I could only deal with so many unknowns before I gave up and I didn't want to be stuck here, or as a boy, in case this wasn't a dream.

"Dude, wait up!" My roommate scoffed at me but stopped, waiting as I turned the corner, chasing him half-dressed.

"Chase, fix your clothes before you get a demerit! Honestly! It's like you woke up a different person or something!" He huffed at me but grabbed my clothes and began to fix them as he straightened my shirt collar. It was then I saw his bag with the name tag on the side.

Logan Hawthorne.

Holy shit! I had gone back in time. What year did that make it then? I blinked, the time not coming to me as I tried to recall. Maybe I wasn't supposed to know, a time travel precaution so you didn't screw up timelines or something. Though, I wasn't me, so how much could I screw up? Actually scratch that. I was me, just not in my body. I could screw up a whole lot.

Logan straightened my tie and turned to walk the other way, and I had to jog to catch up again. More kids filtered in around us as we neared a building, and I looked to see if I recognized anyone. Not that I would, but it was one of those habitual things you seemed to do when faced with a crowd—look for a familiar face, so you didn't feel alone. Or at least it was something I did.

I was surprised when I actually found one.

Victoria—my adoptive mother.

I stopped in my tracks when she approached, but her eyes were only for Logan. Swallowing, I tried to think of something extraordinary to say to my mother. I hadn't seen her in over five years, and there had been countless times I'd wanted to tell her something. But standing in front of her teenage self, they all seemed to evaporate.

"You okay there, Chase?"

I realized she was talking to me a moment later, and I nodded, not trusting my voice not to come out sounding like I would cry. She glanced at Logan, and he rolled his eyes, clearly fed up with my weirdness.

"I think he had some bad cheese or something." He placed his arm around her shoulders, drawing her into him. It was weird seeing my mom with someone who wasn't my adoptive dad, Scott. But she looked so happy, I couldn't fault her happiness, especially knowing how their story ended.

They began to walk toward the double doors I assumed led to a cafeteria, and for some reason, it struck me that we were at what now was The Aldridge School. Everything looked familiar but not exactly the same. Updates and renovations had occurred from whenever this was to current.

Shit, I wondered if there was an underground site here already?

Someone bumped into me, pushing me along, and I dropped the thought as I caught up to Logan and Victoria. I smiled at her, trying to keep it cool. I didn't want to weird her out since I was currently in the body of a teenage boy. I followed through the food line, grabbing some cereal and milk, not sure I could eat with this much occurring at once. My mind swirled all around as I tried to gather all the information I could.

It had to be the reason I hadn't considered until we got to the table that I'd be smacked in the face with my biological parents as well.

Samson and Isla were already seated at the table and were… kissing. I stopped midway to my chair, my jaw opening as I took in the scene in front of me.

"You okay there, dude?" Logan nudged me, and I closed my mouth, nodding. I couldn't quit staring at them though. So, when they pulled apart, Samson found me watching and raised an eyebrow in such a similar move to Rhett that I almost choked.

It also brought the realization the guys weren't with me, and I sobered, focusing on my breakfast. I tried to eavesdrop as I crunched my cereal, intent on learning what I needed to so I could return back to my time and the men I loved. It seemed there was a Christmas party tonight and a gift exchange. I hoped whoever I traded bodies with had been a planner and already bought a gift. No way could I manage to do that for someone I didn't even know.

Everyone started to gather up their stuff and get up, so I rushed to swallow the last of my food, downing my juice. I didn't know if I'd get another chance, and maybe if I drank something different, it would reverse whatever voodoo spell that lady had placed on me in case that was the cause. An elbow nudged me and I found myself staring at Victoria.

"Oh, um, hi." Why were my cheeks reddening? I wanted to push my hair back, the nervous energy needing an outlet, but the short tresses I had as a boy didn't really lend to the fidgeting action. The realization my mother might think I was flirting with her, had me sobering, and I cleared my throat, standing tall.

That was when the fact I was tall, like really, really tall, sunk in. At this height, I had to look down at her, her head coming to only my upper chest, and I found her smiling kindly at me.

"I know you have practice now," she started, and I inwardly began to freak out at the thought. "But I was hoping afterward, we could go into town and you could help me pick out the hockey thing I'm getting Logan."

"Oh, yeah, sure. Um, I'll text you?"

Victoria tilted her head, her nose scrunched up in confusion. "Text?"

Shit! This was the 90's or something. "Oh, ha! Just kidding, who has minutes, am I right?" I spluttered as I tried to remember what form of communication they used back then. Every movie I'd ever seen that took place in the late '90s began to scan across my brain. They definitely had cell phones in Clueless, maybe no one used them here. Wait, what was that messaging thing they used? AWOL? No, that was something else.

"You're so funny, Chase. Just call my dorm phone or send me a message on AIM if I'm online. Just don't tell Logan, it's a surprise."

Nodding, I waved as she left, stunned and feeling like the biggest idiot. If I didn't figure out how to get back to my time, I would never survive in the '90s. Nope, it wouldn't work at all. I was a product of my generation and I needed my technology. The thought of not having Netflix had my whole body trembling.

Glimpsing around, I noticed everyone was gone, and I cursed. I needed to find my way to the hockey rink if I did have practice. In no way did I want to screw this guy's life up just because he'd been unfortunate enough to have me steal his life. Shitballs, I hope he wasn't in my body!

Cringing at that though, I headed out of the cafeteria. Two seconds later, I shrieked, jumping back when Aggie appeared directly in front of me in all of her ghostly fashion. "Oh my God, woman! You're going to actually kill me if you don't start announcing yourself!"

"Oops, sorry, dear. I'm still getting the hang of it. Have you figured out what you need to do yet?"

"Seriously? It's been like an hour since I last saw you!"

"And?"

"Ugh, no. I haven't. I'm late for practice and I don't know where that is, and then I have to go shopping with my future adoptive mom, who probably thinks I have a crush on her because I can't stop blushing or losing my words. Why was I sent back here? Can't you just help me out?"

"Sorry, dear. It doesn't work that way. You've gotta figure it out for you."

"Ugh, fine. Is there anything you can do?"

"Oh, I know!" She snapped her fingers and I was immediately transported to the hockey locker room. For the first time in my life, I didn't want to be. Naked dudes, upon naked dudes, surrounded me, and I stumbled my way to a spot near the wall that was free so I could shut my eyes and avoid all the juvenile peen.

"Chase! Come on. What is with you today?" Logan yelled out, slapping me on the back as he stalked off.

"I'm coming," I grumbled, throwing my bag onto the bench. Thankfully, I knew how to put on all the hockey gear, having played with Ty several times in high school. As long as I wasn't the goalie, I'd be fine. Pucks flying at my head wasn't a situation I wanted to be in regardless if I was 6 ft something. Once the room cleared out, I looked around and found a locker with the name Chase O'Daniel on it. Lacing up the black skates, I finished up and wobbled out the door, one of the last people left inside.

A whistle blew as I stepped onto the ice, and it immediately made me miss Ty and Ollie. The memory of Oliver taking me to the rink to show off flashed through my mind, and how it ended with me kissing Tyler made me smile. That had been a good day.

"Boy, what's got you smiling?" An older man bellowed, and I sobered, realizing he was talking to me.

He gave me a perplexed look when I didn't move, so I scurried, getting in line with the others, and began to run through the drills with everyone else. Amazingly, my natural balance from figure skating over the years lent to me not falling on my ass. Not to mention, hockey was so much easier at this height! Moves I usually struggled with, I found I could do easily now, my long arms and leg strength adding to the effortlessness of each movement.

Somehow, I managed to survive the practice, resulting in a dripping, sweaty mess a few hours later. I followed the horde back to the locker room and remembered to shut my eyes this time to avoid the free dong smorgasbord I was about to walk into.

Gathering my stuff, Logan gave me another weird look, his hands on his hips as he stared at me, his blue eyes observing me closely. However, there was no way I would be showering with that many teen boys. Nope! Gonna have to pass on that experience. Logan kept looking at me, waiting for a response.

"I, uh, got a thing. I'll, um, see you later."

He nodded slowly, his face scrunched up in thought as I practically ran out of the locker room, my head in my bundle of clothes as I made my way out. Once I hit the outside air, I slowed, relieved to be out of the stinky boy fest. Unfortunately, a few seconds later, Logan caught up to me, a question on his lips.

"What's going on with you? You're acting weird."

"What? Me? Nah, I'm cool."

"Uh-huh. What's up?"

"Nothing! I swear. I just didn't feel like being around that many dicks! Okay?"

"Are you homophobic or something, Chase?" He stepped back, his face changing to disgust at the thought, and I filed that away. It sSeemed Logan was all for love, even as a teen.

"What? No! Ugh, this is going in the wrong direction. I had some bad cheese last night or something, remember? And now I have tummy problems. So, you know, I gotta take a shit and I'm a nervous pooper. Happy?"

He stopped in his tracks and I took the advantage to stalk off, hiding my face as best I could without long hair. Seemed even when I was in a different body, I still had code orange moments, even if this was a size 12 foot in the mouth one.

Thirty minutes later, I'd showered alone, changed, and was now trying to figure out this archaic system of sending a message on AIM. Clicking on the AOL icon, I groaned when the icon wheel spun as it loaded, taking over ten minutes to open. Seriously, the patience of this generation. No wonder none of them had it now when it came to driving. They'd spent it all as teenagers waiting for dial-up internet and pages to load.

When it finally came online, I searched through the contacts, but of course, no one had an easily identifiable username. After flicking through *bootysmak, hockeylover009,* and *iceskatersarebetter,* I gave up, deciding to take my chances at the girl's dorm instead. Thankfully, the dorms were in the same place as they were now, and I found it easily. However, I kept forgetting I was no longer a girl, but a boy now. The dorm mom at the front desk kindly reminded me.

"Excuse me, young man! Boys are not permitted on the upper floors!"

I stopped, face flaming at my blunder. "Sorry ma'am, um, I'm here to see Victoria." I left it at that because I couldn't remember if she went under her real last name here or if she had a different one, her name changing over the years almost as impressive as mine had been.

"Hmph," she snorted, but nodded, pointing to a waiting area.

I waved thanks, and took a seat, wiping my sweaty hands down the legs of my jeans. Geez, boys sweated a *lot*. I could already feel it building under my armpits, and I'd reeked after that two-hour practice. Why did I think it smelled so good on my guys? Must be a pheromone thing, because I did not find myself smelling seductive and masculine at the moment.

"Chase!"

I stood as Victoria descended the stairs, shuffling my feet as I waited, again not knowing how to interact with her. I'd spent fifteen years of my life with the woman, but at the moment, she felt like a stranger. We walked in silence for a few minutes and I thought about all the things I'd wanted to ask my mom, but hadn't gotten the chance to after the night my world had changed. But now that I stood here with her in my presence, none of it seemed important anymore.

"So, um, Logan, you seem to like him, huh?"

Victoria looked up at me, probably curious as to why I asked but nodded. "Yeah, I do. He's much better than his cousin."

Her whole body did a shiver and it hit me that Alek was here as well. I whipped around, afraid he would be directly behind me, wanting to kidnap me. Of course, he wasn't there, but the dreadful feeling his name dredged up stayed, and an even bigger sense of urgency to return to my timeline hit me. I didn't want to be in a place where he existed.

"You don't like him either?"

"No!" I shouted, then immediately cleared my throat, toning it down. "No."

"That's smart of you. Most of the other boys hang on to all of his words acting like he's a fucking king, especially, Robert." She rolled her eyes, and I so badly wanted to tell her everything that would transpire. But I didn't. I couldn't risk screwing anything up and not being where I was twenty-odd years later, lying in a bed surrounded by men who loved me.

As much as I wished Victoria could escape what life had in store for her, I knew I couldn't sacrifice everything else for it. The mother I'd known wouldn't want me to do that either. She'd sacrificed her life for mine, after all.

We arrived at the store in town a few minutes later, and she led me over to the wall of sticks she was considering. The problem now I realized was I had no knowledge of hockey sticks. Looking at them all against the wall, I started to panic when I couldn't tell the difference between the red one or the black one outside of color.

"Um, you know what. Hockey sticks are lame and impersonal. You should get him..." I nervously scanned the store, hoping something would stick out to me. Out of the corner of my eye, I saw something shiny at the front. Walking over to it, I found myself drawn there like a magpie, that or the ghost of Aggie jumping up and down pointing to it led me there. You take your pick.

"How about one of these with his jersey number on it?' I picked up the dual crossing hockey sticks keychain and held it out to her. She looked at it, and smiled, nodding.

"Yeah, you're right. This would be much better. Thanks, Chase." She hugged me briefly, then headed to the engraving station to personalize it. I'd wanted to hold on for longer when she'd wrapped her arms around me, but figured it would've been weird. Instead, I tried to remember how she smelled and felt to lock away in my vault of memories for my mom.

She returned a few minutes later, a huge grin on her face as she carried the small gift bag. "Come on, coffee's on me."

We walked out of the store together, and around the corner to the coffee shop, and I almost tripped when I saw which place it was—the coffee shop I'd met my friend Ace at.

The door jingled when we entered, the sound eerily familiar. It looked similar to how it did now, not much had changed in the years. The espresso machine looked dated, or I guess, it wasn't for the current time period.

"What are you thinking?" she asked, peering out the corner of her eye.

"I know you said coffee, but I'm kind of feeling tea. It's something I used to do with my mom." My voice dropped, becoming soft at the end, and I tilted my head away so she wouldn't see the tears that were wanting to spring to life. I couldn't cry here.

"Oh, that sounds perfect. I love a good pot of tea."

Relieved, I smiled and nodded. She ordered one she liked, and we took it over to a table, sitting down and arranging our dishes. It felt nice, even if I was a boy, to do this.

"You said you do this with your mother?"

"Yeah, we would have heart to hearts and tea. It was nice. She died a few years ago, though. So, it's been a while." I shrugged, concentrating on fixing my tea, knowing if I looked at her then, I would sob my eyes out.

"Oh, I'm so sorry Chase, that's awful. But wait, I thought your mom visited last month for the alumni thing?"

She asked, and my head snapped up in panic. "I mean my grandmother. She was like a mom to me."

"Oh, that's cool. I'm not that close to my grandmother, and my mother died when I was eight. My family hasn't always been the best of people, though. My dad, he's very strict and hard to please. I came to this school to be my own person, but he's wanting to pull me back again. Just when I think I can make different choices for myself, I find myself falling back into old habits."

I nodded, understanding what she meant. "I've felt that way before. Once, I was in a new place, and I felt like I couldn't trust anyone. Life was really lonely during that time, but I survived. Then I came here, and there were all these amazing new people and I had to decide if I wanted to trust them or keep living a life where I was only half living."

"How do you get past the fear?"

"I don't think you do. Life is always scary. I think the more important thing is who you have in it to help you through it. I know my life is fuller now because of them."

"You're very insightful, Chase. I'm glad I got this chance to get to know you better."

"Yeah, you too. And listen, if I act differently after this, it's just because it's hard to be vulnerable."

"Oh, sure."

I relaxed at her acceptance, not wanting to set Chase up for failure. We drank the rest of our tea in silence for a while. I wasn't sure why Victoria had fallen silent, and I was kicking myself for being so different from the real Chase and potentially making it awkward for him. When nothing but leaves remained in our tea cups, we grabbed our coats and started to walk back toward campus.

"I think I'm going to do it," she said eventually. "You've given me the courage to pave my own way, and I'm going to take it."

"Wow, that's awesome. I'm glad I could be helpful."

"You really were. I'm glad we did this. I feel like we're better friends now. I'm happy I got to before we all left school."

"Me too, me too."

Something in my chest tingled at the feeling, the sound of bells ringing in the air, and I wondered what the sensation meant. I didn't get the chance to explore since the next second I spotted Aggie, and she winked before snapping her fingers. I prayed I'd learned what I needed to send me back to my body and timeline. But most importantly, to my BOSH boys.

CHAPTER THREE

SAWYER

This time when she transported me, it was thankfully back to my own body and bed. Gasping, I sat up with a start, relief washing through me at the familiar bedding and surroundings. A shadow moved in the corner, and I swiveled, the momentum causing me to almost fall out of bed. Thankfully, an arm wrapped around me, pulling me back down to safety.

"Babe? You feeling better?" A sleepy Soren mumbled, cracking his eyes open at me. I was so excited to see him, I bent down, kissing him passionately for a minute. He took my kiss as my answer and rolled me under him.

"I'm gonna take that as a yes," he confirmed when he pulled away. His eyes lit up, his blonde hair falling down around his face as he stared down at me in delight. I tucked the hair back behind his ears, the tresses touching his shoulders now.

"I like your hair this length. Gives me something to grab onto."

He raised his eyebrow, his pupils dilating at the thought, and he thrust his lower half into me. "Is that so?"

Soren bent down to nibble my neck when the pain returned, and I grimaced. "Ow, ow, ow."

He moved off me at lightning speed, and I rolled into a ball, clutching my stomach. "Shit, this pain makes me almost not want to have sex ever again. Ugh, I have to pee, and if it hurts again, I'm cursing you all!"

Soren only chuckled, not taking my threat seriously before he scooped me up and carried me to the bathroom. "Thanks, but there's no way you're staying in here."

"No worries, sweet pea. Golden showers aren't my thing. Yell if you need anything, though. I'm sorry you're going through this. I'll get you some water and meds for when you're out."

Nodding, I gave him a brief grimace before the door closed. Bracing for the pain, I gritted my teeth as I emptied my bladder. It wasn't as painful as the first time, but it wasn't a walk in the park either. Washing my hands, I was relieved when I found my green eyes, blonde hair, and no facial hair staring back at me. I'd assumed I'd returned to myself when Soren hadn't freaked out when he was making out with a 6ft bearded guy, but then again, he was pansexual, so he loved me for who I was as a person and not my gender. That was comforting, actually.

Still, it was nice to have my body back, short stature and all. "It'd been nice being 6ft tall, Chase. Hope I didn't screw anything up for you."

With that, I exited and found a lot more people in my room than when I'd left it. "You're all courageous to show your faces after I just had to breathe through peeing," I pouted.

"Love, we feel awful, so we're here to cheer you up. A whole day where you can decide what you want to do. If you're feeling up to it." Elias looked at me, the challenge thinly threaded through his words, the familiar fire burning inside, and not in my vagina this time.

"Hmm, I might be up for it. My fever appears to be gone, though it made me have the craziest dream. You guys won't believe it."

"I once dreamt I had tiny hands like a T-rex," Ollie stated, demonstrating as he tried to grope his boyfriend, Ty, making us all chuckle.

"Well, I don't know what it means," I admitted, walking over and sitting on the bed, "but mine was weirder."

"How so? I'm impressed you remember it too," Henry asked.

I turned to him, and he pulled me closer. "I woke up in a boy's body and back in time. I got to meet my biological parents and Victoria as teenagers. I'm guessing the combination of reading her journal and watching old Christmas movies." I shrugged, not wanting to admit I didn't think it was only just a dream. It had felt so real. But, even if it was all a fever-induced delusion, it was nice to see my mom again.

"Wow, that's pretty out there," one of them said, but I snuggled into Henry, not caring. I fell asleep again with the hope I wouldn't wake up in a different person's body.

Thankfully, when I woke up later, I was still me. After another dose of antibiotics, I felt back to my usual self and took the guys up on doing something. I really wanted to go to the ice castles, but they wouldn't be open until January, so we added it to our excursion list for next year.

Instead, I found myself staring at a 1,200 ft wide lane of snow, on top of a mountain, as people careened down it in colorful tubes. "This was a bad idea."

"You're not scared, are you, *Dulzura*?" Mateo pulled me closer to him, my sweet, nerdy boyfriend having stayed by my side.

"Um, maybe, a little."

"You'll do great. You've skied. This will be even easier."

"Yeah, you're right. It just seems so much faster."

"Yeah, but I think you'll love it. Come on, it's our turn."

He tugged on my hand, pulling me toward the front, our tubes dragging behind us. I watched as a few of the guys took off, heading down the slope. Swallowing my fear, I nodded, and we dropped our hands and grabbed the handles of our tubes.

"Belly?"

"Belly," I agreed. Smiling, I faced the front, and we counted together. "One, two, three." We took off, jogging a few feet before we launched ourselves into the air. A scream ripped from my lungs, the rush of the exhilaration filtering through me as we flew. With a thump, we landed close together, skidding a few feet as our momentum took us sliding through the snow.

Laughing, I turned my head to see Mateo. "Okay, this is awesome." He smiled, and I returned to paying attention to where I was headed, not wanting to run into anyone. That would so be my luck.

Rhett and Elias were waiting at the bottom, and I heard the other four behind me. Rhett bent down when I stopped, scooping me up. I would never get over him doing that. "You have fun, baby?"

"I did! Let's go again."

"Smalls, we gotta do the two-person one, or all go in tandem!" Henry shouted as he and Soren came to a stop. Ollie and Ty were behind them a few seconds later, and we all headed to the lifts together. We spent the next few hours taking turns, trading off who went down the slope. By the time we left, we were all smiles and worn out.

Ty held my hand as we waited for Rhett to pull the car up. It was dark now, the sun having set off in the distance. The mountain was lit up with lights allowing tubers to continue to sled.

"Today was a lot of fun, wildcat."

Tilting my head up, I smiled wide as I agreed. He bent down, kissing my nose, and I couldn't help the blush that rose to my cheeks. Ty was so sweet at times, and he made me feel all the butterflies. Arms wrapped around from behind me, encasing us both, and I looked up to see Ollie.

"Hey boyfriend," I cooed, loving how much Ollie had changed since he'd told us about his family.

"Hey girlfriend, hey boyfriend," he sang back. He reached over my head, kissing Ty before looking back at me. For a second, I'd been completely enclosed in their arms, like a Ty & Ollie igloo and it was nice.

"So, I was thinking," Ollie started, and Ty and I groaned. "Hey! Not all my ideas are bad." Ollie attempted to pout, but he couldn't pull it off. Mainly because he couldn't stop his own laugh from bubbling up. "Anyway," he continued, ignoring us, "we should have a party at the house. But make it like a Christmas extravaganza. We'll have a bunch of contests. Cookie baking, gingerbread house making, snowman creating, Christmas charades, ornament decorating, and oh, we'll end it with a Secret Santa party!"

I looked at Ty, and he had the same look of disbelief as I did on my face. "What's the catch, because all that sounds fun?"

Ollie looked down at me, a twinkle in his eyes, and I knew this was where the twist would be. I didn't think Ollie could do anything without making it into something extreme. "Ye of little faith, Sawyer." His grin did not go away, though, and instead, it spread wider, and I wondered what the hell he was up to. If I knew Oliver Windsor as well as I thought I did, he'd wait until we were all gathered and agreeing to it before he dropped the bomb on us. I guess he'd learned that trick from his family and the training through the Council. Hopefully, he would use it for good and not to embarrass me, one of his favorite pastimes. I did that well enough on my own.

It had been a whole week since the body switch and UTI fiasco. I was officially through all my antibiotics, and it no longer burned when I peed, thankfully. As much as I said I wasn't ever going anywhere near their dicks again, the week of no sex was getting to me. At first, the guys were respectful and kept their distance. But once I'd been back to basic working order, their touch hazing began.

And it was hazing, no matter how they tried to spin it.

They were all slowly driving me mad with the torture. It had been almost a full week of nothing but edging! In the beginning, I hadn't noticed. Their casual grazes seemed innocent and nothing out of the ordinary. But by mid-week, they'd dropped all pretense and were straight out revving me up and then backing away. Each and every single one of them, even my sweet Mateo.

"You've been corrupted, Mateo," I panted as he casually passed his hand over my center as he nonchalantly took some popcorn from the bowl. Which was nowhere near my vagina, mind you.

"*Oh*? Whatever do you mean, *Dulzura*?"

"Don't you dare *'Dulzura'* me! What's going on? Either you've all gone crazy from no sex for a week, or there's something to be won by edging me this hard. Though, I wouldn't put it past Ollie or Soren whispering in your ear either."

His hand stopped midway to his mouth, and he glanced at me, gulping. "Uh, Wh-aa-tt?"

"Ha! I knew it!" I jumped up and straddled him, knocking the popcorn to the floor, not caring if it scattered everywhere. "Two can play this game, babe. So, what's it going to be? Are you going to tell me, or will I have to torture it out of you?"

"I don't know what you're talking about," he hedged, but I saw the way his Adam's apple bobbed as he swallowed, along with his cock hardening beneath me. Leaning down, I nipped his ear before whispering into it.

"You really want to play this game, *Teo*?" I rocked into him, and his breath caught on a gasp in his throat. His hands planted firmly on my hips, and he didn't stop me as I rocked again before pulling back. I'd started to call him Teo in moments when we were alone, and I found he liked it, his dick thickening even more as I pressed into it.

Heat seared me from his eyes, his glasses a little skewed from the movement. Slowly, I began to lift my shirt over my head, my breasts on display right in front of him, and he groaned. Taking his hands from my hips, I placed them on the mounds, encouraging him to explore. Mateo had come a long way in the time we'd been together, but sometimes he was still shy until we were in the heat of the moment.

"Sawyer, you're the most beautiful woman I've ever seen. Some days, I pinch myself to make sure I'm not dreaming, but there's no way my imagination is this creative."

He leaned forward, his breath skirting my skin, and my nipple pebbled at the sensation. I ran my fingers through his hair, loving how curly it was becoming. All of my guys had the best hair, and I wouldn't admit I was half jealous of it. The silky strands fell through my fingers, and I pressed the tips of them into his scalp, alternating pressure. Mateo groaned, the vibration echoing around my breast in the process, and I rocked forward, needing some friction.

"You ready to tell me?" I knew I wasn't being fair as my hand skirted down his chest, but they'd been touching me all week and then leaving me hanging. I'd use my womanly wiles if it got me both the D and information. When my hand grazed his jeans, I rubbed the length of him, and his breath hitched more. In his excitement, he bit my nipple, and I was the one moaning this time.

"Oh, God."

The need in me rose to a new level, and I no longer cared about information. I just needed him in me. Slipping my hand down his pants, I found his cock ready, and began to stroke. He was hard as steel, his head falling back as I stroked him. Unzipping his pants, I freed him, giving his dick a few good strokes.

"*Dulzura*," he moaned, his fingers tightening on my hips where they'd returned to.

Lifting up on my knees, I pushed my sleep shorts over and lowered myself on him. When he felt me start to slide down, his head snapped up, hunger in his eyes. Mateo's fingers tightened on my hips, and he pulled me the rest of the way down. Together, we moaned at the connection, both needing it. Kissing him, I mussed his hair as my arms tangled around his head, pulling us closer, knocking his glasses off in the process.

Mateo took over, thrusting up as we worked together to climax, our breaths panting out between kisses. When he bent down to kiss my neck, I opened my eyes and found a grinning Soren to the side of the couch. Feeling extra needy, I beckoned him to me as Mateo used my ass to direct me. He'd at least gotten comfortable around a few of the guys by this point, Soren and Henry being the ones he felt the closest to, so I didn't think he'd care if he joined in. Leaning forward, I whispered in his ear, making sure it was okay.

"Soren's here. Care if he joins?"

He lifted his head slightly, looking over my shoulder, shaking his head no. Soren took it as the all-clear and began to strip as he moved closer. An idea sprung to my mind, and I wondered if Mateo would be game.

"Teo, feel like checking off another thing on your sex bucket list?"

He smiled, trusting me to guide him. "If it's with you, I'm always willing."

This sweet boy, he killed me sometimes with how pure he could be. Cupping his face, I spread my thumb over his cheek, just enjoying the moment between us for a second. His eyes closed at the touch, his lashes fluttering against his cheeks. He had the most beautiful long lashes. Kissing his nose, I slowly slipped off him and discarded my clothes entirely.

Soren's hand fell to my hips, his cock jutting between my ass, the piercing rubbing me there. Instinctively, I arched my back at the feel of him. Pulling his head down, I wrapped my arm around the back of his neck so I could whisper into his ear. "Let's help Mateo pop his anal cherry... with *me*."

Soren lifted his head, a smile on his face at the idea. He kissed my shoulder and pulled away to hopefully grab some lube. Mateo had chucked his jeans and shirt, his lean body on display as he watched me walk toward him. He had a way of making you feel like every time was the first time and that he would never get enough. It was addictive and something I hoped he never lost.

Reaching out a hand, I pulled him to his feet, our naked bodies touching as he came closer. "I think it's time you claim the last hole." His eyes grew big, but he nodded, a smile forming.

Soren returned and picked me up, throwing me over his shoulder, surprising me at the swiftness. "Ah! Soren!"

"I got you, sweet pea." He tossed the bottle of lube to Mateo and laid down on the couch, pulling me with him. Snuggling in close, I kissed his neck, his golden skin a tempting sight. I knew Mateo had to be nervous, so I focused on Soren but lifted my ass up, so Mateo could reach me.

His hand shook at first, but when I didn't back away, he kept exploring, letting his fingers dip into my wetness, plunging his fingers deep while I made out with my golden sunshine boyfriend. Tentatively, he began to spread my hole, using my own juices to lubricate and prepare. I lost myself in kissing Soren, his cock piercing rubbing against my clit with each rocking forward. I heard Mateo's breath as he started to push forward, and I tried to stay still, giving him what he needed. I moaned out, the pressure finally beginning to satiate the need I've felt all week.

When he was seated, he groaned, his hands stilling on my hips. Lifting my head, I peeked over my shoulder, and I found him breathing heavily, his eyes closed. "You okay, Teo?"

"So good."

Giggling, I wasn't prepared for when Soren decided to slide into me from the front, his piercing rubbing me in all the best ways as he did. My giggle morphed into a moan, and I fell back to Soren's chest, letting them hold me up at this point. They began to move together, finding a rhythm, and it was everything I'd been needing. It didn't take me long, the orgasm having built to a precipice for a while, and I fell over the edge, bursting into a cacophony of tingles. When I opened my eyes, I was surprised to find Henry had joined us.

He winked at me, then bent down to kiss me, all the while thrusting his dick in Soren's mouth. Every time I saw those two together, I simultaneously melted and became aroused. I loved the love they held for one another, their connection genuine.

"I love you, Smalls," he whispered, pulling back from the kiss.

As the three of them worked, I found myself beginning to rise up again. The air smelled of sex, our bodies slapping together in the most delicious ways, our moment full of love and heat. I knew without a doubt I loved all three of them. Each time we were together, it wasn't just a carnal thing, but a declaration of our love for one another too.

I could tell they were close now, and when Mateo banded his arm around my midsection and pulled me closer to him, I knew he was about to cum. He kissed me quick, staring into my eyes as he thrust deep once and stalled. The hand on my hip tightened as he spilled inside of me, and I watched as he came undone.

Soren thrust up, hitting me in the best way, and I tipped over quickly, the feeling so exhilarating, it felt like I was falling. A minute later, Henry's groan followed, and our bodies stilled, nothing but the sound of our breaths in the room. When I opened my eyes, I realized I was on the floor. I looked around, the guys a mess of tangled limbs with me. They all laughed at my confused expression.

"I thought we were on the couch?"

"We were, Smalls. Somehow when you and Soren came, your body trembled so much from the orgasm that it tilted us over the edge.

"Huh, so I guess when it felt like I fell, I was really falling."

They burst out laughing with me, the moment too lighthearted not to. As our laughter died down, I heard someone coming closer to where we all were. None of us had the energy to move though, and we'd all seen each other naked, so we weren't concerned at the moment.

However, when a screech rang out, I knew the day had finally come. Finley had walked in on her brother post-sex.

"No, no, no! Shit balls! I did not need to see my brother's balls! I'm scarred for life. I need some brain bleach!"

"It could be worse, Fin," I started, sitting up. "He could've been balls deep in me." She lifted her hand a smidge to glare at me. Her eyes were squinted so hard, I didn't know how she even saw me.

"That is not funny, Sawyer Sullivan! Don't forget I can get you back. I'm dating your brother too, after all."

Cringing, I held up my hands, not wanting to picture that. We might have only known we were siblings for a few months, but no one wanted to see their twin's balls.

"How about we all get dressed and quit talking about balls," Henry grumbled, not keen on his sister talking about sex. She stuck her tongue out at him, even with her hands still covering her eyes. I hoped to get to their level one day with Asa.

"Speaking of balls," Soren started, and we all groaned. "What? I was going to suggest making some coconut ones." He cheesed, and I rolled my eyes, not buying it.

We all dressed and joined Finley in the kitchen, where she told us why she'd come over as we made coconut balls. Apparently, there was a rival party on the same night as ours, and she wanted to rally, making ours the best. Throughout the night, I never remembered to get Mateo to tell me what they were planning.

CHAPTER FOUR

SAWYER

The next time the crazy Freaky Friday thing occurred, I was walking through town with Elias. One minute I was enjoying my hot chocolate and holding his hand; the next, I was slipping on ice. My foot went up, my momentum sending me backward, but I never hit the ground. Instead, I landed on a bed. A very soft bed, in fact.

Feeling the sheets, they were silky, and the texture felt nice under my hands as my fingernails dragged across them. The realization I had nails, something I never had in real life, had me bringing my hand in front of my face. Except, I couldn't see. Or well, I could see, but it was blurry. Sitting up, I couldn't make out anything else in the room; it was all blobs and muted colors.

Glancing around, I found a nightstand close by, and I reached out, hoping to find some glasses, assuming I'd woken up in the body of someone who was practically blind. I really should've paid more attention to Mateo when he woke up because as I reached out to find the object, I knocked it off, sending it to the floor.

Fucking great.

Throwing my legs to the side of the bed, I tentatively placed my feet down on the ground, making sure I didn't step on them. When it was free of objects, I put the rest of my weight down and stood. Squatting, I started to feel around for the glasses, excited when my hand connected with them. Pulling them up, I placed them on my face, and the room finally came into focus.

It looked like a hotel room, and I wondered where I was this time. Standing, I looked for any signs of my whereabouts. There was a notepad on the floor next to the nightstand I'd knocked the glasses off. I picked it up and sighed in relief. I was still in Oak Crest Peak. In fact, I was at Rhett's mom's B&B. An awkward thought entered my head, and I rushed to the door in my room, hoping it was a bathroom. When I saw my reflection in the mirror, I relaxed. Phew! I hadn't woken up as my future mother-in-law or sister-in-law. That would've been hella awkward.

Instead, I was a woman with dark hair, average height and body, and wearing a pink silk pajama camisole and short set. The glasses I'd found sat crooked on my nose, and I straightened them, remembering the nails. Looking down at my hand, I took in the beautiful french manicure with a little diamond on the ring fingers.

The door opening from the other side had me turning in shock as a man, a very familiar and bare-chested man, entered. He was rubbing his eyes, so he hadn't seen me yet. He was only partially dressed with a pair of lounge pants on, but I was thankful he was at least wearing them. Thankfully, they weren't the grey sweatpants my guys wore that I drooled over. I'd be upset if *those* had been ruined for me.

"Mr. Hawthorne!" I screeched, covering my eyes. I heard him stop, and I peeked through my fingers, finding him gaping at me.

"Gwen, apologies, the door wasn't locked. Let me know when you're finished."

He spun, shutting the door behind him, and I found myself breathing a sigh of relief again. Well, at least some things had been cleared up for me. I was someone named Gwen and staying in a joint suite with Mr. Logan Hawthorne. Logan appeared to be the common denominator from my previous body-switching experience so far.

Using the bathroom quickly, I knocked on his door and then scurried out of mine, closing it behind me. I heard the other side open a few seconds later, and I stepped away, not wanting to eavesdrop while my pseudo-uncle relieved himself. In fact, I should get dressed and figure out what year I was in and see if I could manage to get Aggie to show.

Pulling open the wardrobe on the far wall, I found it full of fashionable dresses. Whoever Gwen was, she had style. Selecting a deep red sheath dress, I found a drawer of undergarments and hosiery. Screwing up my nose at the hose, I decided to brave it without. Seriously, those things were evil. Sorry, Gwen.

I ignored the idea I was wearing someone else's underoos because, actually, Gwen's body was the one wearing them, not mine, so it was only a mental thing. When I heard the shower turn off in the bathroom, I waited a few minutes until I heard his door open and close.

"No courtesy knock, huh, Logan?"

Popping my head in, I checked it was clear and made sure to lock the other door this time. Quickly, I got ready, styling my hair as best as I could and applying the makeup as professionally as I was able. Finley always helped me with this stuff, so without her here, I was lost. "Sorry, Gwen," I muttered again, cringing.

Unlocking the door on Logan's side, I hurried out of the bathroom again and exited the other door. I was brought out into a sitting room area and found Mr. Hawthorne sitting at a table, drinking a cup of coffee. I didn't know how to act; I wasn't sure who I was to him. As far as I knew, he was single, but again, I didn't know what year it was. I should've looked for a phone while I'd been in the room. I turned to go back and look when he called out, stopping me.

"Gwen, everything okay? You seem a little off this morning?"

Spinning, I gawked at him, not sure what to say. "I, um, just didn't sleep well. That's all. I'm gonna grab my phone." I pointed back toward my room, hoping what I'd said wasn't too out there like last time.

He raised his eyebrow at me, and I froze, scared I'd stepped in it again. "I mean," I started, backpedaling.

"It's over here, where I told you to leave it last night so you wouldn't work."

"Right, you did say that."

Walking toward it, I tried to hide my face, the heat rising to the surface at making a fool of myself in front of him, even if he didn't know it was really me. Every moment in this man's presence had been weird. I'd verbally assaulted him the first time I ever met him, the second he'd watched me almost shoot his cousin, and the third had been when I had a UTI. Between waking up as his roommate in the past, and his pseudo roommate whenever this was, I was beginning to suspect my assumption it was connected to him was true.

I spotted the familiar device on the console table, and I sighed in relief at recognizing the model. It had to be around the same time as my own. Unplugging it, I clicked on the calendar and relaxed when I found I was still in the year 2020. Okay, so same year, different body. Not as horrible to deal with.

Scrolling through the phone, I tried to figure out just who I was to the man. I started with pictures, but Gwen didn't have much in her albums besides photos of a fluffy white cat, shoes, and dresses. Next, I clicked on her messages, but they were mostly from Logan about work and people who appeared to be her family. Okay, so she must work with, or for Mr. Hawthorne.

The problem was, I had no clue what he did other than take down corrupt agencies. A knock on the door had me jumping, but I recovered and walked over to it. When I opened it, I had to restrain myself from hugging the woman standing there.

"Good morning, Ms. Norton. I wanted to check that you and Mr. Hawthorne had a good evening and if you needed anything else from me today?"

"Oh, it was wonderful, thank you."

"Excellent. Will there be any special meal requests or requirements this evening?"

"Um," I stuttered, turning my head, peering at Logan, who gazed at me, an odd expression on his face. "Any special requests?"

"You know all my preferences, Gwen. That's why you're my assistant."

"Right, yes, that." I nodded, pointing a finger in acknowledgment.

Glancing back at Rhonda, I tried to hide the grimace, and stepped out into the hall, pulling the door behind me. "I'll have to get back with you. I'm having a little bit of a memory issue this morning, and nothing is ringing a bell."

"Okay, dear. Just let me know."

She patted my hand, the familiar gesture making me calm even if she didn't know it was me. Tapping the phone in my hand, I wondered if Gwen took notes on things. I opened it up to search when a ghost of Charlie appeared directly in front of me.

"Oh, God!" I gasped, clutching my chest as I stepped back, hitting the wall. Rhonda stopped, looking back at me in concern, her face worried as her eyes creased.

"You okay, dear?"

"Yes, sorry, thought I saw a spider, but it was just a shadow," I said, awkwardly chuckling. "I'm good."

"Okay." She accepted my response, but walked off, giving me furtive glances as she did.

Once she was gone, I gave my former guardian the stink eye. "What do you think you're doing, old man?"

"Waiting until you were dressed and away from spectators, Sawdust. I didn't particularly want to walk in on you, you know." He waved his hand up and down, and I cringed at the thought, even if it wasn't really me.

"Yeah, okay. Good call. But what are you doing here? What's going on? I thought I was hallucinating when Aggie visited, but now you too? Am I secretly in a coma somewhere?"

"No, Sawdust, you're just experiencing reality from a different perspective."

"Thanks, that clears it up so much," I deadpanned, leveling him with a look that clearly stated I wasn't buying it. I started to ask a question when the door opened, and Logan looked at me strangely.

"Who are you talking to?" he asked, looking up and down the hallway.

"Oh, just taking some dictation notes." I waved the phone in front of his face, my smile a bit manic, but I was struggling to keep it together.

"Are you sure you're okay, Gwen? You're acting strangely."

"Totes, fine." I cringed as soon as the words left my mouth, but I owned it, walking back into the room. Wonderful. Charlie had given me no info on what I needed to do to get out of here, and I was stuck with a man that gave me hives. And this time, I wouldn't have either of my mothers here to distract me.

Sitting down at the table, I buttered a croissant and stuffed it in my mouth. Chewing, I turned to Logan, who had a piece of bread held halfway to his mouth, gaping at me.

"What?" I mumbled, then remembered I had food in it. Grabbing some coffee, I filled a cup and swallowed, turning to look at him again. "Something on my face?"

He cleared his throat, shutting his mouth as he shook his head. "No, sorry. It's just, I don't think I've ever seen you eat carbs before."

Looking at the croissant in my hand, I almost pouted at the thought of not getting to enjoy it. I didn't want to disrespect Gwen's body, but maybe she deserved a day where she got to eat a carb. Shrugging, I finished the croissant, enjoying every last bite. Logan cleared his throat, and I turned to him, hoping he'd give me some information on what in the world I was supposed to do here.

"Are you ready for our meeting?"

Swallowing, I nodded, wiping my hands on the napkin. "Yes, um, let me grab my things real quick."

He tilted his head slightly, the stoic man watching me closely, and I tried to get up from the table gracefully and walk back to the room without falling on my face. When I shut the door, I sighed back against it. Charlie needed to get his ghost butt in here and tell me what the fuck was going on.

"Charlie," I whispered. When he didn't appear, I hissed it, "*Charlie.*" Still nothing. Stomping my foot, I let the expletives rip. "Old man! Get your ass in here, pronto. I'm not naked, and I need your help. Aggie was such a better ghost friend than you! Is there a Ghost HR I can complain to?"

He finally popped up, right in front of my face, the turd! Jumping back, I knocked my head on the door. "Ow."

Charlie crossed his ghost arms smugly and dared me to say anything. "You *rang*?"

"Don't give me any of that crap, sir! Now, do your mojo thing and tell me what the heck I'm supposed to do! I can't ruin this woman's life."

He rolled his eyes but snapped his fingers, and I was transported to a conference room. Seriously! I was going to have to talk with him about his attitude. Thankfully, I didn't make any noise when I came to my awareness and peered around the room. I checked the phone in my hand and realized a few hours had passed. Logan was sitting at the long conference table, scribbling some notes down in a leather portfolio. He looked up and found me watching him.

"Gwen, did you hear me? My next appointment is here."

"Yes, sir, sorry."

Standing, I smoothed the dress material down and started for the door, hoping it would be obvious where I needed to go and grab this visitor. Thankfully, there were only a few other doors and an open area for a lobby when I exited. A man stood in a suit looking at the wall, so I hoped he was the one I was meant to get.

"Sir?"

He turned, and I almost tripped over myself when it was Elias. He looked so handsome in his attire. He smiled at me when I said his name and walked toward me.

"Gwen, so good to see you." He reached out to grab my hand, and I mistook it and hugged him. Awkwardly. He patted my back, but I found it hard to let him go. He cleared his throat, and I pulled back, my face flaming.

"Um, sorry. Christmas cheer and all that. This way," I blurted, spinning toward the door.

He tilted his head oddly at me but thankfully didn't comment. I berated myself to get it together as we made our way into the conference room. I'd been hopeful when I saw him, thinking it would give me some clues why I was Gwen, but as they started talking about business, I found myself zoning out. Shit. I was going to get this woman fired! Focusing back in, I tried to listen to what they were saying. When I heard my name, I perked up.

"How's Sawyer doing?" Logan asked.

"She's good. Still adjusting, but she's on the mend."

"That's good, that's good."

"Are you going to attend the Christmas party?" Elias asked, watching his mentor.

"Oh, no. I don't think I'll have time." Logan cleared his throat and began to pick up papers, avoiding Elias. Okay, this was interesting.

"You sure you're not just avoiding getting to know her?"

"What would ever make you think that, Elias?" Logan smirked.

"Oh, I don't know, Mr. Hawthorne, the fact you seem to be avoiding getting to know her."

"She doesn't want to get to know me. I'm no one to her. I was in love with her adoptive mother, but I failed them both in the end. I can't believe Alec had her, I—" he stopped, taking a breath. He looked up at Elias, searing him with a sharp look. "I gave her the journal. There's not much more I can do. I'm not going to force myself on her. She's already had that done by too many others."

"Hmm, that sounds admirable, sir, in theory. But I know for a fact, Sawyer doesn't realize how much you've looked out for her and how you kept her off the Council's radar for those five years she was in Iowa. Or how you faked her death to provide her with that reprieve."

I sucked in a breath. Elias was right. I had no idea Logan had been so instrumental in my life. I knew Samson had interfered; his role had been easy to identify, but this. I didn't know what to think. He was a stranger to me, but it seemed I meant a great deal to him, or at least my mother had.

"It doesn't matter, Elias."

"If you say so, sir." He gathered his stuff, and I wanted to follow him out and ask him about us; if everything else in this reality was the same. But I stayed put, the temptation was too great and I didn't want to mess up anything.

"Gwen?"

Looking up, I found Logan staring at me expectantly. "Yes, sir?"

"I asked if you were ready to head out?"

"Oh, yes." I stood, gathering the few things around me I hoped were Gwen's, and followed him out of the room. I spotted Charlie leaning his ghost body on the counter, and when he saw me, he snapped his fingers, winking, and I was teleported again. He was getting coal this year, for sure!

When I opened my eyes, I found us at what appeared to be a children's home. Logan was standing next to me in the corner, his arms crossed as he watched the children talk to Santa. An older woman with grey hair walked over, a big smile on her face, grasping his arm when she was close.

"Mr. Hawthorne, we can't thank you enough for all you've done for us. The kids are having a wonderful Christmas. Are you sure I can't announce you so they can all tell you thanks?"

He shook his head no. "That's not necessary. I'm glad they're having a good Christmas, though, and I enjoy seeing them happy. That's the only thanks I need. Please let my assistant know if you need anything else in the upcoming year."

"Of course, Mr. Hawthorne. Have a Merry Christmas."

He titled his head once and headed for the door. I followed, smiling at the woman who patted me on the arm as I passed. "He's a good man. Take care of him."

I nodded, not sure how to take what she was saying. When I went out the door, the cold air whipped around me, and I cursed myself for not wearing the hosiery now and scurried to the car that was waiting. Logan was standing next to the door, holding it open for me. I scooted in, and he followed me, the car taking off as soon as his door closed.

"We have two more places to go, and then you can have the rest of the night off, Gwen."

I nodded, not sure what to say. He peered out the window, lost in his own world. We ended up going to a children's ward and a soup kitchen. Each visit, he refused to be acknowledged but enjoyed watching the people getting to celebrate the holiday. At the last place, a woman walked up to him, taking his hand.

"Mr. Hawthorne. I just wanted to thank you for your assistance in getting the city to back down on the closure of this place. You really were the Hail Mary we needed."

"Of course, Sherry. It's what I do, after all."

"Well, you went above and beyond. We wouldn't be able to help all these families without you."

"I'm just glad you're enjoying the holiday. Please let me know if you need anything else, but you shouldn't be hearing from them anymore."

"Thank you. Merry Christmas, Mr. Hawthorne."

He tilted his head again, not saying anything as he set off toward the door. I followed him closely, information rolling through my head. "You paid off the city, didn't you?"

"I don't know what you mean, Gwen. I met with them and renegotiated the terms. That's all."

"Mmhmm."

He kept walking, dropping the subject. I still didn't know what I was meant to do here, but I was learning a lot about the enigma that was Mr. Hawthorne. Logan did a lot for people but never wanted the credit for it. And yet, he seemed lonely. I wondered how much he'd closed himself off after my mother's disappearance from his life, the knowledge of her death another burden he carried.

The car pulled up to the B&B, and he made no move to get out but turned to me when I didn't either.

"You're free to go for the evening, Gwen. It's Christmas Eve, go and spend it with your friends. I know you have plans."

I nodded but stopped. "What about you, Mr. Hawthorne?"

"I'll be fine."

I opened the door and stepped out of the car, turning before I closed the door. "Merry Christmas, Logan."

He looked up but didn't say anything, and I shut the door. It took off as soon as I was clear from it, and I wasn't surprised when I found Charlie standing next to me. He had a sad look on his face as he watched the car disappear. He held out his arm this time for me, looking at it for me to take.

"You'll want to hold on for this one."

The moment my hand touched his ghostly arm, we were transported to a cemetery. At least, I no longer felt the cold, and I wondered if I was now a ghost version of myself. When we stopped next to where the black car I'd just exited was rolling to a stop, I figured I'd guessed right.

Logan stepped out, a bundle of white roses in his arms as he made his way toward a grave. Charlie nodded for me to follow. Cautiously, I did, despite not needing to be quiet since he couldn't see me. Something about being in the cemetery made me want to be, though, in order to respect the sanctity of this place.

When he came to a stop in front of a new headstone, I had a pretty good guess who it was for. I wondered when he had this done and why he hadn't told me. He placed one rose on top of the stone and the rest at the foot. He crouched down, brushing the snow off so he could read it.

"Hey Tori, I hope you like your new resting place. I finally got the call today that the stone was here. I'll tell Sawyer tomorrow, but selfishly, I wanted to be the first to see you. You'd be so proud of the daughter you've raised. She reminds me so much of you. It almost makes me feel twenty years younger. Some days I wish we were, and all the different choices I could've made were still out in front of me. But I know that's unfair. Our paths were the ones we were meant to take, even if I don't like how they ended. I miss you, and I'm sorry that in the end, I wasn't able to save you too. I hope I can at least make it up to you by keeping her safe."

Tears rolled down my face, and ghost Charlie patted my back, handing me an invisible handkerchief. When I gave it back, he placed his arm out, and we were transported again. This time it was back in the B&B. Logan sat in front of a fire, a tumbler of whiskey in his hand, the lights off. I could hear the TV, a newscaster giving the weather report.

"It's going to be a cold Christmas, but the snow will be perfect for everyone's Christmas sledding or skiing activities."

"He's alone on Christmas?" I asked, looking up to Charlie. He nodded, placing his hand over mine.

"He's always alone."

With that, he winked, and I was whisked away again. This time, when I landed, my back hit the snow as I was transported back into my body.

CHAPTER FIVE

SAWYER

"And she's down!" I blinked, trying to orient myself to the world around me. Snow fell around me as I laid in it, the cold, wet feeling beginning to absorb through my layers. A face appeared above me, his sparkling chocolate eyes shining down on me.

"You okay, baby?"

"Mmhmm. I think so."

"You got hit with that snowball pretty hard."

Rhett reached down, lifting me, and setting me on my feet, brushing the snow off. I blinked again, trying to align myself back to my time frame. A tear escaped, the remnants of the last thing I'd seen with Logan hitting me. Rhett wiped it away, squatting down to my height to look at me.

"Sawyer, are you okay? Did you get hurt?"

"I'm fine. Just emotional, sorry."

"You don't have to apologize, baby. Is this too much too soon?" he asked, but before I could answer he continued to mutter under his breath. "I knew this would be a bad idea. I should've told them all no." Rhett carried on for a few minutes this way, including several methods of how he wanted to maim Ollie, concluding in me giggling at his creativity.

"No, I promise," I assured, cupping his face."I've just been thinking a lot about Victoria. I've been reading her journal, and it's made me feel closer to her, but it's also made me miss her more, you know?"

Rhett nodded, rubbing his face against my gloved hand."Yeah, baby, I get that."

"And, well, it's made me wonder about Logan. He was important to her, and he helped save us all. Maybe I should get to know him more. I feel like he might be alone." I bit my lip, not wanting to admit I knew the truth, that he was alone.

I was still having a hard time reconciling the time jumps to reality. I could easily explain away the first one, the weird cider and medication making it plausible as a dream. But now, I had no idea how I could walk, drink hot chocolate, slip on ice, and then wake up in the snow? This time it felt like I'd missed a whole day.

The rest of the guys came over when they realized we weren't joining back in the massive snowball fight I'd apparently woken myself in.

"Sawyer? You okay?" Soren asked, a little out of breath as he looked me over in concern.

"Yeah, fine."

"Let's head inside, guys. I think that's enough practice for today."

"Practice?" I asked but then immediately regretted it when everyone looked at me in concern.

"Alright, Smalls, let's go. Coach Maggie will kill me if we miss any more practices since we have an invitational coming up next month."

I nodded absently, following them all inside. Finley was there baking with my brother, Asa, when we entered the kitchen.

"Sawyer, save me! Your best friend is a cookie nightmare!" He cringed, as Fin laughed, swatting him in jest.

"Ah, you've been introduced to Finley 'bossy pants' Reyes?"

"Hey! I'm not bossy! I just happen to want things a certain way. There's nothing wrong with that," she huffed, planting her hands on her hips. I watched as she joked, all smiles, but I saw the strain behind it and wondered if I'd pushed my best friend too far.

"You're right, Fin. You're amazing."

She smiled, but I could still see a little anxiety around the edges, and I wanted to kick myself. I needed to check in with my friend to make sure I hadn't screwed anything up between us. Since she'd been taken and drugged, Fin had been maintaining that she was fine and hadn't skipped a beat, and we all let her. She was so good at showcasing what we wanted to see, I forgot how she dealt with difficult things.

She didn't. Fin was an avoider, and tended to bury things, thinking it would go away if she ignored it. I knew from experience how that strategy never worked. I'd have to steal her away and go to the ice cream place Asa had taken me. Nobody could be sad when eating sprinkles. Plus, the woman's magic at guessing the perfect combination was too awesome to miss out on.

"How did your practice go?" she asked, changing the subject.

"Good until Sawyer got hit in the face with a snowball."

"Who do I need to beat up?" she huffed, narrowing her eyes at the guys. Laughing, I walked over and hugged my bestie, glad to have her back in my life after five years. Her arms wrapped around me, and we held each other for a few seconds, both just needing the comfort, apparently. I held her tight, wanting to infuse my own comfort into her.

"Thanks, Fin, but I'm fine, promise." Pulling back, I watched her nod as I observed her, giving her a look only best friends had. The one that said we had a gab session in our future. "So, what are you baking?"

Asa launched into the different kinds of cookies they'd been working on, and Ollie huffed and walked over, taking control. "This is the wrong kind of flour, and you're doing the icing incorrectly. Here, hand over the spatula."

When Ollie went all bossy in the kitchen on his knowledge of baked goods, it always made me hot and bothered. He was so funny and jokey any other time, but was all business when it came to hockey and baking. I loved watching him geek out over different recipes and was always willing to be his test subject.

As Ollie took over, Finley outlined the schedule for "training" for the rest of the week for us. Apparently, part of her plan to make our party the best, was to make it into a weekend competition between the houses. Only Fin would consider a competition a way to solve someone else having a party the same night. I didn't know how she had the time or the energy to do everything to the level she did, but she was Fin, and she always made it awesome.

We broke off into two units and began to tackle the rest of her list. I was paired up with Elias as we attempted to build a gingerbread house.

"Love, I don't think that's how it's supposed to work." I stood back, looking at the piece of gingerbread I'd just added, using the frosting to seal them together.

"What do you mean?" I kept staring at it, but I couldn't see anything wrong with it outside of being wobbly. He walked over, a sexy smile on his face, and I fell into his gaze, still getting used to seeing Elias enamored with me instead of our fighting.

He wrapped his arms around my waist and pulled me to him, placing his head on my shoulder. Elias held me for a few minutes before he said anything.

"This is better."

"So, you had me thinking I'd put a piece of the house up wrong when really, you just wanted an excuse to hold me?" I scoffed but laughed, not at all mad about it.

"Hmm, that doesn't sound like me."

"I do like this position better too, but it might be hard to win the contest if both of our arms are occupied."

"I've already won in life, love. I don't need to win anything else."

He kissed my cheek, and my heart took off at his words, the butterflies filling me every time I thought about Elias Turner. A realization occurred as we stood there looking at our crooked gingerbread house.

"Speaking of, what can you tell me about Mr. Hawthorne, or I mean, Logan?"

"That was not what I'd expected you to ask." He chuckled. "He's been a mentor to me for a long time. Our relationship has changed over the years, but he's pretty private, keeping most of his personal life to himself. Logan is generous and smart, and I've yet to beat him in chess. I know he loved your mom and hasn't ever recovered from her leaving. He's been single for as long as I've known him, only pictured with his assistant, Gwen, or occasionally some other upper-class women at events. Nothing ever permanent."

"Gwen, yes, of course."

"You know Gwen?"

"Um, I'm sure I met her once."

"Hmm, well, she's the only one I know to be consistent in his life. She travels with him everywhere. Logan keeps busy, always working on a bunch of different projects through his foundation. He has a knack for helping people out of tough situations. Outside of work, he plays hockey on occasion, enjoys bourbon, brandy, and whiskey, and has a penchant for fast cars. Other than that, he's a closed book."

Nodding, I filed the info away, determined to learn more about the man I was beginning to care for. Finishing our gingerbread house, I didn't know if it was fortunate or unfortunate we didn't meet Fin's expectations. She left us with a disapproving eyebrow, as she went in search of her next gingerbread builders. I excused myself from the Christmas festivities and took some solace in my room, Lucky joining me on the bed.

Laying on my stomach, I petted him as I prepared myself to dive further into my mother's past. Pulling out the journal, I hoped to uncover more about the man my mom had loved first.

Today, Logan and I went to get hot chocolate together. I know I'm falling in love with him. I just don't know how to tell him. At least he liked the keychain I'd picked out with Chase. I'd been nervous, thinking the better bet was the hockey stick, but as Chase had said, he had a lot of those, and the keyring was more sentimental. When I hugged Chase later at the party, telling him thanks, he looked at me weirdly and said, "sure." I swear, boys do not make sense.

Shut the front door! I stopped reading as the realization of the incident I'd body swapped with had been real. Or had I only read about it before and osmosis was at work, the words seeping into my brain as I slept? Looking back at the journal, I kept reading for more clues.

The pressure my father is placing on me continues to increase, and I know I'll have to make a decision soon. I want to tell Logan, but I'm worried that doing so will put him in danger or invite him into a fight that isn't his. He wants to be an environmentalist and have a family he comes home to. I know his life has been displaced most of his life, and he wants to settle down in one place and go to sleep in the same bed each night. If I tell him what I'm going through, it will change the future he wants for himself.
I don't know if I'm ready to destroy his dream yet.

The reality of the situation, how Logan's life was irrevocably changed anyway and set on a completely different course, hit me, making me feel even more for the man. I could no longer deny the facts. Even if my out-of-body experiences weren't real and only my imagination, the realities of Logan's life told the truth.

He was alone, and I had an idea on how to change it.

I'd fallen asleep with Lucky on my bed, and when I woke, the light in the room had faded, indicating it was evening. Checking my phone, I found a few messages from the guys and Fin. Some of them were going out to grab more supplies, and others were finishing their last-minute shopping. I hope some part of me had managed to get shopping done because I couldn't remember at this point with all my possible time jumping what I had and hadn't done. Let's pray it was when I was in Gwen's. Stretching, I got up and decided to go see who I could find. Lucky lifted his head but decided to stay where he was all curled up in my blankets. I swear, that dog was a comfort hog, always finding the squishiest places to curl up in.

Walking down the hall, I found the first few rooms I checked empty. When I walked into Ollie and Ty's room, I stopped, immediately turned on by the scene I came across. The first thing I noticed was a naked ass. The second waswere the hands palming said ass as they rocked into one another. Ty's boxers fell just below his cheeks, his upper body bare as he and Ollie kissed one another, and grinded their lower halves. Their moans and movements were erotic, and I found myself panting from the view alone.

I debated on what to do. Did I jump in and join them? Did I stand here and just watch? Or perhaps, I would have some solo play while I viewed?

Ollie and Ty continued to rock into one another, and I knew I wouldn't be able to leave. Decision made, I took my shirt off as I tiptoed closer and pushed my shorts and underwear down as well. I was headed to the chair when an arm snaked out and pulled me close. Gasping, I looked down at my captor and found both of them taking me in with hungry eyes.

"You weren't thinking of only watching, were you, wildcat?"

"Well, yeah, I mean, I was going to have some solo play because you're both too hot not to."

"You hear that, babe? Sawyer thinks we're hot."

"Hmm, what I heard was, she was going to touch herself to us."

As they were discussing what I'd planned to do, Ollie's hand slipped lower, cupping the globes of my butt. Ty's hand smoothed up my back, sending tingles over my spine. They both worked my body over with their touches while rocking into one another and having a mundane conversation at the same time.

"I don't know, I think what she was saying was… " I tuned them out, Ollie's hands dipping lower now, and I spread my feet a little, lifting up to give him the angle I wanted. When his finger brushed my wetness, I moaned, and they both stopped their nonsensical arguing and turned to me.

"Oh, someone is ready to play. What do you say, Ty? How should we play with our girlfriend?"

"Hm, I have some ideas."

They hauled me up on the bed, and I landed in the middle with both of them on the side of me. I pouted, though, the beautiful man sandwich now gone.

"What's wrong, bite-size?" Ollie asked, teasing me with his nickname for me.

"I liked watching you two together. It's why I didn't interrupt. You guys were sexy, and I wanted to watch the show."

"Mm, is that so?" He leaned forward, taking my breast into his mouth, and I surrendered to his touch for a second before I refocused.

"Yes," I panted.

"Okay, wildcat. We'll put on an appetizer for you, and then you can be our main course."

Nodding, I licked my lips in anticipation as Ty rolled across me, shucking his boxers completely off this time. I focused on his cock, and watched it as it bounced with his movements, completely entranced by it as it moved. Ollie laughed at me, but I wasn't embarrassed, shrugging as I wiped away the drool. I didn't call it dicknotizinged for nothing. All these beautiful peens to enjoy, it was bound to happen.

Ollie shoved off his boxer briefs, his cock jumping up and ready to join the party as well. I moaned at the sight, my hands already starting to travel my body. Leaning on my side, I placed my head in my hand and bent one leg up so I could watch and have access.

It didn't take them long to fall back into their passionate kiss, and I marveled at how beautiful it was to watch them both embrace this relationship between them. Ty rocked into Ollie again, their dicks rubbing up against one another with each thrust. Slowly, I drifted my hand down, finding my center soaking wet and using some of my own lubrication to swirl around on my finger before I started rubbing my clit.

I loved how they kissed, their tongues and hands more aggressive with one another as they sought what they wanted. Dipping lower, I found my pussy hot and throbbing as I plunged two fingers inside. Licking my lips, I moved my fingers in and out, and I found my eyes closing as I began to approach my orgasm. Pushing faster, I laid my head on the pillow so I could pinch my nipple, squeezing my breast to my chest as I built up speed. Opening my eyes to watch them before I tumbled, I was surprised to find they'd stopped, both panting as they watched.

The look in their eyes held wanton passion for me, and it sent me careening over the edge. As soon as I tumbled, they both snapped and pulled me into them, no longer willing to leave me out. Ollie kissed me, his playful tongue skipping all around as he devoured my mouth. His hands were in my hair, possessively gripping my head as he reminded me I was his too. Ty moved down and began to alternate between sucking Ollie and licking me.

I could hear us both moaning as he changed back and forth, and I was a gasping mess. But this time, I needed more.

"Fuckety fuck, I need someone to fuck me hard, *now*."

"Well, when you ask so nicely," Ollie teased, chuckling. He stopped, his face turning serious for a minute, and pulled me close to whisper. "I'm ready to take a step with Ty, but I'm a little nervous. Would you help me, babe?"

Smoothing his auburn hair back, I nodded, kissing his nose. "Of course, Ollie bear. What do you need me to do?"

Ty had other plans, though, and a side I didn't often see from him emerged, knowing what Ollie really needed. "Are you doubting me, Ols? You know what position to take. On your back, legs braced."

Ty's voice came out darker than usual, a little domineering in his tone, and I found myself wanting to obey as well. Ollie whimpered, doing as he said, and I saw how his cock jutted up at the thought. Reaching over, I stroked him, and his head rolled back, eyes fluttering closed. Ty winked at me as he got the lube out, and began to prep Ollie. They were each other's firsts, and I knew this had to be a momentous occasion for them. I was honored to be part of it.

Tilting my head in the other direction, I stroked Ollie and cupped his cheek. His eyes opened, looking straight at me as he smiled softly, at such odds to his usual cocksure one. Leaning forward, I captured his lips with mine, the gentleness of our kiss being a healing balm to my soul. When I felt him tense a second later, I kissed him deeper, wanting to distract him from the uncomfortable part. Squeezing his cock at the base, I slowly drew my hand up as I swirled my tongue with his.

Ollie pulled away when it became too much, panting as he tried to center himself. "You're doing great, Ols. Fuck, it feels amazing. I'm almost there. Just, hold on." Ty's words reassured him, and I watched as he took a deep breath and let it out. Once Ty was seated, they both stilled. I looked to Ty to see what he wanted me to do next.

"Your choice, wildcat. You can lay back on his chest and ride him or sit on his face?" He smirked, and I couldn't help but laugh at the mischievous nature he was displaying. The feeling of still needing one of them in me rose, and I found myself straddling his chest and laying back as I braced my legs outside his. It was a bit of a jungle gym, but it worked and when I slid onto his waiting cock, Ollie and I groaned, my pussy still wet from my orgasm. Wrapping my arm around his neck, he banded one under my breasts, and we locked our lips together.

They somehow managed to communicate when to move, and they both started to rock. I could feel each of Ty's thrusts into Ollie as they pushed me in the opposite direction. It felt like a reverse see-saw in a sense, but it was the most incredible orgasmic see-saw that had ever been invented.

"Fuck, I'm not going to last much longer. Watching you two and feeling you so tight around me, I'm about to explode," Ty moaned.

"Same," was the only word Ollie managed to get out before he pushed me down on his cock, holding me in place as his whole body tensed. Thankfully, Ty was still aware of enough to flick my clit, helping to send me over the edge again. When Ty came a moment later, I worried he might pass out as his eyes rolled back. He fell to the side a second later, and we all three laid there a sweaty, naked, and cummy mess.

"I gotta catch you guys in action more often if that's the result."

"Is it you catching us if we knew you were there the whole time?" Ty asked, lifting his head slightly with a smile.

"Semantics," I mumbled, causing Ollie to laugh, the rumbles lifting me as the vibrations traveled through my body as well.

"I think I'm dick drunk," he finally slurred, causing Ty and me to laugh with him.

"I just thought of your next t-shirt slogan," I mumbled, my eyes getting heavy.

"Oh?"

"Dick the halls and messy balls."

"Babe, that doesn't even make sense."

"Sure it does."

"No, it would be better as Dick the balls with howls of jolly."

"How is that better?"

"It actually rhymes!"

"You're both hopeless."

"Love you too."

The three of us managed to play silly Christmas sex games the rest of the night, and I never had so much fun thinking of words to rhyme with balls.

CHAPTER SIX

SAWYER

When it happened this time, I was more prepared, expecting the switch. What I hadn't been ready for, though, was finding myself on an airplane. At least I wasn't flying the plane. That would've been a disaster. I wasn't sure what the rules were for these alternative timelines either. If I'd mess up something in my future, would it still happen? Or even if I could die here and not in my timeline?

It was too complicated to fathom. Stay alive, Sawyer. That was my motto. One that had served me well so far in life considering the amount of people who'd wanted me dead at one time or another.

Taking in my form, I had to guess I was a nurse or someone in the medical field based on my attire. I wore blue scrubs and comfortable shoes. Whoever I was this time, they were about my same height, and I'd guess older, the wrinkles on my hands pointing in that direction. Glancing around, I didn't see anyone else near me, and I had a brief second where I wondered if this was how I died—alone on a plane in the future. Fuck, I sure hope that wasn't how I went down.

It was a private plane, the open and elegant space different from any commercial flight I'd taken. Twisting in my seat, I pushed up the window screen and was met with the night sky, lights of a city below.

We'd either just recently taken off or were landing soon. A door opened from behind me, and I turned, finding my father walking toward me.

Samson looked older as well, probably in his late sixties. He'd greyed a lot but still had a full head of hair. His face was scruffy, the unshaven look patched with grey as well. When he saw me watching, he nodded and took a seat across the way from me.

"He's resting but will probably need more medication when we land."

I nodded, not wanting to sound like an idiot since I didn't know who he was referring to. The plane started to descend, the overhead speaker coming on and announcing our arrival in Salt Lake City, Utah. Well, at least we were still close to Oak Crest Peak.

When we landed, I unbuckled and followed Samson, hoping he'd know what was going on since I hadn't had a visit from my always helpful ghost friend yet. He started down the steps but stopped when he noticed me following him. Giving me a curious look, he stopped on the step.

"Don't you need to check on the patient and help him off the plane?"

I froze, oops. "Yes, I just wanted to see if it was raining. Holy shit, I'm British."

Samson squinted at me, more concerned now. "You feeling okay, Ethel?"

Nodding quickly, I realized my immediate mistake when my head didn't snap back like usual, and I found myself dizzy, needing to grab onto the railing, so I didn't fall. Once it cleared, Samson appeared like he was about to offer me to sit down, and I didn't want that, so I turned and huffed down the aisle to the back room I assumed my "patient" was in.

Opening the door, I quickly entered, shutting it behind me, and I found myself in a dark room. There was a bed and a body laid in it, hooked up to an IV and a bunch of other wires that hooked into a machine. It beeped, causing me to jump, and I startled myself, clutching my chest. I decided to ignore the wetness I felt below. Fuck, was this what happened to women? I was not looking forward to that. Hopefully, I wouldn't be in this body long, determined to figure out my purpose before I had to deal with it.

"Hello."

"Shit balls!" I jumped, squealing a little as the curse flew from my mouth. I spun around and found my ghost friend. She was a little girl, sitting on the edge of the bed and swinging her feet. Thankfully, they didn't seem to actually make contact with the bed, keeping it from moving with her movements. She was cute, about five, her blonde hair in braids on the side of her head. She could be me for all I knew. The resemblance was uncanny.

"Um, sorry, don't repeat that."

She giggled, watching me. "You're funny."

"Ha, sure, little girl. Are you here to help me? Can you get us from the plane to wherever we're going? I don't know how to do any of this medical stuff, and I'm bound to kill him if it's left to me."

She shrugged her shoulders, and I tried to rein in the urge to shake her tiny frame for answers. Whatever ghost training they did, needed to be revamped! Or were the people in my life just insufferable? Yeah, probably fair.

"I don't remember being this stubborn," I muttered, only making her giggle again.

Sighing, I turned to the man, not sure I wanted to find out who it was, but I needed to so I could get back to my timeline. Besides, I was 98% sure I knew.

Stepping closer, I peeked around the machine and found Logan Hawthorne. He looked awful. Rail thin, with a sickly pallor, it wasn't surprising to see him needing all these machines. A pit formed in my stomach, and I swallowed as I tried to figure out what to do. Maybe I just needed to be there for him?

Picking up his hand, I patted it, unsure what to say. He blinked his eyes open at my touch, a strained smile crossing his lips.

"Ethel, are we here?"

Nodding, I didn't trust myself to say anything else until I could swallow the tears, my sinuses burning as I tried to hold them back.

"Yes, sir. We've landed. Samson is getting the car, I believe. I'm to help you get off the plane."

Somehow, I'd known what to say, or at least how to fake it. Logan nodded, so I'd been close enough, at least.

"Very well. Help me sit up, and then I'll get myself into the chair." He nodded to the corner, and I saw what he was referring to. Relief rushed through me. I wasn't going to need to carry him out of here. I'd been wondering if I needed to find that slide thing they used when planes crashed. Knowing my luck, I'd break this old gal's hip in the process. That couldn't be good karma.

Focusing back on Logan, I could tell it pained him to ask for help, and I bet his insistence to get into the chair by himself was for his own pride. I panicked for a second when I went to unhook him but realized there was only one thing other than the IV hooked up to him, and he pulled it off with ease. Grabbing under his armpits, I helped him sit up, and when he felt stable, I turned to grab the chair. The little girl was now sitting in it, watching me. I shooed her, and she shook her head.

"Ugh, you're annoying. I really hope you're not me." She giggled at my statement but still didn't move.

"You say something, Ethel?" Logan asked.

"Nope, sir."

I pulled the chair and pushed it closer to the bed, and ignored her sitting in it. She could get a face full of bum for all I cared. I noticed the IV hook on the back of it as I pushed, so I transferred the bag over when I stopped, feeling proud of myself for figuring it out. I looked down at Logan watching me.

"You seem different today, Ethel."

"Oh? Same, ol' me." Curses! These damn observant men.

"Hmm, well, for one, you're way more chipper than usual, and two, you never call me sir. It's usually ol' chap or dear."

I paused with my fiddling, panic surging through me. "Ha, ha. You got me, sir, I mean, dear. I was testing your togetherness, and well, yay, you passed. You have it together!" I might've done a little jazz hands, but I'd deny it if anyone asked.

"Hmm, I think my illness has taken a toll on you, Ethel. At least it will be over soon, and you can have some time off."

I stopped, looking up at him, shock registering over my face. "Wh-at?"

"Don't give me that, Ethel. You know what this trip is, my last hoorah." He started coughing, the activity taking a lot out of him, and he pointed to a bag as I stood gaping. Shutting my mouth, I grabbed it and opened it, looking inside. A million bottles littered the inside, and I had no clue which to give him. I pulled one out, the name Eloxatin not meaning anything to me.

"The Tramadol, please."

With relief, I looked for the one he said and found it, handing it to him. He looked at the bottle and then at me. "Um, Ethel. I can't open these, you know that. My grip isn't what it used to be since the chemo. Plus, I need water."

"Right, sorry."

I grabbed it back from him, twisting it forcibly when it went flying, pills scattering everywhere. I looked up, worried I'd just ruined everything when a smile broke out over his face, and he laughed. It was a simple guffaw, but it sounded hearty, and I found myself relaxing and smiling.

"So, sorry, Logan. I don't know what's gotten into me. Maybe a little jet-lagged. Here let me clean this up."

I started picking up the pills, putting them back into the bottle. The little girl jumped out of the chair and picked one up. I watched as her little hand went to put it in her ghost mouth.

"No!" I shouted, causing Logan to jump and topple over. "Fucking hell! This would be the perfect time to use your ghost fingers and get me out of this mess!"

The ghost child giggled, putting the pill in her mouth, and then snapped her finger, the little shit.

I was transported to a room, thankfully, not the one on the airplane. I was glad my thoughts were still American. How odd would it be if I suddenly started thinking, "bangers and mash! My rocket is skint!" Or, "the baine is bawling! I'm chuffed to bits!" I'd have no idea what I was doing *or* thinking then. Though, it would be the perfect time to use some of Elias' cuss words.

Peering around the dark room, I'd guess it was still nighttime. Shoving off the covers, I wobbled to the side of the bed, the muscle definition I was used to missing from my legs. Balls, this sucked. I was not looking forward to getting older now. Rocking myself up, I hobbled over to a door, the standard check myself out in the mirror routine becoming common at this point.

I looked about how I felt—rough. My hair was shorter, a classic bob cut. It was a dark color, no grey insight. I'd guess I was maybe in my 60's, but I sucked at guessing ages, so who knew. I still had a little youthfulness to me, but the bags under my eyes, the bird's nest in the back of my hair, and the paleness of my skin made me want to rub moisturizer all over myself. I was so going to up my game with a good skincare routine when I got back to being me. Sorry, Ethel.

Since I was dressed, I decided to explore and hoped to gather information while everyone was asleep. It was the only reason I could find the child ghost would send me here. I couldn't exactly do anything else. I found some house shoes and a robe back in my room, and thankfully, a brush. Once I was moderately respectable-looking, I peeked out the door, finding it clear.

The first room I came to was a standard living room and the next a kitchen. My stomach growled, and I wondered when the last time Ethel had eaten. Taking a detour, I started to rummage through the fridge when I heard someone come up behind me.

"Couldn't sleep either, Ethel?"

Thankfully, I'd heard Samson. Otherwise, I might've dropped everything I'd just gathered. Turning, I took the items I held to the counter. "Nope. Jet lag is a real bitch." I cringed when I realized I said bitch. Samson merely chuckled but grabbed a glass from one of the cabinets and filled it with water from the tap. I kept making a sandwich, and when I finished, I found him watching me.

"My daughter makes the same type of sandwich," he mused.

I paused with it at my mouth, stopping before I took a bite, the realization slamming into me. Crunching down on the bite of Nutella, pecans, and ham, I tried to think of a plausible reason. "She must watch the same cooking show," I finally uttered through my bite, smiling with the food in my mouth, making my cheeks puff out.

"Logan's right. You're different, Ethel."

"Jet lag." I shrugged, like that explained everything.

"Hmm."

"So, how's Logan? Is he feeling better?"

"He's dying, Ethel. You know this."

I coughed, almost choking on the bite I'd just taken. The Nutella stuck to the roof of my mouth as the bread turned to sawdust. I didn't know Logan all that well yet, and this was the future, but something about the news made me sad, and well, apparently, Ethel was a crier. Once they started, she was sobbing, big loud mouthfuls of wheezing, mournful sounds. Samson panicked and patted my back, hoping it would calm me. I waved him off, taking the glass of water he'd sat down instead.

"Sorry, I thought you knew Ethel. You were there when he got the news."

"I, sorry, it just still hits me, you know? I can't imagine a life without him."

"You seem awfully close to Logan for only working for him for 2 months now."

"Well, that's my gift. I care too much."

He nodded, not buying it.

"So, yeah, he's dying. I guess I blocked it out."

"He should've died weeks ago, according to the doctors, but I think he's been hanging on to make it here. His life hasn't been an easy or happy one. I think he's been alone more than he's been with people. I thought once we took care of the Council, he'd slow down, put some roots down. But it was like he worked harder, pushed himself more, and everyone else went on living life without him. I was so caught up in rediscovering my own family that I didn't even notice. He risked his life, and then we all forgot about him."

Samson had tears in his eyes, and when he noticed me watching, he turned and filled the water glass back up. Grief for a life that hadn't even been lived yet hit me. "What about his assistant, Gwen? Wasn't she in his life? And all the organizations he helped?"

"Gwen? Oh, yeah, she left after a few years. I think she was in love with him and kept waiting for him to notice, but he never did. She met someone else and moved, no longer free to keep following him around. He never found anyone to fill her spot and began traveling alone after that."

Always alone. The words ghost Charlie had said echoed in my head.

I started blubbering again. "That's just really sad." Samson looked like he was going to panic again and handed me a tissue. "Thanks." Blowing my nose, I reined in the emotions. Fuck, what if Ethel was like menopausal, and that was what the waterworks were for? Or was it the opposite?

"So, why are we in Utah?"

"I think you hit your head, Ethel."

"Maybe." I shrugged, taking another bite to shut myself up.

"This is where Logan wanted to die. You called me three days ago, telling me his plan, and asked me to join you. Apparently, I was the only number in his phone book that answered."

The thought of that was even more sorrowful.

"So, I rescheduled some things, and you guys picked me up yesterday. He wants to go sledding down some mountain he never got around to and then be buried next to Victoria."

Nodding, I swiped a tear off my cheek. I'd read something about sledding in the journal the other day. So, at least that tracked. Samson stood for a few more minutes, collecting his thoughts, before tossing the rest of the water back and gesturing goodnight as he headed back to his room.

I sat down on the stool, wondering what I needed to do here. I'd come out here to find information and stumbled upon things I hadn't really wanted to know. But I guess that was the point.

The child ghost appeared next to me on the other stool. I didn't jump this time, expecting it.

"Why am I seeing this? Why didn't I ever get to know him?"

She shrugged, spinning back and forth on the chair.

"Why are you my ghost companion? You're no help at all."

Huffing, I turned back to stare out the big window on the back of the house. The sun was starting to rise, the surrounding area becoming visible in the dawn light. We were near a mountain, the backdrop showing a few in the distance as the snow fell around us. It was peaceful.

"Mama sad. She cried when papa called."

I turned on the stool, looking at the little girl. "Mama?" I asked, but she only nodded.

"What was she sad about?"

"Never trying."

"Never trying what?"

She shrugged. "That's all I heard her tell daddy."

"What's your daddy's name?"

She smiled, her little kid smile, and I knew she wouldn't tell me. I watched her grab a cookie before looking at me, waving. Her last words made my heart skip a beat before she snapped me back to my timeframe.

"Bye, mommy."

CHAPTER SEVEN

SAWYER

A gasp escaped me as I came back to myself this time, the tears falling down my face at the scene I'd just left. Except apparently, I'd managed to cry from my whole body in the time I'd been gone, the tears streaming down my entire body. Opening my eyes, I sighed in relief when it was only the water from the shower pouring down over me and not tears escaping my body. That would've been a weird thing to develop.

"Baby? Are you okay?"

Rhett's voice rang out through the bathroom, and when a sob escaped, he immediately stepped into the shower, clothes and all. Wrapping his arms under me, Rhett scooped me up into him, holding me close to his chest. I couldn't stop crying, and I didn't know why it was hitting me so hard. My words came out in a mumbling mess of nonsense, making it impossible for Rhett to understand anything I said. So, he simply rocked me in his big arms in the world's best teddy bear hug.

When I finally calmed down, he wiped my cheeks. It was then I realized we were sitting on the edge of the tub and no longer in the shower.

"How about I draw you a bath and wash your hair?" he asked.

Memories of the last time soothed me, and I knew it would bring me the soft reassurance I was okay that I needed. Nodding, Rhett stood up and sat me on the counter so he could turn on the bath and put some bubbles in. He peeled off the wet shirt he wore, and I watched as his back muscles bunched, moving together as he twisted.

Fucking hell. I think my mind conveniently forgot how sexy this man was at times so I could get work done. Because each time he showed me his body, it was like getting slapped upside the head with a sexy stick. At 6'7", the man was all muscledy perfection. His Greek heritage provided him with thick dark hair, some intense eyes, and his golden bronze skin, making up one delicious man. His grumpy nature had to be the only thing that kept women away, because Rhett was as delicious as man candy got.

"Like what you're seeing, baby?"

Peering up, I realized he'd turned his head to look back at me while I'd been staring at his butt. Shrugging, I smiled and licked my lips. His famous eyebrows that had their own language lifted as heat flared in his eyes. It was like he remembered I was sitting on the counter, naked, all of a sudden. Rhett turned off the water, the massive tub half full, and I wondered how long I'd been out of it staring at his butt. Eh, worth it.

Apparently, I'd dozed off again because Rhett lifted my chin with his finger, the heat no longer there as he stared down at me in concern. "Come on, let's take a bath, and you can tell me what's troubling you."

He picked me up again, placing me in the warm water, before stepping back. I started to whine, thinking he was leaving when he smirked, unzipping his pants instead. He peeled the wet fabric from his legs and then scooped them up with his shirt and walked into the shower to hang them to dry. It was the simple things like this that always surprised me about Rhett. He was meticulous and thoughtful, never rushing anything as he took time and care to pay attention to the details. I knew it was from years of taking care of his mom and sister, especially after Rowan had been diagnosed with Lupus, but I still found it sweet as fuck.

Moving forward, I made space for him to slip into the water behind me, the level rising to almost the top now, and I understood why he hadn't filled it all the way, again making me smile and go all gooey for the man. Leaning back on his chest, I sighed in contentment.

"Sometimes I wonder if you're even real, you know."

"Why is that?" he asked while scooping up water to pour over my hair.

"Because of this. You're romantic and sweet, caring and protective, and sexy as all get out. You were the first to suggest I could date you all and didn't get mad when I kissed Mateo. You care for all the guys and always make sure everyone is safe. You're the mother hen of the group."

"I'm just being me, nothing special I'm doing."

"And yet, the fact you don't realize that what you do without thinking it's special, makes you even more special. You don't do it for applause or accolades, but because you care. I'm just glad I met you and get to be part of it."

"Baby, you're my whole world. I didn't think girls like you existed, but I hoped, and then you swaggered out of an airport, hitting me with all your confidence, and I couldn't help but fall in love with you right then. Of course, I would do whatever I needed to make sure I got to be with you. The fact we've all made our own little family, has just made life better."

He kissed my temple, my eyelids fluttering closed at the sweet gesture. Rhett Taylor was one of a kind, and I was glad he was mine. Rhett proceeded to wash my hair, taking care to rinse and lather each strand. I never felt as cared for as I did when I was in the arms of my guys. They truly made me feel adored, all the years of self-doubt and feeling replaceable, washed away a little more each day.

When he'd rinsed out all the suds, he pulled me back to his chest, and I laid there, listening to his heartbeat for a while. Finding my words, I said the things I'd feared out loud.

"I don't know if it's real or if I've been having weird hallucinations since the day at the Christmas store, but I've been experiencing moments where I'm not myself. And each time, I'm someone in Logan's life."

"Mr. Hawthorne's?"

"Mmhm."

"Are you saying…?" he asked, not finishing his sentence, the words croaking on his tongue.

Laughing, I shook my head understanding his fear. My cheek rubbed up against his pec with the motion, and I smiled at the sensation, the smoothness was a soft balm to my face.

"No, it's not like that. I told you, no more dicks for me. Besides, he's like an almost father to me, I guess. No, what I'm saying is that each little experience gave me some insight to who he is. I might've been dreaming it all, but it felt real. And…" I stopped, not sure how to formulate the last bit.

"And?"

"I think, no, *I know,* that I'm meant to be a part of his life. He needs me, all of us probably. Logan's all alone. He never got over Victoria and then made his life a mission to help others and take down the Council. When we all needed him, he was there, saving us. And now, he's just what? Pushed to the side because he's done his part?"

"I don't think anyone meant to. It's been a bit of a whirlwind since that day, baby."

"You're right, I know you are, but I also feel guilty. When he stopped by the other night, I didn't really want him here. I felt weird that he was trying to form some relationship with me because he dated my adoptive mom back in high school."

"I think you're being too hard on yourself. It's a natural reaction to someone you don't know that well. Most of your life has been about hiding who you are and not trusting people. Until you arrived here, that is."

"True. I guess I forget it's my natural reaction because all of you bulldozed into my life, and I never looked back."

"It's not too late to reach out to him."

"Yeah, I'm going to. I fear if I don't, then he'll live a short and lonely life, dying with only Samson and a nurse as witnesses. I don't want that for anyone."

"Yeah, Samson isn't the best conversationalist."

The laugh escaped me, and I looked up at my mountain of a man. "Those words did not just escape you?"

"Why? Because I'm not allowed to make jokes or make fun of the fact I'm also not a conversationalist unless it's with you?" He raised his eyebrow, and I laughed again.

"I love you, Rhett Taylor."

"I love you, Sawyer Sullivan, to the moon and back."

"To the moon and back."

Sitting at the counter, I waited for Elias to get back. He'd gone into town apparently to do something for my dad. Just thinking that thought had me realizing how much my life had changed in a few short months. Coming to Utah, to The Aldridge School, to train the junior level figure skaters had been the best decision of my life. Not only had it given me the answers I'd sought for the past six years now, but it also brought all these incredible people into my life. I had a twin brother, a mother and a father, and seven boyfriends. Not to mention reconnecting with my best friend and making other ones with Rowan, Ace, and Chloe. With Charlie moving here and dating Aggie, everyone important to me was here. It was odd how such an unassuming place had become my home.

My life was full and overflowing with people I cared about.

But I still had room for Logan.

I'd pushed him away earlier, thinking he was trying to connect out of his guilt for my mother. I didn't think I needed anyone else in my life. And maybe I didn't. But he did. Logan needed someone to pull him into their sphere and not let him escape with a polite, "thank you, but I'm fine."

I wouldn't forget him.

Elias walked in, and I jumped up, scaring Lucky, who'd been asleep at my feet, in the process. He scattered to a standing position and we both ran to Elias. Wrapping my arms around him, I peered up at his face. My distinguished boyfriend looked down at me, a wry smile on his face.

"Love, what can I do for you?"

"Help me save Logan."

"Save Logan? From what?"

"Loneliness. It's awful, Elias. We all forget him, and then he dies alone, only Samson and his nurse there to witness it."

"I don't know what you're talking about, Sawyer, but I believe you. What do you need help with?"

I smiled wide. "I love you. Thank you for not fighting me."

"I happen to only enjoy fighting with you in the bedroom nowadays," he said, bending down to kiss me.

The urge to give in to the desire in his eyes at that moment and throw caution to the wind was strong. But the look of Logan on his last day, the grief and regret I saw in my dad's eyes, and the words of the little girl about not trying haunted me, and I knew I couldn't rest until I knew he wouldn't die alone. If not for those reasons, for Victoria. She'd been my first mom, after all, loving me as her own, and now it was time for me to love someone she'd once thought she'd have forever with.

"First, I need Gwen's information."

"Easy. Next?"

"How do you feel about sledding?"

Elias quirked his eyebrow in question, and I grinned, the plan coming to me after reading more of Victoria's journal.

"Why do I get the feeling this isn't your typical sledding like we did the other day?"

"No, that was tubing for fun. This is extreme."

"Well, loving you is a bit of an extreme sport, so you know I'm in."

"Seriously, who knew this sweet guy was under all the bullshit in the beginning? I'll never forget how you thought I was a 'rando hook-up,' though." I laughed, the sound traveling through my whole body.

"I was a tosser, love. Obviously, I needed the love of a sassy pixie to set me straight."

"Well, save all the sweet words for now. We've got a trip to plan." Kissing him on the nose, I pulled him over to the conference room. We didn't have to use it anymore for Operation Toe Pick, so it had reverted back to a regular meeting space.

I already had the information for the mountain and the plan to get everyone to the Christmas Party. Elias looked over it, a smile coming to his face.

"Alright, love. This is brilliant." He handed me his phone as he went back to looking at the details.

Pulling up the details for Gwen, I took a deep breath as it rang. When she answered, it took me a moment to respond as the sound of her voice sent a familiar chill down my spine.

"Um, hello, Gwen. This is Sawyer, Sawyer Sullivan."

"Oh, yes, Elias' girlfriend. How can I help you, Sawyer?"

"Well, you see, my adoptive mother Victoria, she and Logan were very close, and I'd like to get to know Logan better. He brought me her journal last week, and well, one of the things mentioned in there is how Logan and Victoria had plans to go to some crazy mountain and drink hot chocolate by the fire. And well, I want to make that happen."

"I don't think I understand. Why are you calling me then? Do you need Mr. Hawthorne?"

"No, you're who I needed. First, I wanted to make sure you keep him in Oak Crest Peak and put our Christmas party on his schedule. And second, to cancel anything he had for the weekend."

"But... "

"I know, he'll probably be mad, but I'll take the blame. This is important. I feel if I don't take this chance, then I'll never get it."

She was quiet for a few seconds, and I bit my lip as I waited.

"You care about him?"

"I do. I don't want him to be alone or forgotten."

"Okay, I'll do it then."

"Thank you, Gwen."

"You're welcome, Sawyer. Is there anything else I could do for you today?"

"Yes."

"Okay, what is it?"

"Make sure you schedule yourself as well. I'd like you to come with Logan to the party."

"B-u-u-t-t, me?" she sputtered.

"Yes." I smiled, nodding to myself, not caring she couldn't see me. "It's important I get to know you too, and I'd like you to be here."

"Oh, well, that's very kind of you. I just don't know if Mr. Hawthorne will like that."

"Well, too bad. It's for me. Please, Gwen? It's Christmas, and you can't be alone on Christmas."

"Well, I guess you make a valid point."

"So, you'll come too?"

"Yes, I'll come. Just send me the details."

"I will. Thanks again. Bye."

"Bye. And Sawyer," she hesitated, before finishing, "thank you."

She hung up, but I heard the thanks for what it was, and it filled me with warmth, the Christmas cheer and sense of magic wrapping around me. This was what life was meant to be like all the time. Christmas just reminded us it was possible.

I turned back, Elias watching me. "Do you have some free time?" He nodded, and I took his hand, pulling him out to the garage, only stopping briefly to get my boots and coat.

"Where are we going, love?"

"Shopping!"

"I feel like this is a setup."

"Nah. I hate shopping most of the time, but this will be fun. First, we gotta stop at the pet store for Lucky. And then I have a perfect idea for my secret Santa and a gift for Logan."

"Hmm, I guess I could grab a thing or two."

"See, I'm a life saver."

"You're something alright."

Sticking out my tongue, I laughed, knowing Elias was only

pretending to hate shopping, and in fact, loved it. He just had to grumble about it first.

We made it to the pet store a few hours later, and I smiled when Megan greeted me. I'd like to deny she knew me on a first-name basis, but since October, when I'd picked up the gift for Elias, I'd been back at least once a week. It was a bad habit, but I kept finding new things for him to love. Lucky was the most stylish and well-pampered dog in Oak Crest.

"Hey, Megan. Just picking up some last-minute gifts for the pooch."

"You got perfect timing, Sawyer. I was just about to call you to say your customized gift was done."

"Yay! That's perfect."

"Do I want to know?" Elias asked, a smile on his lips, though.

"Nope."

I picked up a few things I'd been eyeing, avoiding Elias, knowing I'd cave if he tried. When she brought it out a few minutes later, I shoved it in the bag, not wanting Elias to see it until it was time. I placed the other few things I wanted on the counter and paid quickly, ready to get home.

Walking out of the store, for a brief second, I flashed to the first time I'd been here and how R had shown up, threatening to kidnap me. Gah, I was so glad he'd been taken care of. Getting into the car, a message from Gwen came through, the final piece in place.

Gwen: It's on his schedule and I booked him off. He'll just think it's something he's forgotten. Everything is set.

Me: Perfect. Thanks again, Gwen. See you on Friday.

Gwen: You're welcome. See you then.

Smiling, I sang along to the Christmas songs on the drive home, hopeful Christmas magic existed and would grant me this one wish this Christmas.

CHAPTER EIGHT

SAWYER

It was the perfect Winter Wonderland as we walked through the house one last time before the final day of competitions started. Rhett had been working overtime this week to get the house even more "Christmasey," if that was even possible. Though, somehow, he managed to squeeze in one more tree and a 6ft Santa that scared the shit out of me every time I walked around the corner.

"Ho, ho, ho." He chuckled, and my body shivered at the sound of his voice, making me want to kick him in his animatronic junk. If I could, I'd roast his chestnuts on an open fire any day.

"It's cute how much you hate that thing," Henry whispered in my ear.

"Yeah, well, it's a larger version of Chucky just waiting to come alive and bash my brains out."

"Smalls, I don't understand half the crazy things your mind makes up, but it always entertains me."

"That's what I'm here for, the entertainment," I snarked, then cringed, not meaning for it to come out so sharp.

Henry, of course, heard it and pulled me to him. "Hey, what's really going on?"

"I'm just worried he won't show."

"He'll show. Gwen confirmed and everything. Now, tell me, what's really wrong?"

I peered up at Henry, his eyes softly showing me his patience and love, and I sighed, knowing he was right. Wrapping my arms around his waist, I snuggled close to him, just needing the boy who loved me first, to hold me.

"I'm scared he won't like me. I'm a bit much. I say the wrong things and tend to go either all in or nothing at all in things. What if he thinks I'm not worth it and regrets saving me? He could've spent all that time looking for Victoria instead. I'm also just sad she's not here. The past Christmases were hard, but they also felt like any other day. Until I met Charlie, I didn't even get a present. This will be my first Christmas with family and friends, making me miss both of them so much more. You remember what they used to be like at Christmas?" I asked, blinking the tears off my eyelashes.

Henry nodded, wiping them before they could fall. "Yeah, I do. I wondered if this would be hard for you. Your mom, Victoria, she had a way at Christmas. She didn't go hog crazy on the decorations, but she always made sure to make it special with the events and things. Where do you think Fin stole all of her ideas?"

Thinking about that, I smiled, liking that she'd made an impact on my two best friends and neighbors, even back then.

"And your dad, actually, are we calling him Scott or Brent?"

"Um, I dunno. I guess Scott, that's who he was to me. Victoria became a whole other person, and reading her journals and learning about her life, it just felt right to call her that, I suppose. My dad didn't really change much other than his name. I don't know him as Brent."

"Fair. Well, Mr. Brennon," he teased, winking, "he was the best at lights. Scott went all out each year, and no matter how much my dad tried to beat him, yours won the neighborhood award each year."

"Yeah, Christmas was always fun even if we spent a lot of it practicing for our competitions. I always loved the little traditions we did."

"Then let's incorporate some of them now. You can keep the spirit of Victoria and Scott with you, even now that you have a room full of family. I know Samson and Isla would understand. Besides, you're doing a big one tonight for Logan. I think that will help once he's here to see it."

"You're right. Thank you."

"Anytime, Smalls. I just have one question."

"Okay?"

"Who did you get for secret Santa?"

"I'm not telling!"

"Fine!" Henry rolled his eyes, a playful smile on his lips. "Come on. I think the gingerbread and cookie-making contests are wrapping up. All that's left after that is the present wrapping and ornament decorating. Fin's got everyone on a schedule, so all the parents should be arriving in thirty minutes or so."

"Yeah, okay. Just one thing." I smiled, stealing his words.

"Yes, Smalls?"

"You going to kiss me under this mistletoe, Henry Alexander Reyes?"

"I'll kiss you everywhere."

"Good answer."

Leaning down, he kissed me softly, his lips pressing into mine, and I tasted the mint from the candy cane he'd had earlier. Henry was the epitome of first kisses and loves. "Love you."

"Love you too, Smalls."

We walked into the dining room and heard the judges scoring the gingerbread houses, and amazingly, Soren and Mateo had come in first place, with one of the Ashleys and her roommate coming in second. I still needed to figure out which Ashley was which and not just refer to them as one of the Ashleys. With Adelaide gone, they'd become friendly toward us, no longer part of her 'Alphabets' girl group.

Henry pulled me into the kitchen, and we found the cookie baking/decorating contest going strong. Ollie had insisted Ty help him, but as I watched Ty lick more frosting off his finger than what made it onto the cookie, I wondered if Ollie had made that decision dick-drunk. The fact he kept looking at Ty and blushing made me realize he didn't care. It was a softer side of the fuck boy persona, and I found myself loving all the ways Ollie kept growing and surprising me.

The blonde judge was being a little handsy as she walked between the two guys, and a part of me wanted to march up to her and show her who they were with, but Henry tugged me, locking me to his side. Of course, Ollie handled it better than I ever could have in the end.

"Ma'am, I did not give you consent to touch my chest. It may be on display, but it's not for you to have your way with me. Not to mention, my boyfriend is standing right there."

The girl blushed, embarrassed, and began to apologize profusely. Ollie turned and winked, and I knew I had nothing to worry about. Not to mention how hot it was to see him stand up for consent. My whole soapbox spiel I'd given him my first week here when he'd undressed me with his eyes seemed to really stick.

Fake wiping a tear, I joked as I looked up at Henry. "Our Ollie is growing up."

Shaking his head at me, we kept walking through the house, meeting Rhett, Elias, Finley, and Asa as they came in from outdoors. The other events were held at the other houses to spread out the congestion and make it fair for home-field advantage or something.

"Hey, how did we fare?"

"Elias and Rhett got first place in the snowman building contest, and Asa and I got second in Christmas Carol charades," Fin answered as she removed her coat. All three guys gave me big eyes at her news, and I knew my bestie was not taking that news well. Fin did not like to lose.

"Asa, maybe you can help Henry with the ornament decorating in my place?"

"Sure, sis."

He kissed my cheek as he walked past, squeezing my shoulder as I approached Fin. She was messing with all the coats, straightening them every which way. I still hadn't had an opportunity to talk to her. It looked like now was my time.

"Hey, I'm sorry you didn't win."

"It's fine."

"Fin, cut the crap. I know how much you hate to lose. I have a scar on my shin that says so."

She laughed, but then tears started to flow, and I pulled her into my arms. "Hey, what's going on, really? I don't think this is all really about charades."

"I'm just, I don't know what I'm doing anymore, Saw. I can't seem to get my groove, and I'm messing up everything. I don't even know why your brother puts up with me. I'm a mess."

"None of that. Asa loves you. It's clear as day. And you're not messing up everything. You do so much. I imagine it's just all catching up with you. I think you need to stop spinning so many plates in the air and focus on a few things and see if that's easier."

"It's more than that, though," she whispered, looking at me with fear in her eyes. Fin opened her mouth to profess whatever had been weighing on her for the past two months when the door opened, cold air blowing in and bringing with it both our parents. She quickly wiped her eyes and turned to greet everyone, the perfect and poised Finley back on display.

"Mom, Dad, I'm so glad you made it. Samson and Isla, it's so good to see you too," she greeted, hugging them all.

"Mr. and Mrs. Reyes." Hugging Fin and Henry's parents, I helped take their coats and directed them where to go. Samson and Isla had hung back, waiting to give me a hug in private.

"Hey Mom, Dad, it's good to see you too." I embraced them both, always amazed each time I got to. Learning I was adopted two weeks before my sixteenth birthday, I never thought I'd get to say that to my biological parents after the story my parents had told me. To be here now was one of the best things about the past three months.

"When does the competition end and the party begin?" Isla asked.

"It should be in about twenty minutes. The ornament decoration and wrapping contest were the last events, and they just started."

"Excellent, point me in the direction of some cookies. Ollie promised me some good ones!" Samson exclaimed, rubbing his hands together. The change in him was remarkable since the whole take-down. Remembering kicking him in the junk like I had when he'd made me mad had me laughing now.

"Come on, I'll show you."

I grabbed Isla's arm and pulled her with me into the living room. "Thanks for your help in getting everything together."

"Oh, sweetie, it was my pleasure. Victoria and Logan were my friends too. This means just as much to me."

Nodding, I laid my head on her shoulder as we watched the last of the competitions. Finley stood off by herself, watching Asa and Henry, her fidgeting making me anxious from observing her. Charlie and Aggie were competing in the gift wrapping, and watching Charlie try to get a ribbon to curl had me chuckling. Finley exhaled in relief and relaxed even more when the time was called, and Henry and Asa came in second. I assumed it meant we had enough points, but I hadn't been keeping up, like Fin apparently was.

A few minutes later, one of the new board members announced the winners. In third place was Ashley's house, second place was one of the hockey guys' houses, and we all held our breath as we waited to hear who'd won.

"And in first place, Rhett Taylor's group." We all cheered, the first official Christmas BOSH extravaganza a success. Hoots and hollers rang out around us, as we all congratulated the teams.

"Well, that's all folks, now the Christmas parties will begin, but our hosts of this house have asked everyone who isn't family to clear out as they have something else planned. However, everyone is welcome back tomorrow for a surprise. Merry Christmas."

"Merry Christmas," rang out, as everyone began to pick up their belongings, hugging friends goodbye. Once they were all gone, we all jumped into action, running around the room to pick up things that had been knocked over or moved. Five minutes later, we all ran back into the living room, panting but in place for when he was to arrive. I spotted Rhonda and Rowan to the side, and was glad everyone had made it.

Gwen: We just pulled in.

ME: Perfect. Just walk in and go straight.

"That was Gwen. They're here. Places everyone! Places!"

We were probably a sight to behold as we all ran around attempting to get into a hiding spot. I didn't know why I thought a surprise Christmas carol party would be the entrance he needed, but something in Victoria's journal had made me think it was the right move, and Rhett had helped me decorate the front room to fit it.

Tonight, Logan took me to a Christmas village. He held my hand the whole time, and it was one of the most magical nights. It was simple, but that was what I liked about it. We talked, and for that one night, I could pretend I wasn't a girl from a family that sold weapons to the highest bidder, among other criminal activities. We walked around, taking in the sights, talking about our favorite things about Christmas. I confessed that one of the things I missed about Christmas at home was my mother's snow globe collection. My father had bought her one each year, and even after she died, he still did. My father wasn't always the best, but he loved my mom, and Christmas was when he showed it the most. Logan listened intently, not interrupting once, and after my story, he dragged me to a store.

It was a little antique shop, but there was a wall of snow globes in the back. He told me to pick out the first one for my collection, and he'd buy me a new one each year until I had my own room full of them because that was my dream.

It was the happiest and saddest moment because I knew it would never come to be, but this snow globe, the one he bought me tonight, will go with me everywhere. The tiny figure skater on ice with snowflakes on it is a perfect representation of my time here, and I'll cherish it forever. If only I could take the boy with me too. At least, I'll have my memories. It would have to be enough.

I remembered the snow globe she spoke of, and she would pull it out every Christmas. I wish I still had it, but running away in the middle of the night didn't leave much time to dig through the Christmas decorations. So instead, we all went out and bought a snow globe, making a room full of them to represent all of us and the Christmas we'd spend with each other from here on out, making

Victoria's room come alive. It was probably dorky, but I hoped he liked it. It was my way of saying I wanted him to be part of our tradition too. Henry was right, I could feel Victoria in this room, and I hoped it meant Logan could as well.

"Gwen, are you sure the party was to take place here? It's too quiet."

"Sawyer said her house. Just go, Logan. I'm sure it's fine."

I smiled at the fact Gwen was giving him grief and hoped he'd see the woman in his life for what she could be. I didn't want him to miss out on things, living life alone. I couldn't fix his love life, but I hoped my willingness to be in his life showed him he could also open his heart for others.

When he stepped into the room, the music started playing softly, and I suddenly felt weird, like I was waiting to propose to him or something. Motioning for the others to join me, I smiled when his eyes landed on me. They started to sing behind me, staying in their spots as their caroling of "Have Yourself a Merry Little Christmas" became a soft backdrop to the scene.

"Sawyer, what's going on?"

"Merry Christmas, Logan."

"Merry Christmas. I still don't understand what's going on."

"Well, since no one will join me," I groaned, narrowing my eyes at the people hiding, "I guess I will have to share myself. Sorry, it sounded like a good idea in my head, but now I feel like I'm waiting for you to take me to a dance or something." Blowing out a breath, I relaxed when he smiled at my word vomit. "I read the journal you gave me, and I wanted to thank you for giving me that piece of her. I read about the time you took her to the Christmas village and how you bought her—"

"A snow globe," he answered, a realization falling over his face.

"She did keep her promise to pull it out each year. And we had fun picking a new one each year. She ended up with over twenty before we had to leave them all behind." My voice croaked on the last part, and I stopped to gather myself so I wouldn't break into tears. Before I could, though, Sofia, Henry and Fin's mom, stepped out, a box in her hand.

"Actually, I think I might have something for you. After you guys left, I was tasked to box up all of your belongings for the Agency, and well, look for clues for the Council." She stopped, clearing her throat. Talking about her dubious past was still difficult for her. "I didn't find anything worth turning over to the Council, your father had done a good job not leaving any clues, but I did take a few personal items when packing that I thought you might want someday, if we were ever to cross paths. I didn't remember until I got Fin's message, and well, I think you might want this."

She handed me the silver box, and I knew immediately what it was. Nodding, I turned to Logan with it. "Well, it looks like we do have one more to add. Would you do the honors and mark your spot in our snow globe family? And well, our family as well?"

Logan stared for a long moment, and I worried he'd say no, and my anxious need to fill the quiet exploded out of me, code orange style, and I awkwardly emotion-filled word vomited all over him.

"I'm not like propositioning you or anything. I mean, you're a lovely looking man, but you're kind of old and dated my mom, and I don't know if you two like you *know*, and yeah, I can't do that. Besides, I already have my own cock express, and it's pretty full. I just didn't want you to be alone and thought it would be cool to do something, but if it's too much, just tell me, and I'll shut up. Shit. I'm doing that thing where I make it worse, aren't I?"

Face flaming, I didn't resist the arms of Elias or Ty, who were the closest to me, as they cuddled me in my embarrassment. Everyone else laughed, and I heard Charlie, Samson, and Asa make comments about not wanting to know anything about me and dicks ever again. Once the laughter died down and I pulled my head out of Ty's armpit, I found Logan smiling at me.

"This is the best Christmas gift you could ever give me. Would it be weird to ask for a hug?"

"Not at all. Iif you can accept me saying awkward as fuck things, then you deserve a hug."

Elias and Ty let me go, and I handed the box to Gwen when I walked forward, smiling at her. It was weird seeing this side after being her, but I'd keep that to myself. Logan opened his arms, and I hugged him, and it felt right. He smelled of hot chocolate and peppermint, and I immediately felt comforted. When I stepped back, I didn't miss the mistiness in his eyes.

"I think you're up, old chap," Samson said, handing Logan the snow globe. He took it, looking around the room to find the perfect spot. When he walked up to the mantel and placed it, I smiled.

"Perfect."

"Okay, now that the mushy stuff is out of the way, it's time for some secret Santa shenanigans!" Fin directed,

"And food!" Ollie shouted.

Everyone cleared out, leaving Samson, Isla, and me with Logan. "There's one more thing. Tomorrow, we're all going to Mt. Crest Peak, and we're all going to do the plunge together."

Logan's eyebrows raised, his mouth open as he looked between the three of us in shock. "But, I don't understand. I thought it was closed?"

"It is closed because we reserved it."

"That was something…" he started, before trailing off.

"Victoria mentioned you wanted to do it together, so we're all going to do it in her honor. What do you say, Uncle Logan?"

He froze, and I wondered if I'd stepped in it again until he rushed forward, pulling me into another hug, the tears no longer content to stay in his eyes. "Thank you, I never realized how much I missed her until you showed me it was okay to."

It was the perfect thing for him to say, and I knew without a doubt that from here on out, Logan would be part of our group, our family. It was the best Christmas gift I could've gotten.

CHAPTER NINE

SAWYER

It couldn't have been more than a few hours when someone was waking me up. We'd stayed up late, exchanging gifts, and just being together under the Christmas lights. Rhett had strung them up in the movie theater, and once all the grown-ups had left, we'd congregated there to celebrate together. We stayed up until the early hours, and I barely made it to Rhett's bed before I fell asleep.

I was about to roll over and give someone my best grinch impersonation for waking me up when I came eye level with a red bow. A red bow that was attached to a very erect cock, pointing right at me. Blinking, I covered my eyes and then moved my hand to ensure I wasn't imagining things. I even touched my body to make sure I was in the right one this time.

"Baby, is there a reason you're playing peek-a-boo with my cock?"

Rhett's voice had me looking up into his eyes, an unusual carefree smile on his face. Sitting up, I licked my lips when I realized I was still me.

"Not particularly, just, you know, making sure I wasn't imagining it, and honestly, I didn't expect it from you. Not that I'm complaining, I'm just shocked."

"I can affirm you're not hallucinating. I won the stupid game Ollie made up, and the prize part of it meant having to wear this stupid thing. But," he stopped, his eyes heating even more. "It also meant I got you for Christmas morning. So, are you going to unwrap your present? Or do I have to keep standing here with this stupid bow on my dick?"

"She hasn't even noticed me." The slight British accent had me turning around where I found Elias sitting on the other side of the bed, reindeer antlers on his head, and a red circle nose covering the tip of his tattooed cock.

"What in the Christmas Hell is going on?"

"Well, apparently, you can't get your stocking stuffed by Santa without riding his reindeer too."

"That is the corniest Christmas joke, but sign me up for whichever list gets me this!"

"Then come and unwrap your gift."

Turning, I crawled on my knees toward Rhett, who stood at the end of the bed. He was stark naked, only the red bow on his cock and a Santa hat on his head. He was hands down the sexiest Santa I'd ever seen. The shirt I'd fallen asleep in rode up over my hips with my movements, and I heard Elias groan behind me, my ass now in his face, bare.

"Bloody hell, love."

I smiled, finally reaching my target, and I plucked the bow off of Rhett's tip, placing it on my head instead. Leaning forward, I licked up his length, and he groaned, his monster cock bobbing right in front of me. When I felt Elias' hands on me, I joined in the moaning, my lips wrapping around Rhett, taking him as far as I could. Rhett's fingers threaded in my hair, and he helped guide my mouth down over him.

Elias surprised me a second later, and I jerked forward a little when I felt his finger tracing a line up my slit, the wetness already gathering there. "You're always so wet, love."

I couldn't respond, my mouth full of Rhett's dick, but as Elias began to play with me below, I felt my eyes roll to the back of my head as I attempted to take Rhett further. I was probably only half to three-fourths of the way down, his palm holding the base.

We stayed in this position for a few minutes as I sucked Rhett's monster cock, and Elias plunged his fingers into my pussy from behind. I was beginning to feel the start of an orgasm when in some weird coordinated movement, I was beginning to expect from the duo, Elias pulled out of me, and Rhett stepped back, and I wondered what they were up to now. The two of them had discovered their enjoyment of watching and performing in front of others, as well as sharing me between them. They didn't cross swords, but it was still always an epic fuckfest.

"It's time to tell Santa what you want, baby." Rhett grinned as he sat back on the bed, patting his leg for me to climb on.

"I just can't take you seriously with the puns." I laughed but moved over to him anyway. When I got there, he turned me, so I was facing Elias, my back to his chest. Holding me tight to him, I spread my legs over his thick thighs as I lowered myself down. Each time I took Rhett in me, I was always amazed at the capacity the vagina could stretch to. Moaning, I stopped once I was fully seated, needing a second to pant through the sensation of being fully stuffed.

"Shit, fuck."

"With that mouth, you're being awfully naughty. I think it's time I show you what happens to naughty girls," Elias whispered, inching closer to me. I was locked into Rhett's arms, my legs positioned on the outside of him, stretching me wide. Rhett started to plunge in me, and I was helpless to do anything but moan out my pleasure. I went a little dick-dazed as usual, the room fading into nothingness as Rhett fucked me with short thrusts. When I felt a finger on my clit, I opened my eyes to find Elias smirking at me.

He cupped my cheek, bringing our lips together, and kissed me passionately while I fucked his best friend. The exoticness of that thought, the feel of his finger on my magic button, and the huge cock pistoning into me ignited the orgasm that had started to build, sending me careening over the edge. Neither of them let up, and I soon found myself bent over on my elbows as Rhett grabbed my hips and pulled me down on his dick with greater force.

It was the perfect eye-level position for Elias to tease me with his tattooed cock, and rub the tip over my lips as he stroked himself. Sticking my tongue out, I tried to capture it, but he kept mocking me, only bringing it forward when my mouth was closed and pulling back each time I tried to take more. Rhett's movements had me moaning out as he thrust forward, and I peeked over my shoulder to see him intently watching where he slid in and out of me.

When I turned back, I found Elias waiting, and this time when I stuck my tongue out, he didn't budge, and I was able to take him into my mouth. Each of Rhett's thrusts pushed me onto Elias, and I found the perfect rhythm to suck him. When Rhett was close, he pulled me up, locking his arm around me again, but this time he tilted my head back so he could look in my eyes and kiss me.

His hand traveled down to my clit, and as his tongue tangled with mine and he rubbed my nub, I felt him stutter in me, thrusting up once more before he locked me down on him as he came. Rhett moaned into the kiss, only pausing briefly before he kept on kissing me, riding out the orgasm as his tongue devoured my mouth. I began to spasm around him, my second orgasm leaving me a boneless mess. When he stopped, he carefully pulled me off him and laid me on the bed.

Elias was waiting for me and pulled me to him. Gently, he brushed the hair back off my face, cupping my cheek as he leaned forward to kiss me too. "I'll never grow tired of kissing you, love."

My heart swooned as his lips met mine in a passionate kiss, and I soon found my body craving to be closer to him. Hitching my hip over his, I wrapped my arms around his neck, needing to feel every inch of my body next to his. Elias slid into me easily at the angle, and in a move unlike him, he slowly thrust in and out of me in short movements. This was what I was beginning to discover about Elias.

Most of the time, our lovemaking was the passionate, rough, dominating, make you scream in a few seconds type of fucking, and every now and then, he would also do the sweet, make you so wet, heart-melting ones. It was the perfect representation of him, and I loved every minute of our time together.

Rolling me onto my back, he put my ankles on his shoulders

before he moved back, leaning on his haunches, lifting my ass up off the bed. "It's a good thing I'm flexible," I moaned as Elias began to fuck me at a fast pace.

"It's a great thing, love," Elias barely panted out before he pounded into me harder, his grunts echoing around the room. The reindeer antlers on his head bounced with each thrust, and I found myself watching them, wondering how long they'd stay on. Soon, my eyes were closing as I drew close to the edge, and when he pushed into me one more time, I lost consciousness as I orgasmed again, so close together.

I was wrapped up between Elias and Rhett when I came to, one in the front and one in the back. Rhett faced me, and I smoothed my hand over his cheek as he watched me.

"Well, Santa, what's your decision? Am I on the naughty list? Am I your favorite ho, ho, ho?"

"Baby, you're on all the lists and always my favorite everything."

"I don't think that makes sense, but I'll take it."

"Love, go to sleep for a little longer before we have to go and try not to die falling down a mountain."

"Okay, Grinch."

"I don't even care what you call me if it gets me some more sleep. I think you stole all my energy with that fucking."

"Oh, so I'm a succubus now?"

"Ssh, sleep."

"Fine."

Somehow we did manage to sleep for another hour and then were woken up by the other guys. Ollie was like a kid, excited for Christmas morning, and he'd even made us all special Christmas cinnamon rolls that were amazing. It was one of the best Christmas mornings, as we all sat around drinking coffee and eating buns in our onesie Christmas pajamas Soren had gotten all of us. As Lucky lounged in his bed, his own Christmas shirt on, I knew I wanted this a million more times.

A few hours later, I found myself staring down at the 100 vertical foot drop, and I was beginning to question my sanity. Logan was pumped, though, the biggest smile I'd ever seen on the man as he looked out all around him. It was only this fact that got me to sit on the sled, wrapping my arms tight around Soren, who was in front. I figured the snowboarder had the best odds at keeping me safe, but it could just be wishful thinking.

"You ready, sweet pea?" Soren asked, patting my thick gloves with his.

"No, but let's do this." His chuckle didn't comfort me, but I looked over at Logan on his, and he winked before he pushed off, and I knew I'd do this a hundred times if it meant he wouldn't take his last breath on this mountain alone. Taking my own deep breath, I squeezed Soren's middle, and we took off.

I'd like to say I enjoyed it once we were going, but that would be a lie. It was as terrifying as I'd thought, and that was coming from someone who was used to flying through the air, spinning, and then landing on thin blades of metal, on ice.

If I never had to sled down that mountain again, it would still be too soon. Ty apparently felt the same, so when everyone else opted to go again, he stayed down at the lodge with me.

"Thanks for sticking back, though I would've been fine to sit here by myself."

"Are you kidding? I didn't want to go again, but now I get the bonus of cuddling you all to myself. Come on, let's get some hot chocolate and make this fantasy a reality."

Chuckling, I followed him to the stand, the woman operating it looking familiar. When I went to grab a cup, she stopped me, handing me one instead. I looked at her, realizing she'd been the lady back at the Christmas store. Opening my mouth to ask her if she'd been the cause of my body-swapping issue, the question got stuck on my tongue. Instead, I heard the tinkling of bells as my hand wrapped around the cup, and somehow, I knew, my task was done, and I wouldn't be swapping places anymore.

She winked and then moved on to the next customer. I stood frozen for a second, Ty tugging the hand he held, and I followed in a daze. He picked a comfortable couch in front of the fireplace, with the Christmas tree next to it by a big bay window. As the soft Christmas music played, I curled into his arms, sipping my drink, and I knew that this was only the beginning of all the wonderful Christmases I would have, and I couldn't wait to see what epic tales and fails they brought. Because what was Christmas without a bit of magic, a dash of laughter, and a heap of love.

"I think BOSH Christmases are my favorite."

"Mine too, wildcat. Mine too."

As I stared out the window, the familiar feeling came over me, and I turned to Ty, a smile on my face. "It's going to snow."

"Oh? How do you know?"

"I just do. It's something my mom taught me."

"Hmm, I don't know if I believe you."

"Well, you'll see."

"I think that's my favorite part."

"Why?"

"Because seeing means I get to be there, and anywhere with you is where I want to be."

"Well, I'm glad. Merry Christmas, Ty."

"Merry Christmas, wildcat. One of many more to come."

As I snuggled close and waited for the rest of my boyfriends and family to return, I knew that no matter what, we would always have this, and it was the perfect wish I could ever have for myself. Only it was better than a wish because it was already true.

EPILOGUE

Closing the journal, I smiled at the last passage, knowing that the tradition would continue. If my life had taught me anything, it was that traditions and family were the things you could hold onto. Life would be messy, love might get complicated, and sometimes evil would triumph, but if you held steadfast to the ones you loved, nothing could take that away.

"You ready, babe?"

"Yeah, I just need to check on the twins real quick."

"I'll go with you." Nodding at my husband, I took his hand, and we walked into their room together. The twins were sleeping soundly. I brushed back the blonde hair, a soft smile on my face as I stared down at my daughter. My son snoozed next to her, his little cheeks rosy from being out in the snow all day. My husband pulled me close to him, and we both stood, watching them breathe for a few seconds, content to relish in the joy of our children.

Picking up the silver snow globe, I turned the dial. The sweet melody played out quietly as snow fell down around an ice skater. Setting it back on the shelf, I grabbed my husband's hand, walking out to join the rest of our family. Before I shut the door, I whispered, "Merry Christmas, Victoria. Merry Christmas, Logan."

Today, we played in the snow, and the two of you had so much fun. You both laughed so much when you got to go sledding with Grandpa, and when your favorite Uncle showed up, you were bouncing so much, I thought you would take off like a rocket into the sky. Grandma and Nanna visited, and you all made so many cookies. I think we have enough for a week! The best part, though, was picking out your snow globe and adding it to the Christmas village we'd created. I love doing that with you each year, and I hope it's something you continue to do as well. Sleep well, my loves. I love you both so much.

Love

Your mother

BONUS EPILOGUE

HENRY/REY

Smalls giggled as Ollie tackled her to the ground, the pillow bed around us providing a soft landing. The adults had just left, and we'd all congregated here to do our Secret Santa exchange. We'd drawn names in an attempt to decrease our holiday shopping, but I know most of the guys hadn't stuck with the rule. Soren had ordered Christmas onesies for everyone, and even though I hadn't drawn Sawyer, I'd still gotten her a gift too.

It was still fun to do the Secret Santa though, especially because Fin and Asa had joined in. I liked seeing my sister happy, and I wanted to get to know Asa more. Both because he was Small's brother, but also because he was dating my sister. I knew it was important to both of them.

"You okay?" Soren asked as he wrapped his arms around me. I never thought I'd be the one snuggled, but when your boyfriend was taller and broader than you, I seemed to keep finding myself in his arms. Not that I was complaining about it.

"Yeah, I'm just reminiscing and all that."

"Hmm," he mumbled into my neck and I had to remind my dick my sister was in the room. Soren didn't appear to have the same reservations and brushed his hard cock against me. Groaning, I pulled away, needing the distance to stop me from turning around and ravishing him.

"Okay, let's circle up and start unwrapping!" Fin clapped, and everyone followed her lead. Sitting down on the pillow, I smiled when Smalls sat next to me.

"Can I sit here? I feel like I haven't seen you as much lately."

"Smalls, you never have to ask. Sit your cute butt down." She stuck her tongue out at me, but happily sat. I linked our fingers together, happy to be spending this Christmas with her. Soren sat on my other side, stretching his long legs out in front of him, and leaning back on his arms. He'd turned himself at an angle so he was behind me, his shoulder touching mine. Soren was determined to kill me with the small things, no doubt about it.

"Alright, so, I think it'd be fun if we open the gift and then try to guess who it's from first before we're told."

"Yes, Fin, we understand. We all got the 10 emails you sent about not putting who it was from on the tag. Now, can we start?" Sawyer teased, smiling at her.

"Ugh, alright. Here," she said, picking up a gift and handing it to Ollie. "Looks like you're first." Fin sat down then, and it was the first time I noticed her anxiety peeking through. Hmm.

"Yippee! I get to go first. It better be good," Ollie shouted, pulling me from my observation of Fin. He tore into the beautifully wrapped gift, paper pieces flying everywhere. He was such a kid at heart and was the perfect person to start. Everyone watched with huge smiles on their faces, his exuberance filling the air with Christmas cheer as we waited to see what he got.

"It's a... " he unfolded the material and read it, a joyful laugh leaving him. "'*I'm a weird dough.*' Oh shit, this is good. It's an apron, and it's punny." He beamed wide as he turned it and showed the rest of us, chuckles ensuing as well at the gift. Cupping his chin, he peered around at everyone. "Hmm, who would've picked this out for me. Sawyer?" he asked.

"Nope, afraid not." She grinned, shaking her head.

"Well, fuck, I have no clue then. Who was it? I need to hug the genius behind this!"

"Now I don't want to say," Elias muttered, but Ollie heard and grinned wide. He launched his 6ft frame up and at the broody asshole before he could refuse, wrapping the man in a big bear hug.

"Oof." Elias patted him on the back, giving everyone a wide-eyed stare. "I'm glad you like it," he said, clearing his throat. "There's a gift card in the pocket for some baking utensils I didn't understand but felt you should pick out."

"Ahh, I knew you got me, Eli-Cat!"

"Do I even want to know?"

"You're like an alley cat, all skittish, but leave out some food, and you become all soft and purring."

"Uh, sure, mate. Can you get off me now?"

"Oh, sorry!" Ollie moved back, a slight blush on his face, and I found it endearing knowing the once brute could find something sentimental.

"Okay, great, well, Ollie, pick a gift for someone to unwrap," Fin suggested, wanting to move the game along.

We watched as he critically moved back and forth, looking at all the packages. Finally, he bent down and selected a red gift bag with black tissue paper sticking up. Inwardly, I smiled smugly, attempting to hold my laughter in. He read the nametag and grinned toward Ty. "You're up, stud."

Ty shook his head but took the bag. Tossing out the paper, he lifted the item up for everyone to see.

"Well, I think I know who my Secret Santa was," he commented, looking toward me. I couldn't hold back the laughter anymore and fell over, as it tumbled out of me. Ty held up a pair of boxers and socks that had my face on them, and I'd scrunched up my nose, indicating something smelled terrible. Cackles went out around the room, and I found myself laughing so hard, I couldn't breathe for a second.

When I finally managed to calm down, I wiped tears from my eyes. "Sorry, I couldn't help myself."

Ty had pulled the socks on and pulled the boxers over his pants, posing with his hip out. "What? I think your face looks great on my feet."

When the laughter died down again, he walked into the center of our circle and grabbed a flat gift in basic brown wrapping. "Mateo," he read, grinning before he walked it over to him. Sitting up, he blushed a little before accepting it. He'd come a long way since his first day here, but there were moments he still became shy around everyone, especially if he was put on the spot.

Unwrapping it carefully in a very Mateo way, he took his time and made sure not to bend the corners. When he unfolded the paper, he stared at the gift in his lap quietly for a moment, taking it in. I leaned around Soren so I could see what it was.

"Wow, it's beautiful. Thank you, Rhett."

The man in question simply nodded. "I thought you could use it for the tattoo you'd talked about getting."

"I will, thank you. It's simply perfect." Mateo held it up now for everyone to see. It was a combination of different elements from Disney movies all mashed together. It really was cool to see Simba on a magic carpet with Jiminy Cricket on his shoulder. Rhett was talented.

"Outside of Ollie, you guys are no fun," Fin huffed, crossing her arms that the last two people had immediately guessed.

"You said no name on the outside. You didn't say anything about the gift itself," I teased. Fin stuck her tongue out at me but settled back against Asa.

"Well, I guess I'll pick then," Mateo cut in, quickly selecting a box wrapped in Christmas trees and handing it to Asa.

Unwrapping it, Fin peered over as he did, waiting to see what his gift was. The music continued to play in the background, the lights Rhett had hung adding the perfect Christmas ambiance. Asa laughed, the sound jolly as he turned the box of hot sauces around. We'd all recently discovered his penchant for spicy things.

"I love this. Especially because of what they're named. Too Hot to Handle, Ass Blaster, Nukey No-No, and Choke Your Chicken hot sauce. This is great. I can't wait to try them out."

"Just maybe stay away from me when you try the Ass Blaster one. I don't need any of that," Fin teased. Asa beamed at her, and I could tell how much he loved her, his eyes displaying all of his feelings. He leaned forward and kissed her cheek before turning to guess who had his name. I relaxed when I realized I hadn't wanted to punch him when he kissed her. I guess I approved.

"Hmm, I'm going to go with Soren?"

"Nope."

"It was me!" Ty barked, and Asa turned to his teammate, bumping fists with him.

"Well, thanks, man. I love it. Okay, I guess I get to pick the gift next." He sat the sauces down and leaned forward, picking up a purple gift bag with snowflakes on it. "This one is for you, Finster."

"Ah, thanks." She smiled big before pulling out the paper and holding up a coffee mug. She read it and then turned it around for us to see. "I code like a girl. Try to keep up."

"Oh, that's cool," Sawyer said, smiling at her friend.

"And there's a bunch of pens and post-it notes inside with the same phrase. Hmm," she muttered, tapping her finger on her chin as she looked around the room. "Soren?"

"Why does everyone think you got them?" I mumbled, a little sour despite my gift being obvious.

"Obviously, because I'm thoughtful and kind," Soren responded, kissing my cheek, brightening my mood.

"It was me," Mateo admitted in a soft voice. Fin grinned wide and got up and hugged him. "Thank you." He nodded, his cheeks reddening some.

"Now, let's see, I'm going to pick this one," Fin sang, plucking up a small box wrapped in silver wrapping paper.

"It's for you, bestie." Sawyer sat up straighter, stretching her hand out to grab it. I knew what this one was, and I turned to watch her open it. Smalls unwrapped it quickly but was mindful not to tear anything in the process. She opened the small box, lifting the lid to uncover a rope bracelet with an oval shape in the middle. I felt Soren casually move his arm behind me, and in the next second, the oval lit up, causing Smalls to gasp.

She peered up, looking around the room to find who was the gift giver. "I mean, I want to say Soren too, but everyone else has been wrong, so maybe, Ollie?" she guessed.

Oliver chuckled, shaking his head. Soren lifted his wrist, showing an almost identical bracelet on his wrist, only in black rope instead of the rose gold Smalls was in. He pushed the center again, and the light on hers lit again, and a smile came to her face.

"They're 'thinking of you' bracelets. Whenever you think of me, or I of you, we just hit the center, and it will light the other person's bracelet, letting them know the other is thinking of them."

"Oh my God, I love it!" Smalls launched herself over me, wrapping her arms around Soren's neck. I smacked her butt since it was on my lap, and she squealed at the sensation. Smalls turned her head, her eyes narrowing at me, but was cut off by Fin.

"As sweet as that is, I don't want to see any of what else is about to occur. I've already been scarred enough for a thousand lifetimes."

"Haha, Fin."

"No fair, I want one of those," Ollie pouted.

Soren rolled his eyes. "I'll send you the link."

Smalls crawled to the center and grabbed a present. There were only four left, the pile diminishing with each gift. I started to go through who had been revealed in my head to see if I could figure out who might have my name.

"Here, Elias, this one has your name on it." Smalls tried to hide her smile, but it was evident to me at least she'd been his Secret Santa. The corner of his lip lifted, and he took the gift from her, waiting for her to sit back down before he opened it.

Unwrapping the present, which had been wrapped with Christmas dogs in funny Santa hats, he took his time, much to Sawyer's dismay. She was practically bouncing on her knees as she waited for him to pull out the gift. The first item he brought out was a small disc held by a string, and if I had to guess, it was an ornament. He read it, smiling before looking at her.

"It's perfect, love."

He turned it around for us to see, and we all leaned in close to read it. "Most paw-some dog dad" was engraved with a sketched drawing of Lucky below it. Smalls beamed, happiness almost protruding from her pores. The second item he brought out was a travel mug. Elias read it, a guffaw leaving him as he did. "Thanks for picking up my poop. I ruff you."

Everyone joined in with the laughing as Sawyer bounced in joy. "That one's technically from Lucky." Elias nodded, looking over to the dog, who was conked out under a bed of pillows.

"Well, I appreciate it. Clever girl picking it up right under my nose too."

"Yep! I told Megan to wrap it up so you wouldn't see."

"I love it. They're both perfect. Thanks, love." She nodded. Elias got up to grab the next gift but walked over and kissed her briefly first. I watched as she blushed, and I pulled her into me, loving seeing her finding her happiness.

"I love you, Smalls." She tilted her head up, peering at me.

"Love you too, Henry." I kissed her nose, and we both turned to look at what gift he had grabbed. He picked up another gift bag, this one with an ugly sweater pattern on it, and handed it to Rhett.

We all watched as the giant grump opened his gift. He pulled out a black t-shirt and grunted when he read it, a smile breaking out over his face. "This is clearly Ollie, but I actually like it, so thanks."

Ollie laughed, nodding as we all waited for Rhett to share. He turned it around, and it said, "This is my normal face." It had an outline of a frowny face on it under the words, and we all laughed along with him when we saw that. Rhett placed the shirt back in the bag before he leaned over and grabbed one of the remaining two gifts. His long arms allowed him to reach the pile without even having to move.

"Damn," Smalls whispered, and I swear she licked her lips too.

"Henry," he read, handing the gift to Elias to pass over toward me. Once it made it past a few people, it made it to me, and I smiled as I unwrapped the box. It was heavy, and as I lifted the lid off, I was stunned by what I found.

Beautiful blank sheets of music paper laid in the box. There was a note on top of it. "So you can keep making beautiful music for all of us to hear."

"Wow, I'm so amazed. If I didn't know better, I'd say it was from Soren too," I joked, trying to dispel some of the tears that wanted to fall at the thoughtful gift. Looking around, I tried to remember who was left. Only Fin and Asa remained if I'd done it correctly. Swallowing, I looked to my sister. "You?" She smiled but shook her head. Shock registered in me before I looked at Asa.

"Asa, wow, thank you. It's a perfect gift."

"You're welcome. I know you don't want to sing, but I thought your song at the birthday party was great, and I wanted to help you follow your dream. Plus, you owe me a song for next year, so I figured I'll make sure that happens."

Laughing, I nodded, grinning from ear to ear. "You got it, man."

"Well, that leaves one person, Soren," Fin stated, biting her lip as she held out the gift. I couldn't place what would make my sister nervous until I realized she wasn't just getting a gift in the game, but it meant something to her to buy it for my boyfriend.

"Thanks, Fin. I'm sure I'll love it."

She sat back down, and we all watched eagerly as the last present was opened. Soren pulled four boxes, laughing as he did, and sat them down. He turned them around, and I realized what they were, Funko Pops from Schitt's Creek.

"These are amazing, Fin. They'll go perfect with my others."

She grinned happily, sagging in relief that he'd loved it. I picked them up, looking them over and recalling how I'd been so confused about my feelings for him when we started the show. Leaning over, I kissed his cheek, happy to be where we were now. "Merry Christmas, Sor."

"Well, that's our cue to head out," Fin said, interrupting our moment. She pulled Asa up, and they gathered their gifts, saying their goodbyes to everyone. Kissing her cheek, I held her close, hoping she knew how much I loved her.

"I love you, little sister."

"I love you, big brother."

Pulling back, I observed her eyes, trying to answer the questions I didn't know to ask.

"I'm okay. Promise."

Nodding, I let her go and watched as she left with Asa. Before exiting the room, he stopped, looking back and giving me a look. For a second, brother to brother, we shared a look, and I knew he'd look after her, just as he knew I'd look after Sawyer. Nodding, I accepted his concern for what it was, the knowledge giving me a solace of hope Fin would rebound from this and let us in. If not, I didn't know if she'd be able to survive the fallout this time.

Shaking the morose thoughts, I leaned back into Soren's arms, the rest of the BOSH crew around me, and I snuggled in for a long winter's nap. Or at least, a Christmas Eve one. Rhett had set up movies, the lights dimming as they began to play. Over the next few hours, one by one, everyone began to fall asleep, either choosing to head up to bed or hunkering down in the Christmas dreamland.

As my eyes fluttered closed, I couldn't help but think, "Merry Christmas to all, and to all a good night."

Want to know how the BOSH gang developed? Read their story in the Council Series, and Fin's next year in Stiletto Sins.

LETTER FROM THE AUTHOR

To all my readers, new and old, I hope you enjoyed this Christmas Novella, and it filled you with all the squishy feels. If you're a new reader, check out their story, and for all the BOSH fans, there's more to come in this world in 2022, so make sure to stay tuned to see what's next.

Thank you to Emma, Amber, Kayla, and Tory for helping me get in the Christmas spirit and make sure the story was true to the characters, and adding that bonus epilogue.

ABOUT THE AUTHOR

Kris Butler writes under a pen name to have some separation from her everyday life. Never expecting to write a book, she was surprised when an author friend encouraged her to give it a try and how much she enjoyed it. Having an extensive background in mental health, Kris hopes to normalize mental health issues and the importance of talking about them with her characters and books. Kris is a southern girl at heart but lives with her husband and adorable furbaby somewhere in the Midwest. Kris is an avid fan of Reverse Harem and hopes to add a quirky and new perspective to the emerging genre. If you enjoyed her book, please consider leaving a review. You can contact her the following ways and follow Kris's journey as a new author on social media.

Join the newsletter

Join KB's Mavens of Mayhem

ALSO BY KRIS BUTLER

THE COUNCIL SERIES

The Council Series

(completed series)

Damaged Dreams

Shattered Secrets

Fractured Futures

The Order (Council Spinoff)

Stiletto Sins

Summer 2022

Sinners Fairytales (standalone)

Pride

Dark Confessions Series

Dangerous Truths

Dangerous Lies

Dangerous Vows

Coming 2022

Tattooed Hearts Duet

Riddled Deceit

Smudged Lines

HOLIDAY FROM THE HEART

A STANDALONE FROM THE SWEET RIVER ROMANCE SERIES

AVERY LAWRENCE

CHAPTER ONE

The air felt stagnant as I entered the terminal. There was weight to it.

The assuring words to "I'll be home for Christmas" bellowed from the overhead speakers. This version, with a full orchestra and a bass-baritone offering the words, carried an ominous tone. Where were Frosty and Rudolph when you needed them?

Exiting towards baggage claim, I saw the deep red velvet ribbons trimmed in gold lining the ceiling. Their presence brought a smile; then led my eyes to a sad tree in the corner. It was lacking ornaments and had seen better days. The twinkling lights and their joy fought through the dust and slight decay.

"I feel ya, buddy," I muttered under my breath.

Flights from secondary cities in Oregon to mid-sized cities in New Hampshire were a tad scarce. The flight I came in on was the last one in the terminal for the night. I was a little groggy and admittedly, part of my mind was still back in Oregon—back with Dr. Andrés Morales. I was still beating myself up for insisting he didn't need to get out of the car. Telling him I could just get my bag. *What was I trying to prove?*

We should've been standing by the trunk, me thanking him for going out of his way; him comforting me with a lingering hug.

Savoring it as he watched me walk into the airport. In this imagined reality, his wave and that thousand-watt smile would be my last image of Oregon. Instead, I jostled my bag, trying to get it to stay upright, found multiple ways to apologize for the early hour; and completely fumbled everything.

I tried to blame my nerves on everything that awaited me in New Hampshire. I was worried about getting from the airport to the hospital. Wondering if my mom was as bad as her friend Stacie made it sound. Curious about how long I'd have to stay. Which was certainly part of it; the fact the deep brown of his eyes completely disarmed me was the majority.

The terminal was quiet, other than the music and the monotonous thump and spin of luggage. Only one baggage carousel was in motion. My steps were brusque as I moved towards it, moving forward towards the next steps and solutions.

Out of the corner of my eye, I caught a sudden movement. A frozen figure animated as I passed and seemed to fall in step behind me. My grasp on my backpack straps tightened. My fingers fumbled the length of my body to double-check the zipper on my purse. I discreetly padded my pocket to check for my cell phone.

Their pace quickened and before I could decide if running and screaming was overkill, I felt a hand on my shoulder.

I whirled around; wielding my purse as a weapon. I aimed roughly at where I thought a face might be. In the slow-motion moments before the purse made contact, I tried to slow its speed and gasped.

"Trent!" I dropped my purse and covered my mouth. His fingers felt his face, assessing the damage.

"You sure know how to make an entrance."

"What are you doing here? -Why were you following me?" His sarcasm melted my sympathy. Annoyance crept in.

"Slow down, slugger." Trent put his arms up, blocking another advance.

Raising his arms in mockery gave me the sudden urge to strike him.

"I'm here for *you*." He paused, as though expecting a response, then continued, "I'm your knight in shining armor."

Trent took a step back, making room to bow with a flourish.

His raven locks grazed the length of his chin as he lowered his head and then tilted it slightly up. His steely gray eyes balanced his playful grin.

Those eyes could make everything else melt away, but I needed to focus.

"How are you here for *me*?" I countered.

"Isn't it obvious? -I'm picking you up. I ran into your mom's friend Stacie at Market Basket. She mentioned she was worried about you not having a ride to..." he fidgeted with the seam on the side of his jeans and his voice drifted off.

Was he scared to say hospital, or was he unsure if I still called Newhouse home?

"She didn't know when I was arriving."

He massaged the back of his neck and then released his arms in a shrug. "I may have been here a while—but there weren't many flights coming in late."

I squinted at him. *What was this?* I hadn't seen him in... *wow—over seven* years, and he just shows up at the airport to pick me up? As if we haven't missed a beat?

That was Trent, though. Oblivious to anyone but himself and always pursuing what was best for him, regardless of how it affected others.

My chest heaved with a deep sigh. It wasn't worth questioning. Whoever he was doing this to impress, whatever his motive, I was too tired and emotionally drained to figure it out. I held his eyes a second longer and turned on my heel, headed straight for baggage claim.

CHAPTER TWO

"Sure, you don't need help with that?" Trent reached again for the suitcase.

My eyes seared into him, "I said I've got it."

It took a slight swinging motion to propel the bag up on to the tailgate, but I got it in.

"I can't believe you still have this 4Runner." I traced my fingers along the side as I walked up to the front of the vehicle.

"I'm keeping her until she's a classic."

"I think she's already there," I muttered softly.

He leaned into the vehicle. The door perfectly framed him. His hands held the top edge, the rest of him angled back. His head and chest floated, and those smoldering eyes barely upstaged his flirtatious grin. My breath caught in my chest. I was right back to the first day of being a junior in high school when he'd offered me a ride home. He looked about the same, only the jacket was thicker and better tailored. There was also a trace of a five o'clock shadow framing the angles of his chiseled chin.

"What's that you're saying over there?" He cocked his head slightly to the side and attempted to give me an accusatory stare. His lips stayed curled and outweighed the hazy glare.

I sat perfectly still. Taking in the moment, holding those eyes. There was this instinctive part of me that wanted to reach my hand out to him, knowing he would take it. Wondering if he would still kiss the back of my hand and inner wrist—or if he would just hold it for a second and let go.

I shook my head and filled my lungs.

Good gravy, I was so tired, my brain was no longer functioning.

I needed to release that image. Trent's slammed that door shut years ago.

I was here in the present. A present where handsome doctors drive me to airports and ask me to holiday parties.

"Come on, I'm exhausted. You're here to give me a ride. Now, get me to the hospital."

"You don't want to head to your mom's and get some rest first?"

"Hospital." I turned my gaze forward into the shroud of darkness.

CHAPTER THREE

The sanitized air and buzzing silence hit me as soon as we entered the hospital. Even with a recent remodel, the laminated floors were straight out of the 80s. The shapes were geometric, but the pattern was illogical and disruptive. It was a small hospital. Stacie, my mom's best friend, had texted me the room number. It was easy to follow signs and find our way (though at this hour we had to sneak in through the emergency room entrance).

"You should've left me here and gone home." I tried to keep my voice low as my feet scurried down the hall.

"You wouldn't have a ride home. It's almost 2 a.m. Besides, your bags are in my truck."

"I would've figured it out." I scanned the doors, putting on the brakes quickly when I found the right number. Trent was three steps past me when he realized I'd stopped.

I drew in my breath and reached for the door.

"You can't go in there."

I spun my head left, then right. The voice came out of nowhere. Behind us, a nurse tapped her foot, arms crossed, peering down her nose.

"Uh..." I stammered.

I was contemplating ripping open the door and locking myself inside. She was far enough back; I was pretty sure I could do it.

"Nurse Higgins," Trent said gently.

His sly glance at her badge was so smooth he had me thinking for a moment that he knew this woman. Her look made it clear; he did not.

"Willa has traveled all day from the other side of the country. She just wants to peek in and see if her mom's okay." He had stepped closer to nurse Higgins. His hand outstretched and his head tucked as though approaching a growling animal.

"Absolutely not. Visiting hours are from eight to eight. Simple as that. She is resting, and she *needs* her rest," nurse Higgins peered around Trent, "I'm sure her daughter would agree?"

My hand dropped from the handle and guilt washed over me. I nodded slowly.

"You can come back tomorrow," nurse Higgins pursed her lips in triumph.

Trent's eyes bore into me as I stared at the ground and shuffled my feet back towards the exit.

CHAPTER FOUR

"How could you let her get the best of you like that? That's not the Willa I know."

The comforting cone of silence had only lasted to the car. Here it crashed to the ground. My shoulders dropped and my head fell to the headrest behind me.

In through your nose. Out through your mouth.

What else had I learned in years of Social Work training?

Connect with your senses, something you can-

"Willa, are you ignoring me? What's happened to you?"

My chest tightened. My hands balled into fists. I turned towards him.

"What's happened to me? The Willa *you know*? You disappear from my life for years, randomly show up at an airport, pretend you still *know me,* and when *you* are inaccurate in your projections, something must have *happened*? Are you even listening to yourself?"

There was heat in my eyes, the flames leaping out at him, each word intended to sear into the recipient.

He stared gently back at me, unscathed.

"Come on, Willa. I'm just trying to help."

He lifted his hand briefly as if to reach towards me and instead reached towards the dash and fidgeted with his keys. He turned fully towards the opaque sky ahead of us and ran his fingers through his hair. He gave me one last glance and started the engine.

CHAPTER FIVE

There was a couple of inches of snow on the ground, enough that the tires made a satisfying crunch as Trent turned up our driveway. Funny, I still thought of it as "ours" even though I hadn't been home in years. The last year and a half I'd been settling into Oregon. Before that, well, I didn't have a good reason for before that.

Before that was graduate school. I was only in Boston, but it was incredibly hectic, and I told myself there was no time. We were also in a cute little apartment and no longer had the seasonal shifts of the dorms. Sierra and I loved our little place, and I frequently got mom to visit. I convinced myself that mom was the one that needed to get away. So, she always came to me. I couldn't comprehend any reason that I would intentionally stay away.

When they'd built the house, they tucked it into a grove of trees. It made it feel like there was no one for miles, even if the home was only on a modest acre. Darkness engulfed it tonight. No porch light, no Christmas lights, no signs of life. Trent's headlights bouncing across the stonework were the only way to know we were at the right place. He parked at a strange angle so that the light shone down the walk to the front door. For that, I was grateful.

We got out in silence. When he pulled out my suitcase to carry, I didn't raise a word in protest. I followed silently behind him. I felt like an electrical wire torn down in a storm. Perfectly docile until crossed. Then I was flailing and dangerous. I needed to be grateful for all he'd done. I needed to let the past stay in the past.

"Do you have a key?" He set down the bag and turned towards me.

I maneuvered around him, turned the handle, and pushed open the door.

"Some things never change." I smiled up at him and realized how close we were. I immediately tried to take a step back, forgetting the planters that line the doorway.

His arms were around me before I could even find a place to put my hands, or my brain could process a solution. I may not have crashed into the planters or the ground, but this seemed an equally dangerous scrape. It was an embrace that felt more like coming home than this house did. One more second under the spell of those dusky gray eyes, and—

"Trent-" my body stiffened, and I secured my feet back under me.

"I've gotcha, that's all Willa. You just need to know that I've got you." He dropped his hands slowly away. No sudden moves. He pushed open the door and grabbed my suitcase as I felt for the light switches. The porch illuminated immediately, but the hall light was missing bulbs and it remained cast in shadows. He walked my bag into the darkness of the front room, maneuvering around the coffee table my dad built like he knew the exact dimensions. Like we were eighteen again, and he'd been over earlier in the day. As though one of his scarves might still be errantly tossed over the couch. My feet led me near him like a lost puppy looking for the way home.

"Here you go. Need anything else? Do you want me to pick you up in the morning? I didn't see your mom's car in the driveway."

It exhausted me; figuring it out, processing, solving. My lips parted, frozen for a few moments before they could find the words.

"I'd appreciate that."

He stepped closer and lifted his hand to sweep the hair back from my face. He tucked it behind my ear and drew his finger along my chin line.

"You've got this Buttercup, there's nothing you can't handle."

The moment he called me Buttercup the tears welled in my eyes. I bit my lip and tilted my head back, trying to withhold them. I felt his hand trace the length of my arm.

"Come here." His words beckoned me, but he was the one who moved. He stepped forward and fully enveloped me. One hand cradled my hand and brought it to the soft cool material of his coat and the other wrapped around my waist. A torrent ripped loose, and the tears poured out of me. I hadn't realized how much I needed this, and melting into Trent felt like the safest place I could be.

I hadn't cried like this the day before, maybe because it started so simply. It was a call from a police officer telling me they were taking my mom to the hospital, but even with the kerfuffle, I could hear coughing and declaring in the background, "I'm fine. Stop your fussing!"

She'd slipped on ice coming out of the Post Office and couldn't get back up. The angle she was at concerned the paramedics. She may have broken her femur or hip. They were taking her in for x-rays. I was her emergency contact. They wanted to let me know she would be at Exeter Hospital, and since her cell battery was low, I would have to call there for updates. Stacie was like an aunt to me—I called her immediately. She went to the hospital to be with mom, and I was helpless. I spoke to colleagues at the clinic where I work, learning a little too much about how serious a hip fracture and recovery could be.

By the time Stacie called to tell me it was a fractured hip, I could barely process that they may postpone surgery to place the pin because of her pneumonia. *Pneumonia?* I was too shocked to get worried, to even ask the right questions. By the time my head cleared, the time zones were working against me—it was too late to call anyone and learn more. The fractured hip was the reason she'd need help. The pneumonia was why I needed to rush. I booked a ticket, packed, canceled plans, stared at walls, problem solved. There wasn't time for crying.

Maybe this was making up for all that. The lack of sleep, the shock of seeing Trent, not being able to see mom, the fear and unknowns with mom's health, being back in this house, my disrupted life in Oregon. Or the stress of contacting clients, giving up my plans with Sierra for Christmas Eve, missing the Christmas party with... Andrés! What was I doing wrapped up with Trent when I was finally making progress with Andrés?

I snapped my body straight and smeared the tears from my cheeks.

"Thanks, Trent. I'm not sure what got into me."

"It's okay to cry, Willa," he leaned back, moving from left to right, trying to catch my eyes, "I think you are the one that taught me that—remember? When my mom die-" Trent dropped the word like a hot potato, realizing the danger of any unintentional parallels.

We both wanted him to take it back, so we both ignored it. With a shared history, you can do things like that.

"Um, I should get to bed. What time works best for you tomorrow?" I was halfway to the door by the time I finished asking.

I needed him out of here.

"7:30 a.m. work?" He ran his fingers through his hair, and my mind conjured memories of when my fingers had done the same.

"That's great—or even 8. Let's just make it 8. I'm beat, and the hospital isn't far."

"You'll be ready by 7:30. I'll see you then." He gave a half wave, a nod of the head, and he was out the door.

Ordinarily, I would process what just happened for hours. But right now, I was so wrecked that I didn't even take off my clothes. I didn't even bother to see if my old room was an option. I left my luggage in the front room, only pulling my charger out of my backpack. I walked straight to my mom's room, plugged the phone in, peeled off my coat, and collapsed in a pile of pillows and her Sherpa-lined duvet cover, that I'd loved since I was a kid.

CHAPTER SIX

"I can't believe you found Apple Cider Donuts. And this coffee! This coffee is perfection." I was talking with my mouthful and with anyone else this behavior would be mortifying. Trent was laughing under his breath and gleaming like the first grader who just won the spelling bee.

"You've been gone a while. We have fancy new establishments, and one carries Apple Cider Donuts into January."

"What! That might be sacrilege. But if sacrilege tastes this good, I think I'm gonna be bad."

I quickly wiped the crumbs from my scarf as I stomped my feet on the mat just inside the automatic doors. This time we came in the front and things were bustling. There were wheelchairs, scrubs, and conversations. The vibe was less ominous than it had been the night before and made me ache for our clinic back home with familiar faces and fewer serious concerns.

I flung my head from side to side to dislodge the little bits of snowflakes we caught on the walk-in. It reminded me of an unfulfilled ache I had for snow in Oregon's wet, yet more temperate, winters. I made a mental note to get to the mountains this year—they were a bit of a drive, but I'm sure it would be worth it.

I let my breath out when we reached my mom's hallway, and although there were more people around—there was no sign of nurse Higgins. The donut and the bustle made me ready to see whatever was behind that door.

There was a small amount of filtered light fighting its way in through the blinds, and a small glow from what appeared to be a nurse's area. Otherwise, the room was dark. I moved closer to the mound covered with sheets and blankets. I could make out her arm and the IV lines going to it, but she had her face turned.

"Mom?" It was a loud whisper. I didn't want to wake her, but there was a chance her eyes were just closed.

"Oh, Bug!" she reached towards me, and soon let out a little yelp. Her hands went immediately to her side and leg.

I made a beeline for her side. "Oh, mom."

"Stop your fussing." She was batting me away faster than I could do anything effective. "I just moved a little too fast, that's all."

"I just worry about you. Have they said anything more about the pneumonia?" I still fluffed her blankets and was grateful that Trent had turned on the light.

"It was hardly pneumonia. They like to make a big deal out of everything around here." When she waved her hand for emphasis, you could see it moved at a slightly dulled pace.

They were taking care of her. Overall, she was much better than I'd expected.

"It's just good to hear your voice and see you in person, mom."

"I tried calling you yesterday, but it went straight to voicemail. You know I hate leaving messages on machines." She was a tad more suspicious than usual. I wondered if that was the medication.

My shoulders stayed tight even as I released my breath, "I'm sure I was on a plane, mom. Flying here."

"Well, this is all a bunch of nonsense. You get it, don't you Trent?"

Out of the corner of my eye, I saw Trent's head bob in agreement. I turned my head towards him and the nod halted before our eyes connected. He was always trying to please everyone. That charmer.

"I'm just glad it isn't as bad as it sounded. We need to get some color in those cheeks."

My mom tilted her head to the side, trying to shield, and no doubt minimize, a cough. She winced when her chest convulsed. I couldn't tell if it pulled against things still tender from the surgery or if the cough itself was that painful. I laid my hand on her shoulder. I was glad it wasn't as serious as it sounded before. I'm also glad I came.

"I am sure you want to keep Willa all to yourself, Mrs. Jones-"

"Ugh, Trent. Don't call me that. It makes me sound old. Call me Vivian or Viv."

"Okay, Viv," he cocked his head and bowed it slightly, "as I was saying. I know you are going to want to keep Willa all to yourself, but I am sure you know they are having the Newhouse Nights of Christmas on Saturday and Sunday. I would love to show Willa some ways Newhouse has grown and changed."

"Oh, I don't have time for anything like that," I interjected.

"Nonsense," my mom said and paused for a slight cough. "If you are going to insist on being here—I'm going to insist you go to that festival with Trent." She waved it off as a closed topic.

I filled my lungs with air and tried to exhale evenly.

I turned to Trent. Just as I said "Thank you-" before I could muster words of argument or add in a "but", my phone rang. My heart quickened when I saw Andrés's name flash across the screen. My cheeks flushed crimson. It still felt scandalous to call him Andrés instead of Dr. Morales or Dr. M.

"Um, I need to take this," I said the words without looking up and exited the room. I was such a coward. I wasn't good at explaining myself. Likely because I didn't know what I was doing half the time.

I ducked down an adjacent hallway and laid my hand on my belly as I sucked air in slowly.

"Hi, this is Willa." I rolled my eyes. I was terrible at this.

"Hey Willa, it's Andrés. I just wanted to check in. How's your mom? I hope it's not too early."

"Too early. I am three hours ahead of you. It isn't even dawn there, yet."

"I like to get up early. I work out before I head into the clinic." He said it casually. I made a note to conjure a mental image of that later. "How are things going? It didn't sound like you had much info before you left." The words were simple and showed little, but his voice was like cashmere wrapping around my shoulders.

"I just got to the hospital. There's still little I know. She looks far better than I expected and better than her friend Stacie made it sound."

"I'll be thinking of you. Uh, both. Pneumonia can be serious, especially for someone her age. I am surprised they did the hip fracture repair."

I didn't have the heart to tell him my mom was only forty-five. She was twenty when she had me, which wasn't *that* young. After all, she and my father were married and madly in love. Since we were both from a small town, you would think it would be easy to tell Andrés that, but his years in medical school seemed to make him a little more out of touch with those things. In his defense, it was a reasonable mistake; being widowed, breaking her hip, and having pneumonia made her sound like she was a little old lady in her sixties.

"I probably should have known if they were doing a hip fracture repair, the pneumonia wasn't that serious. She's just terrible about taking care of herself." My fingers were twirling my long hair like a schoolgirl, my body turned towards the wall like I was hiding a call from my parents.

"Well, she is lucky to have you. You are very reliable and a good person."

Reliable? Good person? Not exactly the words you want your crush to use.

"Um, thanks." My fingers dropped from my hair. I crossed my arm across my chest, rubbing my fingers on the arm holding the phone.

Silence hung between us. He finally broke it, "Well, I don't want to keep you-"

"Oh, my word!" I jumped so quickly my head bumped into the wall. I spun around. Trent's sheepish grin communicated his apology.

How could he think that just putting his hand on my back wouldn't scare the crap out of me?

"Is everything okay?" Andrés's voice emanated concern.

"I am *so* sorry, someone bumped into me. It surprised me, that's all. Nothing concerning." I waved it off with my hand. "I'll let you get back to your workout."

"Alright, take care."

And then he hung up. Without saying goodbye. *Did that matter?*

I kept the silenced phone lingering by my ear.

"It was great talking to you, too. Thanks so much for your care and concern. Yeah, I'll keep you updated. Talk soon." I paused. How far was I taking this charade?

Maybe a little further, "Aww, you too. Bye." I spoke into the silence.

I tucked it back into my purse.

"You might want to check that." There was a mischievous glint in Trent's eye.

What was he getting at?

"What do you mean? Check What?" I asked.

"Your phone lit up while you still had it up to your ear. Maybe a message came in."

"I'll check later. Do you need something?"

He stood there waiting for the pink in my cheeks to warm to scarlet and make it clear he had won that round.

"The festival—what time and where should I pick you up?"

"When is it?" Annoyance was edging into my tone.

"Oh, don't even start. You heard your mom. You are doing it for her. It's tomorrow. Here, give me your phone."

"What?" I clutched my purse to my side.

"Seriously?" He rolled his eyes and tilted his head back. "I was only going to program my number in. Whatever." He pulled out his phone, "Just tell me your number."

"617-227-9176," I rattled off the numbers.

"Kept with Boston 'eh?" He chided.

"The beauty of cell phones." I returned.

"You should've kept with New Hampshire." He finished typing, never looking up from his phone. Maybe there wasn't a double meaning to those words.

"I just sent you a text, so you have my number. We'll figure it out tomorrow. It would be nice to get there by about 5:30/6:00 p.m. But we'll play it by ear since you don't know your obligations or schedule yet. Later, Buttercup."

He waved his hand over his shoulder after his body was already walking away.

CHAPTER SEVEN

"What do you mean, he's obnoxious?" Stacie surveyed me closely. Clearly, I had chosen the wrong word.

"Not so much obnoxious, maybe relentless? I don't know." I poured another packet of sugar into my coffee. The hospital cafeteria was stark, and the wallpaper meant to look like cloth felt suffocating. I usually only took one packet of sugar in my coffee, but this coffee needed all the help it could get. I wrapped my fingers around the rough texture of the Styrofoam cup, hoping it would warm them.

"He's a sweetheart. You used to think that too." Stacie neatly cornered off a piece of her blueberry muffin with her fork. "Did you know he visits your mom most every week?"

"He *what?*" My forehead puckered at the idea.

"Usually on Sundays. He brings her firewood in the winter, mows her lawn in the summer. She gives him iced tea or hot coffee- sometimes makes him her famous gingersnaps or picks him fresh strawberries from her garden." Stacie mopped the muffin in her pat of butter, completely oblivious to the impact of what she was saying.

"I'd no idea. Mom never mentions it."

"Really? She's always prattling on about it to me. I've been there a few times when he's stopped in. Running the flower shop means I don't see your mom near as much as I'd like, but I can usually get away on the weekends." She glanced up at me and paused. "Oh dear, did I say something?"

My eyes were glossy with tears, and I was a little confused why. Was it the betrayal that neither of them had told me? Or was it the fact that Trent hadn't spoken to me in years, and yet he saw my mom weekly? What was so wrong with me that Trent hadn't even wanted us to be friends? My chest was so tight it made my shoulders slump.

"It's nothing," I stammered and blinked my eyes hard. "It's all… overwhelming."

I sucked air in through my teeth and pinched the bridge of my nose. I was just emotional—lack of sleep will do that. I needed to get this conversation back on track. "Mom looks better than I imagined. Is she putting on a show?"

"I think it only developed into pneumonia because that woman wouldn't sit still. She wouldn't even admit to being sick when she got to the hospital. Kept claiming it was allergies. The nurse noted again and again that this wasn't the time of year for allergies and that coughs often indicate something else. Your mom was unyielding—they stopped asking her questions and just ordered the chest x-ray at the same time as the pelvic x-ray, diagnosed her, and started treatment. It was why the hip surgery happened the next afternoon, though. They wanted to make sure that she stabilized, and her fever came down."

"Why didn't you tell me any of this on my layovers? It all sounded so dire on Tuesday when we spoke."

"It all felt dire on Tuesday. She looked terrible. The whole reason she fell was that she had a coughing fit and slid on the ice. She never should've been out of the house. I knew nothing else until I came last night after work—I'd called the hospital during the day, but they didn't say much. By the time I'd seen her—I figured you'd be at the hospital any minute and see for yourself." Stacie stirred her coffee and seemed unfettered by the acrid taste.

"My flight got in crazy late. By the time I got here, they wouldn't let me see her. Which reminds me," my eyes squinted at her, "you were the one that told Trent to go to the airport."

"He went to the airport?" Her knitted brow made it clear this was new information to her.

"Yes, you sent him. He ran into you at the store or something...?" I asked.

"I saw him outside Market Basket the day it happened," the stirring paused, and she fixed her eyes on an invisible point near the salad bar. "I told him about your mom, that you were flying into Manchester, and I wish I knew when you were landing because it was late and it'd be hard to get a ride." She raised her hands slightly and went back to her cup.

My shoulders went slack. *He did that completely on his own.* I stared at my half-full coffee cup as if it might evaporate and tea leaves with all the answers would magically appear.

"So, what is this your mom tells me about some doctor? Auntie needs details." Stacie wiggled in her seat like a kindergartner at Sunday School.

My face brightened. "It's probably nothing. How do you even know?"

"How else? Your mom."

Stacie and my mom had met in elementary school. Stacie had trotted the globe most of her life doing merchandizing for a high-end fashion brand. My mom married a year out of high school and never left this town, apart from trips to Boston. In some ways, they were as dissonant as jazz and 80s rock, yet they remained solid as sisters. Stacie had a brownstone on Beacon Hill in Boston—though she traveled so much, I am sure her mailman was there more than she was. She had expansive windows, comfy furniture, and a partial view of the Charles River. Visiting her was like sneaking into someone else's life for an afternoon. I loved it.

That brownstone was her one constant; until my father died. She claimed her return to Newhouse was because she was in her early forties, and it was time to grow some roots. She had always wanted a flower shop, and she loved being her own boss. I think her family and folks in town fell for that line, but it was unequivocal to me—she had returned to be there for my mom. I'd always cherished her, and with that gesture, she reached icon status. I was deeply grateful. Her doing that is probably the reason I could move to Oregon unencumbered.

"I can't keep anything from you two," I commented.

Her reply was simple, "Yeah, but isn't that the beauty of it?"

I shook my head. I valued their friendship; I just hated being the center of their conversations.

She persisted, "Go on, tell me."

"There's nothing to tell really," I shrugged, "I have an unrequited crush on an aesthetically pleasing pediatrician."

"Aesthetically pleasing pediatrician, huh? Do you realize you do that?"

"What?" I asked.

"You do that when you want to change the subject." She was pointing her stirring stick at me.

"What?"

"You use big words hoping people will lose interest. Doesn't work with me. It sounded like there was some *requited* interest from what I heard. Weren't you going to a big party together?" The corners of her eyes crinkled, and the corners of my mouth dropped.

"That's tomorrow night. We planned to go to the work Christmas party together. Clearly, that isn't happening."

"Oh love, I am so sorry," she reached over and patted my hand, "that is an unfortunate turn of events. The fact he asked shows interest. But that's it? You've had no other dates or time alone together? You work together, right?"

My face flushed with a pang of guilt. Why on earth was I interested in someone I worked with? This—*this* was the challenge of small towns. Not enough options.

"We go on walks at lunch together all the time—just the two of us." I tucked my hair behind my ear and leaned in. "He's actually the one who offered and drove me to the airport well before dawn yesterday. He's already called to check in on things too."

"Sounds like he's interested," Stacie offered.

"Or it sounds like he cares and is compassionate." I steeled myself and continued, "But there are moments when our eyes fuse, and it feels like we are communicating entire conversations. We brush each other in passing and there's a kinetic energy. It takes effort to compose myself if he flashes me a grin during a staff meeting. It sounds absurd, but I swear his voice drops just a little lower when he speaks to me."

I release the breath I've been holding and look directly at Stacie. "There is a connection, but we're taking it slow. We want to make sure it doesn't get complicated." I swirled my coffee in the cup. "I guess that is why the Christmas party had me so excited. It was a move forward. It was our first date. He was picking me up, we would show up at a party *together*. Now he's going solo—and I'm here."

"I'm sorry, love. That must be frustrating." Stacie was always good at listening. My mom was always good at correcting and telling me to get over things.

"It is what it is. It's sweet. Sweet and uncomplicated. It meant a lot that he took me to the airport."

"He did." She gave a half shrug. "So it should also mean a lot for someone to pick you up at the airport."

I gave her a blank stare. "Really? My mom is chasing that lead hard enough."

"I just find it intriguing, that's all. It's quite a gesture. I know he's an immense help to your mom. Though I've lost track of your opinions about Trent since you were in college. You shed some tears for that boy. I didn't realize you two patched things over." She didn't pause long enough for me to interrupt her. "Since you and Dr. Mysterious haven't started anything—there are no limits to your options." I felt her eyes on me. I was studying my cuticles.

"He disappeared Stacie." It was a relief to say it out loud, "I thought he was the love of my life and that we could overcome anything. Then he stopped talking to me. Wouldn't answer my calls. Vanished. I was naïve back then. I've learned my lesson. I know what he is capable of, and he can just do it again."

"You were young. People don't handle relationships well when they are young. I'm sure he didn't entirely disappear. How much have you spoken since then? Did he ever explain?"

My head shook from side to side. "The first time we spoke was at the airport. Prior to our breakup, we'd spoken every few days on the phone after I'd moved to Boston for undergrad, seven years ago. I thought everything was fine. I came home for a visit, thrilled to see him. He wasn't at my parent's house. He wasn't at his house. His dad said he was off camping with his buddies. That was it. Afterwards, I called him a few more times, sent emails—he never responded."

"But he came to your dad's funeral; I remember seeing him there."

"The whole town was there. Everyone loved my dad. I was so focused on mom; I didn't pay attention to much else."

"I'm so sorry, love," she reached out and put her hand on mine again. She waited until I looked her straight in the eyes. "The way he talks about you, it feels like you guys must still talk once a week. I never would have guessed he closed you out like that."

"We were kids, Stacie." I drew in a breath and moved my hand away. "I thought our relationship was something that it clearly wasn't. I've learned a lot about dating since then. He's just the first boy I fell in love with. I hadn't learned people could fall out of love or treat you like that."

She squeezed my arm. "Sounds like you've thought it through. You'll figure it out, you always do."

I took in a sharp breath. Everyone always thought I had it all figured out. Right now, nothing made sense. I was still spinning about my mom's surgery and health. Her recovery had a lot of implications for my life. My love life (or lack thereof) was hardly a factor.

I wondered if there was some way to get out of going to the festival with Trent tomorrow.

Talking about how things ended seven years ago had me feeling raw. It also made the last twenty-four hours seem trite.

CHAPTER EIGHT

"I know your mom said you *had to go,* but right now, you look like a prisoner of war. Should I take you home?" Trent's olive branch and way out made me feel slightly better. Which made it harder to answer the question. I didn't want to see him, but I needed a change of scenery. My body ached from being cramped up in that hospital room and that one uncomfortable chair.

"No, I could use a little fresh air. I've been there every hour nurse Higgins has allowed."

Trent threw his head back and laughed at the mention of nurse Higgins. "How is that dear sweet woman?"

"I avoid her when I can, but she comes in starting at 7 p.m. counting down the minutes to the end of visiting hours."

"What've you been doing once you're kicked out?"

I looked at him for a moment and considered whether he should ask that question.

"Mmm... Thursday night I unpacked and settled into my old room."

I left out the part where I ran across a box of old memories. Wouldn't want him to suspect I had spent most of the evening reading sweet notes he'd sent me in high school and reminiscing over old pictures.

I kept with the safe details. "Last night Stacie came over and we watched chick flicks."

"Which ones?" He was glancing over at me and then rotating back to the road.

"Um, *Twister* and *Sweet Home Alabama,*" I told him.

"*Twister*? You consider that a chick flick?"

My lips curled slightly. "I guess I use the term loosely. Sometimes it's when chicks watch a flick together, though it has an interesting love story."

"Never thought about it like that. *Sweet Home Alabama,* isn't that the one where she comes home and chooses her childhood sweetheart over some fancy rich guy?"

I glanced at him sideways, "I guess you could boil it down to that."

When we walked from the lot onto Main Street, my jaw fell open. Twinkling gold lights had it completely transformed. The glow of dusk hid the flecks of dirt in the banks of snow. All that remained were reflections of light and merriment. It was bustling with excitement and there were more people than I had ever seen on these streets. The park at the end of the way was lit up with multi-colored lights and you could hear the carols being played live. At the moment, it sounded like the high school jazz band with some lyrical accompaniment. I had always loved my small town, but tonight it was magical.

Trent placed his hand on my lower back and silently guided me through the crowd.

"Do you remember this?" We stopped in front of a high-end store that had mannequins dressed in sequined formal gowns. It was completely unfamiliar to me. I shook my head.

"This used to be The Corner Shake, where we would all grab sodas after school. Do you remember that time we stopped in after camping at Crawford's Notch and Richie knocked over your hot fudge sundae?"

"That's not something you forget." I gave a half laugh at the memory.

My focus remained fixed on the renovation. The front windows and the door were the same, but everything else about the space was completely different. I tried to look past the mannequins to see if there were any remnants I might recognize. The intricate pattern on the wall with gold thread laced in, the plush carpet, the chandelier. It was the furthest thing from my memories of high school.

"A lot has changed," I muttered.

"In a lot of ways." Trent's fingers swept across the longest strands of my hair.

I looked up at him, searching his eyes. Everything my aunt said was flashing through my mind, along with the pictures of how he used to look at me.

I broke from him and continued down the sidewalk.

I rubbed my temples. I probably shouldn't have agreed to this outing. It was strange spending time with him. It was just like it'd always been, and yet completely disparate. It was so out of sync with my current life.

My mom had been so excited when Trent picked me up at the hospital. It was the most pep I'd seen in her since I arrived. We'd talked to the doctors at length today and we were both drained. I hadn't seen her smile in hours, and she lit up when he entered the room. As though we had finally found the right salve.

During our lengthy conversations that day, we'd covered all the things she would need for her recovery. It was intense. It would require me staying to give her constant care for at least a month; or putting her into some sort of assisted living facility. Which is the last thing either of us wanted. We passed the time playing gin rummy in between talking to the different specialists; respiratory, physical, occupational, orthopedic, pulmonology, and more. The cards were a welcome distraction. The last time I remember us playing, I was still a child. We'd started playing the day before—when there was room for chatter and light laughter. Today, it filled the silence as we each soaked in all we had heard.

Maybe it thrilled her to see Trent because it meant I was leaving soon. She could be alone with her thoughts. We loved each other dearly, but three consecutive twelve-hour days was a lot. I couldn't imagine how taxing twenty-four/seven for a full month would be.

Or maybe her excitement at seeing Trent was separate from that. His boyish charm made everyone fall in love with him—at least a little. I needed to remember that.

When we got closer to the park, I could see the collection of booths. There were homemade cookies, felted caps, handmade ornaments that glistened in lights, and, of course, old-fashioned fudge. There was even a jolly old fellow with a white beard, complete with a mob of little ones scrambling to see him.

They hadn't cleared all the snow from the ground, so it still crunched underfoot if you walked over the grass. They had pressed it artistically against the booths to add to the ambiance. The air swirled with hope and spirit as we entered the little wonderland.

"Do you wanna grab some cider?" The holiday lights danced in Trent's eyes, reflecting a bit of mischief. He casually kicked snow up onto my boots.

My eyes scowled, but my lips were still curled into a smile.

His playful nature was one thing I appreciated about him.

"Is cider the new code word for a snowball fight?"

He shrugged. "I try not to talk in code. I think they are two separate things." And he kicked more snow at me.

"Trent Darby, don't start something you can't finish."

He threw his head back and laughed, "Willa Jones, let it be recorded that *you* incited this."

In one swift motion, he scooped up a chunk of snow, balled it, and pulled his arm back. He was ready to throw before I'd even decided to defend or counterattack.

He propelled his arm forward, but only pretended to throw and instead took a few steps back; allowing me to end this or spur it forward. I guess he had grown up a bit.

I hesitated a moment and then flipped my purse to better secure it on my other shoulder. I took a few steps to my left, partially shielding myself with a bush. Then squatted down to prepare my artillery.

Trent responded in kind—though he wasn't wise enough to seek shelter.

As soon as he bent his head down, looking at the snow—I hurled the first snowball directly at his head. I hit him square on.

He laughed and shook the snow from his jet-black locks. He swiftly pivoted to launch a counterattack. In his haste, it was only a half-formed snowball. It disintegrated mid-air.

I stuck my tongue out like a third grader and quickly ducked behind the bush. I craned my neck to assess his next move. I'd barely gotten past the edge of the bush when a small chunk of my hair whipped back. The snowball had skated through and continued behind me.

"Sorry, Mrs. Adams!" Trent's voice rang out, and I turned to see Mrs. Adams turning around, trying to examine the snowball that had landed on the arm of her coat. My shoulders shook with a giggle. The look on her face was priceless.

I turned back to wag my finger at Trent, only he wasn't there. I stood to find him. Before I was squarely on my feet, I felt him pulling at the neck of my coat and sweater. Shivers went down my spine as something icy and slushy slid down my back.

I whipped around and seethed through clenched teeth. "Trent Darby, please tell me you did not do that!"

I arched my back and shook the bottom of my sweater, trying to quicken the snow's trail before it melted any further.

Daggers shot from my eyes.

Trent's jaw was slack, and his face was ashen.

"I didn't think that through," were the muffled words I heard. It was hard to make out because his gloved hand had moved to cover his gaping mouth.

I took the remnants of an unused snowball, still in my right hand, firmly grabbed the waist of Trent's jeans, and pulled it towards me, releasing the snow to glide down.

His eyes grew to saucers. I was the one with my mouth ajar.

His hand snapped down to remedy the situation. I muffled my

laugh, turned on my heel, and sprinted away—having no clue where to go. I headed towards the darkness closer to the fire station. I'd barely escaped the merriment of the park when I felt him closing in on me.

He caught me up from behind, fully encapsulating me, and spinning me around. I am not sure if he was tickling me, or if I devolved into giggles at my own accord.

"I'm sorry, I'm sorry, I can't believe I did that!" I squirmed in his embrace; laughter punctuating my words.

"What am I going to do with you, Willa Amber Jones?" His face was beaming, and his eyes were foraging the depths of mine.

My body stilled and the giddiness of our frolic settled into something deeper.

"You'll think of something."

I was breathless, my heart was pounding, and I could feel every point where his body met mine. His lips pressed against mine, and his clasp intensified. I had kissed these lips more than any other and tonight they felt softer than I remembered and more passionate. It was a kiss to be lost in. Where the snow, the carols, the buzz of the nearby crowd, the hospital, the decisions; just melt away.

We floated outside of time. We could have been kissing for moments or half an hour. When he eventually pulled away, he'd leaned me to a 45-degree angle at the waist. His fingers were caressing my cheek, and I felt a snowdrop on my nose. I looked up and belly-laughed at the cliché snowflakes that were decorating us both.

I smoothed my hair and coat, lacking for words.

"I guess that is one way to warm up," I said with a smirk.

He held my eyes for a long moment, "And the other is cider, let's get to it."

He took my hand in his as though this was a kiss among hundreds. As though we'd never stopped doing this and the past seven years didn't exist. He guided me back to the merriment of the park, stopping at the edge near a booth.

"You wait here. I'll be back." The booth was full of baubles, ornaments, and an assortment of fudge. Quite the variety. I stepped towards the display, but my eyes followed him.

He chatted, his head bent intently, with the elderly lady running the booth. There was no one else over there. I guess hot apple cider wasn't the most popular beverage at a holiday festival. She needed to add a drizzle of caramel or carry a macchiato option as well.

He patted the women's hand and listened intently as she prattled on, patiently waiting for the simple drinks he had ordered. He had such a way with people. I still can't believe what Stacie told me. He came to see my mom every week. I hadn't asked my mom about it. It felt like it would invade her privacy. His name came up more today than it has in years. It was as though she had to see me with him before she could speak about him with me. To see that he and I were okay. I wondered how harshly I'd reacted historically any time his name came up. His disappearing like that was the cruelest thing anyone had ever done to me. The more you love, the more you hurt. And there is no love like a first love.

"Did you know they have a Ferris wheel?" Trent's voice startled me, and I looked to see his hand extending the cider to me. I wondered how long he'd been like that.

I snatched it from him. "Seriously? Where'd they hide it?"

He tilted his head back towards the way we'd just been near the fire department.

"It's over there. Hidden by the building. We may have to check it out later," he said with a sheepish grin.

"I'd like that."

I studied him for a moment. His steely eyes were harder to read when he was serious. When he was playful, the light would dance in them, and you could read him like a book. There was a strong angle to his jawline that contrasted the fullness of his lips. His build was similar to when I saw him last. He was always tall and lean, though from that embrace he felt more substantial. There was strength behind his grasp. It's hard to tell under the layers of winter clothes, and we'd hardly spent enough time indoors together to even take off a jacket, but my body had felt what my eyes had yet to see.

"First, we shop." He flung his arms out, encircling the surrounding space.

I hooted a quick peal of laughter. "Why, yes. Of course."

He offered me his arm, and we set off to exploring.

CHAPTER NINE

The Ferris wheel was larger than I had imagined. There were a few other rides as well. The music overhead had changed to that of a typical carnival. It was as though we were attending two discrete events on the same night.

We were no stranger to the Ferris wheel. We had gone to the County Fair both summers we spent together and even traveled to the Fryeburg Fair in Maine our senior year. Being here had transported me back to those years more than anything else. Perhaps it was the teens surrounding us, or the way we walked arm in arm like high schoolers, or maybe it was all the chiding and chuckling.

The whole evening had been flawless. As though we were in a play and had only gone to intermission seven years ago and seamlessly came back to the second act; at the Newhouse Nights of Christmas. None of the torment or tears. Just the passage of time, and the natural maturing that comes with age.

I had forgotten how much he made me laugh. I'd already laughed more this evening than I'd laughed the entire year and a half since I'd been in Oregon. Oregon was lovely, the people were sweet and caring. The work was important; I was happy—I just didn't laugh like this. I don't think most people laughed like this.

"Do you remember the first time I called you Buttercup?" Trent pressed into my palm, massaging my bare hand, the glove sitting in my lap. We were at nearly the top of the Ferris wheel looking out over the lights below and the few scattered on the hillside up and into the woods, all of which comprised Newhouse.

"It was a long time ago." I worded it carefully as not to lie. Of course, I remembered. I remembered everything.

"We were on the Ferris wheel that first summer. We'd been inseparable for nearly a year at that point. You, sassy as always, threatened to push me off for some little thing I did. I bowed my head and said, 'as you wish Princess Buttercup'. You had no clue what that meant. So, I made you watch *Princess Bride*. I called you Buttercup ever since. I think you only allowed it because she had long hair like yours and everyone thought she was beautiful."

"I think I got used to it. Used to it and liking it are two different things." Even if they were both accurate. He also used the phrase "as you wish" incessantly. Strange that I never started calling him Wesley.

I rested my head on his shoulder and tangled myself up close to him. He wrapped his arm around me and continued massaging my palm with his free hand.

He kissed the top of my head, and I lifted my face as he made his way to my lips. The kisses started slow and soft and then built in intensity. I took back my ungloved hand and ran my fingers through his hair.

Was there anything more reminiscent of high school than contorting ourselves to kiss on a Ferris wheel?

As I shifted to better align with him, I felt something sliding on my leg.

"Hey, that ain't cool."

I gasped and then burst out laughing.

The voice was that of a teen far below.

"What? What happened?" Trent asked.

I could barely make out the words- "My glove!"

CHAPTER TEN

Trent purchased popcorn and hot chocolate for the teenagers my glove had assaulted. The ride operator almost didn't let us retrieve it. My incessant giggle ruined Trent's credibility as he relayed the story. I may have been compensating for the heat creeping into my face and coloring my cheeks.

"Good thing you never did that in high school." Trent shook my arm when he said that.

"We were smart and rode the Ferris wheel when it was warmer, fewer things to drop."

"If I remember correctly, there was once a shoe you almost lost." He tilted his head as he looked down at me.

"You remember too much." I smiled back.

His face had gone dark. "Maybe I do." He was looking down at the snow now.

"What's that?"

"Why'd you leave, Willa? It was right when I needed you." He'd stopped walking and his eyes had an intensity that I didn't recognize.

"Leave? You think I left you? That doesn't even make sense."

"You went to Boston. You went away when I needed you." He pushed back.

"Trent, I went to college. We both knew I was going away for college. That I always wanted to go to college in Boston. That was something I'd decided before I ever met you."

"Then things changed, Willa. They changed and you should've stayed."

I physically separated myself from him. My mind was reeling. After all these years, he was trying to pin this on me?

"What are you talking about, Trent? You disappeared. I came home for the weekend to see you and you'd disappeared."

"We were talking on the phone twice a week, Willa. That wasn't a relationship. You were an hour and a half away and we were worlds apart. I needed you here. You could've at least waited a term."

"A term? What are you talking about, Trent? What difference would a term have made?"

"My mom had only been dead a month when you left, Willa. I couldn't stand being in that house, being in this town, but my dad needed me. Why couldn't you see I needed you?"

I rocked back on my heels. It was as though a slap had landed across my face. His mom. How could I have forgotten his mom? I thought he was fine; he acted fine.

How *could* he be fine? We were eighteen.

"Trent..." I said his name, but had no other words. My mouth gaped open, while my eyes danced around, trying to collect thoughts. I'd spent seven years blaming all of this on him. How could I make room for the fact I may have let him down, that somehow I was at fault.

An unremitting tone from his phone broke the silence.

I closed my eyes and took a deep inhale. My mind was in a whorl.

The least I could do was find the words to apologize.

I looked him square in the face, but his features had hardened. His eyes fixed on a distant point.

I couldn't tell if it was in response to what he read on his phone or our conversation.

"I've gotta go," he said.

"Really? We're not gonna finish this?" I pulled back.

"I'm sorry, Willa, I… I just can't right now." He stammered as he took strides backward. He stopped. I could see the hesitation, but the clouds continued to storm across his face. He turned and left.

CHAPTER ELEVEN

I was sitting on my childhood bed, with a box of memories sitting beside me. I'd only made it home because Stacie came and got me. She asked a lot of questions and respected my lack of responses. She gave me a long hug. That must've been why I chose her over Uber.

Emotions overwhelmed me, and I wasn't sure how to process any of them. I had spent seven years covering over and trying to forget all the beautiful things about Trent and Willa; only to have them come rushing back over the last few days. All I had was the bitterness and the anger at him for disappearing. What he told me tonight was completely bewildering. It was rewriting a story that was engrained in me. It hurt to carve it out.

I kept trying to piece together that fall seven years ago.

He said nothing. He never told me he wanted me to stay. Had he? Had I been so focused on my goals that I didn't hear him? Had I never considered it? Would I have stayed *if* he had asked? I know Stacie came back for my mom in a heartbeat. Was I willing to put someone else before me like that? I was eighteen. It's not like I went across the country. I didn't desert him—I went an hour and a half away.

He was right, though—I hardly had time to talk. I was setting boundaries and making sure I didn't let my high school boyfriend distract me from my college education. That I didn't let my past keep me from my future. Had I already categorized him in my past? Maybe I was more to blame than I ever realized.

But he vanished.

Just like he had tonight. If we had talked. If we had fought, if he had told me... Would that have changed the outcome? I can never know for sure. I *do* know it would've changed the next seven years. It would've changed how I saw him. How I saw us. How I saw myself. How I framed our ending and our entire relationship.

This new way of trying to conceptualize things exhausted me.

I needed someone to process this with. Not my mom or Stacie, whose biases were clear, but someone outside and neutral. I called Sierra. She was my roommate from graduate school who was whimsically staying with me in Oregon. She knew me. She would help me sort through this.

When she answered the phone, the loud background noise surprised me.

"Sierra? It's Willa."

"Hey Willa, hold on."

She muffled the phone slightly as she seemed to move to some place quieter.

"Hey girl, what's going on? How's your mom? Your texts make it sound like she's doing better." I'd been keeping everyone back in Oregon updated via text. I wasn't up for phone calls.

"Um, yeah. She was better than I thought she'd be. There are a lot of big decisions about her care we need to figure out though." I let out an enormous sigh. Maybe that was weighing on me as well. Guilt over letting her down if I didn't stay; compounded by what Trent had brought to light. "That's not why I called, though. It's for silly boy stuff." I pulled us back on track.

Sierra was uncharacteristically silent.

"Sierra, are you there?" I asked, but I could still faintly hear the background noise, so I'm pretty sure she was.

"Is this about Dr. M?" Sierra's voice was muffled like a shielded whisper.

"No," I mused, "It's about this guy from high school. Do you remember me talking about Trent?"

"Oh, good. Whose Trent?" Her response confused me. I looked at my watch. It was 11:00 p.m. here and 8:00 p.m. there.

"Where are you, Sierra?" I tried to keep my tone neutral.

"Oh, well…" her words were halting, "Izzy worried there wouldn't be many people at the holiday party, so I agreed to come along."

"You went to the party with Izzy and her boyfriend?" This was odd. The third wheel on a date? Izzy and I worked together—Sierra didn't work with us. I'd introduced them when Sierra came to town, but I wouldn't consider them friends. It made little sense she was at a Christmas Party being thrown for the staff of the clinic where I worked.

"Well, actually Andrés, um… Dr. Morales drove me." I nearly dropped the phone. She continued. "I just think Izzy didn't want to be the only one with a date—and knew I was lonely with you gone, so she talked her brother into bringing me."

Izzy was Andrés' younger sister and dates being allowed at the event was new this year, so it's possible she wanted someone else there who wasn't an employee. Regardless, I couldn't skip the part where Sierra had essentially called herself Andrés' date. My Andrés. And they were at the party that was supposed to be my first official date with Andrés.

Before everything overwhelmed me. Now I was spinning past my limits.

"Willa, you there?"

"Um, yeah." The knot in my stomach was making it harder to breathe. "This connection isn't very good. Why don't you get back to the party and we'll talk tomorrow or something?"

"That works!" Sierra's voice was much cheerier now that she had an escape.

We exchanged our goodbyes. I sat staring at the phone.

This was too much to process. I pushed the box aside, flipped off the lamp, and climbed under the covers.

I could brush my teeth in the morning.

CHAPTER TWELVE

"Seriously, mom?" I would've glared at her, but I was keeping my eyes on the road. "This isn't how I normally drive. I'm driving like this for you."

"Well, if this is for me. You can cut it out. It's incredibly annoying," she said.

"I'm going to pretend you didn't say that."

I fumbled without looking at the knobs and turned the radio up louder. Christmas Carols didn't have quite the same effect as the music from my teens. She stopped talking though, so I think she got the message.

I was still stopping a little sooner than normal at every light. I was taking every corner slower. And more cars might have passed me this morning than the whole of my life before today, but it was necessary.

Traffic was light since it was Christmas, but it wasn't about traffic.

I was taking my mom home. She and we had been through enough. We needed to make it home safely. It was the first day of the four weeks she was under my care. I was taking this seriously. Sunday had been quiet. I snuck in a DVD player so mom and I could watch Christmas movies starting with *While You Were Sleeping* and ending with *The Family Stone* (that one always made me cry). Both were good movies. Both made me glad I was an only child.

I'd brought the fudge I'd picked up at the festival. She was good at settling for my vague description of how beautiful downtown was when she asked about my night. No follow-up about Trent. His name had hardly come up over the last couple of days, which helped. Somehow in the bustle of Christmas and trying to get my mom out of the hospital; all mention of men went to the back burner.

Monday was Christmas Eve, but all the specialists were working. They were there with last instructions, guidance, and preparing discharge papers so we could go home on Christmas. They kept us there for a few hours this morning, but thankfully we were now released. I had thought to order a take-and-bake meal from Market Basket I could pick up tonight. Other than that, we may just need to find more Christmas movies to round out our lack of festivities.

As we rounded the corner towards our house. I took a second look. The house was aglow. Every light seemed to be on and there was a twinkle of colored Christmas bulbs gleaming off a tree you could see in the window, right where mom always put the tree. Someone haphazardly wrapped lights around the front porch; as if they had run out of time before finishing. There was no car or evidence to divulge the identity of our mystery helper. It, of course, would be Stacie.

"What is this?" My mom's voice filled with excitement. "Did you do this for me?"

My eyes were still wide with wonder. I shook my head. "I had nothing to do with this. I'm as surprised as you are."

"I'm not surprised. I am thrilled. Someone knows how much I love Christmas!"

I rolled my eyes and pulled into the driveway.

"Well, I'm going to go see if your Christmas elf is also helpful. I'd feel better if there were two of us getting you in the house, even if there is only one step."

Stacie had cleared the snow up the sidewalk. It impressed me. Stacie wasn't much of one for manual labor. I swiped a bit of fluff over to the small bank of snow and realized she must've paid somebody else to take care of it.

I called for her as I entered the door, "Stacie, you are either the best person ever for doing this, or the worst person ever for making me look bad. I haven't decided which yet."

The house smelled like fresh cinnamon rolls. It propelled my steps as I neared the kitchen. I rounded the corner—and got goosebumps.

There was food on the counter that separated the kitchen and dining area. There were cinnamon rolls, a plate with tight little curls of ham and cheese, and some rather haphazard deviled eggs. Next to them was Trent, drying a dish with a towel.

"I think the best person ever would be my preference." He said, with a beguiling twinkle in his eye.

"Trent, what are you doing here?" My chest tightened and yet the rest of my body felt a wave of relief.

"Well, I guess I could have left before you guys got home." He set down the dish and towel, drawing a little closer to me, "But part of the point was to see you. I need to apologize."

He searched my eyes, but my face was indecipherable. How could it show emotion when I wasn't sure what to feel? No word for two and a half days, and he just shows up in my mom's kitchen? On Christmas?

"I know I left quickly Saturday night." His eyes downcast, he rubbed the back of his neck.

"Left quickly? You essentially sprinted out of there—in the middle of our conversation. You left me without a ride."

His eyes widened at the mention of the ride.

"Ouch, I forgot I was your ride. I'm sorry, Willa. I wasn't thinking."

"Clearly." My arms folded across my chest and the self-satisfaction heated the judgment in my belly.

"I just didn't know how to explain things. And we were on an important topic, so I didn't want to change the subject abruptly. I knew I didn't have time to explain things, or fix things, and…." There was a soft thud as he dropped his hands to his side, "I have a 2-year-old daughter."

I rocked back on my heels and blinked hard. "What?"

"I know I should have told you, but there was no room for it to come up. We'd hardly spent time together yet. So, when I got the text that her fever had spiked and they might take her to the hospital—I just had to go."

"Is she alright?" I asked.

"Yeah, Kelly's mom made it there before I did. Apparently, Kelly didn't know to give her Children's Tylenol. So, once we did that, her fever went down just fine. Which makes it even more embarrassing that I left like that."

I tried to let his words sink in. It was a justifiable reason to leave. I could see why he hadn't explained in the moment, but it was more than just his sudden departure Saturday night. I was still reprocessing that seven years ago I was part of the reason this ended—it wasn't all him. I was dizzy with how easily we fell back in step, how one kiss could ignite the spark of the many before. And this, this was a whole different level. He had a kid. I'd never dated someone with a kid.

"I know that's gonna take a bit to sink in." His feet moved in slow steps towards me. "But I needed to be fair and let you know. She's the greatest little girl you'll ever meet. Her enthusiasm is as contagious as her giggle."

"Trent, how could you kiss me? How could you come on to me without telling me something like that? Do you keep this from all the women you date?"

"Does that mean we're dating?" He flashed me his most charming grin, but it disappeared as soon as it didn't get the reception he'd hoped.

"Willa, I didn't plan any of this. I didn't expect to kiss you. It surprised me how strongly I felt about you. I knew I missed you. I knew you'd been in my thoughts. Especially the last year when I was seeing your mom more, but I thought our story was done. That book was closed. Then I saw Stacie at the store; she told me about your mom and that you were coming. All I wanted was to be there for you. I cared so much for you it ached, Willa. Before I knew it, I was sitting at an airport trying to guess when you might land. That's when it all started flooding back. Us. There was so much more to us than I'd let myself remember. But it was clear you had long shut that door. Then at the festival, I saw a glimmer of us, Willa. I saw the playfulness in your eyes. You looked at me like you used to. I wasn't thinking of all the reasons why not or the warning labels I should clear up. I was thinking of you and me. Willa, I felt it when we kissed. It is still there. You and I have been connected since the first time we locked eyes across the commons area at Newhouse High. It was no coincidence that you needed a ride home that day. I know you better than anyone. Even the pieces you've forgotten. Let me help you remember. Let me help you laugh again."

I took in a sharp breath. Those last words flooded my eyes with tears. The burning in my chest spread to a warmth coursing through me. My hands instinctively shielded my face. Then Trent wrapped himself around me and I buried my head in his chest. It surprised me how soft his sweater was. When we were younger, it was always cheap scratchy t-shirts.

"I've got you, Willa. I'll always have you."

He tilted my chin so he could see my eyes.

"I'm incredibly sorry, Willa. I shouldn't have taken off like that. I'm done disappearing."

I drug my palm across my cheek to clear the remaining tears and find my words.

"And I'm sorry for not realizing I played a part in things, too. I guess I need to-"

The shrill blare of the horn on my mother's car interrupted us.

My hands leaped to cover my mouth. "I forgot about her! I'm a horrible daughter."

"Come on, I'll help you get her."

CHAPTER THIRTEEN

"Trent, where did you learn to cook like this?" My mom had gushed over Trent the second she saw he was here.

"I've got a few tricks up my sleeves." His eyes twinkled.

"And the tree—it's beautiful."

I gave a slight chuckle at my mom's mention of the tree. It reminded me of the one at the airport. It was probably the last one available, but still needed a home. Trent had scrounged up lights, but that was the only decoration. I wasn't sure if that was a lack of time or lack of knowledge. What could he have done? Found the boxes in the attic? Come up with a theme?

We deemed the recliner was too low for my mom so she was sitting in a dining room chair with arms. Her eyes had a little sparkle, her lips curled in a slight smile, but she looked pale and was fidgeting a bit from discomfort.

"Okay, that's enough for you. Off to bed." I walked over to her.

"That's ridiculous. I just got home!" she argued.

"Mom, it's been almost forty-five minutes. It's supposed to be closer to half an hour for sitting."

"But it's Christmas." She whined just as a small child would when they wanted to open just one more gift.

"Come on, Viv—I'll help." Trent walked over and joined us.

"Now how can I say no to that?" She reached her arms up to him.

"Mom, it's going to be a long month if you'll only listen to him."

"That's okay, you can put me on speed dial." Trent winked at me. I was going to use this to my advantage.

"Now, Willa, have you met his adorable daughter, Sophie? She has his beautiful hair and peppy blue eyes." I looked at each of them.

"Funny how she hasn't come up until now," I said.

"Oh bother, did I mess things up? It's the pain meds. Trent came to the hospital after things didn't go well at the festival. I think he was looking for you, but we had a pleasant talk." She admitted.

My mouth was agape. Not only had he looked for me that night, but the two of them had kept that to themselves. I wasn't sure what to make of this new information.

"We agreed I should give you some space to process things." Trent was good at reading me.

I settled my mom in and set her up with the Hallmark channel and enough Christmas movies to keep her entertained for the full four weeks.

I headed to the kitchen to clean up.

"Hey, come here a sec."

Trent was in the front room and was pulling a small box out of the tree. One magically cloaked in the branches. I guess there was a bit of ornamentation.

My steps were hesitant. "Is that for my mom?"

"It's for you. It's something small I should have given you years ago. Come sit." He patted the seat beside him.

"Oh, no…" my head was rapidly shaking back and forth.

Trent looked down, taking in the size and shape of the box, "Oh, no, no, no. That's not what it is. Though I am honored that's the first thing that came to mind."

I was both silenced and scarlet because of his words. I meekly sat beside him.

"Open it."

The bow on top obscured most of the box beneath it. As I turned it over, a smile spread across my face. The excess of tape clarified that this was a job he'd done himself. It impressed me he had a scrap of Christmas wrap, even a simple red and black plaid with holly.

"I didn't buy presents for anyone, except my roommate- and that's back in Oregon." I said.

"It's not something I bought—let's just call it a something from the heart. Now, *open it.*" His tone was more demanding this time.

I fought with the tape and ended up having to tear every bit of visible paper to get it open. Inside was a velvety clamshell heart-shaped box with no specific markings on it.

I paused a moment, catching his eye before I flipped it open.

I gasped.

It was not the first time I'd seen this. Inside was a simple gold box chain. Hanging at its center were delicate scrolls and swirls surrounding a W on a gold oval locket. When I separated the two halves, the bottom portion still held a spattering of sand.

My connection to this simple object welled inside of me and poured out as tears.

"How did you?... Where did you?" The words stumbled out of my mouth, "Trent, I lost this."

He wrapped his arm around me and let me lean against him as I remained mesmerized by the small treasure.

My dad had given me this trinket for my thirteenth birthday. In it were the grains of sand from the first time I dipped my toes in the Pacific. My dad took me to San Diego the summer I turned ten. We visited the beach almost every day and would splash in the surf and run in the sand. He'd have to drag me away to get food or surrender and feed me a hot dog from the vendors. I would make him stay until after we watched the sunset. It was one of many adventures with him, and the furthest we'd ever traveled. My mom didn't share our wanderlust, so the trips were only us two.

The empty space in this locket carried the whole of a little girl's memories of journeys with her dad. When I arrived in Oregon and first looked out from Cascade Head to watch the sunset, I could almost feel him next to me.

I curled into Trent and let my body heave with sobs. I don't think I'd admitted to myself that the hole left from losing my father was the biggest reason I stopped coming home. It hurt too much to be here without him. How could I not have realized the loss Trent felt when he lost his mom at eighteen? Why didn't I know he needed me?

Trent smoothed my hair. It was minutes before the storm had subsided, and I could sit upright and speak again.

"Where did you get this?"

"Crawford's Notch."

I'd lost it at Crawford's Notch just after graduation, and weeks before Trent lost his mom. It hadn't thawed just yet, and we bundled ourselves up when we went hiking. When I got back to our yurt, the necklace wasn't around my neck. We searched half the day until dark and again the next morning, with no luck.

"Along the trail?" I asked.

"I wish I could take that level of credit," he gave a half shrug, "but it was hanging in the boathouse a couple of summers ago. They'd framed it and it had a poem behind it. I tracked down the owners and they gave it to me once I answered their trick question."

"Trick question?"

"They asked me to describe the photos inside," he beamed, "and I told them it was nothing but sand. Apparently, people had been trying to claim it for years. Usually, they claimed the W was a family name and would describe photos of people."

Even my fingers were warm from the smile that lit my face.

Without a word, he took the locket from the box and placed it around my neck. The cold metal felt so familiar against my skin. I ran the pads of my fingers over it again and again.

I pivoted back to him.

"Trent, we still need to talk."

He hung his head down and avoided my eyes. "This is complicated. You don't do complicated."

"Why don't you let me say it?" I took his hand in my lap and held it with both of mine. I looked straight into his eyes. "Trent, I had forgotten what home was to me. I had forgotten so much about this place, about you. It's taken a bit for me to figure it out. I still don't have all the answers, but being with you feels like home to me." My voice cracked and I could feel the tears rising again. "It's about time I stop avoiding things because they are complicated. I want this. I want *you.* I want to laugh again."

His eyes glistened, and as the first tear fell, he swallowed me in his brawny arms.

CHAPTER FOURTEEN

FIVE MONTHS LATER

"Where are we supposed to put all of this?" my mom was turning in circles, wobbling slightly on her cane as she surveyed all the movers had unloaded from the van.

"Um, the shed for now." I shrugged.

"Willa, I finally got that cleared out for me." My mom narrowed her eyes.

"It's just temporary, eventually I, or Trent and I, will get a place—I promise."

"I want my shed back before summer." She pointed emphatically as she walked back towards the house. She still used her cane occasionally, including days like today, but her hip had healed well.

The noise level behind me increased, and I spun around. Sophie and her infectious laugh were corrupting the movers. Trent waved at me.

I crossed through the maze of furniture over to them. Trent leaned down for a kiss and then Sophie leaned down, calling out, "Billa, Billa." My mom was Biv, so at least it was clear we were related.

"Hey, Sophie—are you going to help move these big boxes?"

She nodded enthusiastically. She was up for anything.

My mom peeked her head out the door. "Did I hear Sophie?" They both lit up when they saw each other. "Get in here with me!"

Sophie was wiggling in place to escape her dad's arms. He carried her over and set her inside the door. The two toddled off, discussing a baking project. Mom was doing most of the talking.

"This place is a disaster!" Trent chided, as he took in all the piles. "Where are you going to put all this?"

My head fell back, and I raised my hands, "Not you too, is anyone on my side?"

Trent moved over and wrapped his arms around my shoulders, engulfing me. "I am always on your side, Buttercup. What's up?"

"You guys are right, space is tight, but it's hard enough to be moving my stuff across the country. I don't need discouraging commentary."

"Enough said." He kissed my forehead. "How can I help?"

"I don' know. I am thinking most of it can go in my mom's shed."

"Why not put all of it in my garage? There is plenty of room there."

I hesitated. At some point, I'd mentioned that I didn't want to move in together unless we were engaged. I didn't want to bring it up again. I wasn't quite ready for that, and I didn't want him to feel pressured. Things were great as they were, and I didn't want the untimely arrival of my stuff to push things in a direction they weren't ready to go.

The last few months had been amazing. Enough so that when my Family Medical Leave was up, I put in my notice. I went back, packed up, sold my car, said my goodbyes, and moved permanently back. Newhouse was home again. I hadn't decided if I should get my own place or what the next step was. I just knew I didn't need to be paying rent when I wasn't living in Oregon.

Trent was tracing the outline of my face and stopped at my chin, lifting it slightly. "Willa, we both know what this is. We both know where this is going. We are just giving it a little space to grow. It makes sense to put your stuff where it is going to end up, anyway."

"Talk like that and I might make you buy me a promise ring."

Trent gave a single belly laugh, "That would certainly pick up right where we left off."

"Just because high schoolers are the only ones who give promise rings doesn't mean it shouldn't become a thing." I half-joked. I loved jewelry, and he knew it.

"I will give you anything you want, but since we need to tell the movers to change direction right now—can we settle for a pinky promise? Then after I set them up at my garage we can go to the jewelry store?" It all flowed out of Trent's mouth casually, as though charting the path for the rest of our lives was as natural as choosing the restaurant for dinner.

My mouth was hanging slightly agape, but I think all of me opened in this little casual conversation. I put my pinky up. Trent raised his and linked with mine.

"I, Trent Aaron Darby, do solemnly promise that every decision I make is for us and our future together. That as we grow and reach new stages, my intent is, and always has been, to make you laugh; aka safeguard your happiness, be here to support you, and ultimately to make you my bride Willa Amber Jones."

I ached with love, with happiness, and joy. It spilled out as tears. I pulled him closer to me and buried my head in his chest.

He shook my finger, "Hey, your turn."

"Um," the depth of emotions I was feeling made words hard to muster, "what he said. I promise that."

"Oh, Willa." Trent messed my hair up a little and pulled me in, rocking us back and forth.

"Do I at least get a kiss?" he asked.

"This one and thousands more."

ABOUT THE AUTHOR

Avery has always loved writing. Writing, snickerdoodle cookies, her two cats, the ocean, and dark chocolate; not necessarily in that order. She grew up on a farm in a small Northwest town; which informs much of her writing. She has a stack of journals she kept through college and can't decide if she should burn them... or mine them for material! In junior high, she talked her church into performing the Christmas play she wrote; filled with themes of love and redemption.

Then there was adulting, graduate school, and an award-winning career; and little time for creativity. That's partially why it has taken a couple of decades for the writing to take center stage. It also helps (when writing romance) that she finally found her own happily ever after. With that, it was easy to write with authenticity. Her favorite part of writing is creating a world to warm the heart of her readers and let them get swept away. Thank you for supporting her and being part of this journey.

Reviews are the lifeblood for authors and help others to find their work. If you enjoyed this story, please take the time to leave a review!

Are you ready for what's next?

Order Fire from the Ashes: Rose River Romance Book 1 (A Small Town Cowboy Romance) now! mybook.to/FireFromAshes

–Release February 2022-

Learn more about Rose River when Willa first arrives. You'll meet many new folks, including Dr. Morales' best friend from childhood, the brooding cowboy Logan Roberts. After injuries and destruction from a wildfire; he must figure out how to rebuild and heal old wounds. Is it possible he might ignite a new flame along the way?

To keep up to date about giveaways, releases (like Fire from the Ashes), and learn more about Avery—join Avery's Avid Readers: https://storyteller.ck.page/0df2fb67a9

Follow Avery on social media:

www.facebook.com/AuthorAveryLawrence

www.instagram.com/AuthorAveryLawrence

(Hint: If you like cats – you'll like her Instagram)

WARM DAYS

KATHERINE MOORE

CHAPTER ONE

HOME FOR THE HOLIDAYS

He met her at the arrivals gate, smiling and holding a bunch of flowers as he swept her up in a big hug. And that broke Moira's heart because he had brought her irises and she knew they were out of season, so she knew he'd spent a fortune on them.

"I missed you so much," he said into her hair and she forced herself to smile back but couldn't quite make herself say something reassuring because she knew it would be a lie.

She'd never been good at lying and the last person she wanted to lie to was John.

"Baggage claim is this way," he said, starting to steer her in the direction of some moving stairs.

"I'm good," she said, holding up her backpack by the straps. The straps were adjusted to fit over her California clothes. When she'd tried to put it on in the plane, she couldn't get it over the bulk of the new puffer coat she'd bought. She'd finally given up in frustration and decided she would carry it.

One of the first things she'd noticed about life in the Pacific Northwest was that you just had to get used to wearing so many more clothes. It had been sixty-seven when she'd left Los Angeles and all she'd worn to the airport was a light sweater over her scoop-neck tee. But she knew it would be cold and rainy—possibly snowy—when she arrived in Seattle, so she'd bought the coat online and had it delivered to her office at the last minute. She didn't want to be stuck borrowing something that Jennifer had outgrown, or some patched up item that her mother-in-law had worn out but had never gotten around to donating to Goodwill. *Like last time,* a voice in her head reminded Moira.

Last time.

Last time had been an utter disaster, but she wouldn't think about that.

"You didn't bring any other luggage," John asked, his voice carefully neutral.

"I told you I was just coming for the weekend," she said, trying to match his tone. Trying not to sound defensive.

"I see," he said, and that was all, but there was so much weight in those two words.

They headed for the exit doors, John slightly ahead of her. "Why don't you wait inside," he suggested. "I'll bring the car around."

"I've got my puffer coat," she said, trying to make a joke of it.

"You don't have any gloves," he said. "I'll text you when I get close."

And then he was gone before she could stop him and in a way she felt relieved that the moment she was dreading had been postponed, if only for another few minutes.

Traffic was heavy coming in and out of Seattle, so the normally ninety-minute drive to Silver Birch took more than two hours and the atmosphere in the car was heavy the whole way.

John had tuned into a radio station that was playing nothing but Christmas songs, picking a volume that was a little too high to encourage conversation. That was fine with Moira for a while, but the fourth time they heard "It's a Holly Jolly Christmas," Moira snapped and turned the radio off.

"Sorry," John said, and though it sounded like he was apologizing for Burl Ives, Moira knew he meant he was sorry for the traffic and the travel and the whole thing. He knew she was in a bad mood and was trying to be thoughtful, to give her some respectful space.

John was thoughtful like that. He was a kind, sweet, thoughtful man and the knowledge that she was about to break his heart nearly broke Moira's. But in the hour-long flight from Los Angeles, she'd done nothing but look at the situation, run the pros and cons.

She loved her job as an executive at a small production company located on the Universal lot. She loved looking out the window in her office and seeing the city spread open around her. She loved driving down Ventura one way and meeting friends for Indian food or sushi or drinks or the best hamburger in town. Or she could drive down Cahuenga in the other direction and be in Hollywood for a premiere or Thai food or drinks. Everything was spread out but it the city was a collection of small towns bound together by the freeways and the pure fizz of adrenalized creativity.

L.A. was dirty and noisy and messy and expensive, but she had moved there after college and felt like she'd come home.

Ten years later, she still felt like that.

Trouble was, John didn't.

They'd met on a blind date and their connection had been immediate and electric. He was someone she never would have met just on her own because he didn't go to clubs or frequent the restaurants she did and their work didn't overlap at all.

In fact, just about the only thing they had in common was a love of movies. Any movies. All movies. John had gotten a kick out of seeing movies with her for free—screenings and openings and the ones she got into with her Producers' Guild card. He liked going to the parties and the events and happenings. He wasn't too hip for the room the way so many of her colleagues were. Even better, he wasn't in competition with her. He just stood by her and admired her and supported her and loved her. And when she came home too exhausted to do anything but nuke a tortilla with cheese for dinner, he was always there with a salad (in the summer) or soup (in the winter) to make sure she was ingesting some kind of vegetable along with her carbs and dairy.

She loved John more than she'd ever loved anyone, but the idea of moving up to Silver Birch full time made her want to jump out of a window.

CHAPTER TWO

WHAT HAVE YOU DONE FOR THEM LATELY?

They'd gone straight to John's mother's house because the electricity wasn't yet turned on in the house John had bought for them. The purchase had been a virtual experience for her because she was in the middle of a project, but he'd kept her updated during each stage, filming his walk-throughs and sending her gigs of pictures. She had given him a wish-list of things she wanted in the house—a list that that covered two pages, single-spaced—and he'd managed to find a house that covered all but two—the washer and dryer were in the garage and not in a separate laundry room, and there wasn't a double sink in the kitchen.

"But we can install one," he said. And what could she say to that except, "thank you."

She had gone along with the plan because she couldn't really think of a way to derail it—except for her absurdly long wish list—and because she felt like such a selfish bitch not wanting him to follow his dream.

Because that's what he was doing. Following his dream.

"Who grows up dreaming of having a small-town dental practice," Moira's friend Chazz asked her. "What was he even doing in L.A. anyway?"

"Capping teeth," Moira deadpanned at the time, and that was part of the problem. John was working with a Foundation that provided cosmetic dentistry to kids who needed it and he loved that work. But to pay the bills, he was a partner in a practice that had celebrity clientele on a waiting list that was two years long. The night he covered some rapper's teeth with diamonds, he'd come home, drunk a bottle of wine by himself and nearly cried when Moira asked him what was going on.

"I need to go home," he said. "I need to do work that means something, even if it means some little kid won't be self-conscious about his smile."

"There are plenty of role models with gaps in their teeth," she had said, trying to make him smile. "Vanessa Paradis. Stacey Abrams , Lauren Hutton, Michael Strahan."

"And they're all awesome," he said. "Đr. Hankins is retiring next year and he's asked me to buy his practice."

Moira had never met Dr. Hankins but he'd heard plenty about him over the years. He'd been John's mentor all the way through college and dental school. They'd met when John had brought his best friend into his office to replace a tooth he'd lost playing football and the dentist had not only hooked him up with a new tooth, but convinced them both that if they kept playing football they could end up with injuries that were a whole lot worse, injuries that could not be fixed.

They'd both finished the season—it was almost over anyway—but when Ken broke his leg in the last playoff, they took it as a sign that the dentist was on to something and in their senior year, they pursued other interests.

"What would that look like?" Moira had asked him, because even though she made a good salary, they lived on his and banked what she brought home. They were renting a home for four thousand a month and that didn't leave a lot left over at the end of the month.

"He's offering very attractive terms," John said.

"So you've talked about it," Moira said, feeling ambushed and angry.,

"We've just talked about it," he said and then he went to take a shower, which was what he did when he was really upset and didn't want to talk about it.

And then Dr. Hayden died of a massive heart attack and suddenly, the offer wasn't just hypothetical or theoretical or any other kind of "cal." It was real and there was a time limit on it. The dentist's widow wanted to pack up and join her sister in Arizona and she wanted to settle her affairs quickly. Before Christmas if possible.

John and Moira sat down and drank some wine and talked about the situation and Moira found herself saying, "If you want to, we should do it," but not really thinking that he meant to live in Silver Birch full-time and figuring she could arrange some sort of remote working situation with her boss for the weeks they'd be in Washington.

Except that was not happening.

Her boss was being a real dick about things and that was saying something but her boss was a woman.

"Your life is not a Hallmark movie," she'd said, when Moira had first broached the idea of working out of the office. "You cannot throw away your career to go grow lavender in Silver Bitch."

"Three-quarters of what I do does not require me to be in Los Angeles," Moira said, ignoring the snotty comment about the town's name. "I can make a phone call from anywhere. I can send a text from anywhere. We're in the same time zone."

Moira was pretty sure she was valuable—she had brought the company a book in galleys that they'd snapped up on her say-so and it had turned into a streaming hit the size of *Bridgerton*—but she didn't make the assumption she was indispensable. Pretty much no one in Hollywood was indispensable. Except maybe Tom Hanks.

If Tom Hanks wanted to live in Silver Birch he would, a voice inside her said. And she seemed to remember that some hot young director had moved to Silver Birch after attending a film fest.

You could live in Silver Birch, she thought, and so she said, "Buy the practice." John had been ecstatic.

She'd joined him in Silver Birch for the big party to celebrate his new ownership and it seemed like half the town had turned out to wish John well and drink to the memory of his predecessor. And right in the middle of the party she'd been called away to deal with an emergency involving the leading man on her current project who had been caught in an intimate moment with a man not his husband and a Rottweiler that belonged to neither of them but seemed quite cozy with them. There were pictures and TMZ was about to splash them all over.

She never did get back to the party. In fact, she'd headed back to L.A. on a red eye and didn't see John for three more weeks. He had been understanding but when the crisis made way for another involving an on-set accident when a burn bar accidentally tipped over, he had made sure she knew what he thought about the continual cycle of crisis and drama.

CHAPTER THREE

IT'S GOING TO BE A WHITE CHRISTMAS

The night Moira arrived, she and John slept in the room that had been his as a boy. He'd had a double bed but it still felt small and at some point in the night, he left the room and did not come back. Moira turned up the heat on the electric blanket and went to sleep.

When she came downstairs the next morning, John was nowhere to be seen.

"He's at the house," John's sister Jennifer told her.

"He's meeting the contractor there."

"He didn't tell me," Moira commented as she poured herself some coffee.

"Yes he did," Jennifer said. "Over dinner."

Moira looked at her sister-in-law. She was ten years younger than John, just out of college herself and as far as Moira could tell, wasn't really in any kind of a hurry to do anything special with her life.

"I was really tired last night," Moira said, wondering why she was apologizing to Jennifer when it was obvious the girl had a chip on her shoulder.

"Is there Uber in Silver Birch?" she asked. Jennifer gave her the side-eye.

"Of course there's Uber," she said. "But right before Christmas? You're going to wait forever and rates are going to be sky high. It would be faster to walk." She looked at the brand-new hiking boots Moira was wearing. "Oh, I forgot. Nobody walks in L.A."

"You're too young for that reference," Moira said, amused.

"Mom will be back later," Jennifer said. "I'm sure she'll let you borrow her car."

"No, that's fine," Moira said. "I really should take a walk." That last time she'd walked more than a dozen feet from her car to her house was...never...but Moira was willing to give it a try.

"It's a pretty small town," Jennifer said. "But if you get lost, just give me a call."

Not if you were the last person on earth, Moira thought.

She went back up into John's room and pulled out a sweater to layer over the thin sweater she was wearing. She put some wool socks over the silk ones she was wearing underneath, added a beanie hat and some gloves and felt like she might survive the outdoor ordeal.

Don't be a wuss, she scolded herself. *It's 34 degrees outside,* her inner voice replied.

By the time she walked all the way to the quaint downtown area that defined the small city, it hadn't warmed up, but Moira had. She was so warm she was sweating inside her layers but she knew better than to take off any of the clothes. She'd read about paradoxical undressing in hypothermia cases. She passed a small used bookstore that was closed and the art-house theater next to it, that had some sort of notice hung up on the door.

She kept going and ran into a pretty substantial Christmas market sprawling over the heart of the town and bought a little bag of star-shaped cookies to much on since no one had offered her breakfast.

She wandered into a vintage store that seemed to double as some kind of bath goods place and surprised herself by buying some goat milk soap that the proprietor told her was made locally by a co-op that owned a small herd. There were pictures of baby goats on the label. They were adorable.

Eventually, Moira realized it was getting colder. She ducked into a local supermarket to get warm and call John to come pick her up.

But the call didn't go through.

And for some reason, that was just the last straw. Moira started to cry. Soundlessly and unobtrusively but with tears rolling down her cheeks faster than she could scrub them away.

Suddenly a tall elegant woman with white hair and a straight back, took her by the elbow and steered her into the little food court set up in the corner of the supermarket.

"Sit there," the woman directed. "I'll be right back."

That's strange, Moira thought but it was very warm and she was chilled to the bone so she didn't complain.

The woman came back a moment later with two large cups of steaming hot chocolate. and a small paper bag with grease spots on it. Some kind of chocolate cookie with nuts and coconut. Moira really didn't like coconut but there was something about the woman that compelled her to accept the gift.

"My name is Nella Halliday," the woman said quietly as she shrugged off her coat. "You're Moira Sandford, right?"

"How do you know that?" Moira said, a little freaked out.

"My friend sold your husband the house. I hope you like it."

"I haven't seen it in person yet," Moira admitted.

The old woman looked at her sharply. "Why not?"

"I don't want to fall in love with it," Moira said, wondering where that had come from.

"Silver Birch is a beautiful place once you get used to it," Nella Halliday said. "I moved from Hollywood to be here with my husband and it took me about a year to fall under its spell."

"You were an actor?" Moira asked, not really surprised. The woman had to be in her late eighties or nineties but she was still beautiful.

"Oh, in those days, they called us actresses," Nella said, taking a sip of her hot chocolate. "It never bothered me."

"They don't call female writers writeresses," Moira said.

"Fair point," Nella conceded and took another sip of her hot chocolate. "The Pacific Northwest is different," she went on. "Strong women are a part of their heritage."

Moira smiled and sipped her own hot chocolate. "Are you the mayor?"

Nella laughed. "No, but I am passionate about the town."

She glanced at her watch, a dainty Longines, Moira noticed. "Oh look at the time." She gathered up her belongings. "It was nice to meet you Moira," she said. "I hope you'll change your mind about Silver Birch."

Moira couldn't help but smile at the old lady's enthusiasm.

"If I do, you'll be the first person I tell," she promised.

Nella patted her on the arm in reply and left.

Moira gathered up her things. She knew there was still time for her to walk to the house John had bought and although she was dreading it, she made herself go back out into the cold.

Her phone buzzed with a text before she'd even taken two steps. She checked it.

Her boss. Of course Sharon was texting her during Christmas week.

And then she read the text.

She'd been fired.

Immediately.

As in, *we'll box up your stuff and deliver it to your house.*

She immediately hit "call" but no one was picking up.

CHAPTER FOUR

WHITE CHRISTMAS ALL AROUND.

The next person Moira called was John. He sounded a little wary when she picked up.

"Are you still at the house?" she asked him.

"I'm coming by. Is there heat?"

"Yes," he said. "I can come get you."

"No," she said, "I need to walk." And she ended the call. She really did need to walk because if she didn't do something to work off her rage, she was going to kill the next person who crossed her path. And she was afraid that was going to be some sweet old lady walking her dog like the one she'd seen on the street a few minutes ago.

She made it to the green on green Craftsman in under ten minutes and was stunned to see that it was completely decorated for the season, with a wreath on the front door and electric candles in all the windows.

John spotted her coming up the walk and threw the door open wide. "Wait there," he said, and came to her so that he could pick her up and carry her over the threshold. *NO no no,* Moira thought. Don't be charming. I can't stand it if you're charming.

"I'm so glad you're here," he said, sounding really happy, which only made Moira feel worse.

"I want to show you something," he said as he set her down in the entryway.

"Show me," she said and he took her through the living room and opened a French door into…a wonderland.

"It's a Florida room," John said. "Or in your case, a California room."

The walls were made almost entirely of glass and Moira could see snowflakes drifting down. But that's not what caught her eye. Inside the room it was a green house, with unobtrusive heaters and sunlamps and plants everywhere.

And there was a comfy-looking sofa there, flanked by reading lights and two end tables that had built-in bookshelves on them.

"I know how much you like to read in the garden," John said, and Moira knew he was saying, "I love you."

She was touched beyond belief.

"I love you too," she said. "Where's the bedroom?"

Later, when they went back to John's mother's house for dinner, she and Jennifer seemed to be in a much better mood. Her mother-in-law asked her if she'd enjoyed her tour of the town and she'd mentioned meeting Nella Halliday.

"You met Nella Halliday?" Jennifer said, exchanging glances with her mother.

"Tall, silver-haired?" Moira asked.

"That's her," her mother-in-law replied. "But Nella Halliday died last Friday. Her funeral was today."

Moira was still processing that when her phone rang again. It was a former intern of hers who had heard the news she'd been fired. He wanted her to produce his first movie.

"I live out of town," she said.

"So do I," he said. "L.A. was killing me."

"Let me call you back," she said, smiling at John. And just before she ended the call, she added, "Merry Christmas."

If you enjoyed this story, please consider leaving a review.

ABOUT KATHERINE

Born in Washington, D.C., Katherine Moore now lives in a small Pacific Northwest town. She has worked as a food writer, a caterer, and a movie extra as well as a freelance lifestyle reporter and staff writer for magazines in Honolulu, Los Angeles, and Richmond, Virginia.

Connect with Katherine

- **Amazon**
- **BookBub**
- **Facebook**

More by Katherine Moore

- *The Christmas Experience: Meredith Manor Hotel #1*
- *The Prodigal: Meredith Manor Hotel #2*
- *His Heart Belongs Here (A Silver Birch Story)*
- *The Pumpkin Patch (A Silver Birch Story coming November 2021)*
- *Snowbird (A Silver Birch Story)*
- *Dream House (A Silver Birch story coming December 31, 2021)*
- *Holiday Hijinks: Halliday Theater #1*
- *Halloween Hijinks: Halliday Theater #2*
- *The Christmas Experiment*
- *The Flamingo Mote1: Mermaid Beach #1*

Xmas at the Flamingo Motel
The Seadog's Wife
Secret Santa
Mysteries of Christmas Past
Tis the Season
Sweet Dreams
Fake It Till You Make It, vol. 2
Pleasure Cruise (Cruising Around Series)
Suddenly Forever
Second Take (Be My Valentine Series, out February 2022)

THE HAND OF FATE

STEPHANIE SCISSOM

CHAPTER ONE

Georgia slipped onto a stool at the end of the bar, positioning herself to watch the door. Noqoìlpi wasn't in town yet, but she had been promised that he was coming. According to locals—if there was a game to be found—it would be here at Chonky's. That appeared to be true, judging from the rowdy poker table beside her. She ordered a Jack and Coke, then glanced over at them.

One of the players looked up and met her gaze. Although he'd been bantering with his buddies, he immediately fell silent and gave her a half-smile before lifting his beer in salute and pressing it to his lips. Georgia quickly looked away, but couldn't resist another peek. He was still staring. This was a supernatural town, and it was likely she was the only human in the room. He could be any number of creatures, but she was willing to bet he was some god or another's prize creation. Chiseled jaw, unruly brown hair that hung past his shoulders, trimmed beard and the most startling pale blue eyes she'd ever seen. He wasn't a vamp--too tan for that--and his features weren't delicate like a fae's. He was big, dressed casually in a red flannel shirt and jeans. Maybe a wolf, but that didn't feel right either. All she knew was that he was unnervingly handsome and it was somewhat a relief when he had to turn his attention back to the game.

The guy to his left, who someone referred to as Leo, was definitely a wolf. When Leo scratched behind his ear, the cyclops made a joke about him having fleas, to which Leo retorted, "Chonky, keep your eye on your own cards."

Interesting. The bar owner. She might need to make his acquaintance.

They were playing Texas Hold 'Em, and it didn't take Georgia long to figure out that, whether they were supernatural or not, she could run this table. A couple of them—the goblin and Leo—played so amateurishly that it took her a few hands to get a decent read on them. Chonky and Mr. Handsome were somewhat better.

Suddenly, Mr. Handsome leaned down, talking to something under the table. "Are you awake, Mel?"

A flash of bright orange and black darted up his arm to curl around his shoulders. The small, orange-eyed cross fox was as beautiful as his owner himself. He scratched its head and it licked his face before directing a hiss at Leo.

"Fate, you better keep that thing under control," Chonky warned. "Or I'll skin it and wear it for ear muffs."

Fate. It suited him. Was he a witch, and the fox his familiar?

He caught her looking and winked. "I like redheads."

Georgia's face heated until she feared it was as bright as her hair, and worse, she couldn't think of a suitable retort. But she got herself under control as they turned their attention back to the next hand.

Henny the goblin folded early, leaving three-handed action. In Texas Hold 'Em, there were four rounds of betting. Each player had two cards in his hand and there were five to be turned up in the middle, community cards. After the last one of those turned up, Fate ended up pushing all his chips to the middle, calling "all in" and both his opponents folded. He glanced at her in time to catch her smirk.

"What?" he said. "I saw that look. You don't think I had the goods."

"It's not my business."

"No, come here." He motioned her over. "Talk to us."

Georgia feigned reluctance as she slipped off her stool, but this was what she was hoping for. She would need both money and connections when Noqoìlpi came to town.

"Leave your cards where they are," Fate told the others as she approached. "Okay, Red. First of all, are you a witch?"

"No," Georgia replied. "Are you?"

Leo snorted and grabbed Fate in a headlock, tousling his hair with his fist. "Eees a filthy demon, this one!" He nodded at Georgia. "And she smells human. Don't see many of those around here."

Georgia nodded. "I'm just a human. My name is Georgia, by the way. But I know the game. My father was once a professional player."

Fate leaned his chair back, looking at her with unabashed interest. "And you think I was bluffing?"

"Not entirely. I think you had maybe a low pair in your hand. Twos or threes. But no more than that."

Fate blinked and she turned her attention to Leo. "I put you on a busted straight draw."

"And you." She nodded at Chonky. "You had the best hand. I'm thinking maybe the board hit for you, but bottom two pairs. Sixes and fours? The way Fate bet on both the turn and the river made you think he had Kings and a lower pair."

They all looked dumbfounded. Fate flipped over a pair of deuces, and Chonky cursed before looking at Georgia and saying, "Excuse my language." He revealed a four of clubs and a six of diamonds.

Reluctantly, Leo flipped over his cards, showing his busted straight that lacked only a five.

"How did you know all that?" Fate asked, and she shrugged. "Betting patterns, body language." She laid a hand on Henny's shoulder. "The hand before, when they put you on a flush … you didn't have two hearts in your hand, did you? You made bottom pair on the flop, but you had a high card, too. That's why you didn't fold right away. I'm guessing ace-four?"

"Why do you think that?" Henny asked, scratching the side of his pointy nose.

"Because you looked back at your hold cards before betting the flop. You would've remembered if they were suited."

"Lovely lady, that is correct," he replied.

"Would you like to join us?" Fate pulled a chair from a nearby table without waiting on her reply and placed it between him and Henny.

"Oh, no. I couldn't," she said. "I'm on the road. Need to conserve my cash."

Fate pushed a stack of chips in front of the empty seat. "I'll spot you. The way you read, I don't think you'll have any trouble."

Indeed, she did not. Even though she slowplayed it, her chip pile grew steadily.

It was a bit distracting sitting next to Fate. He didn't smell sulphuric like a demon, or act like the ones she'd known. But she hadn't exactly grown up around society's finest, either.

Fate's fox abandoned him, moving to curl in her lap, much to the consternation of the rest of the table. Fate tried to get it to come back to him, but it closed its eyes like it was taking a nap.

"It's fine," Georgia assured him, stroking the little fox's orange and black fur.

"You have to be some kind of magic. That hateful thing just hisses at the rest of us," Chonky said.

"To be fair," Leo said. "Georgia smells remarkably better than any of us. I can't blame Mel."

Georgia felt a bit sorry for Leo on the next hand. Everyone else folded on the first three cards, then he checked on the turn card. She looked at him, puzzled.

"Why would you do that?" she asked. "Why would you check aces on the turn, with a straight draw and everything?"

Leo froze. Absolutely froze. He was so flustered that he didn't even bet the last card when he got the three he needed to make his straight. Chonky howled with laughter at his deer-in-the-headlights expression. Georgia was almost tempted to bet him, just to see what he would do, but she'd just told him he had the best hand, so she folded.

The next few hands passed without much drama, then she found herself pitted her against Fate. He bet modestly, given the cards she was almost sure he had. She decided to try the same thing she'd done on Leo.

She studied him so long that he finally looked at her, though he'd been trying hard not to make any movement at all.

"You've got kings, don't you? I feel like you've got kings." She watched him another moment, then made a huge bet.

Georgia loved the psychology of the game. She could almost hear the thoughts bouncing in his head.

If she put me on kings and still bet like that, she has to be the best hand. She's made that flush.

She had not made her flush, didn't even have a club in her hand, but he didn't know that. He folded kings, and she had nothing at all.

"You had it, didn't you?" he asked, grabbing for her cards. Laughing, she jerked them out of his reach and sent them sailing toward Chonky, because it was his turn to deal. The top one floated over, showing a diamond, and Fate groaned.

"Oh, that hurts. I'm sick now," he said. "You should buy me a beer after robbing me like that."

She laughed and handed Fate his fox. "Okay. I need to run to the restroom anyway."

Georgia stopped by the bar on her way and sent a bucket to the table. She left her chips there, showing trust, wanting them to think she was as at ease with them as they seemed to be with her. There was no reason to think Noqoìlpi would give her another match—he'd refused so far-—but she knew what a vain god he was. If she could get even one of these men to publicly question his courage to his face, he would have to accept her challenge.

When she returned, they were having an animated conversation that was presumably about her, since it ceased as soon as they noticed her. It was Fate who spoke first.

"I have a proposition for you."

Georgia gave him a slight smile. "You'll bet a fiddle of gold against my soul?"

They laughed and Fate said, "Uh, no. You could never tell by looking at this place, but the Chonky Tonk—"

"Beersheba Springs Tavern," Chonky interjected.

"No, it's Chonky Tonk," Fate said, and Leo laughed. "Anyway, it's maaaaybe ..." He wriggled his hand in a side to side motion. " ... not the most reputable place in town. Chonky wants to change that. There's a big charity Christmas event this weekend, benefiting the town's underprivileged children. Since he's not exactly a cakewalk and parade kind of guy, I had an idea of another way he could help."

Fate glanced at Henny and said, "How can I make this not sound offensive?"

Henny shrugged, and Fate rolled his eyes.

"Anyway, it's hard for supernatural people to play cards together, unless you are as unskilled as we are, because our senses are different than humans. It would still be okay if everyone was trustworthy, but ... you know. So, I thought that we could have a tournament with human players, supernatural sponsors." He smiled. "And since it was my brilliant idea, I called dibs on you. I would be thrilled if you would be my—"

"Chonky Tonk woman," Leo interrupted.

"Champion," Fate supplied, and cuffed the werewolf on the back of the head.

Georgia hesitated. Noqoìlpi would be through here soon, but she couldn't imagine he would be interested in any Christmas charity tournament, and she couldn't afford to tie up her schedule. Luke was counting on her.

"I'm sorry," she said. "I'll be leaving town soon, so I'll have to decline."

He smiled, but she saw the disappointment flash across his face. "That's too bad. I think you would clean up, just like you have here."

They played a few more hands, but the lighthearted mood from before seemed muted. Fate took the last pot of the night from Henny, earning a raised eyebrow from Georgia. He winked and raked the chips.

"Lady and Dimwits, I hate to break up a good time, but it's getting late and I need my beauty sleep," Chonky said.

The men muttered their agreement.

Chonky stood and gave Georgia a little bow. "Even though you took my money, it was nice to have some class in here for once and I hope you'll come back."

"Thank you," she said. "Can I wait inside until my Uber gets here?"

They laughed.

Henny said, "The only taxi around here at night is Old Clem, and he probably went to bed at dark."

"Are you staying at the Moffett Bed and Breakfast?" Fate asked. "I'll take you there."

She opened her mouth to refuse, but she didn't relish the thought of a long, cold walk to the B & B, especially when there were vamps out. "Thanks. That's kind of you."

"Wait right here," he said. "I'll go warm the truck."

They hung around, chit chatting and watching the spitting snow through the smeared front window of the tavern until Fate said, "It's probably good now."

The cold wind hit Georgia like a slap in the face, and the coat she'd bought on the way up from Texas seemed woefully inadequate. Fate took one look at her, shrugged out of his coat, and wrapped it around her shoulders. Mel darted over to her and she tucked the young fox against her chest.

No, Fate definitely didn't smell like a demon. He smelled clean and woodsy and deliciously male. He opened the passenger door of his gleaming black Dodge for her to climb inside.

The inside of Fate's truck smelled as good as his coat and was immaculate. He was the neatest demon she'd ever met.

"That last hand," she said. "You had top pair?"

He grinned. "I had nothing."

"Nice. You played it well."

He chuckled. "You know what I said about supernaturals having some advantages? Centaurs and werewolves have really amped hearing. Did you know horses and wolves can hear a human heart from four feet away? I knew if he heard my heartbeat go up, he'd think I made my flush."

Georgia laughed. "And how did you make your heart beat faster?

He gave an awkward chuckle and she didn't think the red in his cheeks was just from the cold. "Uh, I'll plead the fifth."

Her own cheeks heated, and she ducked her head to coo something to Mel, letting her hair hide her face.

"So," he said. "When is your friend supposed to be in town?"

"He's not my friend," she said. "And I'm not sure. I had a tip from a mutual acquaintance that he was coming through. Do you get many visitors here?"

"This time of year? No." He paused. "You said you came here from Texas? That's a long way to travel in hopes of catching someone passing through. Couldn't your mutual friend get you a phone number or something?"

"The man I'm looking for doesn't want to see me."

"An ex?" Fate asked.

"No, definitely not. He has something of mine and I want it back. Would you let me know if you see any other strangers coming through?"

"Sure," Fate tossed her his phone. "Put your number in and I'll give you a call if I see anyone unusual. What's the guy's name?"

Georgia looked at him, considering. He didn't seem the sort to keep company with Noqoìlpi, but gamblers were gamblers. She didn't want Noqoìlpi to have a heads-up that she was coming, but it would be great to have another pair of eyes in town.

As he rolled to a stop in front of the B & B, Georgia held Mel with one hand and let Fate help her remove his coat. He folded it on the seat and she nestled the sleeping fox on top of it.

"His name is Noqoìlpi. He's a Navajo gambling god. Please don't tell anyone I'm looking for him." She leaned over and brushed a kiss on his cheek. "Thanks for the ride, Fate."

She jumped out of the truck before Fate could speak, or even catch his breath. Her vibrant hair bounced around her shoulders as she hurried inside the B & B.

He scratched his fox's head and cooed, "That one's trouble. Yes, she is. Just like you."

When he got home, he fed Mel, then called his old friend Ojihozo.

"Lafayette!" the Abenaki warrior greeted. "I see you still don't own a watch."

"Stop whining. You're a god. I knew you weren't asleep."

Ojihozo laughed. "Okay, so what's on your mind? You're not one for social calls."

"Noqoìlpi. Do you know him?"

The silence on the other end of the line probably wasn't a good thing.

Finally, Ojihozo asked, "How do you know that name? Lafayette, please tell me you haven't made a wager with him. You cannot win."

"Is he a friend of yours?"

Ojihozo scoffed. "Noqoìlpi has no friends. But *you* are my friend. Do as I advise—steer clear."

"I have a friend who is tangled up with him—"

"Then I'm sorry for your friend. Do you know what the name Noqoìlpi means?"

"I don't know anything about him," Fate admitted.

"'He-Who-Wins-Men.' He plays men for their possessions, then their homes, then their women and children and finally, he plays for the gambler himself. Anyone who loses themselves to Noqoìlpi is consigning themselves to seven years hard labor, moving stones to build his gambling houses. I have never known him to lose."

Surely Georgia was too smart to get caught up in that, wasn't she? What had she lost that was so valuable?

"Why would he be coming to Beersheba Springs?" Fate asked. "Surely not for a dime game at Chonky's."

"I can't think of any reason he'd be coming *to* Beersheba Springs, but I do know why he might be coming *through* there. There's a big tournament coming up in Birmingham. Lots of easy pickings for him. Trust me, Lafayette. Tell your friend to cut his losses."

Fate thanked him and hung up.

Ojihozo didn't play around, and Fate trusted him implicitly. If he said, steer clear, Fate knew he should steer clear.

He just didn't know if he could.

Fate went looking for her around noon.

"Behave!" he told Mel. "No chasing Cham."

Sure enough, the two-tailed cat perched lazily in the swivel chair at the welcome desk of the bed and breakfast. Mel hissed at him and Cham hissed back before taking his human farm.

"Fate, nice to see that mangy thing hasn't given you rabies yet. What are you doing here?"

"The redhead, the one I dropped off last night--"

"Oh, I didn't know she knew anyone in town," Cham said, a smile playing on his lips. "She's attractive."

"Is she here?"

"She's next door. She asked for a map of the town and lunch recommendations. I told her to go there, and save the razzle dazzle for dinner at High Point tonight."

Fate started toward the door and Cham said, "You can't take that beast in there."

"Well, I can't leave him in the truck. It's too cold. Can I tuck him in my coat?"

Cham gave a heavy sigh. "Does he still eat things he's not supposed to?"

Fate waggled his hand. "Ehhhh."

"So I can't put him in Vayla's office. She'd wear our hides like Cruella De Vil if he messed anything up." He paused, then snapped his fingers. "Hang on. There's an old carrier someone left behind. Let me find it."

When they got Mel safely tucked away, Fate went next door to look for Georgia.

"That foxy redhead?" Aaron the greeter asked. "You just missed her. She left with some Native American guy a few minutes ago."

Fate froze.

"Do you want a table?"

"No. Do you know where they went? Did they say anything?"

Aaron frowned. "Ah, no, man. No idea. What's wrong?"

Everything, Fate thought, then ran back to collect Mel and look for her.

"I wish I could do more," Ahiga said, his handsome face strained with worry.

Georgia gave him a fierce hug. "You've done enough. Thank you for getting me into this town, and for the protection ritual. Now you stay clear. Noqoìlpi would not be pleased that you helped me."

He glanced over his shoulder as if merely saying Noqoìlpi's name would summon him. Georgia hated how jumpy and scared he was on the outside, when he had been so defiant and brave on the inside. But he had spent much longer in Noqoìlpi's shadow world than she had. She remembered how strange and hot the sun had felt on her face, and how big and open and alien the world had felt when she first escaped. Some sort of Stockholm Syndrome, she suspected, but her first urge had been to turn back. Ahiga had only been free a couple of months.

"I wish you didn't have to do this, but I understand. You beat him once, you can do it again." Ahiga hesitated. "Your father. Did you look for him when you got out?"

Georgia's heart felt as cold as the snow that crunched under her boots. "I don't have a father anymore. All I have is Luke. And you. You're my brother now, too."

Ahiga smiled and kissed her forehead. "Good luck, little sister. Do you want me to wait with you until your cab arrives?"

"No, I'm good. Take care, Ahiga. I hope we see you soon."

He headed back to his house and Georgia looked at her watch. She was startled at the time, but she and Ahiga had been busy since lunch.

It was so good to see him again, but also sad, because that meant Luke was in that awful place alone.

Not for long, little brother, she thought.

One way or another.

She hadn't even called for a cab yet. Reception was sketchy here, so she decided to head back towards the town hall to see if it got better. As she crossed the yard, she glanced up and saw Fate parked on the side of the road, watching her, his handsome face scrunched in worry.

"Need a ride?" he asked.

She smiled and ran to climb in his truck.

Mel promptly left his spot by Fate's leg to come curl in her lap.

"Fine," Fate said. "I'll eat my doughnut holes by myself."

Mel's ears came up when Fate rattled the cup of bright, multi-colored balls. He still looked hesitant to leave, so Fate handed them to Georgia. She extracted a bright blue one and gave it to the fox.

"Foxes eat doughnut holes," she mused.

"That fox eats everything. He has sort of a reputation, and I always have a vet bill. It's worse than childproofing for a baby. There have been rings, coins, a watch, a cigarette lighter ..." Fate shook his head. "He's ridiculous. So, where are you headed?"

"Chonky's," she said. "Please."

Fate drove in silence, staring straight ahead. Finally, he said, "Was that him? Was that Noqoìlpi?"

That startled a laugh from Georgia. "No, that was definitely not Noqoìlpi. That was my friend, Ahiga. Noqoìlpi is--"

"A gambling god," he supplied.

"Older, intimidating. And yes, a gambling god. You've been asking around."

"I have," he acknowledged.

She cocked her head, studying him. "Why?"

He swung into a parking spot at Chonky's and put it in park. Twisting in the seat to face her, he said, "Because I care what happens to you."

Right.

"You don't even know me," she said. "We met yesterday."

"So, I can't worry about you?"

"No," she said, pulling Mel to her with one arm and reaching for the door handle with the other. "You can't."

"Georgia, wait!" he said, catching her arm. "Can we talk a minute?"

She didn't want to talk, and she didn't like the concern she saw in his blue eyes, because she'd learned it was better not to trust anyone—even family. Especially family.

But he looked sincere, so she leaned back and said, "Sure."

"I know what he is. He-Who-Wins-Men? Georgia, whatever you're planning, whatever you're thinking, don't do it. It's not worth it."

Angry tears surprised her. She didn't cry. She hadn't cried in years. Who did this guy—this *demon*—think he was?

"Yes, it is worth it! *He's* worth it."

Fate said nothing, simply stared at her.

"He has my little brother, Fate. My father lost both of us to him in a game three years ago. Five months ago, I challenged Noqoìlpi to a game for our freedom, and I won. He got mad and let me go, but he wouldn't let Luke go. And he wouldn't play me again."

"Georgia—" Fate said breathlessly, but she shook her head.

"Luke won't live through another four years in the shadow world. He won't. You don't understand how awful it is there. I'm going to get another game, and I'm going to beat him. I appreciate your concern, but stay out of my way."

She climbed out of the truck and stalked inside Chonky's without waiting for him. Chonky and the bartender, Larry, gave her a double take, whether because of her tearstained face or the fact that she was carrying Mel, she wasn't sure. Georgia plopped onto a seat and said, "Hi, guys. Can I get a Jack and Coke?"

"I love girls who order real drinks," Larry muttered, as Fate wandered in behind her. Fate nodded at Chonky and pulled up the stool beside her. He tried to get Larry's attention to order, but he had already stooped to get a can of Coke from under the bar.

"Don't mind him," Chonky said. "He's grumpy because I'm making him do the Bachelor Auction, Singles' Auction, whatever it is."

"They're not seeing eye-to-eye," Leo joked, and Chonky popped him on the back of the head before leaning in to taunt Larry.

"Think of the children, Larry," he said, then snickered.

"It's your bar," Larry groused. "Maybe you should do it, too."

Fate raised his eyebrows at Larry and they both laughed. Chonky scowled.

"What?" he demanded. "I'm sexier than either of you pretty boys."

"He's the one eye adore," Leo said, blowing Chonky a kiss.

Chonky frowned. "I'm not scared. I'm in. But you and Fate are, too."

"Eye, Captain." Fate tapped off a salute and Georgia laughed.

Chonky took it all in stride. He clapped a hand on Georgia's shoulder and said, "You should stay in town, darlin'. You could probably get these three for a dollar, or you could save your money for a real man."

Mel's hackles rose and Georgia felt an instant of premonition just before the door blew open. The easy banter at the bar stopped when a man in an expensive black suit and cowboy boots walked in.

Chonky stiffened, and his smile looked forced as he nodded and said, "Noqoìlpi. Long time, no see."

The gambling god didn't answer. He was too busy scanning the room, looking for a mark. Then his gaze lit on Georgia and his lip curled. He turned to Chonky.

"I want a game. What do you have?"

"I'll play you," Georgia said. "Head-to-head, right now."

He ignored her, and Chonky made a show of wiping down his bar. "Ah, it's a little slow right now. We don't have any tables going."

"What is this?" Noqoìlpi tapped a flier advertising tomorrow night's poker game.

"Nothing you'd be interested in. A charity event, with human players only. That's really all that will be—"

"I'm playing. You could sponsor a human to play against me." Georgia's heart thumped in her ears, but she summoned the courage to say, "That is, if you have a player who can play better than you. I'd like a real challenge."

Chonky gasped and Fate jumped to his feet, positioning himself between her and Noqoìlpi.

Everyone started talking at once. Everyone except Noqoìlpi and Georgia.

She knew he was furious, but his face betrayed nothing. He held up a hand and the room fell silent. He made a brushing motion with his hand, motioning Fate away.

"It's okay," Georgia whispered, touching his shoulder. She faced Noqoìlpi.

Noqoìlpi made another gesture, beckoning Georgia forward.

Her feet felt leadened, but she moved to stand face-to-face with him.

"I assume we aren't just playing for money," he said.

"I want my brother's freedom."

Noqoìlpi gave the barest hint of a smile. "And if you lose?"

Georgia lifted her chin. "Then you get me back. Seven more years."

Noqoìlpi shook his head. "New game, new bet. If you lose, your brother will still go free, but you will belong to me forever."

"Deal!" Georgia said, even as the room erupted in protest.

Either way, Luke would be free, and that was enough for her.

Noqoìlpi smiled. "Very well." He peered at the sheet again, then he left.

Fate grabbed her arm and made her face him. "I'm not going to let you do this. Maybe your brother's tougher than you think. Maybe he can do four more."

"He can't. I know he can't."

Seven years in the shadow world was an eternity. Ahiga had made it, but he was older and stronger and it had still nearly broken him. Georgia wouldn't tell Fate, but seven years or seventy, she didn't think she could make it either.

Strangely, it felt like a weight lifted from her shoulders. The last five months had been torture, but after tomorrow, she wouldn't have to worry about Luke anymore.

Chonky was trying to talk to her, and so was Fate, but she'd made up her mind. She set Mel on one of the pool tables and walked over to the ancient jukebox. All the songs on the pages were older than she was, but that didn't matter either. Georgia was at peace. She fed it a couple of dollars and punched in a few numbers before walking back to Fate and taking his hand.

"Dance with me," she said.

When Fate took her back to the B & B that night, he didn't leave. He lay awake long after she'd fallen asleep in his arms. After Noqoìlpi had left, she'd acted so happy and carefree, while each sip of his beer had made him want to throw up. She was the best poker player he'd ever seen, and he had faith in her, but not so much that he was willing to bet her life. He tried to tell himself that she'd be playing another human, not Noqoìlpi, but still, it would likely be another person playing for his or her life. He barely knew Georgia, but he already knew he couldn't stand to lose her.

They stayed in bed until noon, then he took her to lunch at High Point. She laughed and joked and cleaned her plate, while his food remained virtually untouched.

"Fate," she said, sliding her hand in his. "Don't worry about me. I'm a survivor."

He couldn't look at her, but she caught his chin and made him. She pressed her mouth to his right there at the table, not caring who was watching.

"Are you that sure you're going to win?" he asked.

She laughed. "No, but I'm that sure it's going to be okay."

She wrapped up a biscuit for Mel, who was napping in his heated carrier, and Fate drove them to the school, where the various vendors were set up.

A little boy approached him with a multi-colored selection of roses and said, "Hey, Mister, would you like to buy a flower?"

Fate selected a red one and handed him a twenty. "Keep the change," he said.

Turning to Georgia, he broke it off, removed the thorns and

tucked it behind her ear. "The Chinese think red is a lucky color. Brides even wear it to ward off evil. It even—"

Mel suddenly bounded from Georgia's arms. Fate lost sight of him for a moment, then he heard someone yelling. Mel was in Benny's Donut's display booth, helping himself to a batch of bright, freshly iced doughnut holes while Benny shouted at him and tried to shoo him away with a rolled up newspaper. Mel stood his ground and hissed, his mouth stained green from the icing.

"I'm so sorry!" Fate said, scooping up his pet.

He threw down some cash and a mollified Benny handed him a cup filled with the rest of the doughnut holes that weren't in a container or on the ground.

Fate chastised Mel as they walked away, but in baby talk, making Georgia laugh. She tucked her hand inside Fate's arm and gave it a squeeze.

"Now you know where the phrase 'crazy like a fox' comes from, but I'm not sure they're as smart as people think."

Mel gave him an offended look, which was comical because of the green and pink icing clinging to his whiskers.

"Don't look at me like that. Don't you do it," Fate purred. "I'm not the one who ate a tube of Krazy Glue once. *That* was bad. He couldn't understand why he couldn't open his mouth and he was scared. We were all chasing him around Chonky's. You're ridiculous, Mel."

Fate tried to maintain Georgia's light mood, but found it nearly impossible. How strong she was. How brave. The only time he saw her frown at all was when the fortune teller tried to beckon her inside her booth. She politely declined.

Too soon, she glanced at her watch and said, "I guess we'd better head that way. It's almost time."

"What on earth—" she said, as they pulled into Chonky's lot.

The bar was booming. Fate had to park a block over.

"Surely these people aren't here for the tournament," Fate said.

Inside, there was a definite change of atmosphere. Everyone was carrying around baby pink drinks with umbrellas. Fate held the back of Georgia's coat as she angled through the crowd to the bar.

Fate heard her make a muffled snorting sound and glanced up at a red-faced Larry.

"What has happened to you?" Fate asked slowly, and Larry's face turned even redder. Two glittery hearts bobbed from his headband, and he wore a pink shirt boasting a donkey holding a pink umbrella drink. The logo read, Ask me about our special! The Chonky Donkey … It Kicks!

"HaaaaaHaaaaaa!" Chonky bellowed, and slapped Fate on the shoulder, earning a startled hiss from Mel. "This is what you call Karma!" He launched into babytalk much like Fate had given Mel earlier. "Poor widdle Warry didn't want to make girly drinks, so he invented one and surprise, sucker! Everyone loves it. Larry, get these two a couple of Chonky Donkeys, on the house." He looked at Georgia. "How you doing, sweetheart? It's not too late to change your mind."

"I'm good. And I have to do this. It'll be okay." She smiled, but when Fate took her hand, it was icy.

Larry scowled as he slammed two pink drinks in front of them so hard they sloshed over the side. Fate said, "I'm not drinking anything that color."

Georgia sipped it, then her eyes widened. "Larry! This is delicious."

Fate gave it a suspicious glance, swirled it around, then took a taste.

"Wow!" he said, and winked at Larry. "And it kicks."

"I hate my life," Larry grumbled, then shot Georgia a guilty look. "Hey, good luck tonight."

Chonky pushed his way back toward them, holding the hand of a female cyclops.

"This is my sister, Agnes. We have something for you."

"Oooh, you're a cutie pie!" Agnes said, batting her eyes at Fate before turning her attention to her oversized purse. She presented Georgia with a garish yellow ring. "This was our mother's good luck charm. Chonk said you could use a little luck today, so we'd like to lend it to you."

Georgia's eyes shone and her voice was hoarse as she croaked, "Thank you. I'd be honored to wear it."

Agnes and Chonky both beamed as Agnes slipped it on her finger, then moved it to her thumb when it was too big. Larry overheard them and reached for his wallet to remove a worn penny.

"This doesn't look like much, but for reasons I won't go into right now, this is my lucky coin. I'd also like to lend it to you."

Georgia accepted it and put it in her pocket.

"Thank you all," she rasped.

When they dispersed, Fate said, "I don't have anything lucky to give you. Never really believed in it until the night I met you. But I believe in your skill, and that's worth more than luck."

He kissed her, losing himself in the softness of her lips, the taste of her. Then Mel made a keening sound and the lively bar grew quieter. They turned to see Noqoìlpi walk through the door.

Although the crowd moved aside for him, there were so many people that Fate didn't immediately notice the man trailing behind him, but Georgia did.

Her eyes widened and her mouth opened in a startled 'o' as they drew near. A single tear streaked down her cheek as she said, "Father."

Georgia's father gave her a forced smile that only reminded her of the one he'd given her when he came to collect them and tell them that he'd lost them in a poker bet. She'd hated him then. She hated him even more now.

"Hi, Sweetpea," he said.

"Is it not enough," she said, "that you caused all of this in the first place? Did you come to finish destroying your own children?"

She couldn't imagine what Fate was thinking. Surely even demon parents weren't this cruel.

Her father had the decency to look ashamed.

"Georgia, I didn't have a choice. I played a game after that, trying to win you back. I lost, and now I belong to Noqoìlpi."

"And that is what you're playing for today? Your freedom versus mine? You're such a great dad."

Across the bar, Chonky announced, "Poker contestants and sponsors, please join me on this end. Your seat numbers and positions were assigned randomly and I've hired an outside dealer to preside. Our local coven has taken steps to ensure there will be no magical interference at the table."

Georgia's seat was to the dealer's left, directly across from that of her father. Fate took his seat behind her. Noqoìlpi sat behind her father, gazing at her as he rolled a smooth piece of turquoise through his fingers. She supposed even gambling gods had their lucky charms and superstitions.

Seven contestants had entered, and only one had been eliminated by first break, taken out by a careless all-in against Georgia's father, who was the chip leader. Before the official tally, Georgia surmised herself in third place.

"Let's go outside," she told Fate, when the dealer announced a twenty minute break.

She stretched, her back sore from the two hours she'd been sitting there.

When they made it outside, away from the crowd, Georgia turned and snuggled against him, pressing her face against his chest. He cradled her close, careful not to crush Mel between them.

"You're doing great," he said. "You are so crazy smart and intuitive."

But so was her father. At the table, he was all business. He hadn't even made eye contact with the daughter he'd left broken, left wondering how any parent could treat his children the way he had.

The second round went a little faster. Three more players folded by the next break, leaving only Georgia, her father and a young man hidden behind dark sunglasses and a hoodie that he kept drawn up, nearly covering his face in an attempt not to betray any signs. But Georgia didn't need his face. She'd realized he had a nervous knee. Since he sat beside her, she wasn't sure her father could see it, but she could sense his slight nervous movement and hoped to use it to her advantage.

Georgia got her chance a few hands after they'd resumed play. She was all but convinced from his betting pattern and his shaky knee that he'd made his full house on the turn, but the river had given Georgia her fourth two. Her father had folded after the flop and she knew only two hands could beat her. She said, "All-in," and he quickly called.

And then there were two.

For the first time in the tournament, Georgia had a slight chip lead, and now she was head-to-head against her father. Partly from a desire to make him react, partly from hurt and annoyance, she said, "Have you even checked on Luke? Do you feel any remorse from sending a fifteen-year-old boy to the shadow land?"

Finally, he glanced at her as he checked on the flop. "You don't understand. I never thought I'd lose. I'd lost my money. I'd lost my house. I really thought I'd figured him out and was going to win. I never ..."

He trailed off, and she said, "Raise 400. You never what ... gave a damn? That I believe. I remember nights before Mom left, when you'd shut us up in a motel room and tell us not to go out, when you both would go to the casino and leave us forty bucks to order cheap pizza for the weekend. We were just little kids."

He called, then looked at the turn card and checked again. "It was hard for me, too, after she left. I didn't know how to take care of you, or hold down a real job. Cards and the game are all I know."

Georgia looked at her hand. She had middle pair and wasn't sure what he had. Her efforts to shake him had merely shaken her instead. She was about to get out of the hand when he said, "Remember your Uncle Frank? I'll never forget that wild game in Boise when you were first learning to play. He was so impressed, and you were so happy when you took me out."

What a weird thing to mention.

Georgia stared at him, perplexed.

For the first time, he stared at her. His dark eyes bored into hers. The look on his face pleaded, *Trust me.*

Georgia did remember Uncle Frank, and the game he was referring to. It was the first time she'd ever felt any power at the table, but she'd gotten too cocky at the end, pushed all-in even though her hand was merely modest. Her father had folded, but as he'd thrown the better pair face up in the middle, he'd said, "Could've had you, Sweetpea. I think you've got sixes."

Indeed, sixes was what she'd had, and he'd had tens. Was that what he was trying to tell her now? Was he intending on throwing the game? The pot was pretty big. She knew she should just fold and try again the next hand.

Her father shot her one last pleading glance. "Come on, Georgia Ann. Whatcha going to do?"

She froze, judging him. Maybe this was his way of redeeming himself. Maybe there was still some good left in him, after all.

"All-in," she said.

He smiled.

She knew from the second she saw that smile that she'd been duped and it was all she could do not to lunge across the table at him. She also knew that she hadn't misread his intentions. He had once again played on a daughter's wistfulness. He had once again revealed his selfish heart.

"I call," he said, and flipped up queens.

Georgia watched most of her money being raked across the table, and she couldn't stop the angry tear that slid down her nose.

She barely had enough to even ante up for the next round, but he took that pot, too.

It was over. She belonged to Noqoìlpi for an eternity.

"Can I at least see him?" she said, looking around that vile piece of humanity to address Noqoìlpi. "When you bring Luke back, can I see him for a moment?"

He gave a slight nod in the affirmative.

"Wait!" Fate cried, his chair clattering against the floor as he jumped to his feet. "Play me, double or nothing. One hundred years labor, my freedom for hers."

Noqoìlpi pursed his lips, then shook his head. "Demons are a dime a dozen. I don't need another pet demon."

"I'm not a demon," Fate said. "I'm nephilim. I bet you don't have a pet one of those."

Shocked, Georgia stared up at Fate as his eyes began to glow a brilliant, icy blue. The room erupted in a chorus of surprised muttering.

Noqoìlpi leaned forward, interested.

"No!" Georgia said, and stood to push Fate backwards. "I won't let you do this."

"Deal," Noqoìlpi said behind her. "Choose your game, nephilim."

Fate handed Mel to her and nodded at the pool tables behind Noqoìlpi. "I choose billiards."

Georgia dragged Fate to the corner and said, "You cannot do this! You barely know me. I won't let you die for me."

"It's only a hundred years," he said, and kissed her forehead. "My father may not have given me anything else, but I've been gifted immortality."

What she didn't say, and what she saw on his face, was that in a hundred years, she'd be long gone. If he lost, they would never see each other again.

"I'm pretty good at pool," he said, brushing a wave of hair from her face. "A lifetime of misspent youth." He scratched Mel's head. "You have to take care of him, though. He doesn't like anyone else."

"Fate—"

"Shh!" He kissed her. "I have no regrets, win or lose."

Noqoìlpi stood at the table, rolling the turquoise stone between his fingers and watching Chonky rack. Chonky glanced at Fate and said, "Eight or nine ball?"

"Eight-ball, best three of five." He looked at Noqoìlpi. "Flip a coin to see who breaks?"

Noqoìlpi gave a dismissive wave. "You can break first. We'll alternate each game."

Fate made three balls on the break, two stripes and one solid. He chose to play for stripes.

Georgia's heart pounded as he circled the table, making shot after shot. Chonky, Henny and Leo gathered around her. She looked around once for her father, but that coward was already gone.

Fate ran the table and motioned at a pocket on the opposite side, calling his 8-ball shot. The crowd erupted when he made it. Noqoìlpi's face remained inscrutable as Chonky racked, then nodded for him to break.

Noqoìlpi took the next two games, allowing Fate only two shots, and both of those were trying to shoot around a safety, where Noqoìlpi, knowing he couldn't make his shot, had positioned the ball behind other balls, not allowing Fate a good shot either.

Georgia noticed something about Noqoìlpi, how he held the turquoise stone in his hand with each shot, even if it made it cumbersome to adjust the stick around it. But sometimes when it was Fate's turn, he'd take the stone and lay it on the table. When he did that, Fate would miss his shot.

"Is there any way to know if magic is being used on this table?" Georgia whispered to Chonky.

He shrugged. "Ah, I don't really know. Let me ask one of the witches."

It was Fate's shot and once again, Noqoìlpi laid the piece of turquoise on the rail. This time, however, he turned away from the table to search for a new blue cube to chalk his cue.

Suddenly, Mel lunged from Georgia's arms, darted across the table and gulped down the turquoise stone that undoubtedly reminded him of the doughnut holes he adored of the same color.

"No!" Noqoìlpi yelled, and grabbed for him. Mel scampered down the rail and climbed Fate's arm to sit on his shoulder, where he promptly hissed at Noqoìlpi.

"That's my lucky talisman!" he shouted, for the first time showing any real emotion, and that emotion was panic. "I want it back!"

Fate gave him an exasperated look. "I'm sorry, but I don't think that's going to happen for at least a day or two. You can have it back then. I don't know what else to tell you."

Noqoìlpi removed a knife from his pocket and clicked it open. "We can cut it out right now."

"You most certainly will not," one of the witches said.

"Magic is against the rules in these games," Georgia said. "Since a god such as yourself would have no need to cheat, I'm sure it's just a harmless stone. Fate said he will return it to you—when that is possible."

Noqoìlpi shot her a look of pure malice and she suddenly knew she was right. He had not held the stone when he'd played her, but maybe he hadn't thought he'd needed it then. She had heard others in the shadow world mention it though. The powerful, invincible gambling god was nothing but a cheat, and he was stuck now, because admitting it would forfeit the game and destroy his reputation.

Fate looked at her and she smiled.

Mel, she thought, *stay right where you're at.*

Fate didn't allow Noqoìlpi another shot for the rest of the game, making a beautiful, nearly impossible eight-ball shot.

They entered their last game tied. Fate made five balls on the break, but scratched, so Noqoìlpi got a shot. He clumsily missed a wide open shot in the corner. Fate looked at her, then looked at Noqoìlpi and purposely missed a bank shot. Noqoìlpi scowled, because he knew what Fate was doing. Noqoìlpi missed his next shot as well, and people began to whisper behind their hands.

Georgia caught Fate's gaze and said, "Finish him."

Fate ran the rest of his balls, but lucky charm or not, Georgia could tell he didn't like his chances of scratching on the eight and giving Noqoìlpi an automatic win, so he did a safety, tucking the eight in a cluster by the side pocket.

Noqoìlpi tried to make his five in the corner, but he sent the eight ball shooting down the rail to sink in the pocket. He had lost.

The room erupted in cheers and Georgia darted around the table to hug Fate.

Noqoìlpi snapped his fingers, filling the spot where he was standing with a cloud of dust. People were choking, coughing, and for a moment, Georgia couldn't see anything. But then the dust settled, and a thin, pale, redheaded boy stood where Noqoìlpi had stood. He looked around, bewildered.

"Luke!" Georgia screamed, and ran to him.

"Georgia!" he gasped. "Is this real? Am I free?"

She looked at Fate, who was grinning at her. Mel almost looked like he was grinning, too.

"It is, and you are. Thanks to them."

❄

The party was in full swing at Chonky's when Georgia pulled Fate outside again. Luke sat at the bar with Henny, devouring a plate of wings and fries. Mel sat on the counter beside him, eating the discarded bones. Fate picked her up and spun her around in the cold night air and she laughed before kissing him passionately.

"That dirty cheat," she said ."Thank goodness for that hungry-eyed bottomless pit rascal of yours."

Fate laughed and rubbed the back of his neck. "Yeah, I guess we need to find him a vet, just to be safe, but he's eaten worse."

He held open his arms and Georgia snuggled against him.

"Nephilim, huh?" she said, and looked up at him. "Good angel or bad?"

Fate winced. "You don't really want to know."

"It doesn't matter. You and I are not like our fathers."

He kissed the top of her head and said, "I *am* going to need a favor from you. That auction thing tomorrow night … please bid on me. Chonky's sister was talking about how cute we all were and saying something about a reverse harem and I'm a little scared right now."

Georgia giggled. "She better get that eye off my man."

"Your man, huh?" Fate asked, pleased.

She held up her hand and he pressed his palm against hers.

"Oh, yeah," she said. "I bet all I have on you, Fate. I'm all in."

"I am, too," he said, and kissed her as the snow began to fall.

OBSESSED WITH HER

ALEXIS TAYLOR & BETH HENDRIX

CHAPTER ONE

I was sitting at my desk staring out the window watching the snow fall. It's Christmas Eve and everything outside is white, snow covering it all. The usual blue sky is full of big clouds and even though it's just after two in the afternoon, the street lights are on because of the cloud coverage. It was beautiful, especially when you take in the Christmas lights of the houses in our neighborhood. All except Zander, Jaxon, and Kelvin's.

Zander, Jaxon, and Kelvin. Just thinking of them sends shivers through my body. They were our neighbors and they were definitely strange. Identical triplets who were all handsome, broody, and way too old for me to be fantasizing about. It should feel wrong and forbidden, but it doesn't, so I tried not to think of them.

However, I do fantasize about getting the hell out of this house and away as soon as I can. Daydreaming about someone, or someones taking me away from here. Making me their wife. A new path, a new life...

I would do anything to get out. To live, but I had no choice but to stay here until I finished college. My father kept a tight leash on me and one of the conditions of my inheritance was that I stayed under the same roof as her and finished school.

Wrapping a piece of my blonde hair around my finger, I lose myself in thought. Focusing on all of the things that I would do with freedom.

"Sandra!" My father's deep voice calls from the hallway making me jump. My heart was beating so fast that it felt like it was going to beat out of my chest.

He comes into the room with his usual judgmental and condescending look. It was so crazy to me that you could love someone, but hate them at the same time. It was a good thing he couldn't read my thoughts because most of them did not paint him in a good light. Unfortunately, though, I was stuck with him until I was out of school.

"Yes dad?" I said back, not getting up.

His hair is completely grey, but he is not a man to trifle with. I didn't know what he did for work, but it kept him in peak condition. He was in his early fifties but didn't look a day over thirty-five. I hoped that meant that I would age as well.

My thoughts turned to my mother then. She had passed when I was only thirteen, but she had been dad's complete opposite. She had been a beauty pageant queen. When she would pick me up from school, she would always wave as if she was on a parade float. It had always embarrassed me, but I would give anything to see it now.

She had tried to pull me into pageants when I was younger, but it didn't work out for her. I would freeze completely on stage and after doing it a few in a row, she gave up. I had always preferred to be home. My nose was in a book in my room. It had been something that she had never understood, but she never said anything to me about it.

"The neighbors, Zander, Jaxon, and Kelvin will be coming over for dinner. I need you to prepare something edible." He walked further into my room, and his suit looked freshly pressed, which wasn't surprising.

"When?" I asked, it was just like him to throw something together and tell me at the last minute.

The neighbors had just moved in four months ago, and since then, my father had been obsessed with getting them over to the house. It was weird, but I let it go because my dad was weird. My older sister, on the other hand, panted like a bitch in heat after them. I couldn't blame her though all of them were gorgeous and loaded. We had all seen the Porsches they drove.

They were tall, muscled, and had bright green eyes. Intense eyes that you could feel staring at you, even from far away. Sometimes when I left for college in the mornings, I could feel their eyes on me as if tracking me like I was prey. And I couldn't say that I didn't like it. I had never been with a man before, but all I wanted was them. To feel their mouths on my body, to have them hold me.

I knew it was ridiculous, this little crush I had on them. They would never be interested in me. Who in the world would be? I was a twenty-year-old who still lived at home with her bitchy older sister and overbearing father? They had to be in their late thirties, they would see me as nothing but a child even though I was anything but. I hadn't been for a really long time.

They probably wanted older women who had their lives together, not some silly college student who fantasizes about them instead of doing her coursework. Now I was going to be stuck watching my sister try to seduce them. In my own house. I bit my lip as my stomach knotted, but I keep my thoughts to myself.

"They will be here at five. I expect everything to be perfect." His tone is sharp and I fight to keep my back from going ramrod straight. All he ever expected was perfection, I had already known this wouldn't be different.

"Yes, Dad," I said back, unable to keep the snark from my tone causing his eyes to flash in fury.

"Don't you take a tone with me Sandra. You will do as you are told or you will be punished." He replied with a hard look and I fought to keep the terror off my face. He had never abused me in the physical sense, but we had a basement with no windows that he liked to lock me in when I was bad.

Looking down at the floor, I waited until he left to release the pent-up breath that I had been holding. God, if I didn't need my inheritance so bad, I would be long gone. I fucking hated it here. Taking a deep breath, I close the novel that I had been pretending to read on my desk and head out of the room. Passing my dad who was standing still in the hallway.

"Thank you, Sandra. I know that I can always depend on you."

"It should be the other way around," I muttered as I walked on.

"What did you say?" He asked, but I didn't stop Just went down the stairs without answering.

I loved our house, the house itself that was, it was modest, but completely decked out in Christmas. My sister was in interior design school and took pride in keeping a showroom-worthy room.

There was a huge Christmas tree, covered in ornaments, beads, and tinsel. It looked as if someone brought to life a Pinterest post. Since mom passed, there were no happy memories, as if there was no soul in the house. No amount of Christmas shit could make up for the fact that my sister was vile and my father was even worse.

Putting my hair back into a ponytail, I go into the kitchen. I had been growing my hair out for the last two years and the blonde locks were now halfway down my back. Checking the fridge, I saw that we had the stuff to make fried chicken. Hopefully, the triplets would be okay with that.

Washing my hands, I started to prepare my batter. I was making green beans and mashed potatoes with it. I could have done something fancier if I had the notice, but this was the best I could do with the notice I had been given.

On a whim, I decided to make some sugar cookies. Not just any though, my grandmother's secret recipe. She had taught me when I was younger and now I knew it by heart. I was a little irritated at my father for springing this on me, but I did love to cook. Before long, I lost myself in the relaxing actions.

Singing to myself as I mixed the butter and sugar together, I smiled. Christmas had always been my favorite holiday. I loved everything about it, and it was easy to lose myself in it.

Before I knew it, the dough was ready. Rolling it out on the counter, I leaned down to get the cookie-cutter when I suddenly felt like I was being watched.

Turning around, I looked out the window that faced the Triplets house. Their blinds were shut and my heart dropped. Of course, they wouldn't be watching me. Such a stupid hope. They don't even know I exist.

Shaking my head, I resumed making my cookies and placed the tree and star-shaped cookies in the oven. I turned on a timer on my phone as I put the rest of the food in the warming drawer of the oven. Looking down, I noticed that my Santa tank top and black leggings are covered in flour.

Well shit, I was going to have to change. Heading to my room, I took the stairs two at a time. Once inside, I slid on a pair of black leggings that highlighted my ass. I wanted them to stare at me as I had them.

Maybe it would keep them from looking at Gina, my sister. I caught sight of myself in the mirror and tried to imagine what I looked like to the Triplets. Brown eyes, large breasts, long legs. But with my short height and slim waist, they probably still see a girl and not a woman.

Even though no one will see it, I lift my sports bra over my head and run to my closet. Reaching in the back of my drawer, I grab my red lace push-up bra. I bought it on my last birthday. I wasn't sure why, but I had wanted it.

Putting it on, I looked at myself in the mirror again and smiled. Now I looked sexy. It made me wonder if the triplets would even notice. My timer on my phone beeped at that moment and I panicked. Shit, the cookies were done.

Pulling on a low-cut green sweater with tiny Santas all over, I check myself in the mirror once more before letting my hair out of the ponytail. Running down the hall I tried to get to the kitchen so that my cookies didn't burn.

"Gina, Sandra. The neighbors are on their way over." My father yelled as I hauled ass down the stairs.

My sister stepped out of her room and I cringed. She was wearing a fitted green dress that showed way too much leg and cleavage, but it did look good on her. She had on bright red lipstick and dark eye makeup. If it wasn't for the sneer she had on her face, I would say she was beautiful'

"You couldn't even attempt to dress up? You are such a fucking embarrassment." She snarled as she grabbed my forearm, stopping me from getting to the kitchen.

"Let go, Gina," I said as she pinched my shirt.

"Oh god, you are wearing polyester. Where did you even find this? A second hand shop?" She was such a stuck up bitch. I loved her but sometimes I wanted to shove her down the stairs.

"The cookies are going to burn," I growled out as the doorbell rang.

Whipping around, she let me go as she released an excited squeal that hurt my ears. Rolling my eyes, I rushed over to the oven and pulled out the cookies. I sighed in relief when I saw that the bottom of them were only a little golden. If I had gotten here any later, they would have burned.

Letting out a deep breath, I sat the food out on the kitchen table. Putting the cookies on a cooling rack that was in the middle of the table. I could hear my father as he opened the front door.

"Zander, Kelvin, Jaxon!" My sister said, dragging out each name. "You are right on time. I just finished making us a wonderful Christmas Eve dinner."

Rage rolled over me, but I shouldn't have expected anything different from Gina. She had been taking credit for my hard work for years.

My hands were shaking with anger as I arranged the rest of the food on the table, making it look as good as I could. My anger quickly turned to panic though as I heard one of the triplet's voices. Oh my god, they were in my house. My heart threatened to beat out of my chest as I turned to the door just in time to watch my father, sister and my forbidden crushes walk into the kitchen.

CHAPTER TWO

ZANDER

As I walked into the kitchen, I finally caught sight of my obsession. Our obsession. She watched us curiously. The look in her eyes was strong, but also wary. It was clear to see that the years with her asshole of a father and whore of a sister hadn't broken her. She looked innocent but wise. She consumed my every thought and I knew that it was the same with my brothers.

I wanted to tell her how special, strong, and brave I thought she was. I wanted to do so much for her, have her by our side, and give her anything to make her smile. But we couldn't do that. She wasn't meant to be ours.

When Gina had tried to pass off the meal as hers, I had almost scoffed. I could tell from the looks on my brother's faces that they almost had to. All I wanted, all we wanted, was to see the girl we had come to see.

Even if we hadn't seen Sandra cooking through the window, we would have known that Gina hadn't cooked. No one who looked like that was making Christmas cookies. Gina's Desperation disgusted me, maybe in the past I would have gone for it, before ghosting her. Not anymore though. I could see through her lies and it took everything in me not to grimace at her advances. This was our one chance though so I played nice.

Truthfully, we hadn't come here for Gina or Gregor, Sandra's father. We were here for Sandra. Since the moment we moved in next door, we had all watched her. It had been just a curiosity in the beginning, but now I wanted to know everything about her. We were all obsessed with every single thing about her.

She went to Jacklensen College and left every morning at eight-fifteen and came back at three in the afternoon. Her favorite color was red and she liked to dance. We knew that her car was at least seven years old. There was so much about her that we had figured out just by watching.

The kicker of that was, her father drove a beamer and spent all his money on hookers and drugs. I doubt either of his daughters knew what he was up to. I was sure at one point that he had enough money to send Sandra to a better school, but had chosen not to. He disgusted me. I wanted nothing more than to take Sandra away from here and show her what she deserved.

With every new thing that we learned about her, the more we wanted to protect her. Watch her, take care of her in any way possible. She was so small and she needed someone to have her back, to take care of her because her family was doing a bang up job.

Tonight was our only chance to see her this close. We had allowed this one moment of weakness. We would be going back to watching her from a distance. Back to wanting the one woman we could never have. She could never be a part of our lives. Killers didn't get love, especially not ones who worked for the Bratva. If we let her into our lives, she would always have a target on her back, a weakness that could be used against us. If we brought her in, we would only turn her light soul dark and that was something that I would never be able to forgive.

Not that any of that mattered. She would never want us. We were all older than her, and there were three of us. We had figured out first hand when we were younger just what women thought when we told them we were a package deal. We were complete opposites in every way and she would never see us as more than her neighbors.

Snapping back to the now, my eyes were still locked on Sandra as she wiped a little flour from her face.

"Thank goodness Sandra was nice enough to get my cookies out of the oven. She is such a sweet girl." Gina said while putting an emphasis on the girl as if we didn't know that she was younger than us. She was twenty though a consenting adult. Gina's voice was sweet as she could make it, but to me, it was cringe worthy. If only she used this tone with her sister, but the only thing that Sandra got from her was vile cruel words and harsh snarls.

I knew this because I have watched Sandra in more ways than just through the window. One day, while they were all out of the house, Kelvin had snuck in while Jaxon and I had been keeping watch to plant two cameras in the house. One was pointed at her bed and the other showed the entire room. Every single night since then, we have watched her.

I was aware that made us stalkers and that it was wrong and perverted and so many other things, but we didn't care. We were going to hell anyway, might as well do something that brought us joy.

Most of the time, Sandra danced around her room, read, or binge watched tv. We watched her like men possessed, soaking in everything that she did. My favorite part though, was when she touched herself.

She wasn't like most girls with toys, she didn't have any of the extras. She did it with her fingers until she came so beautifully. I knew we shouldn't watch it, but we had too. It was a compulsion. She was our one and only obsession.

When one of us had to leave the house, we were always sure to record everything so that we could watch everything. Even though she spent most of the time in her room, thanks to the windows we were able to see into other parts of the house. Which is how we knew that she was the one who had cooked.

We watched everything she did. Everything.

It was as if we were addicted and she was a drug we couldn't kick.

We knew it was wrong, but we needed her in every way we could have her. Even if that was just watching from afar.

That was what made it so strange to be in the same room with her. To smell the meal she had made for us. I knew what she looked like nude, what she sounded like when she came, but I had to pretend as if we were strangers because to her we were. She had no idea about any of it. How much we watched her, how we wanted to be with her.

"Hello, Sandra," Jaxon said, breaking the silence as I fought to keep my heartbeat even.

We could kill people for the mob without breaking a sweat, but us talking to her made me nervous. This was ridiculous, but then again we were hiding a lot. We didn't want her to see our evil.

Sandra turned to look at us all, stopping at me and I watched as a blush spread over her body. She was so fucking beautiful. I wanted to be with her so bad that I had to fight to keep myself from going to her. Looking at my brothers, I could tell that they were in the same boat as me.

"Hey, Zander, Kelvin, Jaxon. Merry Christmas and hope you enjoy the meal." She replied, her eyes moving around us almost nervously. I wanted nothing more than to go to her at that moment, but we weren't good enough for her. No amount of scrubbing would get the bloodstains off of our hands.

"It's Christmas Eve, Sandra. Ugh, not even Christmas yet and they will love my meal." Gina replied, trying to sound playful, but anyone could hear the sneer underneath that.

She then turned back to us, before her gaze settled on me. Pushing up her chest as if she wanted her ample cleavage noticed, she placed her hands on my arms, but I didn't fall for it. Not when the woman who consumed my thoughts was in the room.

"It's polite to say Merry Christmas. Does it really matter that it is only Christmas Eve?" Sandra shot back.

I hated that Gina's words had hurt her and I wanted to throw her off me. Instead though, I took her hands and moved them back to her as she stared at me dumbfounded as if unsure how she should react.

"Excuse me for pointing it out." Gina huffed out before turning in her heels and going to the table. "Let's eat shall we?"

While Gina was getting the seating figured out, all three of us moved closer to Sandra. Her scent wafted from her body causing my mouth to water. All I wanted to do was scoop her up and get her out of here.

She had on a tight green sweater and black leggings and I could see it all. The curve of her ass and her cleavage. I almost stopped breathing as she leaned up on her tiptoes to grab the salt from the counter, giving us all a perfect view of her amazing ass. The need to make her mine pounded through me.

"You made an amazing feast," I whispered as I snuck a cookie causing her back to shoot up straight. Looking at me in shock as if she couldn't believe that I was complimenting her and not Gina.

Her eyes were wide and I was close enough to see the freckles across her face. I felt starved for this woman, like an animal. Keeping my eyes locked to hers, I took a bite out of the cookie. Damn, it really was good. She was an amazing baker. I couldn't wait to try the rest of her food.

"Um, no. Uh, Gina." She attempted to lie and I got why she did it, but I hated it. Hated the way they treated her.

"Your secret is safe with me. Don't worry." I replied with a wink and I cursed myself for it. We couldn't have her, so there is no way that I should be blinking at her. I'd have to be on my best behavior the rest of the night.

The meal was just as amazing as I expected. Could Sandra be any more perfect? I couldn't keep my eyes off her as Gina attempted to seduce us and Gregor attempted to pull us into business talks.

Gina jumped up suddenly as soon as we had finished eating and said, "How about we take the cookies and go start up the fireplace? There's a little bit of a chill in here." Before she strutted off with the cookies and I got up, motioning for Sandra to go before me.

"After you," I said with a small wave.

She smiled up at me and I noticed that she still had some flour left on her cheek. Unable to stop myself, I wiped it off. She gasped when my thumb touched her skin, but her eyes stayed latched to mine while her face went red.

She turned away quickly, but I could see the smile on her face as she followed Gina.

"Why can't we have her again?" Kelvin whispered as he got close to me. This was hard enough without them asking questions like that.

"You know why," I growled out as I started walking, trying to keep my eyes from Sandra's lush ass. Last thing we needed was Gina or Gregor to catch me staring at her ass like a man starved.

Gina sat down on the couch and crossed her legs causing her dress to ride up. Even with the lace garter, I wasn't interested and neither were my brothers as we all sat far away from her. Sandra rolled her eyes as she noticed what her sister was doing.

"Don't one of you want to sit beside me?" Gina purred out and I barely contained my cringe.

"We are fine where we are," Kelvin said, his voice was even, but I could hear the undercurrent of anger that laced it. We had known that this would be bad, but fuck, that girl was ridiculous.

CHAPTER THREE

SANDRA

I still couldn't believe they were here. On my couch, in my damn living room. Their large bodies made the room feel smaller. They were so much more muscular up close that I was surprised that the couch opposite Gina could hold them. I couldn't help the errant thought that made me wonder what it would feel like under them.

A blush covered my face and I attempted to force my thoughts onto something else. Literally anything else, but I looked at them again.

I could almost jump for joy. They were all looking at my sister with varying looks of disgust. Nobody ever saw through her act so I couldn't believe it.

They were so different from any men I had ever met. They seemed so in control of everything, the way they moved and the way they thought, but I could still see the disgust. The more I watched them I realized that they must really dislike her for it to be so plain on their face.

It made me wonder why they had come over. Dad had been quietly staring at them, but they hadn't spoken. Surely they didn't come over for me, right?

Just thinking about it made my heart race. I knew I didn't have a chance, but it made me feel like I might have one.

This close, they really were the most handsome men I had ever seen. They had a little stubble on their cheeks and jaw, just enough to shade them a touch. Their hair was a touch messy, but it looked intentional.

Fuck, I just seriously couldn't believe they were here, close enough to touch. One of them had touched me, Zander, and I could still feel it.

"So, how do you afford the cars that you drive?" Gina asked breaking the silence and embarrassment burst through me.

"Gina! That is rude," I protested, but it was par the course for her. She only cared about material objects.

"I'm just making conversation!" She sneered back at me as her smile turned into a grimace because I had called her out. As soon as she turned back to the men though, her smile was back normal.

"It's okay, My family and I own a chain of bars and I manage the ones on the west," Jaxon said as he nodded at me giving me a grin that caused my stomach to clench.

"Which bars? I may have to check them out." Gina purred, trying to get the attention off of me, but they all just stared at me. My body may as well have been a full blush.

Something about that didn't add up to me though. They seemed too smart, too something to just be bar managers. They were all dressed in perfectly tailored sweaters and jeans that you could tell were designers. Bar managers couldn't make that much, right?

"Ronaldo's bar," Kelvin replied as a hint of an accent creeped through.

I knew of the bar, but I had never been. I wanted to think more about it, but it was hard to do when I was at the center of their focus. I wanted to keep them talking though because their voices were soothing.

"How is school, Sandra?" Zander said, changing the subject. My name on his lips almost caused me to moan out loud.

The way they stare at me is intense as if they want to devour me. I didn't know why, but it caused my body to heat. I knew it should worry me, but it didn't. I was more worried that I would throw myself at them and embarrass myself.

"Oh, um, it's going good. Next semester I have some really interesting classes like life drawing."

"Drawing? Are you an artist?" Jaxon asked, drawing my gaze from Zander to him. Fuck they were too good looking.

"I used to draw in school," Gina interjected as she leaned down attempting to draw the guy's looks to her chest that she was pretty much flashing at them. When it didn't work she glared at me, and I knew it meant that she wanted me to leave so that she could get laid.

This time, I completely ignored it. I made supper and the cookies that everyone was snacking on, the least I deserved was to bask in their presence a little bit longer.

"I was asking Sandra," Jaxon said and I felt a jolt of giddiness at Gina being put in her place.

"Um, yeah I think so. I've been drawing for a while and I am hoping to hone it to make it better." I had always loved to draw, but I never showed anyone my stuff.

"I bet you are amazing at it. What else are you studying?" Kelvin asked, and he sounded genuinely interested. As if he wanted to actually get to know me.

They had all leaned forward in my direction and hadn't taken their eyes off me. They were all so much more intense than I expected, but it didn't scare me. It actually only piqued my interest more and I had the strange urge to run away with them.

"Mostly, Literature," I replied.

They all nodded as they reached and grabbed another cookie before turning to look at the room around us. I released a breath I didn't know I had been holding and took a second to gather my thoughts.

However, Gina had enough of me taking her spotlight and had to ruin it.

"Sandra, hunni, I think it's time for you to go to bed. Give the adults some alone time." She sneered as if I was a toddler.

I opened my mouth to say something, but her stare made me back down. I knew just what would happen to me if I didn't obey. Even though I wanted to be near them, it wasn't worth it. It was Christmas eve so I might as well go on to my room that way I wouldn't be able to hear the sounds of Gina screwing them.

I kept my gaze averted as I pushed to stand up, of course, they were sending me away too. They were only being nice to me because they wanted Gina. I should have known, not let my hope see things in their faces that weren't real. I was nothing more than a child to them.

"No," Kelvin said, bringing the attention to him as he stood and turned on Gina. Glaring at her, I could see something in his eyes I didn't expect. It was almost something feral and as quick as it appeared it was gone, and I had to wonder if I was seeing things. " We don't want Sandra to leave. We are enjoying her company."

"God, she is still so young. She would be bored by our conversation."

My hands balled into fists and I fought to keep my composure. I was smarter than Gina would ever be and I actually gave a shit about people.

"Sandra is obviously a grown woman, and we don't want her to leave." Zander's tone was firm and left no room for argument. My stomach clenched and excitement welled up within me.

It was clear that Gina was confused and angry at what they had said. She sneered as she stood up and patted her dress down. She wobbled a bit but moved forward towards me.

"Fine then," She huffed as she shoulder-checked me on her way by.

I stood firm though, not giving in to the force of her, and instead, it made her off balance. She attempted to catch herself as she lost her footing, but those heels betrayed her. Her arms shot out as she gasped, falling right on her ass.

For a moment, there is nothing but silence until the laugh that I had been holding forced its way out of my throat.

"Fuck!" She yelled as she grimaced pulling herself to a sitting position.

All three of the guys start to laugh, and I couldn't keep mine in. All of our sounds blended together.

Gina attempted to get up, but her balance was lost and she fell right back down. Then we really lost it. We started to laugh until we were gasping for air. It was extremely relieving.

"Sandra, You have to take me to the hospital. I think I broke something," Gina yelled at me from the floor. If I didn't know she was faking, I would have felt like an ass for laughing at her, but I knew her too well. She didn't go down that hard.

My father chose that moment to walk back into the room to take in what was happening. "Get off the floor Gina. Don't make a fool of yourself."

I hadn't realized how close Zander was until I felt his side brush against my arm. The electricity from it moves through me and we both stopped laughing. Freezing in place as his eyes locked on mine.

The look on his face made me think that he would pick me up and carry me away. He breathed in, and everything went silent. He was staring at my lips as a shaky breath passed his. I hoped that he would kiss me. That bubble popped because he stood up quickly, and headed towards the door. All of them headed after him and my heart dropped.

Pausing at the door, his breathing was the only thing that we could hear. Gina gave up on her broken act and pushed herself up.

"Is everything okay?" Her voice cracked as she spoke, but she stood up effortlessly.

"We have to go," Jaxon said in a strained voice and I was to shocked o say anything.

Did I do something wrong? Did he not feel what I did when we touched?

Gina moaned and swayed as she stood, and I went to help her up as the door closed. They had just left. Shame, regret, and other feelings all washed over me and I could see that Gina was as surprised and embarrassed as I was.

She finally steadied herself and I crossed my arms, fighting the urge to pout like a toddler.

"I don't know what the hell you did, but you fucked this up for me. I just needed you to butter them up. I should have known that you couldn't do that. You are both fucking useless." My father shouted before he left the room.

Rolling my eyes and fighting the need to cry, I needed to try to figure out what the hell happened.

CHAPTER FOUR

JAXON

It physically pained me to leave Sandra, but we had to get out of there. We all knew that we couldn't have her and Zander was two seconds away from doing just that. Taking her right in front of her fucked up family. The sound of her laughing and the sight of her smile had been too much. We never should have gone to her.

My heart slammed in my chest as every nerve in my body screamed at me to go back and get her. I could tell that my brothers were thinking the same thing. Blood rushed to my cock then, and I tried not to think about her.

We had just left, ran away like fucking cowards. We could never go into her home again, we would have to go back to watching her. My breath was still coming in pants from running to the house. None of my brothers spoke as we made our way to the room that held our surveillance cameras. My brothers and I had always shared our women, so it wasn't odd to me that they were just as affected as I was.

As I sat down beside Zander, I realized that in a way, our skills as hitmen had prepared us for this kind of love. We were all good at making peace with our past sins. We would have to do better tomorrow.

Technically, this house was a safe house, and once we carried out the hit we had downtown. We would have to hide away for a while. It was how we did it. As hitmen, we were used to it.

The house was a modern home, well suited for a family of three or four. The kitchen was large and modern but completely wasted on us because not a one of us could cook. We mostly lived on takeout.

It was decorated nicely in hints of black and silver. I was indifferent about it though, all I felt at the moment was empty. Sandra hadn't made it to her room yet, so I made my way to my room. I couldn't just sit and watch her on the screen. I wanted to see her in person again.

My room was at the end of the hall, but its window looked directly into Sandra's bedroom. As long as I kept my lights off, she would never know that I was watching her. She had curtains, but never closed them.

She might not have been in her room when I was in the surveillance room, but she was now. Maybe Santa had come early because the moment I looked out the window, I was blessed with the sight of her taking her sweater off.

The cock that I had just gotten to go down, immediately begins to harden again. I could see all her pale skin as she slipped it off, but my heart stopped when the sweater was completely off and I could see the lacy bra that held her in.

I would have never imagined that our innocent Sandra would own such a thing. But holy fuck does she look downright sexy in it. Her breasts were round and spilled over the edges. A look overtook her face and before I could process it, she wiped the sweater back on and left the room. I couldn't help the disappointment that welled up in me as she left. I wanted to be with her even if this was the only way to do so.

I laid down in the bed and stared at the ceiling, fighting every urge I had to go over there and get her. To bring her back over here so we could ravage her. I had a feeling that she was innocent, so we would have to take it slow, but fuck I wanted that so much. I wanted her.

I wasn't sure how long had passed, but I heard the front door being knocked on. Heading downstairs, I opened the door to find Sandra. All rational thought left me and before I could stop myself, I pulled her to me and kissed her. I would deal with the repercussions later, right now, I had gotten just what I wanted for Christmas. My Sandra, my Obsession. She would be ours.

Did you enjoy the teaser Obsessed with her? The preorder for the full story will be going up soon!

ABOUT ALEXIS TAYLOR

Alexis is a mother of three demons, from a small town where nothing ever really happens outside of a writer's mind. A huge lover of books, she started to follow her favorite indie authors on social media two years later she alongside her best friend decided it was time to share the crazy dark stories from their minds with the world. Publishing Terror in a friend's anthology their love for writing was born.

A huge lover of the Supernatural, and all things dark and twisted, she has big plans for future stories and will never stick to just one genre or trope. Now signed to BBB Publishings and a featured Romance Lovers Author the next few years will be filled with exciting new worlds, stories, and definitely some more Twisted Rejections.

A self-proclaimed snobby reader she vows to give her readers different, engaging stories that push the boundaries of the normal author. Never one to back down from a challenge Alexis is one of her and her co-authors biggest critics, always determined to be better and do more her fans are definitely in for a treat.

When she isn't busy with her children, working, or writing she will usually be stalking cover groups for pretties or trolling Instagram for inspiration. If you want to keep up with Alexis, come stalk her by clicking on the link below. She loves nothing more than discussing books and ideas with like-minded readers. Plus she has a serious addiction to giving swag, and other goodies away.

https://linktr.ee/AlexisTaylorAuthor

OTHER BOOKS BY ALEXIS TAYLOR

HELL'S WRATH SERIES

Waking the Demon Within

Heart Of Stone

Twisted A Rejected Mates Series

Goddess Of Trickery: Blood Moon Series

Shorts & Anthologies

Terror

Unleashed

Rites Of Passion

Christmas Miracle

BBB Academy (Found in Relentless A bully Romance Collections)

Infernum Academy (Found in Relentless A bully Romance Collection)

Twisted Secret Part One (Found In Twisted Rejection Anthology)

Twisted Secret Part Two (Found In Twisted Rejection Part Two Anthology)

Fractured Minds (Found In The Anthology Tales Of All Hallows Eve)

Silversen Sisters: Minnies's Return (Found In The My Villainous Ways Anthology)

Anonymous Part 2 (Can you guess which story is by Alexis?)

ABOUT BETH HENDRIX

Beth is a single mother of two, who has worked in a custom cabinet shop since she was young.

She always has so many ideas flowing in her head but never thought that writing was a reality until some other amazing authors pointed out that she could.

A lover of all things paranormal Beth loves the darker more twisted books and it shows in her stories. As a mom to a young girl she also wants to write about badass, strong, independent women who don't care about other people's opinions when it comes to love. Which you can expect to see in her books a lot more.

Everything just clicked into place when she met her co-authors in 2018 and between them, they have over 200 works in progress. When she isn't with her kids, writing, or bossing about Alexis she will usually be found with a book in her hand or secretly buying pretty covers she isn't allowed to buy.

Beth loves nothing more than talking to her readers and getting feedback about her books. If you would like to keep up to date on

all projects, talk, or win some cool shit then follow her by clicking the link below. But be warned Beth is a little crazy and she may just keep you.

https://linktr.ee/bethhendrix

OTHER BOOKS BY BETH HENDRIX

Demon Exchange Series

Hoodwinked

Rejected Mates

Twisted

Heart Of Stone

Shorts & Anthologies

Unleashed

Rites Of Passion

Christmas Miracle

BBB Academy (Found in Relentless A bully Romance Collections)

Twisted Secret Part One (Found In Twisted Rejection Anthology)

Twisted Secret Part Two (Found In Twisted Rejection Part Two Anthology)

Anonymous Part 2 (Can you guess which story is by Beth?)

A NOTE FROM BBB

If you want to stay up to date with our releases and parties. Join our groups

BBB Anthology Party Room
Romance Lovers: A Reader and Author Group

Wanna just join in on some Bookish Fun?
Join Sosha & Nichols Book Besties

https://www.facebook.com/groups/631683167794701

Are you enjoying BBB's Anthologies? You can stay up to date by checking us out on amazon or join our newsletter, where we do giveaways and announce future projects.

Like the cover? You can follow Victoria Schaefer from Eve Graphic Design LLC Below
https://www.facebook.com/groups/EVEGardenofEdenCovers

ABOUT BBB PUBLISHINGS

BBB Publishings is the brainchild of two book addicted besties. Sosha Ann and Nichol Smith. When they first met as personal assistants three years ago they bonded instantly.

As the months passed and their friendship grew they would often brainstorm ideas on how to best help the authors they worked with. After a few months of debating, they opened BBB PA Services dedicated to supporting the amazing Indie Authors they now worked with.

One of the main things their clients would ask for was Anthology Opportunities. Finding very few opportunities for their less established authors they decided they had to do something to help.

In October 2018 BBB Publishings was born, the following July they published their first anthology. Two years on they have published 30 anthologies as well as short stories, serials and have big plans for the year ahead.

The year 2020 was a big year for the dynamic duo as they signed eight new authors to their publishing company as well as planning anthologies and shared worlds up until December 2023.

If you would like to keep up with all things BBB, apply to join their ever-growing arc, beta, or street teams, or just want to chat with the girls you can follow them by clicking the link below. They love nothing more than talking to the readers who make doing their job so much fun.

https://linktr.ee/bbbpublishings

Printed in Great Britain
by Amazon

76537640R00319